SERENADING HEARTBREAK

ELLA FIELDS

For the ones who picked me up when I fell.

He arrived wrapped in warning,
  of which I'd never heed.
    Every shade of gray,
      sunshine and rain-drenched days.
     A love that visited
       and never stayed.

Again and again and again.

Hearts are such unpredictable things,
you can never control to whom they might sing.

ONE

A S IF HE WERE SURPRISED BY THE FLARE OF LIGHT ON HIS JOURNEY through the ground, a worm, swimming through the soil, paused.

My lips wiggled, twitching my nose. With my gloved hand, I shifted the brown soil, being mindful of the worm, before dropping the peony seeds I'd gotten for my fifteenth birthday into the small crevice. Moving the dirt from the tiny mound, I recovered the patch and speared my spade into the soft earth.

"Heads up, Steve!"

My head rose in time to see a shirt sailing through the blue sky. It landed beside me, shaking the grass. I peeled off my gloves and fell back on my butt as my brother walked up the drive.

Trailing him on a banged up BMX bike was a boy I didn't recognize.

With my hand cupping my brow to block the sun, I feigned disgust to hide my curiosity. "I can smell your stench from here, Henny."

Hendrix's lip curled at the use of the nickname I'd dubbed him with as kids. A sign not to call him that in front of company. One I often felt inclined to ignore.

I tilted my head, eyeing the boy with a thick mop of dirty blond hair. "Who are you?"

"That's Everett." Hendrix answered for him. "He lives across the street. Just moved here."

Ignoring my brother, I kept my eyes trained on Everett as he flicked some of his shaggy hair from his face, revealing green eyes. Hard eyes. Like twin emerald jewel stones. The likes of which I'd never seen on a boy before. "Hi." I offered a smile with the greeting.

Those eyes narrowed on my face for a beat, and then, slowly, he jerked his head in some semblance of a nod.

"I'm Stevie, not Steve," I said.

Hendrix tossed his skateboard against the front steps, heading for the door.

Everett glanced at my brother, then at his bike, then at me, unsure. "You're both named after rock stars?"

Still smiling, I nodded. "Our parents' fault, not ours."

His lips twitched; it wasn't a smile but a brief display of amusement. "Right." He went to turn his bike around.

Rising from the grass, I dusted the dirt from my cutoffs.

"You coming?" Hendrix called from the door.

Everett paused at the end of our drive with his brows scrunched. "Where?"

"Uh, inside." Hendrix laughed. "Duh."

The screen door slapped shut behind him, and I gestured for Everett to follow as I moved toward it. "You can leave your bike on the grass if you like."

He nodded, and I waited for him to follow, some part of me knowing he probably wouldn't otherwise.

Inside, he kicked off his worn skate shoes. Intense eyes bounced off the faded yellow walls, taking in the pictures and the knickknacks that cluttered the hall table—a key dish, textbooks, a small sloth statue, and treble clef book ends with four books sandwiched between them.

"When did you guys move in?" I asked, turning the faucet on once we'd reached the kitchen and washing my hands.

Body stiff, he was still peering around, eyes aglow with curiosity.

"Everett?"

"Hmm?" He met my gaze, blinking, then shook his head. "Oh, about two weeks ago."

I dried my hands, then fetched the juice and three glasses. "Where'd you come from?"

"Few hours north."

Pouring us drinks, I frowned. The clipped words brooked no room for further prodding, so I slid his orange juice over the countertop and took a sip of my own.

It took him a second, but he stepped forward, nodding his thanks before draining half the glass.

"Here it is." Hendrix entered the small dining area outside our kitchen. "You ever play?" He slapped his acoustic guitar, grinning, his braces glinting in the afternoon light that bathed the dining room.

"No." Setting his empty glass down, Everett took a cautious step forward. "That's yours?"

"Yeah, man. Got it last Christmas. I'll show you some."

I watched, my back pressed into the counter, as Everett stared at the guitar, then shrugged. "You play. I'll probably just fuck it up."

My eyes bulged at how freely he'd cussed, all the while my chest clenched at his words.

Hendrix's smile grew as if he'd found the best type of new friend. Then he was bounding into the living room, muttering about Bob Dylan and other beginner songs.

Everett didn't follow. Instead, he stared after him with shifting feet. There was a hole around the big toe of one of his dirt-stained socks.

"You should give it a try," I encouraged. "It's fun."

"You play?" He slid his gaze back to where I was still standing.

It was heavy, that stare, and I wasn't sure if he knew, or if maybe it was just me. Fighting the urge to train my eyes elsewhere, I shook my head and tucked some of my blond hair behind my ear. "No. I kept trying for a while, but I can't seem to get the hang of it. Hendrix can play any guitar." When he said nothing but continued to look at me with his lip between his teeth, I rambled on, "Some people have a knack for it, I guess. I'm just not one of them."

His teeth released his lip. "You've got a clover stuck to your butt."

Thankfully, he disappeared before he could see my cheeks catch fire.

I brushed the clover from my cutoffs and stared at its crumpled form on the kitchen tiles. How did he notice it when my back was turned... My entire face burned as I remembered he'd followed me inside.

I was about to drag myself to my room when the music stopped, and muffled voices reached me.

Time passed, maybe five minutes or maybe ten, as I listened to Everett fumble over chords in the living room. Dragging my eyes from the clover, I forced my feet to move to the dining table.

Laughter, then Everett's curses followed by more laughter, bounced off the walls. They kept me company while I started a game of cards on Dad's computer, and as the rays dripping over the linoleum floor changed from luminous gold to a burnt orange, a familiar tune drifted down the hall. It was clumsy in the hands of a beginner, but I recognized it all the same.

Reshuffling my deck, I bit back a smile.

Sometime later, Everett emerged with something I hadn't

seen since meeting him on our drive. Something so beautiful, it would continue to haunt me years later no matter what I did to erase it.

A smile.

"I guess I've got a knack for it, Clover." His bottom teeth were a little crooked, hugging each other tightly. His top teeth were perfect, save for a tiny chip on the right front tooth. Barely perceptible, unless you stared a beat too long.

I always stared a beat too long.

TWO

BOUNCING AS THE BUS FLEW OVER A SPEED HUMP, I GRABBED THE seat in front of me. My gaze, unwilling to roam too far from him, no matter how much I tried, was stuck on Everett.

He was a grade above me, so I didn't see much of him at school. But what I did see was almost the same as what I was staring at then. A stone-still boy who looked as though he'd rather be anywhere else in the world. As though his surroundings bored him to the point of semi-consciousness.

Clad in ripped jeans and scuffed boots, he sat behind the driver. From my vantage point in the middle of the bus next to Adela, who was furiously scribbling away in that fluffy pink journal of hers, I glanced at the back of the bus.

Penny and her crew sat in the back with a couple of guys from the football team, laughing and tossing gum wrappers at one another. Though they might've looked entertained, Penny and her friends' eyes kept darting to the front of the bus.

To Everett.

I turned back, sighing as I pressed the side of my forehead to the cool glass.

"What's up?" Adela asked, still writing.

"Nothing."

"Uh-huh," she dragged out. "Sure."

"Your stop."

The bus pulled over, and a tiny shriek left her as she

scrambled to grab her things, shoving the pen between her teeth as she slung her bag over her shoulder and waved.

I laughed, then waved from the window as she dropped her bag to the sidewalk. The other kids walked around her while she took her time putting her journal and pen away.

The doors shut, the bus jerked forward, and I couldn't stop my gaze from drifting back to the boy at the front.

Only this time, he was staring at me.

I startled, and my lips parted, air falling through them until I forced them to curl into a smile.

His lips shifted, just barely, then he resumed his staring match with the front windshield.

Hendrix had been hanging out with Everett outside of school more, mainly at the skate park. Sometimes, I'd catch them riding home before dinner, and sometimes, I'd hear them in his room, playing Hendrix's guitar. He wasn't bad, considering he only played once or twice a week.

The bus lurched and sputtered to three more stops before finally reaching Gardenia Close. I grabbed my bag from between my feet, swinging through the seats as the bus slowed.

Everett got up just as I reached the front and clung tight to the metal pole.

His emerald eyes narrowed.

I offered another small smile, then cleared my throat and threw myself down the stairs as soon as the bus stopped, and the doors smacked open.

As I walked down the street, the soft crunch of Everett's boots sounded behind me, just as they did on every other day. Something about that day felt different, though, as if I was more aware of every little detail in the world. The crisp breeze that swept in off the sea, and the orange hue of the afternoon sun warming my face and arms.

The steps of worn boots and… the smell of cigarette smoke.

Coming to a stop, I looked over my shoulder, about to ask him why he was smoking, but he was already taking quick strides to his house across the street.

No cars were parked out front, but the driveway was still stained with car fluids from the previous tenants. The grass was a little too long. Weeds sprouted between the cracks in the brick drive and the small, mostly empty, garden beds.

Everett climbed the small hill of the front yard and opened the door, the cigarette still between his fingers as he disappeared through it.

I kicked at some rocks on the concrete sidewalk, then turned and headed inside.

I had homework to do, as well as a load of dirty clothes I told Mom I'd start. Hendrix had not long ago begun soccer again, and Mom and Dad were a little uneasy about having me home alone after school since they didn't finish work until five.

Sick of hanging out at Mom's work while I waited for her to finish, I promised them I'd be fine, and that they'd see just how much they could trust me after one week.

They'd looked at me with not a small amount of wariness but had eventually folded. I tried not to grumble about the fact they thought Hendrix was more mature just because he was older than me by sixteen months.

Hendrix was often the furthest thing from mature.

I stuffed the clothes from the hamper into the machine, not bothering to separate the colors from the whites like Dad preferred. I never did on my days to wash, and he never seemed to notice. I had no intentions of wasting my life fussing over items of clothing, thank you. They were to be purchased, comfortable, and worn, then washed and dried. No frills and no fuss.

Digging a bruise-free apple out of the fruit bowl, I chomped on it as I unpacked my bag, setting my math homework on the dining table with my favorite pack of crayons.

Then I put some music on.

That was the thing about living in a house with fellow music lovers and musicians. Rarely did one ever get to listen to their preference for too long, unless we retired to our rooms or used headphones.

Between the end and start of a new song, a knock sounded on the door.

I tossed what remained of my apple into the trash, then wiped my mouth with the back of my hand on my way down the hall.

Everett stood on the other side of the door, blinking slowly and trying to hide a tiny gash on his bottom lip that hadn't been there before by scratching at his long nose.

"What happened?"

He ignored my question. "Hendrix here?"

"He's at soccer practice." I felt a pang in my bottom lip when he stepped back and rubbed a thumb over the cut. "He didn't tell you?"

His golden brows tugged in, and he nodded. "He did, guess I forgot."

I swallowed, unsure of what to do. I knew he needed a place to be at the very least. "Wanna wait for him here?"

He blew out a breath, looking back at his house, then nodded again, brushing past me to head inside.

In the kitchen, I grabbed a bag of frozen peas from the freezer, and while wrapping them in a layer of paper towel, I tried again. "What happened to your lip?"

"Fuck," he hissed, slumping into a seat at the dining table. "Nothing." Within seconds, his fingers were drumming to the beat of "Gimme Shelter" by the Stones. "Just... mind your business, Clover."

I knew he'd tacked on the odd nickname to help soften the raspy blow, but it didn't work. A wave of ice still blew over my skin—pricking, crawling, chilling.

I carried the peas to the table and retook my seat. "At least put this on it."

I didn't wait for his reaction or even look at him before I picked up my crayon and resumed the mind-numbing task of long division.

The music played on, Everett's fingers tapping committedly as he held the ice pack to his mouth with his other hand. Eventually, he spoke. His quiet, rough voice almost inaudible. "You do math in crayon?"

I flipped the page, tapping the tip of the florescent pink on the paper as I stared at the equation. "Yup."

"Why?"

Dropping the crayon, I rested my chin on my hand and met his curious stare. "Because I want to."

"That's not a reason."

My brows jumped, and I held back a smile. "Whatever." I grabbed the crayon and finished the page, feeling his attention hot on my head the whole time.

He waited until I finished to ask again. "So… why use the crayons?"

"God," I groaned. "Is this payback for asking about your lip? Why do you care so much?"

"No." He tipped a shoulder, sitting back in his seat. "I just wanna know because of how six-year-old it is."

"That sentence makes no sense."

"Sure, it does," he said, lip curling. He winced as it split, a droplet of blood bubbling to the surface. He smeared it away with the side of his hand. "Fuck, Clover. Just answer me."

"I don't know," I snapped, irritated as to why it was so

important he get an answer. "It just... I guess it makes me happy while doing something that makes me unhappy."

Satisfaction remodeled his features. Hard was now soft, sharp cheekbones rising and his teeth flashing with his grin. "Wasn't so hard, was it?"

I closed my book. "Go play Hendrix's acoustic or something."

He did, standing from the table and leaving me to get started on my English reading.

Words blurred into gray blobs, my ability to focus sufficiently stolen.

Clumsy strumming echoed from the living room, and then a riff I didn't recognize slowly stitched together.

I ditched my book, pushing back from the table and walking toward the sound as if it was tugging at something inside me, forcing me closer with every note.

Everett had his eyes downcast, fixed on his moving fingers as his body began to sway with their skill. After another minute, he stopped, jotted something down in a notebook on the coffee table, then went to start again. Before he did, he said, "Need something, Clover?"

I didn't realize he even knew I'd been standing there. "Are you seriously going to keep calling me that?" I wasn't sure why I acted as if it annoyed me. Maybe to end the fluttering that was tickling my stomach.

He didn't answer.

"Did you come up with that?"

"I did," he said.

I shook my head with an incredulous laugh. "But you only just started playing, what, not even a month ago?"

"Your point?" He looked up then, golden brown lashes fanning high.

"My point is my parents tried to get me to play a musical

instrument before I could even walk, and I've never been able to play a damn thing. I can't even sing, for Christ's sake." My arms flapped out, hands gesturing wildly at him. "And here you are. Just waltzed on into town, picked up a guitar for the first time, and became some kind of instant genius."

"I'm not a genius." He wrote something else down. "I really want to learn, so I am. Besides," he said, "I don't just practice here. I've been spending some of lunch in the music room at school."

I had no response; my mouth opened and closed, trying and failing to find a rebuttal. "Hendrix won't like you becoming better than him." I had no idea why I said that. Yes, my brother could get competitive, but I didn't know if he would about this.

He had the audacity to smirk. At least, I think that minor twitching of his perfect lips was considered a smirk. An Everett smirk. "We're starting a band. He didn't tell you?"

Shocked, I almost laughed, almost told him this band of theirs wouldn't last, just like all the bands Hendrix had formed before.

But the tiny lilt of excitement in Everett's voice, that cut on his lip... I returned to my homework and left him to his songwriting.

The front door opened and closed some minutes later, and the clack of Mom's heels carried down the hall. I shut the worn copy of *Wuthering Heights* and scowled when she entered the kitchen. "Mom, I told you I've been fine."

"There's a boy on our couch that tells me otherwise. And anyway." She waved her hand, grabbing a bottled water. "My last kid was a no-show."

Mom was a self-employed music teacher. She taught piano, guitar, clarinet, flute, violin, and even singing in a small building she leased above the town's greatest coffee shop. Her words when she'd snagged it a few years ago. She used to work from home, but it soon became too much to manage from here. She'd said our garage was too small and unorganized to maintain a professional atmosphere.

"Ugh." I dropped my head to the table, pretending to bang it on the wood. "He's just waiting for Hendrix." Lifting my head, I peered over at her when she didn't respond.

Mom took a sip of water, then tucked some of her blond hair behind her ear. "He plays well."

"He's supposedly a beginner." I used air quotes.

Mom's lips puckered in that way they did when she was curious. "This is the same boy who's been coming over these past few weeks?"

"Yeah, Everett."

Mom vacated the room, and I cringed as I listened to her introduce herself to Everett, her voice chipper and soft. I didn't hear a word spoken about his split lip, but a little while later, as I was heading up the hall to take a shower and get my things ready for school the next day, I heard them laughing.

My limbs loosened when she began to sing alongside his strumming. Melancholy, velveteen, and smile-inducing. Unique but beautiful, Mom had a voice that could sing me to sleep long after I'd needed her help to.

And when I shut off the shower, I heard something I'd never be able to wash from my ears, or heart, for as long as I lived.

I heard a sound that scraped over your skin like hot gravel, leaving goose bumps instead of burnt flesh in its wake. A sound that was both rich and caustic, wrenched from the depths of someplace deep and carried on waves of turbulent, crackling nerves.

I heard Everett sing.

THREE

FOR MONTHS, EVEN IF HENDRIX WAS AT SOCCER OR OUT WITH ONE of his latest girlfriends, Everett came over after school.

Mom nurtured him, unspoken words drifting in the air between them, and my dad watched him, hesitant to take on the responsibility of some riffraff boy with too many issues.

And me, well, I had a new companion most days of the week. Even though we rarely talked, and when we did, it was stilted. I did my homework and he did his, often finishing in record time so he could disappear into the living room with Hendrix's guitar.

"They were fighting, screaming, at like two in the morning. I heard it, so the whole neighborhood probably did." Mom sounded freaked out. "Couldn't you?"

"Couples fight all the time, babe." Dad grazed a pan with the dish towel before hooking it above the island in our kitchen with the other hanging pots and pans. "It's none of our business."

"It is."

"He's here enough," Dad hissed in a hushed voice, tossing the dish towel onto the island. "Don't you think it's getting to be a little much? We can't afford a third kid, Brenna."

Mom sighed. "I'm not saying we need to adopt him. I'm just saying I see it. I feel it, and I know something's wrong. Very wrong."

Mom's words sent a spark of fear zooming straight for my chest. For weeks, ever since Everett had shown up at school with a violent bruise on his cheekbone, worry had nibbled at my stomach.

The fact she was seeing and feeling it too, no matter how much Everett might want us to ignore it, made me feel less crazy for worrying about my brother's best friend.

"I agree," I croaked, finally finding my voice.

Both turned, mirroring expressions of shock on their faces as though they'd forgotten someone was still seated at the dining table after dinner.

"What?" Dad's thick brows met.

"His parents, or I don't know." I pushed up from the table. "Someone is hurting him." Someone or something was the reason he was growing into a cold young man with an extra-large chip on his shoulder.

"Christ." Dad pinched the bridge of his nose. "Have any of you spoken to him about it? Hendrix?"

"I have," Hendrix said, entering the kitchen, and I almost jumped. "But he's always got excuses or changes the subject." He dumped a bowl with cereal dried to its edges into the sink.

Mom scowled, grabbing it and the scrubbing brush.

Dad spoke above the sound of the water. "You think his parents are beating him?"

Hendrix tipped a shoulder, then crossed his arms over his chest. A sign he was worried, but not wanting to give too much away. "Something's definitely not right. I'm never invited over there, and when I tried to get in the week before last, he told me to fuck off and said he'd see me later."

"Hendrix," Mom gasped.

Hendrix winced. "What? It's what he said."

"Christ," Dad muttered again, hands on his hips as he stared at the ground. He was a tall man, broad and built from working construction all day long. His beard, tinted with silver, almost touched his chest. Mom hadn't liked it at first, but now she smirked this weird way whenever she touched it. "Okay," he said, hands rising into the air as he left the kitchen. "I'll come home early tomorrow to try to catch him before he leaves and see if he'll talk."

Mom, smiling down at the sink, yelled, "Love you, baby!"

"Yeah, yeah," he echoed back, making her laugh.

She shut the water off, and I went to leave after Hendrix. I was supposed to be online already to chat with Adela.

"Stevie, babe?" Mom called before I got two feet into the hall.

I paused, turning. "Yeah?"

"Do you see much of Everett?" She was leaning against the counter, flicking through a cookbook, but I knew she wasn't looking for something or reading anything.

"No," I lied. "Mainly just on the bus. He mostly hangs with Hendrix when he's here or plays guitar for a few minutes until he gets here."

Twisting her lips, she looked up, eyeing me for a stretched moment. "Okay. Bring out your dirty laundry before bed. I'm starting a load in the morning."

I nodded, walking away as the taste of my lie soured my mouth. I didn't know why I didn't tell her Everett came over some afternoons after school when Hendrix was out. But it kept me awake until midnight when I finally realized why.

I liked it. Even if we hardly said ten words to one another most afternoons. I liked that one hour and twenty minutes of just us.

"Go fish."

I slid a card from the deck, inwardly cursing at the three. I needed another four.

"And don't do that."

Brows pinching, I asked, "Do what?"

Everett studied his cards. "Don't go sticking your nose where it doesn't belong, Clover."

Heat engulfed my cheeks, the kind I was unable to stop or hide, so I ducked my head.

True to his word, Dad had come home early two nights ago and cornered Everett on his way out. I didn't hear what was said on our porch, but from the lines etching Dad's pursed lips, I knew he didn't get any answers. Everett had apparently acted confused, then went home as soon as he could.

"It wasn't..." I was about to say it wasn't my idea, but that would've been a lie. It'd been a group idea, and one I hadn't protested. "Sorry." After a few minutes, I set the cards down, not in the mood to play anymore. I wasn't used to this kind of silence from him, and I didn't like it.

"Clover," he said when I stood and went to the kitchen.

Opening the fridge, I grabbed a soda and shut the door with my hip. "Yeah?"

More strange silence and then he sighed. "Nothing."

The front door opened and closed, and Dale's and Graham's laughter reached my ears before they rounded the corner and dumped themselves into seats at the dining table.

"A little early for poker, no?" Dale started collecting the cards, then tried to shuffle them. They all fell and scattered to the scuffed wooden table.

"We weren't playing poker," I said, popping the tab on my can and taking a sip.

"Oh hey." Graham spun his drumsticks between his fingers. "What's up, little sis?"

"I'm not your little anything, ham."

"Ohhh." Laughing, Dale slugged Graham in the arm, causing his drumsticks to clatter to the table and floor.

Graham just grinned, then waggled his glasses.

Glancing at Everett before leaving, I found his eyes stuck on Graham and that familiar rigidness returning to his jaw.

I didn't hang around. Hendrix would be home soon, and I wanted to watch some TV before the house filled with noise.

Settling into the soft brown leather, I flicked through the channels, unable to decide on anything before Hendrix opened and closed the front door.

"Ahoy, David Beckham has arrived," Dale jeered.

Hendrix drifted past the living room. "Shut up, loser."

I knew Dale would've taken that personally, being that he wasn't interested in any extracurricular activities that didn't involve skateboarding, and he wasn't even in the band. Hendrix had tried to include him last time, but it didn't work out. Dale was worse than me at anything that created sound, and that was saying something.

He'd dubbed himself their band manager, to which they'd all laughed at but had still agreed. Hendrix said it was better to let him think he was helping.

They remained in the kitchen for a while, trying to re-vamp some lyrics Hendrix had written a year ago. I kept the TV volume low, awaiting that rare sound. The sound of Everett's laughter.

"No, no, no," Graham practically yelled over the noise of their bickering. "First things first, we need to nail our sound."

"Our sound?" Hendrix asked.

"Yeah, our sound."

Everett seemed baffled. "We're in a fucking band. Bands are full of sounds, you idiot."

"No, you aren't listening," Graham explained. "We need *the* sound. You know, hard rock, reggae, country, blues, alternative rock, pop-rock, hard-core, screamo…"

"You lost me at algae," Hendrix muttered.

"It's reggae." Graham groaned. "Amateurs. Fucking amateurs, man."

"Let's worry about our sound later and actually make sure we can string something together long enough to call ourselves a fucking band."

He had nothing to worry about. Everett had the kind of scratchy, melodic, soul-infused voice that could fit with the Spice Girls and Slipknot combined.

But if they had a sound, I'd call it blues rock with an edge. Everett's voice held too much grief, too much honesty, too much of everything to venture into boy band territory.

"Okay, well what about a name?" Hendrix said. "I can't even with The Studs, Graham. Fuck that."

"Orange Apples," Graham said.

"What?" three voices said at once.

"Orange Apples."

I bit my lips, but when the laughter threatened to burst free, I stuffed a cushion over my face.

Hendrix cursed. "Nice. Real fucking sophisticated."

I could almost see Graham shrugging his shoulders up to his ears as he said, "That's the thing. It can't be too sophisticated, or no one will take us seriously."

Hendrix sounded exasperated. "I'm going to need you to repeat what you just said so you can hear how stupid it sounded."

"No, wait. He's right," Everett spoke up, surprising me. I would've thought he'd be the least enthusiastic to name the band Orange Apples.

"Thank you," Graham practically shouted.

Everett wasn't done. "But I still don't think Orange Apples is the, um, right fit."

"No one will show up to our gigs," Hendrix said. "We'll sound like a bunch of twats." Hendrix's previous failed attempts at forming a band had never even made it this far, so I could see why he was hesitant to seemingly poke fun at something that meant a lot to him.

"Uh, excuse me?" Graham said. "The Arctic Monkeys, Queen, The Doors, Pink Floyd—"

Hendrix cut him off. "Okay, shut up."

"Point made." Graham made a hissing sound, and I could imagine him licking his finger and sticking it in the air.

"Yeah but Queen is sophisticated as fuck," Dale piped up. "Just saying."

Groans sounded, then Everett snapped, "Jesus. Fine. Orange Apples will do."

"Will do?" Graham scoffed. "It's fucking brilliant. I can just see it now… sold-out stadiums, the glowing orange apple on billboards around the globe, stickers to slap on chick's ass—*ouch*."

"Stevie's home, dickhead." That from Hendrix.

"Like she hasn't heard the word ass before," Graham grumbled.

"Christ." From Everett, who I bet was probably rubbing his temples.

"Screw it," Dale said, followed by a thump that sounded as though he'd slapped the dining table. "Let's vote. All in favor of Orange Apples, raise your hand."

"That's bullshit. There's no other option," Hendrix protested.

Tossing the pillow aside, I rose from the couch and crept down the hall to the kitchen.

Graham laughed. "Not my fault you don't show enough initiative. Snooze and lose, bro."

Everett tilted his head, watching me as I leaned into the corner of the counter.

Three out of four hands shot into the air, and slowly, I raised mine too.

Hendrix sputtered, fingers aimed at me and Dale. "Those two aren't even in the band!"

Graham stabbed a drumstick his way. "You never stated the rules before voting. Again, show some initiative earlier instead of whining like a baby after."

"Oh, I'm the baby? Orange fucking Apples? *Really?*" Hendrix turned to Everett. "Rett, are you hearing this crap?"

"Yeah." Everett dragged his eyes off me and cleared his throat. "And I don't care. Let's just play already and quit dicking around."

Grumbling sounded but it was no match for the cheering from Dale and Graham as they raced around the room and stormed past me to the garage.

Everett was the last to leave, and I watched as he scrubbed his hands over his face. He looked tired, the kind of tired that weighed down the spirit as well as the shoulders.

It was on the tip of my tongue to ask if he was okay, but when he looked at me, defeat warring with the fake smile he maneuvered into place, I knew there was little use.

He stood, grabbing the tiny notebook he carried with him in the back pocket of his jeans.

"Can I get a T-shirt?" I asked before he entered the garage. "You know, with the orange apple on it?"

A slight shake of his shoulders was the only sign he'd even acknowledged my question, and then the door closed behind him.

FOUR

CLICKED MY PEN AND SMIRKED AT THE WAY IT MADE EVERETT'S JAW shift. "You hardly ever do homework here anymore." If he sat with me at the dining table, it was to write in that journal of his. "What's got you behaving?"

"Finals," he grunted out, then cursed and put a line through the last sentence he'd written in his book.

I turned my attention back to my own work, noting the countries that bordered Australia on the notepad beside me.

"Why is it you're always behaving?"

"Huh?" I shoved my pen between my teeth to tighten my ponytail.

Everett followed the movement. I spat the pen out, and his lips curled. "You're never out."

I felt my brows lower. "Am too. Adela and I went to the movies just two nights ago."

His eyes turned down to his notebook. "Not talking about the movies. I'm talking about parties. I see girls your age at them all the time."

"Oh." I wasn't sure what to do with my hands or eyes.

"Not interested?" he prodded.

"I am," I said too quick. "I mean, I'm curious, I guess. But I don't know... I wouldn't be allowed to yet. And I'm not like Hendrix. I don't have the guts to sneak out."

"It's good," he finally said after a few beats, "that you don't do that shit yet."

He was still staring at his messy notes, and I laughed. "Okay then."

Sighing, he pushed his things away and folded his arms on the table. "You're too smart to be getting mixed up in the wrong crowd is all. You've got goals."

"I'm not that smart." It wasn't a lie. I was an average student with average plans. "And I just want to be around flowers all day, keep things minimal to better experience what comes. How's that for goals?"

After blinking at me three times, he lifted a broad shoulder, and my eyes dropped to his tanned forearms. "It's a goal, and a unique one at that. Doesn't matter what it is. If it's important to you and it's what you want, don't talk it down." He went to get a drink, and I sat there, stewing over his words.

I was sure it was the most he'd ever said to me in one afternoon in the whole time we'd been hanging out.

"And what about you?" I asked when he came back with two cans of Coke in his hands.

He set one down in front of me and popped his open, taking a sip. "What about me?" He said it so nonchalantly as if I wasn't supposed to expect him to have any plans.

Watching him swallow, the way his throat dipped, I shook my head and scratched my cheek. "Uh, well, your goals. Don't you have any? College? Music?"

He licked his full lips, then smacked them together while studying my face too intently. "Nah."

"Nah?" I repeated. "But you sing like a god, not to mention the way you play the guitar." I paused then, remembering him and Mom on the piano in our living room last week. He wasn't half bad at that either. "And soon, you'll be able to add the piano to your list of skills."

"That's just fun. I'm not equipped for college." He rapped a fist on the table, his knuckles tapping twice, then pausing before a triple tap. "And if I'm being honest, I'll do just about anything that'll take me away from here."

Taken aback, I straightened my spine. "You're leaving Plume Grove?"

"Yeah," he said, pulling his books back and closing them. "It's stagnant here, and I don't know if I can do stagnant. Especially in a place where…" He stopped and blew out a breath.

"Where?" I prompted after a moment.

Standing, he gathered his pens into a pile on top of his books, grabbed his Coke, and stalked through the kitchen to the garage. "Nothing."

"Everett."

"Mind your business, Clover." The door shut behind his cold words.

It was Christmas Eve when Everett Taylor snuck into my room for the first time.

The window opened, and a scream collected in my throat when he hit the floor with a thud that I worried would wake my parents. I held it at bay and scrambled upright, blinking as Everett rose from the ground.

He picked up one of my books and the jar of pens he'd knocked off my nightstand, setting them back on the glossy white wood as I held my breath, wondering if this was a dream. All the while listening for any sounds of the house stirring.

Nothing.

"What are you doing?" I moved to turn the lamp on, but Everett grabbed my hand.

"Don't. I… Can I sleep on the floor?"

I frowned. "The floor? What's going on?"

His hand was cold and large around mine, and kind of rough. I eyed it in the dark, and then he released me. "Just give me an answer. Or else I'll go find a nice porch seat to sleep on instead."

"Fine." I shook my head, still dazed from sleep, his touch, and his sudden invasion.

I got up and grabbed the mink blanket draped over the chair at my desk, then tossed him all the throw pillows I had, and my second pillow. "Why would you need to sleep on a porch?"

I wasn't shocked when he didn't answer. A minute later, he'd kicked off his shoes and was lying there with the pillows piled around him, staring up at the ceiling.

Yawning, I glimpsed the time. 2:30 a.m. I rolled to my back, staring at the glow worms Dad had glued to the ceiling when I was a kid.

"I'm surprised those things still glow at all, considering how old they must be." His words were a little slurred, a tell-tale sign he'd been drinking. Something he, my brother, and the band spent a lot of time doing these days.

I didn't like the way he was trying to change the subject, or how easily he could derail my thoughts, so I said nothing.

"Clover?" he asked after another minute slid by.

"You went out tonight?"

"Some party down by the beach," he mumbled. "Couldn't get back inside, 'kay? No big deal."

"You have keys," I said, unwilling to budge just yet.

"You don't want me here?" His tone conveyed playful humor, a rarity, but I didn't let it fool me.

"I want you anywhere you're safe," I said, then added, "We all do."

Silence arrived, and my eyes were drifting closed when he finally said, "They had the locks changed." A gruff laugh lit my stomach on fire. "Figures. Can't spare enough money to make sure we've got food in the house, but they'll find a way to change the locks."

My eyes widened as all traces of sleep fled. This was the most he'd ever admitted about his parents, who were now widely known throughout the neighborhood for their domestic disputes. As well as the rumors that shadowed them from the town they'd left behind. Though no one ever quite knew what to believe.

Some said they owed money to a huge drug lord and had to skip town or else they'd wind up dead. Some said there'd been an accident, but everyone had a different story on just who it was who'd been in the accident.

I did my best to keep any pity or sympathy from my voice, knowing it'd be the fastest way to make him clam up. "Everett." I swallowed. "Why would they do that?"

I wasn't sure if he'd answer, but he did. "To spite me."

My next breath burned my lungs. "You never said where you moved here from."

His exhale was rough. "Because it's not worth talking about." A moment later, he cursed, hissing through his teeth as he shifted on the floor.

"You're hurt," I said, rolling over to switch on the lamp.

He flinched, shoving his hand up to shield his eyes. "Fuck, Clover. I said not to turn that thing on."

Absorbing the busted lip and his half shut, swollen eye, anger had me shooting out of bed.

"Wait," he said. "It's okay, really."

"It's not okay. They fucking beat you up!"

His lip curled. "Cussing now, Clover? We really are a bad influence on you."

I ignored him and went to the kitchen to fetch an ice pack and some towels, trying to make as little noise as possible.

When I returned, I locked the door and then dropped them beside him. "This needs to stop, Everett."

His emerald eyes were on my stomach, and I glanced down, noticing my tank had risen. I wasn't even wearing a bra, being that I had been asleep and all. Normally, I wouldn't care, but my boobs had grown, and having his eyes on me did something that had my nipples hardening against the cotton.

"Get in bed, Clover."

I did, but I was still too angry, too worried to simply fall asleep. "I'm serious, Everett."

A sigh filled the room, the towel scrunching as he moved the ice over his face. "It wasn't them. Not this time."

Not this time. "Then who?"

"I got drunk, okay? And then I got into a fight with some asshole. That's all you need to know."

I didn't press for more. Judging by his impatient, more sober sounding voice, he was tired and not drunk enough to humor me any longer.

"The glow worms," he said. "I know there's gotta be a reason you still have them up there. Scared of the dark?"

His question wasn't a barb, just a question, so despite my annoyance, I gazed up at the fading worms and said, "I'm not afraid of the dark. Not at all. But I like what something bright can do to the dark, so they stay."

A few minutes later, the small thud of the ice brick hitting the floor had my eyes drifting open, and then the sound of his soft snoring had them closing again.

"Look who decided to show up. Not like it's Christmas or any-thing," Hendrix said, ruffling my hair as I poured some orange juice and nabbed a piece of bacon.

"Didn't sleep well," I mumbled around the bacon that was exploding on my taste buds.

When I woke, Everett was gone. The blanket had been folded and draped over my chair, the pillows set back on my bed, and the window closed as though he'd never been there at all.

But he had been, and that he'd chosen to come to me in his time of need, instead of Hendrix, sent a flood of warmth filling my chest.

"Merry Christmas, honey," Dad cooed, squeezing me in a hug and almost spilling my juice.

"Merry Christmas, Daddy."

Mom placed a kiss on my head, smoothing some of my frizzed blond hair back from my face.

They waited for me to finish eating before we moved into the living room.

The climate in Plume Grove was too warm for snow. But staring at the tree adorned with mismatched decorations from our childhood, I found myself longing for it as slices of light from the sun danced through the window, over the hardwood floor and piles of presents.

Sometime later, with my books, stationery, makeup, new boots with pink hearts on them, and a flat iron piled expertly by the window, a violent silence fell over the room.

Hendrix placed his new electric guitar by the window with his amp and cable leads, his only presents due to how expensive they were, and raked a hand through his finger mussed, dark blond hair.

Mom and Dad shared a look, and finally, after the ticking

of Grandpa Angus's clock became unbearably loud, Mom sent Hendrix over to check on Everett.

I tried to busy myself with my presents and began carting them to my room.

When I returned, Dad was carrying something down the hallway. Not just any something, but a Gibson acoustic guitar with a red and green ribbon looped around its neck.

Hendrix was back a few minutes later, and I retook my seat on the end of the couch, staring at the guitar with tears threatening to cloud my vision.

Mom gasped as soon as Everett stepped into the living room. "What happened to your face?"

Hendrix looked at Dad, who was frowning, his shoulders tense.

"Fight with one of the guys we go to school with." When my parents said nothing and continued to stare with matching looks of concern, Everett sighed. "It's okay. He looks way worse than I do."

That didn't defuse the tension, but Hendrix forced a laugh, choosing to keep his mouth shut about his whereabouts the night before. A wise move. Mom and Dad knew he went out sometimes, but they didn't always allow it. Especially on Christmas Eve.

Mom, tucking some of her curls behind her ear, cleared her throat. "Well, Merry Christmas. Come on." She waved a hand. "Sit."

Everett did, mumbling, "Merry Christmas," as he settled beside me.

He smelled like an ashtray, sweat, and stale beer. I was willing to bet he still hadn't been home, and therefore, hadn't had a chance to shower off the events of the night before. If my parents noticed, they didn't let on.

Dad grabbed the guitar from beside the tree and handed it to Everett. "Merry Christmas. Now you'll have your own to fuss over."

Everett's mouth fell open, his throat bobbing as he looked from the guitar to my dad. "You're joking," he breathed, and my heart pinched.

"I'm not." Dad chuckled. "And don't look too shocked. It didn't cost that much. It's secondhand."

Finally, Everett took the guitar, holding it so carefully as though he were meeting a baby for the first time. "But..." He blinked at it. "I can't just..." Eyes closing, he lowered his head.

Dad reached over to clap him on the shoulder, and Mom started singing to Mariah Carey's "All I Want for Christmas is You" when it came on the TV that sat above the fireplace.

"Hendrix, help him tune it and then clean up this paper. Ma and Pa will be here soon," Dad said, leaving the room.

"He knows how to tune it better than I do, and it wasn't just me who unwrapped presents. That's not fair."

Seeing Everett brush his thumb over the strings of his Gibson caused tears to gather fast and strong, so I started cleaning up to hide them.

FIVE

I COULDN'T HELP BUT PEEK AT HIS FACE EVERY FEW MINUTES.

If Everett noticed I hadn't turned the page in my book in more than ten minutes, he didn't let on.

His pen left indents in the paper of his journal, pressing the lyrics deep into the page. Unable to read them even if I wanted to, I could only glance at him when I felt it was safe.

Sometimes, his head bobbed to an invisible beat, and every now and then, I'd hear his feet shift beneath the table as if they too were helping to create something only he could see.

I knew he could be doing many other things during the short window of time he spent sitting with me. He could watch TV, hang out with friends, or play. He always found time to practice, but as if it was some new routine of his, he made sure to sit in the same room as me first.

In his company, whether he remained silent, I began to watch him too much, and my chest began to fill with flutters. I felt like my presence was needed—as though it comforted him in some way—and I liked that. To make someone smile, especially him, brought something inside me dancing to the surface. But to make someone feel at ease was rare, and I didn't want to walk away from it or take that unspoken trust for granted.

"What makes you unhappy?"

Dumbfounded, I breathed out a laugh. "Why would you ask that?"

"You can tell a lot about a person by finding out what they

don't like." Scratching at some of the hair on his cheek, he lifted his head. "And you don't tend to make a lot of noise about that stuff."

"About stuff I don't like?" He nodded. "There are things I don't like."

He sat, waiting, as if he didn't believe me.

I frowned, trying to think of what to say as his steady gaze drilled into mine, and my stomach continued to jump. "Celery," I blurted.

"Celery?" He repeated on a gruff breath, his lashes rising to his lowering brows. "Really? That's all you've got?"

Nodding, I tried to ignore the embarrassment creeping up my neck. "Celery is for suckers; can you write a song about that?"

A short bout of laughter and then, after eyeing me a moment, he nodded again. "For you, I can probably write something."

"About celery?" I asked, nerves straining my voice.

He tipped up a shoulder, tapping his fingers on the table. "About whatever I want. What else don't you like?"

Caught off guard, it took me a moment to answer. "Crowds." I forced a shiver. "I need space."

"Fresh air?"

"Any open space." Growing more confident, I said, "What about you? What don't you like?"

Seeming taken aback, he slouched in his chair. "Not many things."

That kind of surprised me. Given his quiet, solemn nature, I thought he'd answer differently. "Such as?"

With a smile tipping the corner of his mouth, he huffed. "You really want to know?"

Frowning, I said, "I really do."

"Fine. Sirens and royalty."

"Is that it?"

Another half shrug. "Pretty much."

"Royalty?" I repeated.

He hummed in confirmation, giving nothing else away.

We stared, the drumbeat in my chest increasing with each second. I wanted to ask why. Desperately.

As if he knew that, he dropped his eyes to the table. "You're a flower bound to suffocate without sunshine, fresh air, and tasty nutrients."

I blinked. Hard. "What?"

Pushing up from the table, he said, "You heard me just fine."

Then he was gone, and I was tearing apart his beautifully constructed sentence for countless minutes, the warmth in my chest spreading to my unstoppable smile.

I was sixteen when I saw the boy I'd watched blossom into a young man kiss someone.

Someone who wasn't me. Someone who looked nothing remotely like me.

Why I thought she even would, I wasn't yet able or ready to dissect.

The Orange Apples had finally started booking some local gigs, and even though hardly anyone showed up, those who did took their role as fans pretty seriously.

It had me feeling woefully young and inadequate in my cut-offs, off-the-shoulder T-shirt, and worn Doc Martens.

When rumor spread that their next gig in town was set to bring a higher turnout, the trouble began.

An echoing whine shrieked from the speakers. "Checking, one, two, skip a few, ninety-nine, a hundred," Hendrix said into the mic, chuckling to himself as he adjusted the stand.

Spinning on a stool at the bar with a cherry Coke in my hand, I watched the guys set up.

Adela sat beside me, giggling at my brother's embarrassing antics.

He'd finally gotten his braces off, but ever since, he'd only become more of an idiot. Especially since he'd scored some part-time work at the local garage with Everett after school and on Saturdays. He had no shame in swaggering around in his greased-up wifebeater long after work. The money from that and the tiny amount they'd made from gigs were going toward a sweet ride, he'd said.

Nothing wrong with being confident, Dad had said.

Mom had given him a look that said she disagreed. Me, well, I just did my best to stay away to help curb the temptation to smack him with something.

"Can I break girl code and marry your brother when we're done with school?"

Most would probably be grossed out by the question, and I was, but I didn't care enough to say that. "Go for it." I snorted. "I wish you luck. You'll need it."

Adela grinned, then wrapped her lips around her straw and resumed staring at Hendrix as he fussed with cords on the make-shift stage set up in the back of the bar.

A flash of red caught my eye, and I swiveled to look down the emergency exit hallway, the one leading to the bathrooms. Everett was standing there, his lip between his teeth, all the while the bar continued to fill steadily with each passing moment.

I hesitated, and then I finished my drink and told Adela I'd be back.

He'd snuck into my room twice more since last Christmas. Both times drunk or high. But now, instead of just reeking of alcohol or weed, he reeked of weird perfumes and was often too wasted to say much of anything, let alone explain why he was there. Within a handful of minutes, he'd pass out on the pile of pillows I'd thrown to the floor.

My best guess was his parents never gave him a key, and he had to wait until one of them was up to get inside his own house.

He turned his back to me as I approached, and as I stopped in front of him, he capped a flask and reached behind him to tuck it into his back pocket. Turning, he jerked his head. "Clover."

"Drinking before you play?" I asked, leaning against the wall.

He blew out a breath, and thanks to our proximity, the scent of whiskey hit me in the face.

I licked my lips, and his eyes narrowed on them for a brief second before he made them meet mine. "Can you keep a secret?"

"Always."

He swallowed, eyes darting behind me to the almost full bar. "I don't think I can do this."

My brows gathered, and I straightened from the wall. "What, play?" I shook my head, confused. "You've done it before."

"Not like this." He gestured behind me. "Not with this many people watching. This is just..." He took a staggering step back into the dark hallway. "It's too much, Clover."

"Says who?" As I watched his expression, the battle he was having with fear, my heart clenched and softened. "Who says it's too much? You? Because you should know," I said, voice gentle while taking a slow step closer. "No one gives a shit if you screw up. They're only here to see your pretty face. That voice of yours is just a bonus."

He belted out a laugh, and I almost melted into the wall as the hard edges of his face dissolved into beautiful, softened planes. "You think I'm pretty, huh?"

I twisted my lips. "You know you're pretty, so don't play coy."

His smile slipped, his hands fidgeting at his sides as if he were going to reach for the flask again. And so I did something I'd never had the guts to do before. I stepped into him and cupped his face with my tingling hands. "Look at me."

His brows pinched, hard eyes narrowing over the crooked bridge of his nose. "Clover…"

"Look at me when you play. I'll be sitting in the back near the bar."

"I can't do that," he said, a tad rough. "It's…" His hands rose to mine on his face, but he didn't remove them.

I sighed and almost swayed from the touch. "Then close your eyes when you feel like it's too much, and when you open them and look at the back of the room, it'll be just like home, only better."

The calluses on his hands as they moved, squeezing mine, sent a shiver biting down my spine. Our eyes were stuck, and his breathing had slowed. After a minute, he inched closer, and my heartbeat quickened, my eyes falling to his parted lips.

He dropped my hands and stepped back. "Only better," he repeated, and then he was gone.

The crowd was clapping and hollering before the band even took the stage, and with one shy smile directed at them from Everett as he strapped his guitar around his neck and approached the mic, I knew he'd fight his way through this and do what he did best.

Clearing his throat, Everett checked the mic, then adjusted the stand as he lowered to the stool. "How's everyone feeling?"

Shouts echoed back at him, and he flashed another half-smile, then began strumming a melody I'd recognize in this life and every one after, I'd heard and watched him sing it that many times.

The stars all glow, even when it snows
But I find myself wishing they'd all blink out
Nothing that beautiful is meant to last
Especially in a world this hard and fast
I wish it'd all blink out

Happiness comes, and then it goes
The only constant anyone knows
Is pain
That filthy reminder
I'll never find ya
Yeah, it's pain
The one that comes with knowing
I'll never see you again

Bottle tops, cars, broken stars,
You said we would never part
Smiling, laughing, fighting, and crying
Time is a bitch who keeps on lying
It's here to stay...

His eyes remained closed, and I knew why he'd chosen this haunting song to start with. The same song that had me wondering and desperate to know what made him write it. It was one of the first they'd played as a band. Everett's comfort and evasive heart all rolled into one.

By the time they reached the middle of their set, the stool was gone, and he was staring into not only my eyes, but also letting his gaze drift over the forty some other pairs in the bar.

My throat hurt when they wrapped from screaming so damn loud. Tears were cascading down my cheeks as the crowd hollered and clapped, shouting that stupid name of theirs.

"Orange Apples, Orange Apples!"

"Jesus," Adela said, and I looked over to see her usually tanned skin three shades whiter, her soda hanging precariously between her fingers.

I took it and set it on the bar. "Amazing, huh?"

"They didn't sound like that the last time I came over."

"Different acoustics and a lot less messing around."

"I'll freaking say," she muttered, eyes zeroing in on my brother as he swung his bass guitar around his shoulders, then jumped into the crowd of girls who were pushing toward the stage.

Everett waded through them, and I smiled and clapped my hands near my face when our eyes met.

He laughed, shaking his head. Then a redhead, Lainey Ray, a senior at school, grabbed his arm, and he stopped.

I tried not to let my buoyant heart sink as he gave her his complete attention, but that was shot to hell when she rose onto her toes to whisper into his ear.

I looked away, and even though I knew what would happen next, I couldn't stop myself from looking back.

Of course, he was kissing her. Those large, rough hands framing her petite face. The same hands I'd had holding mine to his just half an hour ago.

Adela bumped my shoulder with hers. "He's a butt ton of trouble anyway, Stevie."

"Is it becoming that obvious?" I worried aloud.

She grabbed her soda. "Nah, I only recently figured it out myself."

"When?" I asked, internally freaking out that I'd made a fool of myself, while also struggling to even care as my heart fissured.

She waved a hand. "Oh, about two minutes ago." A small, relieved laugh sputtered, and she grinned. "Come on, your mom and dad just got here."

I angled my head at the doors and found them making a beeline for the boys who were mixed up in the audience as the next band began to set up. I knew they'd be bummed they'd missed it, but Mom had a late client every second Friday, and Dad had picked her up on his way here.

The band broke free of the crowd, heading straight for the bar.

Mom and Dad looked to be talking with the owner, so Adela and I waited where we were. There were too many people, and I didn't feel like fighting my way through them. My stomach ached, and I wasn't sure why, or why I couldn't let myself search for Everett again. I knew he'd been with other girls. Everyone did. He'd never made it much of a secret. Though seeing it in the flesh was an entirely different kind of hurt. I knew I liked him, but I never realized how much.

"Guys, guess what?" Hendrix rushed over to where Dale and Graham were standing near us at the bar. "Garry knows someone who's trying to get rid of a bus."

"A bus?" Dale asked.

Graham half-rolled his eyes. "To tour after school's out."

"I can't leave." Dale appeared stricken. "I've been accepted into Brown, you fucks."

"They're touring?" Adela leaned close to ask.

I shrugged. "Apparently." I didn't quite believe they would, though I suppose I should have with the lackluster attempts Hendrix had made to apply for college.

Ignoring Dale, they began hashing out plans to meet with the guy selling the bus.

Everett arrived with Lainey by his side. He was quiet as they made arrangements, yet I couldn't help but notice the way his eyes brightened as he listened, or how his hand slowly slipped from Lainey's hip as he drifted closer to the conversation.

We left soon after, walking past the guys packing their gear into Dale's brother's van out on the street.

Before I slid into the back seat of my parents' car, I glanced back at the bar.

Everett was standing outside with a foot propped against the brick exterior, smoking a cigarette. He lifted his hand, flicking his fingers at me, but all I could muster was a glimpse of a smile before climbing inside and shutting the door on the cold.

Graham hit the cymbal just as I walked into the garage, the noise ringing in my ever-adjusting ears. "Some guy is out front, uh, towing a bus?"

All the guys, even Dale who'd been flicking through his Brown brochure on our old couch, leaped from their positions. Hendrix didn't even set his guitar down. Instead, he almost smacked me in the face with it as they all raced by, and I pressed myself into the wall.

Everett was the only one to take his time, and I averted my gaze to the rug covered concrete floor as he drifted past me, smelling of laundry detergent and cigarettes.

"You avoiding me, Clover?" he asked when I'd thought he was gone.

I lifted my head. "What?" I felt my eyes widen, felt my words sputter out of me, and could do nothing to stop any of it. "What do you mean?"

He sucked his teeth for a moment, sliding his hands into the pockets of those ripped jeans. "You're a shit liar."

"I'm not lying," I lied. "Not exactly."

"Not exactly?" Taking an unnerving step closer, he collected some of my hair and twirled it around his finger.

My stomach flipped. My eyes were trapped as I watched him stroke the strands between his fingers. "Soft as silk. I'd always wonder—"

"Rett! Where the hell are you?"

I flattened myself against the wall, and Everett's hand fell away. "Don't ever lie to me again, Clover."

He could've just been teasing, but when I met those dark green eyes, I saw the vehemence in them. The hurt.

"Coming," he called to my brother, still gazing down at me while he plucked his cigarettes out and stuck one between his teeth.

He was waiting for me to respond, I realized belatedly, so I nodded. It was all I could do with my heart pattering against my chest. Since seeing him with Lainey last weekend, I had been avoiding him, choosing to garden or do homework in my room whenever he came over.

He turned and strode outside.

Mom and Dad had arrived home when I'd finally found the courage to check out this beloved bus.

They were all standing on the grass. Well, Everett, Dad, Mom, and Hendrix. Graham and Dale were already inside it, jumping around and making it rock on its two flat tires.

"A school bus?" I asked, blinking at the faded, peeling yellow paint and the rust marks that sprinkled the bumper, windows, and axles. "Does it even run?"

"Why do you think it was towed here, dumbass?"

"Hey," Mom snapped.

Hendrix sighed. "No, it doesn't. But that'll change. Right, Dad?"

Dad didn't look convinced. Scraping a hand over his beard, he shifted toward the bus. "We can only try, kid. We can only try."

Hendrix scowled. "With our mechanical knowledge, plus your construction experience, I think we've totally got this."

"You're just the help, dude," Graham said, jumping down the bus steps and almost tearing off the door when he caught it to steady himself.

"Shut up," Hendrix spat, shoving him away from the door so he could inspect it.

"He's right," Everett said.

"Rett's been working there more than you, grease monkey." Dale leaped down to the front lawn. I cringed as he narrowly dodged the garden bed I'd recently planted some hydrangeas in. "Don't be so quick to toot your bragging horn."

"Fuck off, Chippendale. Don't you have college brochures to beat off to?"

Dad cuffed Hendrix, and he cursed again, grimacing.

Mom just watched it all with her arms folded over her chest and still wearing her work clothes. A black and blue maxi skirt and cream peasant blouse.

"I suddenly don't know if this college thing is going to work out," Dale mused, then laughed. "Who am I kidding? You guys won't get this thing running. I'll come home next summer, and you'll still be trying."

Everett stepped closer to the bus then, his back rippling beneath his grease-stained white shirt. Tension wafted from him, drifting on the gentle breeze as he headed for the rear of the flat-nosed monstrosity.

I couldn't tell if it was Dale's comment that'd bugged him, or if it was the way I'd tried to lie to him. Maybe it was both. I watched him disappear, and then a bang sounded, followed by a screech, as he opened the back of the bus.

He and Dad bent inside, murmuring to each other as the rest of the guys bounced around like a bunch of preschoolers heading on an excursion for the first time.

"Should we order in?" Mom asked, sliding an arm around my shoulders. "I doubt we'll be able to tear them away from this thing unless it involves fried chicken."

I huffed. "Maybe not even for that." Glancing around the street, I noticed some of the neighbors were taking a peek at the monster that now resided half on our front lawn and half in the street. "That doesn't bode well."

Mom sighed. "Looks like I'll be offering free lessons to the McGregor's grandkids again."

I looked over at Mr. and Mrs. McGregor, who were gawking at the bus, and then at Mom, remembering the last time she'd had to bribe them into not causing a fuss. It was when Dad and Hendrix had built a skate ramp. The thing was so big, it had to stay on our driveway. It was now in five rotting pieces in the back shed.

Idly, I wondered if something similar would happen to this bus. Or if it'd do the unthinkable, and take the band—take Everett—away from Plume Grove.

SIX

THE DIRT CHANGED COLOR, FROM LIGHT TO DARK BROWN, AS WATER escaped the hose in my hand.

"You do know that works better if you stand."

Startled, I almost slipped off Hendrix's skateboard, my head snapping back and up. The sun framed Everett's face, too bright to make out his expression.

I blinked and quickly righted the hose, which had been spraying the mailbox. "If by working better you mean breaking my bones and skin, then no thanks."

Chuckling, he propped a drink on the driveway next to me. "For you."

I stared at the cup, then reached out and wrapped my hand around the condensation-soaked cardboard. "A shake?"

"Vanilla."

I didn't ask how he knew. If I'd learned anything about Everett Taylor and his mysterious ways, it was that he paid attention even while seeming perpetually indifferent.

Sipping from the straw, I felt my eyes flutter. "God, so good."

He took it from me, taking a sip, then set it on the concrete. "Hop up."

Tilting my head, I frowned. "Why?"

He didn't elaborate; he just stood there with the sun still disguising his expression. I could guess at it, though. Without needing to see, I knew his brows were pinching with impatience.

Sighing, I got up and went to turn the hose off. When I returned, Everett was standing before the skateboard, holding his hands out toward me. "Get on."

"I was on it. Then you kicked me off."

"Clover," he pressed.

"Fine." I set my bare feet upon the coarse grip-tape and squealed a little when the board rolled.

Everett caught my wrists. "I said take my hands."

"You said no such thing; you merely held them out."

I could see his face just fine now, and the bemused curl to his lips grated. Then, slowly and with our eyes locking, I watched as all humor fled his while his hands crawled down to mine.

They were warm, callused, gentle, and strong. A prickling sensation danced over the nape of my neck, and my belly warmed faster than my face. "I'm going to fall."

"So fall," he said, low and confident. "I'll be here to help you get back up."

I felt it then, that irrevocable shift inside. As if somehow, someway the vibrancy of the world had dripped away, and the only color that remained was us.

Tugging my hands, he helped me roll off the curb to the street. He laughed louder than I'd ever heard before when I screamed, pitching forward into his chest, and breathing hard. "I could've died."

"Don't say that." He sobered, and his arms seemed to squeeze me close for all of a second, and then he was straightening me on the board. "Back we go then, chicken shit."

"No," I said, refusing to release his hand. Staring down the cul-de-sac, I looked back at him and grinned. "Just once."

Watching me for a beat, he shook his head. "This was a bad idea."

"This was the best idea," I said, pushing off with my foot, and then I lost my grip on his hand, my arms pinwheeling as the skateboard carried me faster and faster down the street.

I didn't even have time to scream; the curb was approaching, and my heart was lodged in my throat. It was all I could do to keep upright, my hair coming loose from my braid and tangling around my face.

My eyes squeezed shut as every muscle braced for impact. Then arms came around me, and the inertia sent me and Everett tumbling onto the neighbor's front lawn.

"Ow," I moaned, my ankle protesting the weird angle it'd found itself in.

"Yeah, ow," Everett grumbled beneath me, wincing as he tried to lift his head.

I pushed my hands to the grass, gazing down at him. The second our eyes connected, laughter howled from us both, dizzying and oxygen depriving.

Drawing a few deep breaths, I settled and stared at his smile, hypnotized by the low chuckles still vacating his mouth. "You okay?"

"I'm good." He heaved out a loud breath, squinting at me. "You?"

"Perfect." His body was hard everywhere, and I swallowed, my gaze unwilling to drift far from his. "My hero."

He grinned, blinding and breath-stealing. "I'm no one's hero, Clover."

"You kept your promise."

Huffing, he groaned, cracking his neck. "Guess I did."

"That makes you a hero in my eyes." His body grew even more taut. Sensing the change in his mood, I climbed off him, then went in search of Hendrix's skateboard.

It'd wedged itself before the opening of a drain. I pulled it free and joined Everett, who was waiting for me on the street.

"You were fucking flying," he said.

"It's made the top five most terrifying moments of my life."

He chuckled, sighing as we reached the driveway to my house. "Do me a favor?"

"What?" I used my hand to block the sun, trying to find his eyes.

They refused to be found, and instead, they drifted across the street. "Don't get on that thing again."

I laughed, grabbing the melted shake, and watched him cross the street before heading inside.

I was nearing seventeen when I agreed to go out on my first date.

I'd been asked out a few times, but I'd always said no. It took Adela asking if I was gay or a love-sick fool to finally realize what I'd been doing.

I'd been waiting for something that wasn't ever going to happen.

And so when Clive Went asked me out, I shrugged, and said, "Sure, why not."

He was cute, the captain of the swim team, and best of all, he was not friends with my brother.

Judging by the gathering of his dark brows, my answer didn't exactly thrill him, but he still said he'd pick me up at seven and take me to the drive-in theater down by the beach.

"What do you mean, you need to go to college?" Hendrix shouted from the garage.

My eyes snapped up from my textbook as the garage door opened and the guys filtered into the kitchen. "Mom said I'll be wasting my time, and they can't afford to put me through school. I need to take this scholarship."

"Who hands out scholarships this late?" Everett muttered, nabbing a bottle of water from the fridge.

"Colleges who offered it to other kids who turned it down."

Everett's forehead creased as if he couldn't understand why someone would do that.

"We leave in three months, man," Hendrix said, sounding close to begging.

"Yeah? Leave with what, huh?" Graham spread his hands; his laughter drenched with scorn. "We're all working minimum wage jobs, earning fuck all, and we don't even have a bus that runs."

I closed my book, thinking I'd go and re-check my mascara. Oftentimes, it felt like the band thought of me as wallpaper. They forgot I was there when I watched them play, heard them bicker and fight, and even when they shared details of their weekend escapades.

"What, you just expected it to be easy, is that it?" Hendrix said. "Nothing good comes easy, dick face. Nothing. We need to get our asses out there and work for it just like every other person has."

"That's just it, Hendrix," Graham said, adjusting his glasses. "It's us against a world full of musicians all thirsty for the same elusive thing. What makes us so different that we'll catch a break?" The quiet that followed his words had Graham wincing, tension suffocating everyone in the room. "Fuck it, I'm out."

"Wait," Everett finally spoke, stalking after him.

"Jesus fucking Christ," Hendrix groaned, folding over the kitchen counter like a wilting flower. "Asshole." His forehead banged against the countertop. "What a fucking asshole."

I kept quiet, worried that announcing my presence might only make it worse.

"Steve?" Hendrix asked after a while.

I stiffened. "Uh, yeah?"

"You wouldn't happen to know any drummers, would you?"

"Um," I started, searching for something to say, something helpful. "No, but maybe I can have my friend, Jean, put an ad in the school paper."

Hendrix sighed. "Unless they wanna drop out, they'd be no good."

"You're still planning on going?"

Straightening, he didn't answer and left the room.

The front door slammed a second later, and then Everett rounded the corner as I was checking the time. Clive would be here any minute.

I snatched my purse and stood. "He's gone?" I asked Everett, keeping my eyes from his.

"Yeah. He's just freaked. School's out in a month, and shit's getting real. I get it." He shifted in his skate shoes. "I think he'll come around."

I nodded, praying he did while also hoping they'd part on good terms if Graham decided to go to college. It might not have been what he'd wanted. Graham had been playing drums since he got his first kit as an energetic toddler, but I understood it might not be what he needed.

"Clover, where are you going?"

I still couldn't meet his gaze, but I could feel it. Hot and probing. "Oh, ah…" The doorbell rang, jarring me. No one ever used it, and instead just came and went as they wanted. "Movies," I said, skirting around him.

Everett grabbed my hand, and shocked, I stopped, turning to pull it back.

His brows cinched as he stared at his empty hand. "With Adela?"

I couldn't lie and wasn't even sure why I was tempted to. "No, um. With Clive. From school."

Darkening, his eyes changed to a mixture of black and green as he said, "The asshole on the swim team?"

I could feel my shoulders square. "He's not an asshole."

"Seriously?" Everett scoffed. "He's a player, Clover. He only wants one thing from you."

I rolled my eyes and started walking down the hall.

"Stevie," he said, voice hard, and the sound of my real name had me almost stumbling as I opened the door. "Stevie, don't let him fuck with you."

Clive, dressed in a navy polo and light blue jeans, stepped back, hearing Everett's words, and I inwardly cursed. "Hey, ignore him. Let's go."

Swiping a hand over his slicked back hair, Clive looked from the now closed door to me, and back again. "Yeah, hey."

I didn't know if it was Everett's warning or if he really was being a perfect gentleman, but Clive kept things respectful. Maybe a little too respectful as his eyes stayed trained firmly on the bloodbath decorating the screen three rows of cars ahead of his old Ford.

Bored and grossed out, I plucked my phone from my purse to find a text from Adela.

Adela: He make a move yet?

Pursing my lips, I eyed Clive's handsome, clean-shaven profile, then shoved a handful of popcorn into my mouth.

Me: Negative.

Adela: What gives???

Me: No idea, but I'm bored to tears.

Huffing, I made an effort to seem extra invested in my phone, hoping that might rally some kind of reaction from him.

Adela: Want me to call? Pretend it's your mom?

I snorted, and still, Clive's dedication to the movie didn't waver. I was tempted to go, but Mom had already told me I could text her and have her bail me out.

Me: Nah. I'll call you when I get home.

I tucked my phone back inside my purse, stole the entire box of popcorn for myself, then settled into the seat.

Purse in hand, I opened the door. "I had a nice time, thank you."

"Me too. I'll, ah…" Clive paused, eyeing the big bus through the stream of his headlights, and the males surrounding it. "I'll see you at school?"

Still confused about his lack of interest, I nodded and shut the door a little too hard behind me.

The bus was now in the drive, and I narrowly rounded it, ignoring the snorts and laughter the idiots on the other side of it tried to muffle, and headed for the door.

Mom opened it before I got there. "Well, how was it?"

"The movie was horrible." I crinkled my nose at the

memory of the gore. "So, kind of boring." I kicked off my shoes inside and headed down the hall as Mom closed the front door. "Where's Dad?"

"Outside with the boys. Determined as hell," she quipped, putting on the kettle. "I don't know why. It's not like he actually wants them to leave. Tea?"

"Please," I said, dumping my purse on the dining table.

"So it was boring, huh?" She dunked two tea bags into mugs, pouring water in once the kettle clicked. "Not exactly what I want to hear about your very first date."

"Technically, it wasn't. Remember Ben from the third grade?"

"That was a playdate, honey."

"Try telling him that." He'd never let me forget he was my first boyfriend. Ben was now openly gay but loved to tell our friends we'd once "had a thing."

I sat with Mom a while as we drank our tea, filling her in on Clive's weirdness, the horrible movie, and then we spoke about Graham's probable departure from the band.

She left not long before the front door opened and Everett strolled into the kitchen, taking a seat on Mom's recently vacated stool beside mine at the counter.

"Have fun?" he asked.

I didn't answer and sipped my tea. The airy note to his tone bothered me. The last thing I wanted was to admit to him it was… "Wait." I placed my mug down. "You guys didn't do something, did you?"

Staring at me point blank, he didn't even try to deny it.

"Everett," I growled.

"It wasn't me."

I raised my brows, then stood, glowering at him. "The audacity. You get to go out, do whatever and whomever you want, and I try to go on one freaking date with a perfectly nice guy, and you won't even let me have that?"

He blinked up at me, smooth lips parting. "Clover, what?" He shook his head, and his forehead crinkled. "Hendrix. He texted Clive. Warned him he'd tell the school he'd been hooking up with the swim coach if he so much as touched you."

I fell back, almost missing the stool, my shoulders and heart falling. "What?" I rasped.

Everett poked his lip with his tongue, then sighed. "He told me after you left."

Heat crawled up my neck, infiltrating my cheeks, and I ripped my eyes from his searching ones.

I'd never felt so mortified. I'd basically admitted that I had a thing for Everett by accusing him like that. "God," I breathed, standing and hightailing it to my room.

Everett followed, barging in as I tried to slam the door. "Clover, what you said—"

"Ignore it. It came out all wrong and wasn't what I meant to say." I flapped my trembling hands about, then raked them through my hair. "It's nothing."

He shut the door, striding close enough to halt my pacing. "I told you not to lie to me."

I had nothing to say to that, so I took the pins out of my hair, allowing it all to cascade around my shoulders as I set them on the nightstand. "This is different, Everett."

"Yeah?" He took a life-changing step closer and then another one. "How so?"

He was close now, too close. So close I could smell that clean soapy scent on his skin that mingled with that of tobacco. So close that when I lifted my eyes from his heaving chest, letting them drift slowly up to take in the scruff coating his strong, stubborn jaw and outlining those parted, full lips, I struggled to breathe. It was a task easier said than done when all I could see, smell, and hear was everything I'd been wanting, standing before me, just one word or movement away from touching me.

"Clover," he said, gravel filling the word. "Answer me."

"You really don't want me to do that," I said, finally meeting his eyes.

That was a mistake. I knew it before they even collided, but the wreckage couldn't be salvaged now.

A hissed curse flew past his lips, and then his hands were cupping my face, his turbulent eyes darting back and forth between mine, looking for something I couldn't name. He must've found whatever he was searching for because then it happened.

His lips lowered, landing on my own and stilling. I could feel it, the way both our bodies seemed to turn to stone, the air shifting and warping around us, cocooning us in a forbidden but oh, so perfect bubble.

"Clover," he whispered, mouth parting.

Soft and warm, his lips held mine between them, a hint of mint and whiskey on his breath. Breaking the spell, I raised my arms, wrapping them around his neck as I tilted my head to press my mouth over his gently, carefully until I grew more confident and tried to lick my way inside to meet his tongue. I wanted it so bad, my knees trembled, and I whimpered when he grabbed my shoulders and moved me back a step.

"Look what you've gone and done now," he murmured, though not a trace of regret filled the words, only rough, complicated lust.

"Me?" I asked, incredulous.

He nodded, gripping my chin and kissing my forehead. "Don't go kissing anyone else, or I'll rip their tongues out and decorate your precious gardens with them."

My heart dipped. "Everett." Panic and want warred when

he went to open my door. "What…?" I started, then shook my head. "Ugh, I just… I don't understand."

"There's nothing to understand." He ran a hand over his hair, sinking his thick fingers into the mussed strands. "We shouldn't have done that."

"Huh?" Something began to sink inside me, plummeting and pulling. "You can't tell me not to kiss anyone else and a heartbeat later decide we can't kiss again."

Laughing, he smirked down at the ground, the sound quiet and filled with resignation. "I never said we wouldn't do it again." He opened the door, not looking back as he left me with, "Just that we shouldn't."

SEVEN

"**W**HAT IS GOING ON, THEN?" ADELA ASKED.

It'd been a whole week since Everett had first laid his lips upon mine.

One whole week of waiting and watching, desperate to see what would happen next. Desperate to know if his last words to me meant anything would even happen. He'd been at the garage, though, much to the band's dismay as they tried to squeeze in some practice that week. Everyone was tied up with jobs and school ending for the year, so I hadn't seen the guys together since the week before.

"Two months?" I heard from the kitchen.

"One sec," I said to Adela, cracking open my bedroom door to listen.

"But Graham's out," Hendrix said. "How are we supposed to find another drummer in two months?"

"It doesn't matter," came the voice I'd been waiting to hear. "We'll find someone. If we don't go, we probably never will, and then what? We'll just waste away here with no other plans?"

There was a beat of silence before Hendrix cursed, and then the sound of their voices faded as they no doubt went outside to work on the bus.

Two months until they leave.

My heart thudded hard.

"Stevie?" Adela called.

I pressed the phone back to my ear. "Sorry, the guys were saying they're leaving in two months."

"Wow," she said. "But what does that mean for you and Everett?"

Nothing, I almost said. Instead, I sighed. "Not sure. We're not… something anyway. I don't know what we are or what even possessed him to kiss me in the first place." All true words, yet they still jabbed like needles.

We spoke some more about a date she was going on that night before deciding to chat after she got back.

After I hung up, I tossed my phone onto the dresser, my nails raking over my scalp as my eyes skidded over the posters hanging on my wall. Stevie Nicks—my namesake—Florence Welch, and Joan Jett.

Warring with the urge to lay eyes on Everett, I filled the tiny watering can I kept in my room and gave some love to the succulents that dotted the windowsill.

"Your room looks different during the daylight hours."

Almost dropping the can, I turned to find Everett leaning in the doorway to my room. "Where's Hendrix?"

"Outside. Dale just arrived with some auto electrician friend of his." He moved into the room, closing the door with a quiet click. "He'll be busy for a while."

I nodded, tucking some hair behind my ear as he strode toward me, the laces of his boots undone and slapping against the worn leather.

Warm skin met my chin, tipping it up as the rough pad of his thumb brushed beneath my bottom lip and his other hand took the watering can from me. "Can't look at me now?"

I licked my lips, then moved out of his hold to sit on the bed. "It's just…"

"Just?" A thick brow quirked. My little pink watering can looked tiny in his large hand.

"I haven't seen you since, you know, and I don't know." I let my eyes find his, noticing the red rimming them and littering the white globes. Concern had me forgetting my eager heart. "How are you?"

"How am I?" he asked, setting the can back where it usually sat in the corner of my windowsill. "That's not what I expected you to ask."

"What did you expect me to ask?"

Rubbing his hand over the scruff on his cheek, he exhaled a tired breath and sat beside me. "Don't know. The usual girly shit."

I tried not to be offended or jealous that he'd been in these situations with others. "You look tired."

"I am," he said. "Been busting my ass at the garage. Rent's due and the assholes have decided to stop paying it now that I'm done with school."

"You're kidding," I choked out. "But you haven't even graduated yet."

"They don't care," he said, hands moving behind his head as he fell back over my blue and green patchwork duvet. "As far as they're concerned, I should've already dropped out and gotten full-time work."

A squeezing sensation constricted my stomach. "I hate them."

Everett huffed a laugh. "They weren't always this bad." A pause. "But yeah, I hate them too."

I lowered and turned onto my side, leaning on my elbow to stare down at him. "What made them change?"

His expression tightened, fingers drumming over his stomach to an invisible beat. His black shirt gathered enough to show a glimpse of skin above his jeans and the waistband of his briefs.

My stomach unclenched, leaping at the sight of the coarse trickle of hair that led from his belly button to the depths beyond, beneath his pants. I'd seen plenty of guys with their shirts off, but I'd never seen one I liked this close, one I wanted to see more of. To touch. To feel—

"You're making me hard," he said.

Shocked, I sputtered out a coughed laugh, my cheeks heating as I removed my eyes from his stomach and tented pants. "Your parents," I prompted, needing to know, even if the temptation to maybe do other things was strong.

His gaze shuttered, then he rolled into me, his hand molding to my waist. "Enough about them."

I froze as his thumb started circling my hip, my T-shirt rising and drooping over my midsection. His eyes stayed on mine, watching, studying. "This okay?"

"Yeah," I whispered.

"Can I kiss you again?"

I almost said yeah but stopped. "Why do you want to?"

He blinked, eyes hooding and hand sliding higher to settle into the dip beneath my ribs. Taking his time, he stared, and it felt like someone was blowing bubbles inside my veins. "Because I realized something the other night." I waited, dizzy for whatever it could be. "Maybe even before then, if I'm being honest. That what I feel for you is far more than friendship or brotherly protectiveness."

"It is?" I breathed out.

He leaned closer, nose gentle as it bumped mine, the scent of mint and tobacco on his breath. "It is. It just took me looking outside my own shit for longer than two minutes to actually see it for what it is."

I erased the space, my mouth melding to his, his hand pressing our bodies together. Our teeth clinked as the kiss went from soft exploration to firm detonation. From parted lips to seeking tongues.

"You always smell like a vanilla milkshake," he said, groaning and licking the underside of my top lip. "But you taste way better."

Butterflies exploded like a fizzing bomb erupting, decimating every cell in my body.

And then a bang sounded outside, followed by yelling and cussing.

I pulled away, and Everett dived off the bed, cracking open the door in time for us to hear, "Everett, fuck." Hendrix hollered, "Where are you? Get out here, quick!"

He raced back to the bed, climbing over me to peck my lips. "When I can, mark my words, Clover, I'll find you."

"Don't take so long next time."

His brows jumped in clear surprise, and he grinned, biting my lip before throwing himself off the bed and adjusting his jeans on the way out.

Turning my face into my bedding, I smothered a giggle while kicking my feet in the air behind me.

The creak of the rising window alerted me, and I sat up, blinking sleep heavy eyes as Everett climbed in and stumbled to my bedroom floor.

"Shhh," I hissed. "Want to wake everyone up?"

"Hendrix is still out," Everett said, a little slurred, and rolled over to kick off his boots. "I wanted to see you, so I left."

There were parties down on the beach all weekend to celebrate the end of school. Bonfire smoke tumbled off Everett as he crawled over to the bed, almost as strong as the stench of alcohol and weed.

His hand fell on mine, fingers stroking. "I don't wanna sleep on the floor this time."

"Oh," I exhaled.

Bloodshot emerald eyes rose, long lashes curling to meet his brows. "No sex," he said. "I'm…" He shook his head as if to clear it. "I'm not worthy of that from you. I just want to hold you, Clover, and feel your skin against mine." Still watching me with nothing but the moon to highlight our features, he dragged his teeth over his lip. "That okay?"

Tears pricked at the vulnerable, honest timbre of his words. "That's okay."

He flashed me a grin, then stood and shoved off his jeans, almost stumbling to the floor again.

I grabbed his arm, pulling him onto my bed before he knocked something over and woke up my parents.

His hand moved to my back, ducking beneath my sleep shirt and rubbing. The scent of the night's festivities was almost overbearing with him this close. "Did you have fun?"

"Mmm," he moaned, nose nudging my chin. "Wish you'd been there. Fucking Hendrix."

I held back a laugh, smiling when his head shifted to rest next to mine on the pillow. "You're beautiful, but when you smile, you're a portrait of starlit dreams."

Still smiling, I absorbed his words, knowing he was drunk but knowing that unless he was singing, it was rare to hear such openness from him. My hand found his cheek, my thumb ghosting over the tiny, almost undetectable, scar beneath his eye.

He hummed, his large hand pressing me closer, legs entangled with mine as his eyelids drifted closed. "I love your touch the most."

I kissed his lips, pushing him back when he tried to take things deeper. "Sleep, Everett."

"Not worthy," he whispered. "But I'll probably keep trying to take you anyway."

His breathing had settled into even puffs that drifted from his lips and nose to stir my hair when I whispered, "You're worthy. You just haven't figured that out yet."

"Just hold your nose," Adela encouraged, laughing.

I did as she said, coughing and splattering as the vodka burned a hole in my tongue and throat. "Holy fire."

She fell back to the sand, howling at the moon.

"Yo, Sandrine!"

So used to hearing it directed at Hendrix, I almost ignored the person calling my surname.

Then I remembered Hendrix was playing a gig in the next town over. We were going to go, but Mom and Dad were out for their anniversary, and Adela wanted to drink. I didn't have a car, and I doubted Adela's parents wanted me driving her new Mercedes.

So we'd walked down to the beach. I hadn't planned on drinking much, but that was before vodka.

As the sound of feet crunching over sand hit my ears, I turned, spying Mark from biology.

"Wassup?" I mumbled, my eyelids heavy as I raised them. Adela snorted, and I asked, "How much have we drank?"

She held up the one-liter glass bottle she'd swiped from her parents' mini bar, and I leaned closer to discover it was half empty. "Oh fucking dear."

"Oh dear is right." Adela snickered. "What's crackin', Mark?"

He stopped, flip-flops kicking up sand behind him. "That fucking bonfire over there. Come sit with us."

I looked up at him, squinting, then over at the people dancing and drinking around the fire. "Nah. Too far."

Mark chuckled, then went to take a seat. "I'll just hang here with you gals, then."

"No, you won't. Fuck off, Jones."

All three of us did a double take at the sound of Everett's voice.

"Hey, man. Good show?" Mark staggered back as Everett's shadow darkened the sand in front of me.

"Yeah, great. Bye."

With a wink, Mark saluted us, then jogged back over the sand to the fire.

"Hey, Everett."

"Hi," he said to Adela.

I didn't know what was funnier—Everett telling Mark to fuck off, or the fact that I was drunk and he seemed to be the sober one for once. I laughed at both.

"What's so funny, Clover?" He dropped down beside me. "Shit, you're tanked."

"That's what's funny."

"Oh, look. I think I see Gabby," Adela slurred, non-convincingly. "I'll catch up with you in a bit."

"She's going home," Everett said. "Want us to take you?"

Adela grabbed the vodka, swinging it beside her as she began walking away. "No thanks, three's a crowd and all that." I didn't want her wandering off on her own, but I knew she was likely heading home.

"She knows," Everett said once she was out of earshot.

"Duh, she's my best friend."

"Fuck," he spat. "Clover…"

I turned into him, my finger rising to those decadent lips. "Shhh. She's known for a while and hasn't breathed a word. Chill."

"Chill?" he repeated, taking my finger and depositing it back in my lap. "This can't turn—"

"Gah, don't ruin my buzz, Ever." I got to my feet, swaying until he jumped up and righted me.

"Ever?" His hold loosened.

Fluttering my lashes, I nodded. "Let's go make out under the pier."

He tugged me back to him. "We can't."

"We can, the ocean says so."

"The ocean?" His brow arched.

"Listen to it," I said, hearing the waves crash beneath the sound of humans littering the beach. "It doesn't judge or care."

"You're drunk." His lips thinned. "Let's go."

"I'm not that drunk. I'd want to make out with you even if I hadn't had one drop of alcohol." At his resolute expression, I snatched my hand from his. "Wait, so we can make out in my room but nowhere else?"

Everett cursed, glancing around to see if anyone was within hearing distance. Then he started walking.

I followed, or tried to, slipping over grooves of sand in my flip-flops. "Where are you going?"

"Just keep walking," he said.

I frowned, knowing why he refused to wait but not liking it.

We entered the parking lot, and I saw Dale's car down at the end beneath the bridge that crossed the lagoon to enter town.

"How was the show?" I asked when he stopped, waiting for me to catch up. "You're not drunk."

"Because I wanted to see you, and you weren't there or at home." Annoyance lined his voice.

"Home," I said, smiling. "Sorry."

He said nothing and opened the door of Dale's Camry for me to climb in.

I shut it, then moved into Everett, pressing my mouth to his chin as my hands roamed down the hard planes of his chest, feeling the dips and bumps of his stomach. "I want you," I breathed. "Your hands on me, your mouth on mine, and our clothes off."

"Jesus," he rasped out.

My tongue licked at the underside of his jaw, over the coarse bristles erupting from his warm skin. Grabbing his head, I tilted it down as I rose to my toes to run my tongue over his lips. "Kiss me, Ever."

His control snapped, his mouth opening and his tongue diving for mine while his hands dug into my hair. He moved, and then my back was against the cool metal of the car he was reaching to open. "In," he breathed, ragged.

I knew he was worried someone might see—even though it was dark, and we were far enough away from the beach party for anyone to see a thing—so I did as I was told. Before doing so, I ripped off my dress, laughing softly at the way his eyes widened. Then, in only my baby blue panties and matching frill-laden bra, I crawled over the back seat.

Turning, I leaned against the door and crooked a finger for him to come to me.

He did, and I'd never felt more thankful for the brazenness that came with the consumption of alcohol. I'd dreamed of us in these scenarios for what felt like years, and now, I finally had the nerve to make those dreams a reality.

He pulled the door closed behind him, and I moved forward, tugging his shirt over his head to scrape my nails over his chest. "So soft, like velvet over steel." He chuckled and then lifted me to straddle his lap, the car rocking a little. With his hardness digging into me, I moaned, "I wonder if that will feel the same."

"Fucking hell, Clover. Are you trying to kill me?" His words were choppy, his chest heaving beneath my greedy hands. "I'm not fucking you in my friend's car."

"No?" I pouted, lowering my lips to his and searching for his hand. "Then you need to at least make me come for the first time in your friend's car."

Stilling, he tugged his hand from mine to grip my face, forcing my eyes to his questioning ones. "You've never had an orgasm before?"

"Only by my own hands." I licked my lips, my hair falling over my cheek, tickling the swells of my breasts. "I mean, fingers."

He stared for the longest minute, and I could feel the war raging inside his head. Both heads. To help make up his mind, I began to move over the one in his pants, a tiny moan slipping free as I grinded right where I needed friction.

Transfixed, he watched. His heated gaze flicked over my face, my hands tangled in my hair, my chest, and dipping further. Down, down, down to where I could feel myself damp against him. A caress, a kiss, and a brand, I shivered under the weight of those molten eyes.

Then the cups of my bra were yanked down, and one rough hand palmed a breast while his tongue and lips sucked and nibbled the other.

"Yes," I breathed, my heart racing, the warmth from his mouth stoking the fire between my legs.

Everett's mouth left my breast with a pop, then, staring up into my face, he licked his thumbs before circling them over my nipples. "You wanna come by humping me?" His head was tilted back against the headrest of the seat, eyelids drooping and his chest rising higher and higher. "Or do you want my fingers?"

My chest sparked and spasmed. "Fingers."

His lips curled, and then his hands were shifting me. I took the opportunity to unzip his fly and tug at his pants as his fingers slowly found their way inside the slick material of my panties, shoving them aside.

His cock bobbed up against his stomach, bouncing, and I gasped at the sight of it in the moonlight. Long, rigid, and thick with angry looking veins.

"Shit." I looked from it to Everett's smirking face right as his fingers spread me open and trailed through the mess he'd created.

My eyes almost rolled. His other hand caught my lower back before gripping my chin and forcing my gaze to his as he circled that nub of nerves. "Ever." I swallowed, my voice hoarse.

"Climb, Clover."

His erection stood there between us. I could feel its heat, so even though I had no idea what I was doing, I gripped it and moved my hand up and down as best I could while he evoked sensations that had me trembling.

"Fuck," he hissed. "Look at me. Give me those blue eyes."

I did, and his hand joined mine over his length, moving it up and down as one thick finger breached my opening and dipped inside, but not too far.

He did it again and again, returning to tease the swollen part of me before sliding back in, and then I was drifting. "I'm …"

"On my hand, right now." He groaned, the harsh angles of his face both slack and stark at the same time. He moved my hand up and down, over and around him, faster and harder. My eyes fluttered, my thighs shaking. "Don't you fucking look away."

I didn't, but oh my God, it was hard as my body quaked, and I clenched and curled over him.

Everything frayed and spun, and then Everett was cursing, his eyes bright in the gloom of the moonlit car. "So fucking beautiful. God, fuck."

I'd lost my grip, but he hadn't and was jerking himself fast. Warm liquid squirted over my hand and his abdomen. Hypnotized, I watched, wanting more while rendered immobile.

His breathing started to slow, but that glow in his eyes didn't fade.

Grabbing my cheek with the hand he'd had between my legs, he brought our lips flush, and I tilted my head, giving him everything I had left.

Mind, body, and soul, it resonated with a permanence I couldn't ignore. I was his.

When we finally separated long enough to draw a breath, I blurted, "I love you." Gradually, he'd snuck inside me, imbedding and making a home for himself beneath my flesh and bone.

He was a crescendo, an ever-increasing note, and there was no end in sight.

Like a switch had flicked, Everett's body turned from relaxed to concrete beneath me.

I smiled. "You don't need to say it." I'd known he probably wouldn't, no matter what he might've felt. "I just wanted you to know."

After an excruciating minute of feeling my heart pinch while I struggled to maintain eye contact, he swallowed, nodding.

We helped each other dress and cleaned up with a beach towel that was in the trunk.

"How're we going to clean that?"

Everett tossed it into the small bush behind the car. "We don't." He stepped forward, pulling at my dress until it hung right. With a kiss to my brow, he slammed the trunk and moved to the passenger side door. "We need to get you home."

"What did you tell Dale you were doing with his car?" I asked when we left the parking lot.

"Really want me to answer that?" He turned down some backstreets, then veered left onto one that connected to our cul-de-sac.

No, I didn't want him to. I didn't want anything to rid the euphoric feeling that'd taken over. That'd made the globs of orange swaying from the streetlights and passing homes seem more than ordinary.

We made sure all the lights inside were out, and then he left me with a brief but reeling kiss before I exited the car. I fished my key from the rose bush by the mailbox and walked inside feeling sober and drunk at the same time. Feeling lighter than air.

EIGHT

"But he's still not your boyfriend," Adela said, skirting a rogue soccer ball some kid was kicking down the sidewalk.

His mom chased after him, and I licked the bubblegum ice cream from the side of my waffle cone. "No." I sighed, licking my lips. "And to make matters worse, I'm pretty sure I told him I loved him." It sucked. What we'd done together in the car that night played on repeat nonstop. Impossible to ignore even though I was starting to desperately need to.

Adela stopped, and I winced when I saw her shocked expression. "Bad, huh?"

She started walking again, tossing her half-eaten tub of cookie-dough ice cream into a trash can. "That depends. What did he say?"

"Uh, well," I hemmed.

"Well?" She all but screeched.

"Well…" My shoulders slumped as the admission barreled free. "Nothing."

Adela was stunned into silence, and I tore off a chunk of my ice-cream cone to keep from snapping or screaming.

"Stevie…" she started.

"I blame the beach. And the vodka. Definitely the vodka." I made my feet move faster as the businesses changed to houses, my Chucks scuffing against the cracked concrete.

"Wait," she said, catching up. "It's okay, you know."

"That I'm in love with my brother's best friend?" I scoffed, tossing my cone into someone's trash at the curb, then brushing my sticky hands over my cutoffs. "Or that I let him touch me all over before admitting I was in love with him, only for him to say nothing?"

Adela pursed her lips, her shoulders rising to hug her ears. "You didn't do anything wrong. It's not as if you can help how you feel." She grinned. "It's a stupid rule. I've been crushing on Hendrix for years."

I rolled my eyes. "That's different, Del."

"Maybe," she said. "But have you seen Everett since?"

"No, he's either been at the garage or working on that damn bus. And if he's working on the bus, he's never alone."

"You don't think he wants to talk to you?"

The sound of the ocean, the passing cars, and the kids playing outside blurred with my muffled thoughts as the sun beat a harsh tempo over my skin.

"Trust me," I said as we rounded the corner, then crossed the road. "If he wanted to talk to me, he'd have found a way by now."

We cut through an alleyway, emerging onto my street, which was three streets away from Adela's. "Will you be okay?" She stopped two houses up from mine.

I knew she wasn't referring to Everett not saying he loved me. No, she was asking because they were leaving soon. With or without a new drummer. But I knew. I think I'd always known, even before they purchased the bus, that he wouldn't stay.

"I'll have to be," I said, quiet as I gazed at Everett's house.

The grass had grown two feet since Everett last mowed it a couple of months ago. That wasn't what shocked me, though. It was the sight of what had to be his mom outside. A gray cotton nightgown hung from her thin frame, matching the curls in her limp honey blond hair. Leaning up off the porch steps, she seemed to be trying to shut the front window.

She grabbed it, slipped, and landed in the overgrown, weed-strewn garden, cursing as pain no doubt radiated up her legs from the jarring impact. Her cigarette fell from her mouth, and she shoved the tangled mess of hair from her weathered face, bending over to pick it up.

The window remained half open.

I glanced at Adela, who was worrying her lip between her teeth, then I looked back at the cursing, muttering woman. A woman who had to have been beautiful once upon a time. Before life stole that beauty and the light from her familiar green eyes.

"You need some help?" I called out.

She turned, her empty eyes narrowing on us. "Fuck off, little slut." Then she marched up the driveway. The screen door screeched, slamming closed behind her.

Adela's brows jumped. "Did she just…?"

"Uh, yup."

Judging from her puzzled, creased expression, the same one I knew I had to be wearing, she was thinking the same thing. We wouldn't want to stay there either.

Sighing, I said goodbye when we crossed the road, and Adela headed to the alley that cut through to the next street over.

About to head inside, I paused when I noticed someone had squashed one of my azaleas. Grabbing a spade from the side of the house, I walked around the giant yellow bus that was now painted a solid black and inspected the flower bed behind it.

My stomach drooped when I saw the squashed and wilting cluster. Not much could be done for it, other than to tell someone off. Which I planned to do as soon as Hendrix arrived home.

After taking a shower, I wrapped my hair in a towel, entering the kitchen just as the guys, hollering at each other, bounded inside. They were all here, even Graham.

Everett was the last to arrive and only stalled a second to stare at me before drifting into the kitchen. He didn't stay. Instead, he walked right into the garage.

I swallowed the thorns invading and cutting my throat, and pasted on a smile. "What's going on?"

"This fucker over here," Hendrix said, giving Graham a noogie, "failed to give his beloved college an answer on time. They pulled his scholarship."

Mouth gaping, I blinked at Graham, who was shoving my brother away. "And this is good news?"

Graham shrugged, not looking the least bit disappointed.

"What do you even mean, Steve?" Hendrix laughed. "Of course, it is. It means he's coming with us, duh." He smacked the wall above the door leading into the garage, letting out a hoot as he disappeared.

"Can't let them have all the fun without me," Graham said, following Dale, the sound of Hendrix tearing into his guitar greeting them.

"Well, congrats," I said, belatedly realizing I'd forgotten to harass Hendrix about my azaleas.

I was tempted to go in there. To take the opportunity to see Everett. To watch him. Even if he'd just outright ignored my existence. If only I could've made my feet move.

Something that'd once felt as normal as breathing now felt wrong.

It grew worse, the pain I'd tried to ignore in my chest. But I couldn't bring myself to regret saying those three words to him. It wasn't a lie. It was a truth that'd sat deep for months, that'd grown roots over time, only growing stronger. Once it'd sprouted, there was no way to bury it. No way to smother it.

It was there, out in the open and starving from lack of warmth. And judging from the glances Mom was giving me over dinner that night, not so easy to hide.

Jumping out of Adela's car, I told her I'd call tomorrow.

She turned and sped off down the street, and I slung my overnight bag over my shoulder just as Dale's car pulled up.

I smiled, trying to swallow the memories of the previous weekend that emerged with the force of a battering ram, then halted when the window wound down and a voice that wasn't Dale's called out, "Get in, Clover."

"Everett?" I raised my hand to block the sun, stepping closer. Peering inside the car, I found him leaning over the steering wheel, Ray-Bans and a white shirt on. "Shouldn't you be at work?"

"Called in sick and told Dale I needed his ride to go to the doctor. Get in."

Briefly, I looked back at the house before shoving my duffel into the back seat and then climbing into the front.

"Where are we going?" I clipped on my seat belt.

Without so much as a glance at his own house, he turned at the end of the cul-de-sac, then veered right at the end of the street. "You'll see," he said. "I've been an ass, but even though I'm often an ass, in this case, I want a chance to try to explain myself."

I pursed my lips to hide my smile, but ignored his hand when he tried to reach for mine. "No touching until the talking has taken place." My smile wiggled free. "Maybe."

His teeth slid over his lip, and he took the next turn. "Whatever you say, beautiful."

A dancing sensation prickled my skin at the endearment, and I kept my eyes focused out the window to keep them from gluing to him.

In buzzing silence, we took the highway for twenty minutes before pulling into an old run-down truck stop. Everett came around the car, offering his hand to help me out.

I gave him a look that said no exceptions, then smirked when he huffed a laugh and shut the door behind me.

The little bell above the door announced our arrival, and I felt a thrill shoot through my veins, making each step lighter as I headed toward a booth in the back.

We were out together. In public. Granted, the likelihood someone we knew would happen upon this place midmorning on a weekday was slim, but still, the excitement was real all the same.

A waitress with the name tag Bev took our order, and I hesitated, knowing I only had twenty dollars in my duffel, which was still in the car.

Everett noticed and grabbed my hand. I let him, blinking as he ordered my favorite, two plates of waffles with ice cream and maple syrup, milkshakes, and waters.

"I got it, don't worry," he said once the waitress walked away.

I stared at a cross-stitched rooster hanging on the wall behind his head, then sighed. "We can eat and bail," I joked.

The tic in his jaw and the slight tightening of his hand over mine said he didn't think I was funny. "I don't steal everything."

Hendrix had once told me how Everett easily pocketed candy bars and other miscellaneous items, completely undetected. So I didn't quite know what to believe. I didn't judge; I just didn't want any part of it.

"Okay," I said, leaving it at that.

He removed his sunglasses, noticing the way I eyed them as he hung them from the neck of his shirt. "I paid for them too. Thirty dollars at the thrift store." His lips twitched. "They're not even fake."

"Bargain," I muttered as Bev slid our waters and shakes over the table. I thanked her, smiling up at her weathered face and taking in the beautiful orange curls that hung around it.

She beamed back, then strutted to a table on the opposite side of the diner.

"You're mad. I get it."

"Do you?" I unwrapped a straw and dunked it into my ice water before taking a sip.

Everett's eyes dipped to my mouth, then returned to mine. "I didn't know what to say, okay?"

"I told you," I said, putting the glass down and pulling the shake over. "You didn't need to say anything. You also didn't need to avoid me."

He sat back in the ripped blood red vinyl seat, twining his fingers together and squeezing. His mouth opened and closed, his tongue prodding at his lips while his eyes crawled over my face. "I care about you a fucking lot, Clover." He swallowed, wrenching his hands apart and shoving one through his hair, slicking the messy strands back. "And other than the band, I don't care about anything else, so please believe me when I say that means something."

I did believe it meant something. "You should've just said that. I'm not expecting us to get serious. I know you're leaving. I've known it since you bought that bus." I paused, dropping my lashes to the table. "I think I knew before then."

"Then how is it fair I do this to you? To either of us?"

"It's not fair," I said quietly. "But what else is there to do, ignore it?" We'd ignored it for too long, neglected it, yet it thrived anyway.

He took a long sip of water, eyeing me over the cup. "I've ignored it since I first laid eyes on you," he admitted, lowering the glass and running his fingers over the condensation. "I'm fucking tired of ignoring it, but I can't exactly take you with me when I go, can I?"

"Well," I hemmed, excitement a growing army that couldn't be defeated. "You could but—"

"Hendrix," he said with a rough exhale. "I don't even know how we'd begin to explain it to him."

"Is there any point in saying anything?" I asked. "Not when you're leaving. When you do, whatever this is, it ends."

We stared then, the minutes ticking by as other customers coughed, laughed, and talked quietly around us.

Biting his lip, Everett stole my hand and watched his fingers trace the creases spanning my palm. "Do you really believe it'll ever end?"

Our food arrived before I could answer, and I thanked Bev again, dragging my plate close.

We ate in silence, and being that I hadn't eaten since the pizza Adela and I had ordered at her place the night before, I nearly demolished the whole lot.

"Whoa, Clover." Everett let out a gentle laugh.

I withheld the belch that needed out and drank small sips of water as I watched him finish his food.

"So," he said, pushing his plate away after scooping up the last mouthful of ice cream from it. "No one knows this. Not from around here anyway."

I reached over the table, swiping the ice cream smeared over his top lip. He nipped at my thumb, then grabbed and sucked the remnants from it.

Liquid heat pooled in my full stomach, and I took my hand back, gesturing for him to continue.

Looking around the diner, he cleared his throat, then shifted in his seat. "I had a younger brother. He was eight when he died." My heart dissolved into ash. "That's why… the reason we moved here."

"I'm sorry, Ever." I blinked to keep my eyes clear, trying to accept what he'd said. "God. What happened?"

He shook his head. "Not ready to get into that. I don't know if I ever will be, but my parents…" He sighed. "They were bad before, but at least they had jobs and tried to appear as functioning members of society. Even when they were half-tanked all the time."

"Then they got worse," I said, remembering what his mom had called me just last week.

He nodded, and sensing he was done talking about it, I took his hand in mine and held it.

Staring down at them, he sat so still. I wasn't sure he was breathing until finally, his shoulders drooped a little. "Let's get out of here, yeah?"

He tucked a twenty and a ten under our dirty plates, then held my hand until I was seated back in Dale's car.

We took the long way home, choosing the backroads that gave way to breathtaking views of the ocean. But even that didn't seem to remove the somberness from Everett's expression.

I leaned over and clicked on the radio, searching until I registered the guitar riff from "Start Me Up" by The Rolling Stones.

Sure, I couldn't sing to save my life, but I didn't let that stop me. I wound down the window, belting out the chorus at the top of my lungs until finally, Everett quit laughing and joined in.

Long after we'd returned Dale's car and walked back to my place, Everett was humming the same song while he held me, sprawled beneath me on my bed.

He didn't try to make a move, and content to listen to the peaceful thud of his heart as he hummed, stirring the top of my hair, I didn't either. My eyes drifted closed, my body relaxed, draped over the strong lines of his.

Sometime later, I woke alone to the sound of shouts and screams echoing down the hall into my cracked open bedroom door.

Bleary-eyed and wondering how Everett got out without anyone noticing, I forced myself up and made my way outside, adjusting my tank as I neared the front door and the commotion got louder.

It opened to the sound of a grunting, growling bus engine, and the sight of the guys climbing and jumping all over each other. "America, here we come!"

NINE

CONFIDENCE WAS FICKLE. IT ARRIVED WHEN YOU LEAST EXPECTED IT and bailed when you most needed it.

I couldn't rely on alcohol to see me through every transaction I was lucky enough to have with Everett.

So I'd ditched my classics and tales of young love, and ordered some romance novels online. Mom had a few in her room, but I'd already read those, and given the time period they were set in, I figured it would be wise to learn from something a little more modern.

"Oh boy," I muttered, turning the page. This woman was due home any moment, and her husband was waiting for her. Her angry and betrayed husband.

Somehow, I'd gotten too caught up in the stories to pay much attention to the sex scenes, but I couldn't find it within me to care all that much. Not when this woman was about to be kicked out on the street. I made a mental note to give this one to Adela when I was done.

"What are you doing?"

The book fell as a silent screech barreled up my throat. "Ever," I panted, hand on my pulsing chest. "A little warning."

"Nah." Lips sliding into his cheek, he tapped the windowsill. "I like watching you when you think no one is looking." Before I could even blink, he said, "Meet me out front."

Reaching for my book, I deposited it on the nightstand,

and with only a brief glance at the bedroom door, I threw back the bedding.

After shuffling into a cardigan to hide the absence of my bra, I shimmied out the window and rounded the side of the house.

Leaning against the back of the bus, Everett stomped out his cigarette, then gestured for me to hurry.

"Where are we going? I have no shoes, and I'm in my pajamas."

"The ocean doesn't care."

Laughing, I lit up inside when his hand clasped mine, and we raced down the alleyway and side streets leading to the beach.

The air was warm, the crickets chirping between breaks of the crashing waves.

Everett kicked off his boots at the base of the stairs, then tugged me onto the vacant stretch of sand.

Lying down, his fingers memorizing mine, he murmured, "I get it now."

Tearing my attention from the stars, I peeked over at him. The half-moon gave glimpses of his jaw, his nose and mouth shadowed. His eyes stayed fixed on the night sky. "Get what?"

"The glow worms."

Turning back to face the sky, I smiled. "Oh."

Some minutes passed, and thanks to his hypnotic touch and the lull of the sea, my eyes began to lose the battle, fluttering closed.

"You know, you're probably one of the only girls a guy could randomly drag to the beach and lie in the sand with without wondering why we aren't fucking." He huffed, the sound dry with humor. "Or complaining about sand in your hair."

My nose and chest bunched, my hand tensing in his. "Sorry," he said, quick and soft. "I'm…" he sighed, exasperation coating the exhale.

I sat up. "Let's go."

"Clover, wait."

Tearing off my cardigan, I let the breeze carry it to the sand, and then I stepped out of my sleep shorts.

In nothing but my cotton tank and panties, I waded into the foaming water, shivering as it reached my waist.

"Stevie!"

I ignored him. A wave crested, and I dived beneath it, swimming through cold midnight depths toward the moon. Shoving my hair out of my face, I treaded water, clearing the salt from my eyes.

The roar of the water drowned out his approach, but when he broke through the surface, just in time to keep from being pulled back to the shore in a violent tumble, I smiled.

Confusion swept his brows together, and he raked a hand over his face, ridding it of water and his hair. "A little warning."

Laughing, I spat water at him, my eyes drifting over those broad, naked shoulders. "Nah, I like wondering if you'll chase me."

Water lapped, a gentle push as we stared, and then we both moved at the same time. "What were you reading?" He rubbed at his nostrils, his face bobbing close to mine.

"A book."

Unamused, he hooked an arm around my waist, dragging me closer. Our feet tangled beneath the surface, wanting to join but needed to stay afloat. "You looked more invested than usual."

His curious eyes, coupled with his hand sliding beneath my tank, fingers skimming over my lower back, made me relent. "I ordered some romance books online."

He didn't so much as blink. "Yeah? You like them now?"

Nodding, I admitted, "I wanted some advice, I guess."

It took a moment, but then it registered. Everett chuckled,

his smile both grim and warm. "Does it feel like we need advice?" Pulling me closer, he urged my legs around his waist, and my hands slid over his bare shoulders. "When we touch, does it feel like we need any kind of instruction manual?" Lifting me, he nudged my cheek with his nose as every solid part of him met every soft part of me.

Everything coalesced into a quiet hum. The waves, our breaths, and the rapid beating of my heart. "No." He was right. We didn't. It came alive, this feeling that coursed between us, and when that happened, nothing else was needed. Just us.

Humming, he dragged his lips over my cheek, fire crawling in their wake, and whispered across my mouth, "Being with you, I've never felt anything more instinctual or more natural in my life."

It ached and bloomed, that organ in my chest. How something could grow, knowing it would need to end, wasn't something I was willing to dissect.

I took the moment, the feeling of his skin beneath my hands, his own holding me as if he'd never let me sink, and I drowned inside it.

Our lips collided, our lungs sharing breath as our bodies found purchase among a slippery, perilous environment.

Graham stabbed a finger on the map spread out over our dining table. "I think we should follow the interstate. Go straight through."

I sipped my tea in the doorway, watching on.

Dad scratched at his beard. "It's a solid plan, but you need to remember the money you guys have won't last long. You might need to stop some places longer to make some cash."

Everett stared at the map. Those long, thick fingers stroking the scruff lining his chin the only sign he was listening.

"Between us, we've saved enough," Hendrix said.

Mom didn't look convinced. The fine lines that spread from her eyes, around her mouth, and pressed into her forehead deepened as her gaze bounced from Hendrix to Dad to Everett.

I wondered if I had the same tight look on my own face.

They were leaving.

I probably did because later that night when everyone had left, there was a collection of taps on my bedroom window. I opened it to let Everett in, then made sure my door was locked as he climbed through and kicked off his shoes.

"I got you something," he said, and I raised my eyes from his worn boots. I doubted he'd worn the same pair since I'd known him, but if not, he would have found some other scuffed-up pair at the town's thrift store.

He needs this, I tried to tell myself. We could only love and support him so much. He needed this opportunity to get out and make a better life for himself. And I had to wonder if that was what love was? Did loving someone grant you the ability to smother your own desperation long enough to see theirs? To want to aid in setting them free from their demons within?

His eyes held mine and softened at what he must've seen in them. "Come here." He set the small silver potted cacti down on my nightstand, then gathered me into his arms.

My nose found the dip below his throat, and I inhaled deeply, trying to capture his scent, needing to lock it away. "This is so much harder than I thought it would be."

"It's not forever, Clover," he said, his hand smoothing over the back of my head. "You'll finish school, I'll eventually get my head on straight, and we'll never have to end."

Lifting my head from his chest, I stared up into his somber, resolute face. "Eventually."

My hands found the hem of his shirt, pulling it up and over his head. My nightgown ended up on the floor with his tattered jeans, socks, and boots. As he climbed over me on the bed, I tucked my fingers into the waistband of my panties and pulled them down.

He stilled. "Clover, we can't—"

"You're leaving, I'm seventeen, and I don't know when I'll see you again." I kept my tone gentle, but firm. "I've waited, Ever. For you."

His eyes shut at the name only I called him. When they re-opened, they were infused with fire.

He snatched my panties, tossing them onto his pile of clothes, and then my legs were spread wide, and his mouth was kissing the top of my mound. "Not worthy."

My breath hitched when his fingers opened me to the cool breeze drifting in through the open window, and then the velvet warmth of his tongue was sliding through me, over me, dipping inside me.

I'd never done this before, but then again, before Everett, all I'd done was kiss a few boys and have them make a grab for my breasts.

It was intoxicating, the sensations that thundered through me. The low hum he made deep in his throat every time my legs shook. "You'll come before you let me inside you, so come," he said when I straddled the edge between bliss and euphoria.

Spasms sharpened and blurred my vision, and my thighs clenched around his head while I struggled to breathe without moaning every time.

Then, he was leaning over me, his length breaching my slick opening before he dropped his forehead to mine, whispering,

"This will probably hurt." When I said nothing, he groaned. "Wrap your legs around me."

I did, and his mouth stole mine, his tongue forcing itself inside at the same time his thickness annihilated the barrier of my virginity. A scream lodged in my throat. My entire body tensed, turning to granite as my teeth sank into Everett's lip.

He didn't stop until he was seated fully, his hips aligned with mine, his fingers holding my chin to keep my mouth on his when I tried to pull away. I knew it was to keep me from waking anyone up.

With his thumb stroking my cheek and his breathing ragged, he slowly removed his lips. "Are you regretting it now, Clover?" He was smiling, panting, as he shifted slightly. "Jesus Christ. This is…" Again, he groaned, and I felt my skin and nipples pebble. "I need to move."

The pain was a burn that wouldn't quit scorching, but I swallowed and gripped the back of his head. "So move." I licked the blood I'd caused to pool on his bottom lip, and his hips reared back, then carefully eased forward.

Eyes locked on mine, he did it over and over until he could feel the tension dissipate in my touch, in my body, and in my kiss.

I wanted him like this—always like this—staring at me, making love to me. I closed my eyes before he could see the storm brewing in them and moaned when he kept sliding over parts inside me that made my stomach bubble and quiver.

"Gonna come," he panted through gritted teeth, his pace gathering speed until we could hear the wet sound of his skin meeting mine in the dark.

He pressed a hard kiss to my lips and then rose to his knees, milking himself all over my stomach.

I didn't care; I couldn't take my eyes off his face. He wore an expression of pure, utter rapture I'd never seen before. He heaved and cursed, and then stared at the mess he'd made.

And I couldn't stop myself. The idea of anyone else getting to see him the way I had just now… "Don't leave," I pleaded, knowing he'd listen but choose not to hear.

His throat bobbed as his gaze sank into mine, thick brows furrowing. With a loud exhale trailing him, he left the bed and grabbed some tissues from the dresser, then returned to clean my stomach and between my legs.

Making no comment about the blood I knew had to be there, he wiped, then kissed my mound again. "We should maybe flush these."

Sorrow weighed every step as I got up and threw my night-gown on, then traipsed quietly to the bathroom. I took my time cleaning up, staring at my kiss swollen lips and tangled hair, half expecting Everett not to be there when I returned.

He was, standing in the glow of the moonlight by the window in nothing but his briefs.

I locked the door behind me, drifting close, my fingers lifting to the muscles lining his shoulders and arms, then dipping over the ridges and curved arch of his spine.

Reaching behind him for my hands, he pulled until they met over his abs. He entwined our fingers, and my cheek pressed into his sweat-misted back, his heart thudding a fast tempo. "You know staying would continue to kill me slowly."

A rogue tear escaped, sliding down my cheek to land on his back. I quickly kissed it away before he could tell what it was. "I know."

He sang me to sleep that night, all the while I did my best to keep my heart from bleeding out all over his naked chest.

It was happening.

The bus was loaded and leaving smoky plumes in the humid morning air.

Hendrix sat behind the wheel, unpacking snacks and setting them anywhere he could reach.

"First stop, Ala-fucking-bama," came from behind us.

I turned from where I'd been studying Everett. He'd been rearranging the drum kit below the bus, checking the straps and sandwiching it in the middle of all their suitcases and duffel bags.

"Get fucked." Graham laughed, racing over and slapping Dale on the back.

Hendrix dropped a bag of Skittles and flew off the bus, and slowly, Everett straightened, shifting his sunglasses from his head to shield his eyes.

They were all laughing and back clapping, and then Everett chucked Dale's two bags beneath the bus and closed the door with a sharp bang.

"What changed your mind?" Mom asked when Dale approached to hug my parents goodbye.

"Well"—he clapped his hands together—"they'll need someone to keep managing their dumb asses. I couldn't leave them to the wolves."

Mom's lips were pressed tight, but she relaxed them enough to force a smile.

After another round of hugs, they all filed onto the bus. Nausea rocked me, fierce and dizzying, and I knew I couldn't watch them leave.

With tears blurring my vision, I went back inside.

A second later, arms wrapped around me from behind, and the scent of whiskey, cigarettes, and clean linen invaded.

I didn't have time to ask him why he'd been drinking before noon. Tilting my chin up, he quickly lowered his mouth to mine, his thumbs brushing at the tears dotting my cheeks. "You're ruining me, Clover. Don't cry."

I said nothing, just kissed him again when he tried to pull away.

"Rett! He'd better not be taking a dump," Hendrix called. "Let's go already."

In harsh waves, his chest rose and fell beneath my trembling hands, his grip on my face tight. "Check your nightstand," was the last thing he said to me before he was gone, and everything changed.

TEN

"It's too quiet," Mom said the next morning, sadness visiting her eyes and mouth.

Dad hummed. "How long are we thinking before they break down or give up and come home?"

That made Mom smile, and she speared a piece of melon. "Three months."

"Three?" Dad took a sip of tea, shaking his head as he set his mug down. "That's generous."

I knocked my scrambled eggs around my plate, knowing in my heart they were wrong but wishing they were right.

"I'm giving them two at most. They have Everett's smarts to dig them out of trouble for a while, but they'll eventually find trouble he can't fix."

I pushed back from the table. "I'm going to hang at Adela's for a little while."

Mom nodded. "You okay?"

No. I was far from okay, but I wasn't allowed to be heartbroken because the boy I'd fallen in love with had left. I was only allowed to be sad my friends and brother had gone. "Yeah, it's just weird here without them. I need a shake or something."

My fingers had already started wearing the note he'd left behind with his very first guitar pick taped to it.

In a world filled with thorns and poisonous flowers, somehow, I was lucky enough to find you.

My clover.

He'd found me, but he didn't want to keep me. The selfish part of me hoped my parents were right, and the band would come home sooner rather than later. For good.

Turns out they were wrong.

Hendrix stopped calling home as much after the summer ended, and all too soon, quiet was the new normal in the Sandrine house.

And I hated it.

"Shots, shots, shots," Davis hollered, and I threw them back, feeling lightheaded but alive for the first time in months.

"Yeah, birthday girl!" Adela looped her arm around me, and I choked, laughing as vodka dribbled down my chin.

She'd been by my side through every broken heart fest, supplying ice cream, shakes, hugs, and an endless number of thrillers due to my inability to watch or read anything even slightly romantic.

She was the only one who knew, though I was beginning to wonder if that wasn't exactly the case. Still, I was thankful for her. Grateful I had someone to help pull me through the blur of days that'd passed since Orange Apples took to the road.

I wiped the vodka from my chin, then tossed my arms into the air, dancing my way out of Davis's kitchen.

"Girl, your phone is ringing like crazy," Adela yelled over the music, pulling it from her purse.

I waved her off, and then, through the drunken haze I'd plunged into, it dawned.

Snatching the phone so fast that Adela laughed, I answered with, "Ever?" as I made my way outside onto the back deck.

It wasn't that much quieter outside, but I still heard him. "Happy Birthday, Clover."

"I miss you," I said. "So fucking much." I ignored the people around me who either snickered or moved away.

"Where are you?"

"Where are you?" I volleyed.

"Tennessee," he clipped. "Answer the question."

"I'm at a party." I stopped to hiccup. "Davis's parents are out of town, and it's my birthday, so he threw one." Silence. "Hello?" I checked my phone to make sure he was still there. "Ever?"

"You're drunk?"

I snorted. "Just a little, maybe."

"Jesus Christ." The line went dead and panic shook me so hard and fast, I leaned over the railing just in time to puke into the garden.

Adela found me a minute later as I was sniffing back tears and sliding to the wooden deck. "Shit, what happened?"

"Everett happened." I hiccupped again. "Then I barfed on the poor flowers."

Adela crouched down in front of me, cringing and swiping away some puke with a tissue from her purse. "We need to get you home."

"Mom," I said. "Call my mom."

Adela hesitated. "Are you sure? You're pretty drunk, Stevie."

I nodded, trying to stand. She helped me up, and we waded back through the house, the bass from the music making my head pound.

Mom arrived within five minutes, clad in her nightgown and with her face mask still on. Adela opened the car door, helping me into the front before she climbed into the back.

"That's some get-together, honey," Mom drawled, eyeing the raging party.

"Yeah," I croaked. "It turned out to be a bigger thing than I expected."

Shaking her head, Mom turned the car around and headed to Adela's place.

None of us spoke until we'd pulled up outside the two-story beachside home, and Adela thanked Mom for the ride. "I'll call you tomorrow, see how you're doing."

"Thanks," I told her as she closed the door.

Mom sighed, then started the short drive home. But when we pulled into the drive that once held a mammoth-sized bus, she made no move to vacate the car.

Neither did I, though that was partially due to feeling as if I might be sick again, and mostly to do with not wanting to go inside after I'd just heard his voice. A voice that haunted the halls of our home and the walls of my heart.

"I'm guessing you're finally ready to talk about this if you called me instead of walking home or catching a ride."

I nodded, not sure I was ready, but positive I couldn't lie in this state. Fiddling with my phone in my lap, I admitted, "He called me."

"Everett?" she asked.

"Yeah, and I don't know, he got mad and hung up." Tears welled and came rushing out.

Mom sat with that a moment. "You and him... how long?"

"I can't answer that." I sniffed. "It feels like it's always been there."

Mom blew out a breath, then reached over and grabbed my hand. "I'm talking physical here, Stevie. How long?"

"Not long, maybe a couple of months before he left."

Mom was quiet for some minutes, her hand tense around

mine. "I knew. You've been too sad, and the way you looked at him"—she smiled when I flung my head back to face her—"it was a little obvious."

Fear spiked, and I opened my mouth to ask about Hendrix.

"No," she said. "I mean obvious that you liked him. He was way too subtle with the way he looked at you for Hendrix to suspect anything. Hell"—she rolled her eyes—"your father and I didn't think anything was happening."

"I'm sorry," I said, swiping beneath my nose.

Mom opened the glove compartment, plucking out a pocket-sized pack of tissues. I took one after she'd pulled it free.

"What are you sorry for?" She laughed, but it was a sad sound. "Falling in love for the first time? That's not something you should ever need to apologize for."

"But it's Everett," I said, thinking that was reason enough.

"Mmm." Mom bobbed her head side to side. "That's what you call shit-luck, honey."

I bursted out laughing, and then she reached over, taking the tissue from me and dabbing at the mascara beneath my eyes. "Not Everett. He's damaged goods, sure, but he's still good. I'm talking about him being your brother's best friend."

I nodded. "I know." I flipped down the visor, checking my eyes in case Dad was still awake, then closed it. "Guess it doesn't matter now."

Mom didn't give that a response. She helped me inside and made me some peanut butter toast and tea before leaving me to finally remove her face mask.

I couldn't sleep, wishing Everett hadn't called me from a private number so I could at least call him back. But I couldn't, and what was worse was that I knew, given how long it took him to call me, that I wouldn't likely hear from him again for a long time.

It was hard to describe. The way my heart had adapted with his absence, however slowly, as though it knew the score and thought either way, we'd won.

But as I tossed and turned that night, my brain laced with doubt, repeating his words from our brief phone call over and over, I discovered any small victory in love would only make the loss even more unbearable.

ELEVEN

CHRISTMAS AND NEW YEAR'S PASSED, AND MY PHONE NEVER RANG. Dealing with loss on your own was akin to tying a plastic bag around your head and being expected to breathe. Each breath was shallow, stilted, and I couldn't help but wonder if maybe it was too much to bear, and it'd be my last.

My heart struggled to make peace with Everett cutting ties with me completely. All because I'd attended a party. I refused to believe it was that. I also refused to believe it was just easier for him, but I had to face the truth. And it rang clear and sharp, hardening my heart's soft edges every time I stared at the silver potted cacti he'd left behind.

His parents didn't seem to vacate their house, not that they usually did. Then again, I was busy with school and Adela, and anything I could do to take my mind someplace else. It wouldn't surprise me if I'd missed a sighting of them. Though I did sometimes ponder how they got by on welfare alone without Everett's help.

My mom's phone sounded from her purse. I ignored it, trying to focus on my essay for the college applications spread before me.

I didn't want to go to college, but the idea of staying here, hoping the boy who'd stolen my heart would return and give it back, wasn't very appealing.

At the very least, I wanted to sign up for some business and accounting classes. Getting a degree that could help make my goals happen faster was boring, but necessary if I wanted to run my own business one day.

The phone rang again, and I chewed on the tip of my pen, eyeing Mom's purse. She was in the shower. Dad was taking her out for dinner when he got home. It was a new thing, something they'd tried to make a habit of every Friday night since the band had left and emptiness invaded Mom's nest.

I got up and answered it just before it went to voicemail. "Hey, Henny."

He laughed. "Steve, Jesus. How goes ya? Long time, no talk."

"That wouldn't be the case if you actually decided to call me," I quipped, taking my seat again.

"The phone works two ways. Ain't that a funny thing?"

I smiled, not realizing how good it'd be to hear his voice. "How are you?"

"Fucking broke half the time, but rich on life."

"You called Mom for money?" I asked.

"Nah, just to say hello. I forgot to call last month, and I thought I'd better do it before we jump states again."

The temptation was there, heavy behind my teeth, to ask about Everett. "How're you guys doing?"

"Eh, so-so. Can't complain too much. People are willing to let us play, but going from a town where everyone knows you to big cities where no one gives a shit has been a bit of an adjustment."

"I'll bet," I said, smirking as I clicked my pen.

"We're opening for a band called The Weeds this weekend, though, so we're hightailing it to Ohio." I heard shouting in the background followed by a feminine laugh. My mouth dried.

"Sounds awesome," I forced. "Tell everyone I said hello, yeah?"

"Everyone, Steve says hello!"

Jeers and hollers pounded my ear, and I laughed, pulling the phone away until they'd stopped. "Guess they miss me."

"Maybe a smidgen. How's that friend of yours?"

I paused. "Who, Adela?"

"Yeah, that one," he said, trying to sound indifferent. "Figured she's probably missing being able to ogle me and all."

"Oh, my God. You're despicable, and no, she's got a boyfriend."

She didn't, but it wouldn't kill him to tease.

"She does, does she?" he said, tone rougher.

"Uh-huh. Oh, look," I said as Mom rounded the corner, towel drying her hair. "Mom's out of the shower. Bye, Henny. Wrap before you tap."

"Fuck. Don't ever talk about penis-related shit with me again, Steve."

"What?" I heard in the background, knowing that voice belonged to Everett.

"Nothing, man, she's just being gross."

"Okay, bye," I sang over the feeling constricting my stomach and chest, then handed the phone to Mom.

"Baby boy, you didn't call me last month…"

I ditched my applications and left the room.

"Come on, I'm pretty sure me going to prom with you instead of Gray Adams means I love you more than cake," Adela said, spooning more mud cake into her mouth.

"I still don't believe you," I joked.

"Hey, graduates," Dad said, dipping his finger into the middle of the cake Mom had baked me.

I picked up my cap, throwing it at him. "Mine. Back off."

"Ours," Adela corrected, grabbing the cake and moving it out of Dad's reach.

He chuckled, then went to the fridge and popped open a beer.

A rumble, followed by the sound of screeching brakes, had my eyes bulging, cake trapped and clogging my throat.

I swallowed hard, then looked at Dad, who shrugged, seeming just as perplexed as I felt.

We all raced out front just as the bus hit the curb and bounced over the grass, parking half on the road and half on our lawn.

"Nice park job," Adela said when the door clanged open, and Hendrix leaped down the steps.

"Nice chocolate faces, graduates," he said, grinning from ear to ear as Adela and I both wiped furiously at our mouths.

My heart flapped, then grew wings with talons that pierced each breath.

Hendrix looked much the same, if not a bit broader and hairier in the face. Dale looked like he'd lost ten pounds, his cheekbones harsh slashes and clothes hanging. They both approached to give us hugs.

Graham and Everett were last to get off the bus, the former wearing a hideous Hawaiian shirt, his hair almost reaching his shoulders.

And Everett, he was the same, only larger in every sense of the word. He seemed taller, broader, and more hardened than when he'd left. The cruel cut of his square jaw was rigid, his hair falling over his forehead and tickling his neck.

I hugged them all, squealing when Graham spun me in a circle, my graduation gown billowing in the air before he planted me on the ground.

Everett's hand reached out, steadying me, and I couldn't stop it if I tried. All the pain, anger, and frustration of missing him, of loving him, evaporated, and I threw my arms around his neck, hugging him for far longer than I probably should have as everyone went inside.

"You never called me again." We both knew it, but I wanted to state it. To know why.

"I couldn't," he said, hands tangled up in my hair, and his nose stuck in my neck. "Fuck," he spewed, pulling away.

"What?" I asked.

Those dark greens darted to the open front door, then back to me, his voice low as he said, "I missed you."

My stomach jumped, and I smiled, ducking my head when he grinned that megawatt, perfectly imperfect grin of his. "Congrats, Clover."

"Welcome home," I said, gesturing to the door and leading the way.

Everyone congregated in the living room, and Dad's eyes were bright as the band regaled us with tales from the road. Mom ordered in, and I kept quiet in the corner on Hendrix's old bean bag, my eyes trained on whoever was talking to avoid staring at Everett.

"... thought it was a fucking kangaroo," Dale said, hands in the air.

"In Dallas?" Everett asked, nursing a beer.

If Mom and Dad were bothered by the underage drinking going down right before their eyes, they didn't show it. Graham even handed my dad another beer, and since Dad was distracted by the storytelling, he just gestured his thanks before popping the top.

I guess most of them were nearing twenty, but still. I doubted I could get away with taking one for myself, and I desperately needed something to curb the fizzing in my veins whenever I felt his eyes land on me.

"Dallas fucking shmallas, it looked like a kangaroo," Dale said, next to Graham on the couch, his ankle crossed over his leg.

"You couldn't tell what it was when it was splattered all over the road like that," Hendrix said, tapping away on his phone, probably updating his Facebook.

He was the only one who kept up with that. The rest of them faded from the social media grid after the bus rolled out of our driveway. And I only knew because I'd spent an embarrassing amount of time stalking for any sign of Everett. Most pictures were of them playing, of Hendrix and his flavor of the night, or stupid GIFs used to describe how hungover he felt.

"The damage to the bus?" Dad asked.

"Big ass dent, but otherwise okay," Everett said.

The conversation veered to the gigs they'd played, the small numbers that showed up, and Dale made a comment that made my parents and me cringe. "Didn't hinder finding sweet tail, though."

"Shut up, asshole." Hendrix reached over Graham to slug him.

Dale dodged it, laughing. "It's true, though. Especially mister serious lead singer."

Unable to stop them, my eyes flicked up to Everett, whose jaw shifted as he looked away from me and to the window, and drained the rest of his beer.

Jealousy suffocated me, and the fissures inside my chest cracked wider.

"Parents, dude," Graham said. "Respect."

Dale smiled apologetically at Mom, who shook her head and began collecting the empty pizza boxes. "I just hope you boys don't find yourselves in too much trouble."

Sick to my stomach, I took my chance to leave and did it fast. "I'll see you guys tomorrow."

"Little sis," Graham called. "Congrats on not being so little anymore."

I waved over my head, then all but ran down the hallway to my room and locked the door.

Falling back into it, I covered my mouth with my hand and slid down to the floor, where I stayed until my ass grew numb and the noise outside faded as everyone headed out or to bed.

My face was sticky, my throat dry and scraped raw with the effort it took to keep the sobs silent.

I'd never thought myself all that naïve, but apparently, I was. He was in a fucking band, and here I'd hoped he'd do the impossible and wait, while knowing all along he wouldn't.

Knowing was one thing, but hearing it confirmed was a whole different kind of hell.

The window opened, and the familiar, heart-stopping clomp of his boots hitting the floor penetrated the fog.

Strong hands wrapped around my arms, hoisting me up off the floor, and then he was carrying me to the bed. On his lap, I sat defeated, my head on his shoulder as he crooned, gentle and desperate in my ear, "Don't cry. Not over me, Clover. Never because of me."

"It hurts," I croaked, wheezing. "It fucking hurts."

"Fuck." He squeezed me to him. "I'm sorry."

"Why?" I straightened and crawled off his lap to the bed. "I don't understand. You said… wait…" My eyelids felt like they were filled with cement. "Oh my God, was it after I went out for my birthday?"

His non-answer and the twist in my gut told me yes, it was.

Rage bit at every muscle, every aching part of me. "What happened to one day, Ever? Huh?" I sniffed, rasping out, "What happened to eventually?"

His voice was hard but quiet, eyes blazing as he glared.

"That was before I left, before I realized you still have a life to live. And before I remembered that no matter what, you'll always be Hendrix's sister, and I'll always be no fucking good for someone like you."

Tears arrived anew, and seeing them, his voice softened, sounding pained. "Things don't change just because we want them to, Clover. Why can't you see that?"

I sniffed, leaning forward to growl at him. "Because all I see is you."

His chest heaved, and so did mine, and then our lips collided, refusing to part even as our clothes were torn off.

His fingers found me, and he cursed, discovering I was already drenched, fucking me with one as he rolled over me and kissed his way down my throat to my breasts. "Want you so bad," he mumbled to my heated skin, licking and sucking at my hardened nipples while his fingers sent my body rocking.

"Take me," I pleaded, out of my mind, desperate enough to ignore the hangover for the high.

He licked his wet fingers, then wrapped one of my legs behind his back, aligning himself and pushing forward.

I winced at the tight fit, and he groaned, low and deep, sinking all the way inside in one slow thrust.

Lowering his head, he rolled his hips, and his teeth sank into my neck. My head fell back, the burn subsiding and my hands raking through his longer hair as he slowly tortured me.

I could feel it building when he tucked an arm beneath my back, then sat up, taking me with him. My nails sliced into his biceps, my breathing heavier, and a moan escaped as I adjusted to the depth of the new position.

He licked my chin, trailing to my bottom lip. "That's it, move your hips. Do whatever makes you feel good, Clover."

He had one hand tangled in my hair, and the other held

me over him as I closed my eyes and circled my hips. Feeling his hot chest pressed against mine, his attention fixed wholly on me, and his cock rubbing all those perfect places brought me to brand new heights, and when I fell, I exploded.

He cupped a hand over my mouth to smother my noisy breaths and used the one around my hips to move me, fuck me harder, deeper, and then he came.

His mouth found mine, and he mumbled his pleasure inside it, cussing and groaning words like, "Beautiful, so fucking good," and then we sat in a sweaty tangled heap, kissing and touching and not talking until he was ready to do it all over again.

"On your knees," he said, voice strained. Climbing off him, I felt him leak out of me. "Yeah, like that. Holy fuck." He paused, and I knew why when his fingers started toying with all the wet between my legs. "I'm taking a mental picture so hard right now."

"Put more in me." I didn't recognize the woman who'd said those words, didn't want to acknowledge how careless she became around this man, but nothing else mattered. I needed all of him all over me, imbedded inside me, with a desperation that had my thighs and arms trembling.

"You're not on the pill," he said, knowing somehow.

"No, but I'll get the morning after pill."

He paused. "You haven't fucked anyone else?"

"No." I sighed and sat up, my libido fading and fading fast. "But I suppose I should probably make an appointment at the clinic and get tested, too."

"Clover," he said, hurt piercing the name. "I'm only bare with you. Now get back on your knees."

Swallowing at how fast he'd rekindled the fire, I did as I was told.

Not even a second later, a slap sounded through the room, and pain mingled with pleasure as I felt his handprint bloom on my ass while he slid inside.

Bending over me, he turned my chin to his face as he began to move, slow and deep. His eyes were hooded but alert and wild. "I know I'm an asshole," he panted, "we both do. But don't ever think for one fucking second I'd put you in harm's way like that again."

Feeling bold, I nipped his finger when it brushed over my bottom lip. "So it's just my heart that gets harmed then?"

He stopped, then sat back, taking me with him with an arm around my waist. Using his other hand, he turned my head to face him. "No more talking."

His lips pried mine apart, his teeth scraping over my tongue as his hand lowered, sinking down to where we joined. He circled and teased until he had to hold me still while he rocked from underneath, and I almost screamed, coming harder than I ever had before.

I didn't know if his plan was to fuck me into oblivion. To ruin me until I was a useless pile of beating, simmering flesh unable to do anything but take what he gave until I passed out sated and limp on top of him. If it was, it worked, and I had no energy to find it within myself to care.

As predicted, he wasn't there the next morning, and judging by the shouting and screaming we all heard from across the street, he'd gone to pay his parents a visit. A visit that clearly hadn't gone well and had resulted in Everett storming off down the street toward the beach.

"I'll check on him," Dale had said as we all stood on the small front porch. He'd slept on the bus, still on the outs with his parents for ditching Brown.

The scrambled eggs and bacon wouldn't go down easy as Mom, Dad, Hendrix, and me sat around the table, eating breakfast together before the band was due to leave.

We were but a quick pit stop.

"Graham needs money, so he's gone to his grandparents to ask for a loan. He'll be back soon," Hendrix said, tearing off a bite of bacon. "Jesus, I forgot how good your cooking is, Mom."

Mom smiled, then asked, "And you? Have you run out of money?"

Hendrix shook his head, then took a sip of orange juice. "Nah, I don't hit it as heavy as the other idiots. As long as some venues keep giving us something, I'm good for a while."

"Some don't?" Dad asked, setting the paper down.

Hendrix tipped a shoulder. "If there's not enough of a crowd, no. We make sweet fuck all. But word has spread in some places, and if we keep booking opening gigs with some bigger bands, I think we'll be able to stay afloat." He paused, grinning. "Oh, and Dale has some chick making merch that he's selling on our website, so that helps too."

"Not a bad manager after all," Dad murmured, brows raised.

"That depends." Mom frowned. "What does this girl get in return?"

Hendrix blinked. "Uh… his love? I don't know."

Mom blew out a frustrated breath, and Dad collected her hand.

"Besides, thanks to the stuff Everett has been writing, it's hard for chicks not to dig us."

"Do you need to call them chicks?" I asked.

"Aw, Steve. Don't be like that."

I rolled my tired eyes, sipping my tea.

Mom laid her chin on her hand. "What about these songs, then?"

"Right." Hendrix laughed, brief and quiet. "I'm positive he's met someone on the road." My heart stalled until he kept going, "They're powerful, hey. The kind that only a guy in love, or who's been in love, can write."

"Wonder who it is," Mom mused, reaching for her tea as her eyes slid over to me.

I just about fell headfirst into my eggs, my pulse screeching in my ears as I lowered my gaze to my half-eaten food. I didn't dare let myself read too much into those words. He was leaving. Again. And knowing it and knowing how bad it would hurt, I'd still handed myself over to him like a fool. Again.

"No idea. You know how he is." Hendrix waved a hand, flippant. "He never talks about feelings and shit. The only way you'd know anything about him is by listening to him sing."

"I suppose that's what attracts them, then," Dad pondered aloud. "Gaining knowledge of the mysteriously broken boy who knows a little something about love."

I wasn't sure if Dad knew, but I was willing to bet he didn't, or he'd have said something to me months ago.

I didn't stay to watch them leave again. Thanks to the hours spent possessed by Everett and his magic, hypnotic ways of making me forget last night, I had places to be anyway. I tried not to wince when I got up to take my plate to the sink and scraped the leftovers into the garbage disposal.

In the shower, I washed gingerly between my legs, both reveling and feeling disgusted over the lingering soreness, though it wouldn't linger long. Just like last time, it would fade. But his absence, that phantom touch would remain.

After throwing on a strawberry-colored button-down sundress, I slipped into my Chucks, then threw my wet hair up into a messy bun and snatched my purse. "Can I borrow your car, Mom?" I called when I heard her leaving the bathroom.

She stepped into my room, her brows puckering at my hastily made bed. "Ah, yeah. You're not staying to say goodbye?"

I swiped some gloss on my reddened lips, then grabbed my sunglasses. I hadn't bothered with makeup, as nothing but big square pieces of UV protected plastic would help mask the puffiness beneath my eyes. "I've had enough of goodbyes."

She grabbed my wrist in the hall, pulling me back to her and cupping my face in both of her soft, slightly callused hands. I tried not to flinch under her inspection. Even though I was taller than her by a couple of inches, she still had the power to make me feel six years old with one look. "What happened?"

"You don't need to know," I said.

After assessing, searching my eyes for a beat, she nodded and brought my face to hers to kiss my forehead. "Love you."

"Love you too."

She handed me her keys, and I rushed outside.

I flipped my sunglasses down as I reversed out of the drive, doing my best to maneuver Mom's small SUV around the gigantic black bus with a nasty dent in its front end.

I was out on the street when I saw Everett behind the car and yelped, slamming my foot on the brake.

Dale saluted me, then headed inside. I waved back, watching Everett round the car to my cracked open window. "Where are you going?"

"To the drug store, remember?" My foot eased off the brake. "Bye, Ever."

He slapped a hand on the window. "We're heading out soon."

Offering a tight smile, I said, "I know, but I don't feel like watching you leave."

He reached for me as I turned the wheel and remained standing there as I drove away.

TWELVE

RASLOW WAS A QUAINT TOWN FILLED TO THE BRIM WITH HIPSTERS, retirees, and students from the local college.

As soon as I'd seen the pamphlet, I'd immediately researched local florists and nurseries in the area and found two of each. I scored a job at Petal Power, a florist owned by a couple in their late fifties. It boasted such an array of flowers and plants that even I had to research some of them to figure out what they were.

"Ugh, we need to get that plumber back out here," Adela said. "The tap won't stop dripping. Can you imagine the water bill?"

"It's included with our rent, isn't it?"

"Yeah, but still sucks for the landlord who's paying that sucker."

She had a point. "I'll call them on my break." I finished my coffee and closed my textbook before rinsing my mug in the sink. "I need to go, but I'll grab some milk on the way home."

Adela stuck her head out of the bathroom, her toothbrush hanging from her mouth. "You don't have class until tomorrow."

"I've picked up extra shifts. Gloria's off for the week." I combed my fingers through my hair. "Sinus infection."

Adela disappeared, and I heard her spit and then the running of the tap before she returned. "She suffers from allergies but works in a freaking flower shop?"

I laughed. "That's what I said, and Gloria said we don't

choose who and what we fall in love with, even when it's a hazard to one's self."

Adela cackled, ducking back into the bathroom. "What a woman."

"That's what Sabrina said." Adela laughed again as I grabbed my bag and shut the door behind me.

I jumped down the steps, then hit the sidewalk, the mist from last night's rain heavy in the autumn air. We were leasing a three-bedroom apartment. Though it was old, it was well kept and nestled in the outskirts of the business district of Raslow.

Another reason it felt like the perfect fit was due to its proximity to home. It was a fifty-minute drive down the highway. Not that I had a car yet, but Adela did. I'd wanted to leave, but I didn't want to leave completely.

There'd been nothing but radio silence from Everett, but then again, I hadn't expected any different, and what I'd said to him was true. I was fed up with this feeling hollowing out my insides. Dad said last he'd heard from Hendrix, they were heading farther north to a series of gigs they'd lined up before Christmas.

Another perk that being away from home provided was a break from the memories. No longer did I stare across the street at the run-down house where he'd lived, or the walls of my own where he'd spent most of his time, growing, learning, and making me fall.

Finally, for the first time in over a year, I found it easier to breathe.

Cursing interrupted my thoughts, and I stopped, staring back at a guy who was kicking the tire of his car. "Jesus, Mary, and Joseph, no." He groaned, threading his hands behind his head over his jet-black hair. His eyes were almost the same shade, which made his luminous smile blinding and hard not to notice on that chiseled, clean-shaven face. Not that he was smiling now.

Aiden Prince.

We shared the same business class. He was also on the college baseball team.

"Shit," he continued. "Stinking, putrid shit." Then he turned and saw me standing there.

I winced at being caught and offered a wave, hoping the flush in my cheeks receded.

His lips pursed, those dark eyes narrowing. "You," he said.

"Me?" I couldn't help but laugh.

"Yeah, you." He swung his legs forward, prowling toward me with a glimmer in his gaze. "I'd bet if you were standing exactly where you were not even five minutes ago, the bastard who wrote me this ticket"—he flicked it in the air—"would've been too distracted to even remember what day it was."

I coughed out another laugh. "Distracted, huh?"

"Yeah." He sidled even closer until the scent of his caramel, woodsy cologne reached me, and I could make out a faint smattering of freckles across his straight nose. "In case you haven't noticed, you're kind of really fucking beautiful."

I'd always thought of him as lean; muscular and tall, but lean. However, having him this close, standing feet above me as he stared down into my face with crooked lips and fanned out lashes, I discovered I'd been way wrong.

He was a muscular giant.

My voice was scratchy as I muttered, "That a pick-up line of yours?"

His straight teeth slid over his lip as he studied me. "Uh-huh, I just go round getting tickets on the regular to pick up the ladies."

I laughed again, and his head tilted.

My cheeks tinged under his inspection, growing warmer as he said, "Do that again."

"What? Laugh?" I snorted, then laughed at the fact I'd snorted. Dear God.

"It's music. Anyone ever told you that?"

Feeling like I'd exited my own body, I shook my head, then backed up. "I need to go. Um, sorry for gawking."

"Please." He scoffed, half rolling his eyes. "You can gawk all day long. Stevie, right?"

I nodded. "Yeah."

He licked his lips, nodding too as he retreated a step. "Well, hopefully my dad won't curse up a storm when I tell him I got my sixth ticket for the year. I figure he'll be okay when I tell him the story of how it led to meeting my future wife." Tipping his shoulder, he added, "He's a sucker for true love."

I nearly choked on my next breath. "Excuse me?"

He chuckled, and I noticed a faint dimple in his right cheek. "I'll see you round, beautiful." With a wink, he turned and climbed into his black Audi.

"Girl," Sabrina said, clipping the stems on a bundle of roses as I walked in. "That boy looks like bad news. The kind that'll trample all over you, then return to feast on your remains."

She was wearing purple rain boots today with a white sundress, and a glittery white scarf draped over her graying red hair.

I huffed, mumbling as I took my bag into the backroom, "He basically just did."

I was still thinking about Aiden Prince that night when I got home, so naturally, I decided to do some detective work.

I mean, if a guy declares you're marriage material the first time you have a conversation, I figured he deserved a little stalking.

His Instagram page was littered with shirtless pictures of him either on a yacht, at the beach, playing ball, or even washing his car. My stomach flipped at the latter, spying bunches of muscle tucked beneath his golden skin.

I had to wonder who'd taken the pictures for him, and as I kept scrolling, I realized it was probably one of the many girls he'd been photographed with.

I didn't use Facebook much, but I logged in to find a few notifications before searching for him there too. Empty, for the most part. Only tags from some of his teammates with pictures of him playing.

I had to admit, those pants did great things for his ass, and the ball cap... I shut my laptop, then reopened it when I remembered I hadn't even bothered to check in on the band.

Aside from the usual hangover or partying posts, there were no updates on Hendrix's profile or the page Dale had started for the band.

After putting my laptop away, I showered before curling up on the couch and flicking through Netflix. I'd managed to go an entire day without thinking of him, thanks to Aiden, and then one tiny thing sent me tumbling back down into the murky void that was Everett Taylor all over again.

Did he even think about me when he was gone? The way he'd touched me, looked at me, and fucked me told me he had to be feeling at least half of what I was, and in that case, how could he keep doing the things he did if he'd left half his heart behind?

He's a guy, Adela would say when I brought it up to her. But that didn't matter to me. I thought controlling yourself would've been easy if you had a reason to.

Then Aiden bulldozed his way into my life, and I'd soon learn not everything could be controlled.

THIRTEEN

"BEAUTIFUL." THE HEATED WHISPER STOLE MY ATTENTION from the notebook I'd been scrawling in.

I blinked, and then Aiden was in the seat next to me. Prying my eyes off his curling lips, I smiled straight ahead at the scowling professor.

Aiden's arm slid close to mine, causing my skin to prickle, the tiny hairs rising as they met before the warmth of our bodies did. "What are you doing?" I asked between cracked lips.

"What do you mean?" he asked so casually while taking notes in his messy, barely legible cursive.

After looking at him with narrowed brows for three thudding heartbeats, I sighed and faced forward again, trying to ignore the touch that was causing my toes to scrunch.

We both remained silent until the lecture ended, and we began packing our things.

"Have dinner with me," he stated more than asked.

I laughed at his audacity, then stood and slung my backpack over my shoulder. "I'm surprised you're starting that low. Do you need to pay your ticket before you can buy a ring?"

Grinning, he rose with his book tucked by his side and inched so close, all I could smell was his cologne and all I could see was the golden column of his throat.

I forced my gaze up, and it skated over his clean-shaven, square chin to meet his fathomless dark eyes, as he said, "I've already got one picked out, but I figured you'd at least like to know I'm capable of feeding you before you say yes."

My head fell back, laughter pouring out as students vacated the lecture hall around us.

When I stared back at him, I chuckled some more, swiping beneath my eyes to make sure the leakage hadn't smudged my mascara. "You're a total rogue."

"Rogue?" he questioned.

"Mischievous," I said. "And I'm guessing you're going to make me climb these seats to get out if I don't say yes to dinner."

He puckered his full bottom lip while tilting his head. "You'd be right. But I'm willing to negotiate."

"What?" I laughed out. "Breakfast instead of dinner?"

"I'll settle for buying you a milkshake." All humor left his face. "Right now."

I didn't have any other classes for the day, but he might. "You don't have class?"

"Nope, and I'll take that as a yes." He backed out of the aisle, bowing with a swinging arm for me to go ahead of him.

I sighed, yet I couldn't wipe the smile off my face. "Fine. You're paying."

He scoffed, walking beside me up the stairs. "I may be a rogue, but I'm no scoundrel."

"You're ridiculous."

"I'm smitten."

"You don't even know me," I countered once we'd hit the stairs outside.

He stopped at the bottom, catching my hand gently in his. "So give me a chance to."

I turned to him. Chewing on my lip, I studied the earnest set to his jaw and the honest spark to his eyes. "Okay, but I must warn you..." I pulled my hand from his and headed in the direction of the cafeteria. I stopped talking, unsure why I wanted to divulge my cracked open heart to him. As if any guy wanted to hear about how the girl he was chasing was hung up on someone else.

"Warn me?" he asked, catching up and walking backward as he surveyed my face, then my tangled mess of hair that kept slapping my cheeks courtesy of the wind.

"Milkshake first," I said, pushing open the door. "I'm scoring a freebie before you run for the hills."

He said nothing to that but ordered two vanilla malts, and the sight of them was enough to curdle my stomach.

"So," he said, sliding his wallet into the back pocket of his jeans before taking a seat opposite me. "You've got an ex you're not over or something?"

I pursed my lips, then dunked my straw, eyeing the frothy milk. "Pretty much, but I'm trying." Aiden was quiet, and I looked up to find him staring at me. "Sorry."

He whistled, blinking, and it was then I realized he'd asked the question in jest.

Silence crept in, and I struggled to hold his gaze.

"You don't need to apologize," he finally said. "Everyone's got some kind of baggage to carry."

A little relieved, I smiled, and some passing girls cooed and waved to Aiden. He flicked his head at them, then returned his attention to me.

"You don't seem like the settling down type anyway."

He chuckled. "I'm not, no. I've had one serious girlfriend, and that was in my senior year."

"Uh-huh. How long did that last?"

He pursed his lips, as if trying to remember. "Long enough."

"So." I raised a brow. "Do you offer marriage to all the girls you want to sleep with?"

Leaning over the table, he took my hand in his, his gaze snatching and holding mine. "No. Only the ones I want to continuously sleep with."

"You might not like sleeping with me. You've never done it before," I whispered, and that sour feeling in my stomach made way for heat.

"I'm a betting man, and I'm willing to bet a whole fucking lot on you being the best time I'll ever have." His thumbs brushed over my clammy skin, and then he sat back and drew a lengthy sip of his milkshake.

Still blinking at him, I did the same, too aware of my thighs clenching together.

A lot of boys, soon-to-be men, had tried to do what Aiden had successfully done in a matter of minutes; pique my interest. But I'd never been able to see or feel anything, not even lust, for someone else.

Not until then.

Yet I kept on pushing. "I'm still in love with someone."

Aiden's hand went to his heart, and he flashed a crooked smile. "I see what's going on here." I noticed how quick it fell. "That's fine. Keep trying to deter me."

I sighed. "It could get... complicated."

"Are you still seeing this guy?" A thick brow arched. "Girl?"

I smiled again. "No, I rarely ever see him."

"Rarely?"

I nodded, not wanting to offer any more than that.

He sucked in a hard breath, then drummed his hands on the table. "Okay, how about this? We just hang out."

"Just hang out?"

He shrugged. "Yeah, I mean, you're too easy to stare at, you smell fucking incredible, and I like hearing you laugh. Those are good enough reasons to hang."

I felt my brows gather. "You're suggesting friends, then?"

His expression lost its playfulness, those high cheekbones lowering. "Friends. Who knows, maybe you'll eventually want more. Or maybe, I'll tire of your beautiful face and leave you in the dust."

I laughed, even as the word *eventually* ricocheted in my ears. "You're too smooth, Prince."

"You know my last name," he said, brows ticking up. "Go on, tell me more about the stalking you've been doing."

I bunched and tossed a napkin at him.

Laughing that full-throated laugh, he caught it and grabbed the pen that had been resting atop his book. I watched as he unfolded and scrawled his number on the napkin, then slid it over the table to me. "I lied." He slurped the remainder of his milkshake, then collected his book and pen. "I do have another class. Text me, friend."

"And what if I don't?" I asked, still staring at the napkin.

After another caressing chuckle, he grabbed my hand to press his warm lips to before swaggering out of the cafeteria.

FOURTEEN

"**H**EY, FRIEND."

Smiling, I stopped on the sidewalk, waiting for Aiden to catch up. "Hey, Prince."

"You know," he said, sunglasses shielding his curious eyes. "I've never liked chicks calling me that before, not when all my teammates do."

I twisted my lips, kicking at a lone pebble. "Is that your way of telling me to stop?"

"No," he said, bumping my shoulder with his and gesturing to his car down the street. We headed toward it. "If you stop, I'll be pissed."

Laughter infused my voice. "Noted."

"No school today?"

"Work." I gestured over my shoulder.

Tossing a glance backward, he hummed. "Petal Power. How fitting, you little ray of sunshine."

I laughed loud, almost snorting. "I'm not so shiny these days."

"Could've fooled me," he said. A weighted moment passed before he asked, "Because of that guy you were talking about?"

"Yeah." I exhaled a breath. "I'm okay, though."

Stopping at his car, he opened the passenger door, and I climbed in without a word of protest.

After giving him directions to my place, we spent the short drive in silence until he pulled up to the curb. I wanted to talk, to say something, but words failed me; all the while, his presence comforted me.

"I had this girlfriend once."

"Senior year?" I unclipped my seat belt, then turned in the seat to face him.

His eyes glimmered as he removed his shades and did the same. "You remember."

"It was only last week." I knew saying that would give away that I'd been thinking about him, but I didn't mind admitting it.

With a nod, his attention dipped to the console. "Her name was Darby, and she was my first real girlfriend since anything before ninth grade doesn't count. Anyway, she broke my heart. Haven't tried again."

"What did she do?" I asked, feeling pressure on my chest when he turned to stare out the window.

"Stripped for a living. I could get past that. But then things went awry with a bunch of my friends one night."

I blinked several times, hating the memories that cloaked his features, turning them to stone. "He was my brother's best friend, a damaged soul and a heavy drinker."

Darting his gaze to me, Aiden's eyes narrowed. "Shit."

"He was also beautiful, kind, creative, and talented." I undid my ponytail, rolling the elastic over my wrist. "Besides my mom and best friend, no one knows we had, I don't know, something. It was never going to last. I knew that, and still, I thought that maybe one day…" I cleared my throat. "And now, they're all on the road, playing music."

"Your brother?"

"Guitar, all forms." I smiled, grabbing my purse. "They're really good."

"Searching for fame, huh?"

Pondering that, I looked back at him. "They're searching for something; I just don't know if it's the same thing." Shrugging, I opened the door, then paused. "So I've still got that napkin."

Flashing me a grin, he watched me climb out. "Music to my ears, Petal."

"I don't think your dad will care what you get him as long as he gets to see you."

Aiden snorted into the phone. "You don't know my dad, Petal." He'd called me that ever since he found out where I worked. He paused, and I knew what was coming before he said it. "Oh." Amused laughter bubbled. "That would be too good. You come with, and he'll forget all about the fact I didn't get him a stupid present."

"You can't keep using me as an excuse to get out of shit with your dad," I told him, refilling my water bottle at the sink.

"What do you even mean? He already loves you, and he hasn't even met you."

"Prince," I warned, muttering about the mixtape Adela and I were trying to find the night before as I entered my room.

"What?" He said something to someone in the background, then laughed at whatever they said back. "Wait, did you just say mixtape?"

"Sure did." I tugged out a box from beneath my bed and lowered to the ground to rummage through it.

"I'm sorry, how very eighties of you."

"Shut it," I said, grinning when I finally found it beneath some records. "Got it!"

"Pray tell, what's on this mixtape?" His voice lowered a few decibels. "Hang on, is it a dirty tape?"

I snorted. "No, and it belonged to my parents. Adela and I used to dance to some of the songs on it when we were kids. We were wondering if I brought it when we moved here." I flipped the cassette over, inspecting the back. "It was bugging me, not knowing."

"You're too fucking cute. What songs? Fleetwood, Abba, the Stones?" He started to hum a bad rendition of "Ruby Tuesday," and my eyes widened.

"Dear God, you're a worse singer than I am."

He sputtered. "I'll have you know I was once told I had a brilliant voice." He paused. "And then my voice broke, and it all went to hell."

We both laughed then and settled into a comfortable silence. I could hear him getting into his car, the change of his voice as the door closed and the phone connected to the Bluetooth. "I miss you. Let me come over for another movie night."

"And have Adela watch us like we're two teens who might kiss at any moment? Awkward."

"All right. That was awkward, but I'll break the ice a bit better this time."

"What are you doing?" I asked, changing the subject. We'd grown closer since he'd first come over to our apartment, and it often worried me how comfortable I was speaking to him yet how uncomfortable I got when he was too close.

I liked it a little too much.

"Heading home from the team meeting."

I'd learned Aiden had been accepted into Duke, but he wanted to play ball for a living, and Raslow was the only college that had offered him a full ride. It'd caused some contention between him and his dad, who apparently wanted him to take over the family business, but things were civil, he'd said.

"We can hang tomorrow?" I offered, tapping my fingers on the side of the box. "Maybe grab some dinner?"

We'd been out for dinner a handful of times since I'd met him before Thanksgiving, so I didn't feel like I was leading him on by asking.

"Sure. Bonnie's?" he asked, meaning the little diner we preferred near my work.

"Duh," I said. "Later, Prince." I hung up before he could leave me with a lasting line of his that never failed to make me question why I kept him in the friend zone.

I only had to look at the tape and the records in the box, and recall all the times Everett had sung along to some of the songs to remember why.

"Am I too dressed up?" I asked Aiden, glancing down at my floral skirt, heeled wedges, and plain white tank.

The March air was crisp, and I shrugged on my leather jacket as Aiden eyed me from where he was leaning against the brick exterior of Bonnie's.

His team blazer gave the impression of a young grease monkey with his perfectly swept back hair and tight jeans. "With that jacket, you look like sex on legs. Come on, I'm fucking starved."

He held out his arm, and I looped mine through it, smiling when he leaned in to kiss my cheek and inhale my curls. "I felt like making an effort after embarrassing you in my cutoffs and band shirt last time."

He waited for me to slide into the lime green booth before sliding in on the other side. "I'm not even going to comment because I'll probably call you something stupid. Like an idiot."

I laughed. "You just fucking did."

"Say fucking again, Petal, and I fear I'll need to at least steal a kiss. It turns me to steel within a second." He leaned over the table, his eyes trained on my nude glossed lips. "Every. Fucking. Time."

Wildfire shot through my limbs. My head spun as I grabbed his chin, bringing his mouth close to mine. "You wouldn't dare."

"Careful," he said, sounding dangerously close to the edge. "I might bite."

"I bet you bite." Quickly, I pecked his lips, then released him and sat back before he could take it any further.

"What was that?" he asked, hands spread wide. "Such a tease."

"You wouldn't be here if you didn't want to put up with it."

He sighed. "So true."

We both ditched the menus, opting to order what we always did. He asked for the steak, medium rare, with salad and fries, and I ordered the wedges with sour cream.

"What's happening with your dad's birthday, then?"

Aiden drank some water before answering. "I told him I'll head home for Easter. I have a game tomorrow night, and even if I left right afterward, I'd get there too late." His dad lived four hours north, where he grew up. "That's why the present is so important. He's probably going to be pissed."

"He loves you." I licked some cream from my lip, smirking when Aiden's eyes narrowed, and he mouthed the word, "Evil."

Watching me for an echoing beat, he said, "While that may be so, he can be an asshole about it."

I chose not to comment and kept eating. My phone rang in my purse, and feeling full, I pushed my bowl away and checked it while Aiden finished his steak.

Hendrix.

It was the third time he'd tried to call this week, but I was finally in a good place. Happy.

So even though guilt pressed heavy hands on my chest, I continued to ignore him to keep that feeling from disappearing.

He was probably calling to ask for money anyway. Last time I'd spoken with Mom, she said things were getting tight for them, and they'd had to stop some places for a while and work some cash jobs before they could get back on the road. They didn't make it home for Christmas for that reason, being that they were stuck in some Midwest town for six weeks trying to earn enough cash to fuel the next leg of their tour.

"Where's your mom?" I asked, tucking my phone away.

Aiden was frowning at my purse. "She's dead."

I held in a shocked gasp. Just. "Aiden…"

"It's okay," he said, waving a hand. "Well, no, not really. Suicide. But it's been years."

I took his hand, squeezing it with mine. He offered a soft smile, then plucked his hand back and swiped at his mouth with a napkin. "Wanna go?"

I nodded, finishing my water to wash away the taste of sour cream and sadness.

He paid the bill, and we drifted out onto the lamplit sidewalk, heading to his car. "So no movie night tonight?"

"I guess…" My voice faded. People were streaming out of the bar down on the corner, herds of them littering the street. Thumping traveled to my ears, and then the unmistakable sound of Hendrix and one of his infamous guitar riffs. "Oh, my God."

"Stevie?" Aiden sounded worried. "The color is falling off your face onto the fucking concrete. Does your stomach hurt?" His hand landed on my cheek, trying to turn me. "Maybe food poisoning. Though I don't think it usually sets in so—"

I was walking away before he could finish his sentence,

gliding toward the crooning voice that was calling. The one that always had me crawling back every time I heard it.

Just like now.

I pushed and shoved my way inside, dodging the bouncer who was too preoccupied with the mountain of people at the door to pay me any mind, and then I froze.

By the bar, the lights dim but the men on stage clear as day, I stood rooted to the spot.

"Stevie." Aiden found me. "What the fuck, are you high?"

"No," I breathed, my eyes watering as Everett, almost unchanged, sat on the stage, his knee bent for his guitar to rest over, and the mic lowered for his voice to reach.

Once more, his hair was longer, tucked behind one ear as he sang with closed eyes.

...same toxic beat
Has fucking chains around my feet

Nurse the lyric like a mother
Disguised as a lover
For all the world to see
Through the gaps of your mind,
Your words can bend time,
But baby,
They'll never set you free

Whoa, oh, no
Rinse and repeat

Lifting a bottle of whiskey from the scuffed stage, Everett took a swig, muttering something into the mic as Graham segued into the next song. With a harsh shake of his head, Everett placed the bottle down, his large hands returning to the guitar strings, and his eyes closing again.

There's a blunt edge to the tray filled with ash,
And it sings to that open wound
You call a gash
Night after night,
You feel it coming,
Day after day,
You feel like running

But it's all your fault,
That empty bottle
The overflowing ashtray
It's all just salt
On the festering guilt you made me carry
From city to city
Skipping dreams and solar beams
Yeah, it's all your fault...

I felt every hair on my body rise with his voice as he carried the melody to the rafters, and the room swelled, the audience bottled inside for the minutes Everett held them captive for.

The thundering rumble of Graham on the drums drowned out half the cheering, and when he hit the cymbal with an ending clash, that was when it happened.

Red eyes opened, and Everett looked up. One look made sure I felt it all. Everything I'd tried to suffocate clawed straight back to the surface, and Aiden steadied me as my knees quaked.

FIFTEEN

SHOULDN'T HAVE IGNORED HIS CALLS, WAS THE ONLY THING I COULD think as Aiden turned me to face him, asking again if I was okay.

"I'm fine." Blinking away the mist in my eyes, I waved a hand toward the stage. "I just..." I blew out a trembling breath, knowing I'd have to be honest. "I know them. It's my..." I stopped and licked my dried lips. "My brother's band."

Aiden's dark stare held mine a beat longer, and then his hands left my face as he was wrenched back and shoved into the bustling crowd.

"Everett," I yelled when he advanced on Aiden, predatory intent in every step.

"Who are you?" I heard him growl over the noise.

Thankfully, no one besides the few people at the bar seemed to be paying us any mind.

That changed when Aiden's eyes gleamed. "Her boyfriend."

"Aiden," I pleaded just as Everett swung.

He missed, which was probably thanks to the whiskey and the flask peeking out of his back pocket, but Aiden still tipped, almost falling to the floor when he ducked and lurched back.

"This is the guy you were talking about, Petal?"

"Petal?" Everett snarled, sending a heated glare at me over his shoulder.

It was all I could do to nod, but when I caught sight of my brother and the others heading this way, I made a move for the exit, grabbing Aiden. "Come on. We need to go."

Ignoring me, he sidled right up into Everett's face, and though they both seemed evenly matched, I knew Everett wouldn't fight fair, if he could even fight in his state, so I tugged on Aiden's hand. "I mean it, Aiden. Please, let's go."

Everett's nostrils flared. Though he kept his gaze firmly on Aiden, he no doubt heard me.

"Fine," he gritted, eyes trained on Everett. "Lead the way, Petal."

I didn't like the way he put extra emphasis on the nickname to rile Everett up, but I was just relieved he'd relaxed enough to head outside with me.

Any relief I felt withered and died. We weren't on the street for two seconds before I heard Everett. "Clover!"

Aiden's hand was tense and clammy around mine as we kept walking, rounding the corner to where a group of people were standing around, talking and smoking.

"Clover, don't fucking walk away from me."

"Clover?" Aiden asked, halting.

"Jesus," I said, my hand releasing his to rake through my hair. "I can't believe this."

"You didn't know your brother was coming to town?"

"No," I said, tears starting to resurface. "He'd tried to call, but I didn't want to hear about the band, or anything to do with..." I flapped my hand to where Everett was stalking toward us, a lit cigarette dangling between his fingers. "I didn't know it was to tell me he was coming here."

Aiden cursed. "Want me to go?" I looked back at him, and what he saw on my face had his dropping. "Yeah, okay." He laughed low, shaking his head. "Call if you need me, Stevie."

My feet tripped forward. "Aiden, wait."

He turned, walking backward with his hands tucked into his jean pockets. "That all depends on what you decide to do tonight."

I closed my eyes, inhaling deep and getting hit in the lungs with the acrid scent of tobacco. Turning around, I was met with the bloodshot eyes of Everett Taylor.

He inhaled his cigarette so hard, almost half of it disappeared before he let up and slowly exhaled out the side of his mouth. A pile of ash was flicked to the ground, his eyes narrowing to slits. "That punk, is he really your boyfriend?"

"No, but he's my friend."

Again, he inhaled his cigarette, just staring at me. A stare so penetrating and cold, I struggled not to flinch as my stomach twisted and all the knots I'd undone in his absence retied and tightened.

He had a new scar on his cheek, right on the sharp crest of the bone, and his stubble was a day or two away from becoming a beard.

"You're not even going to talk?" I finally said. "You show up here, all of you, and you act like an asshole to my friend, and then you just stare at me like I've done something wrong?"

Smoke billowed past his lips as he released a caustic laugh. "You have. He's not your fucking friend."

"Oh, I have, have I?" Outrage spiked my tone. "Tell me then, Everett, just how many friends have you had while you've been on the road?" I stepped closer, hissing at him. "Since you fucked my brains out and left me in yet another broken heap almost a year ago?"

His teeth flashed, his voice deceptively calm. "I don't look at any of them the way he looked at you." Leaning down into my face, he seethed, "In fact, I don't need to look at them at all."

Those words had me swaying back. "Fuck you."

He chuckled, the sound void of humor, and then he grabbed for me, looping his arm around my waist. "Fucking right you will be."

"Rett?" Hendrix called. "Hey, Steve. The fuck are you guys doing?"

Disgusted, I pushed Everett away, then raced down the street and across the road, dodging couples and a man on a bike as I found the alleyway that cut through to our apartment.

I should've known he'd follow. I almost had the door closed before his boot wedged itself inside, and I screamed, moving back as tears began to tumble down my face. "Fuck, just leave me alone."

"Never," he said, shutting and locking the door behind him.

Adela didn't appear to be home, or she would've made her presence known by now with the commotion we'd caused.

"Never?" I asked. "It's all you ever do, come and fucking go as you please." My finger shook, pointing at the door. "Not anymore. Get out."

He just stood there, leaning back against the door with his arms crossed over his chest, the stupid orange apple on his black fitted shirt.

"Did you hear me?"

"Oh, I heard you. But you see," he said, straightening and taking his time to prowl down the hall, his fingers trailing over the potted plants on the entry table, "your words don't align with what your eyes are saying."

My heart drooped and my spine curved, my entire body liquefying with every step he took until he was standing before me. Rough fingers grasped my chin, and his thumb ghosted over it so tenderly. "You split me in two, Clover." His head lowered, his hands reaching for my waist as his nose slid beneath my chin, tilting it back to inhale my neck. "You never said goodbye."

"I'm tired of goodbyes, Ever."

"I need all your goodbyes and every hello. Don't fucking deprive me of you."

"Like you don't deprive me?" I grabbed his head, lifting it. "You do it every time you leave."

His forehead dropped to mine, and the scent of rum washed over my lips. "Don't leave." I couldn't believe I'd whispered words I never thought I'd say again, especially now that I thought I didn't need him.

Perhaps I'd always need him. He was a drug, and I'd constantly relapse whenever he was made available to me.

"I don't want to," he whispered, then his lips were on mine. His arms lowered, picking me up and carrying me through the doorway into the kitchen.

His taste was the same, and I worried how much he was drinking now. If he'd resorted to drinking rum as well as whiskey.

We bumped into the counter and he cursed, muttering an apology as he set me on it. Removing my jacket, I could hardly breathe when his teeth sank into my lip. His hands pulled at my tank, tugging it and my bra down over my breasts.

"Fuck." He tore his mouth away, lowering to my chest as he unzipped his jeans.

I gripped his face, needing those lips back on mine, then I reached for his waistband, shoving his jeans and briefs down.

He helped, and then pulled me right to the edge, testing my entrance with his thumb before licking the digit and pushing my panties aside. "I still have your other pair," he said, his breath rattling as he pushed at my opening.

"Wha–oh, shit." He rammed inside, and my head rolled.

He slammed in and out, again and again, one hand around my leg that'd been looped behind him, and the other behind my head as he bent over and hammered into me, sucking at my throat.

It'd been so long, and I felt just how long as the discomfort slowly fled and pleasure began to flood my bloodstream. "I-I think I'm coming…"

Everett chuckled, the sound dark. "You think? Clover, when I'm fucking you, you know damn well you're coming." Then he lifted me and spun us around until my back met the cool exterior of the fridge, magnets digging into my ass while I kept my legs wrapped tight around him.

I mumbled incoherent pleas to his tongue as it slid over mine. Our teeth clacked, his hips jerking up so fast and hard, I was on the edge and shaking for what felt like minutes. "So fucking beautiful. So fucking mine. Say it." He reached between us to flick me into a million shattering pieces. "Say it while you come because of me."

"Yours," I rasped, and he held my face as he jerked and stilled, his forehead hard on mine and his breath choppy as it drifted inside my mouth.

We remained like that, eyes locked, our thundering hearts taking their time to slow and calm. His finger drifted over my cheek, and his cock softened inside me. "You've wrecked me, Clover."

I swallowed, my throat dry.

A loud bang echoed on the door, followed by, "Open up, scumbag. I know you're in there!"

Hendrix.

"Fuck," Everett groaned out, his hands clenching tight.

My heart started racing again in fear.

Then Adela's voice sounded, "I'm sorry! He called me and told me to meet him. I didn't know."

Muffled curses, and then Adela shouted, "No, you shut up."

"Open the door, Adela."

"You open the door."

Silence, then, "Fine."

A boom echoed through the apartment.

"Is he trying to kick the door in?" I choked out.

"Don't fucking kick my door, or I'll kick you, motherfucker."

"You wouldn't dare, tiny one."

A yelp and a groan had my eyes widening, and I patted Everett's shoulders.

His eyes opened, and I frowned. "Were you falling asleep?"

"Maybe," he whispered, groggy. "That Hendrix?"

My eyes stung as realization dawned. I'd just let him ruin me all over again, and worst of all, he probably wouldn't even remember most of it. I pushed, and he fell out of me, his semen dripping down my thighs as he stepped back, wobbling until he caught himself on the counter.

"Are there any days when you don't drink anymore, Everett?"

"Ever," he mumbled. "You usually call me Ever."

I shook my head as he leaned over the counter, head hung low and his pants still undone.

Heading to the bathroom, I locked myself inside to clean up.

Keys jangled, Adela shouted a warning, and then the door opened with a bang as it no doubt hit the wall thanks to Hendrix. "Where are you, sister fucker?"

Shit.

Shaking out my wet hands, I tore open the bathroom door and rushed into the kitchen in time to see Everett doing up his fly, and Hendrix shoving him back into the countertop. "How long have you been fucking around with her?"

"I've never fucked around with her," he slurred out. "She's my clover."

"Jesus Christ," Hendrix said, visibly shaking as I stood behind him. "You're too drunk to even punch."

"Don't," I said.

Hendrix turned, his face mottled and his fists clenching at his sides. "Do you enjoy fooling around with my asshole best friend, Steve? Because he's just that, an asshole. Everyone knows it, and that makes you a fucking idiot for letting him touch you."

"Hendrix," Adela warned, voice and eyes sharp, and moved beside me. "You'll watch your mouth, or I'll watch it for you."

He laughed, dry and drained, and didn't even spare her a glance as he swiped a hand over his chin, his stare hard and pressing into mine. "You haven't seen what he does on the road. He's either drunk or he's fucking his way through the hordes of women who show up at our gigs." He stepped even closer, biting out, "Sometimes two or three at once."

A strangled shout was all the warning we had to step back as Everett grabbed my brother by the shirt and flung him through our kitchen, then hurled himself over top of him.

Adela screamed. "Oh, God!"

The rest of the band arrived then, but it was too late. Everett had landed two punches to Hendrix's jaw before he was flipped, and Hendrix landed blows to Everett's mouth and cheekbone.

"Leave you guys alone for two minutes and then we're racing through some kitschy looking town like a bunch of fucking psychopaths," Graham muttered as he and Dale pulled Hendrix off Everett and tossed him to the floor.

"What the hell is going on?" Dale asked, shoving Hendrix back when he tried to make a move for Everett, who remained on the floor, groaning.

I ran to the freezer to grab some ice and wrapped it in a dish towel, then crouched down beside him to press it to his cheek.

"He was fucking my sister. That's what's going on."

Everett groaned again, pushing my hand away.

"You're shitting me," Graham said, turning to me. "Little sis?"

Ignoring them, I tried again to hold the ice over Everett's cheek. He allowed it this time, squinting up at me.

I brushed some hair off his face, and Hendrix scoffed. "Unbelievable. Look at this shit. She worships him, and he's out there acting like she doesn't exist night after night."

My hand fell away at the reminder, lips and heart pinching.

"Hendrix," Dale said. "Tone it down."

"Get fucked, Dale."

"Little sis," Graham said, still sounding perplexed. "But I always thought if any of us could win her heart, it'd be me."

"Win her heart? What are you, a fucking poet?" Hendrix said, spitting blood onto his hand and frowning at it.

"I'm a rock star. Close enough."

Hendrix rolled his neck, muttering a slew of curses.

Everett was still staring at me when I shifted the ice to his busted lip. "Not worthy," he whispered, so quiet that no one else could hear.

My head shook, and Hendrix groaned, clearly watching us again. "Fuck this, I'm out. Some best friend you are, you giant fucking asshole."

The door slammed, and Dale and Graham stood there a moment, unsure what to do.

Adela entered the room with a glass of water, and then the guys snapped into action and helped me lift Everett to sit as Adela handed me the water.

He took slow sips, wincing as it hit the cut on his lip. "At least that's over with."

Dale snorted. "Ha-ha. Not by a long shot, buddy."

Everett swayed, about to lie back down when the guys swooped in. "Come on," Graham said. "Back to the bus for you."

I was about to offer that he could stay here, but judging by the look Dale sent me when I opened my mouth, I knew it'd be a terrible idea.

"They need to hash it out," Adela said as we watched them head down the stairs outside. Everett was propped between Dale and Graham with his arms slung over their shoulders. "Having him hide away will only cause more tension. They're a team. The quicker they have it out, the quicker they can hopefully move on."

Though I wanted to, I wasn't sure if I believed her.

SIXTEEN

THOUGHTS OF EVERETT, HOW DRUNK HE'D BEEN, AND HOW MUCH he hadn't seemed to care about any repercussions haunted me until I finally fell asleep.

Aiden's crooked smile floating behind my lids had me waking early with an aching chest in the cocoon I'd made of my bedding.

He'd just told me about his mom and how she'd died, then minutes later, watched me race down the street toward another man. The same man who was holding me back from him.

When you want something bad enough, it was too easy to justify all the ways in which you're right, and everything else is wrong.

A steady ache pressed behind my eyes, a fitting companion for the one growing inside my chest.

I could hear Adela moving around the house, getting ready for work at the small cinema in the middle of town.

Eventually, I dragged myself to the shower, then downed two cups of tea as I sat at the kitchen counter, trying to call my brother. His voicemail greeted me five times before I finally gave up and decided on a different tactic.

The sun was bright beneath clouds that tried to smother it, the town of Raslow coming alive as it did every Saturday morning. Families crowded the streets, heading to street vendors, cafés, and the fruit and flower markets.

In the gravel lot behind the bar sat the bus that'd carried my heart away from me and sent us both down different paths.

The paint was fading, and stone chips and small dents exposed glimpses of the original yellow. The big dent in the front still hadn't been fixed, but I suppose they didn't exactly have the funds to go around fixing materialistic things like that.

Dale was where he'd said he'd be, camped out outside the bus on a deck chair. Wearing Wayfarers, checkered Vans, and an unbuttoned black dress shirt, he sipped his coffee while plucking at the strings of the guitar in his lap.

"Decided to try again?" I asked, leaning against the bus.

"These shmucks can't keep bagging all the good chicks," he said, strumming a soft melody that sounded painfully familiar, right up until it bottomed out. "That fucking chord."

"C minor nine." My smile was grim as I remembered Hendrix trying to master it some years ago.

Dale's hand slapped against the strings, and he sighed. "You've created quite the mess, Stevie Nicks."

I tried to smirk but failed. "I know." I toed some gravel with my chuck. "He here?"

Dale leaned the guitar against the side of the bus. "Who, your brother? Or the drunk?"

"It's gotten that bad, huh?" I knew without having to ask, but I still had to.

"Yeah." Dale exhaled. "He can rock that stage drunk, high, or sober. But as soon as he's off?" He rose, stretching his arms above his head before bending to retrieve his coffee. "The shitshow begins."

"All the women..." I trailed off, wishing I hadn't said anything.

"Stevie." Dale gave me a tired smile. "The only time he doesn't have a drink in his hand is when he's asleep." He stopped, a short bark of laughter leaving. "No, even then he'll sometimes nurse a bottle or flask."

I looked up at the bus, worry mingling with anger. "He needs help."

Dale's voice lowered, his hand coming to rest on my shoulder. "He can stop. He just doesn't want to."

I didn't know if I believed that. I didn't know what to believe anymore. "I thought—"

"That he'd be better once he left the two assholes he called parents?"

I nodded.

"We all did. Especially him." He stepped back and glanced up at the bus when movement sounded from inside.

"He took off," Dale said. "Hendrix. Wasn't here when we got back."

Guilt thickened my voice. "Will you tell him I'm sorry? I don't know if I'll get to see him. He won't answer my calls."

Dale wiped a hand down his face, mumbling what sounded like, "Shit, here we go," when the door to the bus flew open, and Everett stumbled out, falling to the gravel lot.

He didn't even see us, and I made to go to him when he rose, steadying himself with a stream of curses. Unzipping his fly, he staggered over to a weed-infested garden to relieve himself.

"We're nothing if not classy," Dale said, grabbing the guitar and heading to the door. "I'll be inside if you need anything. Otherwise, bye, Stevie."

"Thanks. Later, Dale."

Everett swung around then, still tucking himself away. His eyes widened, his hair a stringy mess, falling into his face until he shoved it back. "Clover?"

"Hey."

Zipping his jeans, he trudged over, the laces of his untied boots slapping at the small stones. "What are you doing here?"

"I came to see you and, um"—I straightened from the bus, slipping my hands into the pockets of my shorts—"Hendrix."

Recognition lit those green, bloodshot eyes. "Fuck."

"Yeah."

We stood there a long moment, me watching him, and him watching the ground.

Then a rough laugh had his head snapping up, though he didn't look happy at all. "Thought you would've run back to your preppy boyfriend by now."

That all depends on what you decide to do tonight.

I rubbed at my forehead. "He's not my boyfriend."

"You don't look too sure about that." Everett squinted; his voice soft and rough at the same time.

I ignored him. "What happens now?"

"With what?" He pushed his hand through his hair, clearing it off his face.

I tried not to wince at his words, the split, swollen lip, or the bruise on his cheekbone. "Us."

His brows scrunched, and a hollow laugh tightened my gut. "There is no us, Clover. Just because your brother knows I like to fuck you doesn't mean anything's changed."

Ice-layered thorns wrapped around my heart. "You're serious?"

He lifted a shoulder, then dug his hand into his pocket and pulled out a squashed pack of cigarettes. Sticking one between his teeth, he lit it, then shoved the lighter and pack back inside his pocket. "Yeah," he finally said. His eyes darted behind me and hardened further before he let them settle on my face.

My hands clenched at my sides, and I drew in a scathing, silent breath, trying to keep hold of all that was threatening to unravel. "You know what?" I said, my smile sad. "It's probably for the best."

He blinked, exhaling a cloud of smoke, then nodded. "You're a comfort, Clover. Nothing more, nothing less."

I stepped back, sucking my lips between my teeth. "Right. Well, find some other kind of comfort from now on, asshole."

His rumbling laughter hit me square in the back as I began to leave. "I always do."

Hendrix was stalking to the bus, his hair a disaster and his clothes wrinkled. "Steve."

I swallowed the tears that'd pushed past my defenses. "Tried to call you."

"I know." He stopped.

"You don't want to talk to me?"

He sighed. "Not particularly."

I nodded, biting my lip as we just stood there, not looking at each other.

He yawned, then shifted and gestured behind me. "We've gotta head out. I'll, ah, I'll see you."

"Yeah, okay."

He skirted around me, and I was tempted to see if he and Everett would fight again, but I didn't have it in me to care, so I continued to walk away.

SEVENTEEN

FORGIVENESS WAS A DESPERATE HEART'S MISTAKE.

You didn't forsake the soul to save an organ. Hearts had an expiration date; the soul was immortal.

And I was beginning to fear for mine. This had to stop before the stains blemishing who I was couldn't be removed.

Adela came home to find me in a sea of tissues on my bed.

Without saying anything, she pulled back the duvet, slipped in behind me, and wrapped her arm around my waist until I was ready to talk.

When I finally did, she didn't speak for the longest time.

"You're worrying me," I said.

"Me?" She laughed.

"Yes, you. You're not saying anything."

A sigh left her. "Because I don't know if what I want to say will be of any help, or if it's what you want to hear right now."

We laid there some more, now staring at the ceiling. It'd taken me a while to get used to a bare white with no faded glow worms.

"Tell me anyway," I decided.

"You can't help who you love, but I think it's time to try."

"That's it?"

She hummed. "Yep."

I nibbled my lip, sniffing. "He won't talk to me."

"Who?"

"Aiden," I said, my eyes closing.

"Well, I was starting to worry he was stealing my best friend card, so maybe that's just fine."

We both laughed, and I winced at how the action made my ribs ache.

"Have you tried to talk to him?" she asked.

"I called him earlier when I got home. He didn't answer." Her silence had me rolling my head to face her. "What?"

Her lips were pressed into a tight line. She released them to say, "You left him in the street for Everett, and he probably figures you slept with him. I'm sorry, hussy, but I think it's going to take a lot more than simply calling him."

I blew out a breath, closing my eyes again. "On a scale of one to ten, how horrible am I?"

Adela pretended to think about it. "I'd say a solid seven."

I snatched and tossed a pillow at her, and she laughed.

The bus wasn't in the parking lot when I headed to Aiden's apartment the next morning.

I didn't expect it to be, but seeing the cars parked in that space was a reminder of what I'd allowed to happen. Of what I always allowed to happen.

No more.

I'd only been by Aiden's apartment once, when we'd been on our way to one of his games, and he'd forgotten his lucky ball cap. I hadn't gone in, but I thought I had a pretty good idea which apartment I'd seen him enter from where I'd waited in his car.

I'd thought wrong.

I knocked on four doors, of which only two residents

answered, telling me I had the wrong place, until some guy wearing a gaming headset said I'd find him in apartment eight.

I thanked him, then walked down the end of the hall and knocked before I could chicken out.

No answer.

I was about to try again when the door opened, and a bleary-eyed Aiden ran a hand down his face, his golden skin paling a shade when he saw me.

Trying not to let the shadowed dips and muscles of his bare chest distract me, I started in, the words rushing out of me so fast, I was surprised he heard them. "I owe you about a million apologies. I know that. I'm an idiot. I know I told you it was complicated, and even though you probably won't want to speak to me after what I did, I promise you I'm done with complicated." I finally expelled a breath. "So, so done."

Aiden glanced behind him, skating his tongue over his teeth as his shoulders lowered. "You sleep with him?" My mouth opened, but he must've known the answer. "Don't say it."

"Aiden, I wasn't thinking properly." I laughed, the noise breaking. "I never really do where he's concerned, but like I said, I'm done." My eyes begged. "I swear, and I'm sorry."

"Done," he repeated, dark eyes assessing mine. "Look, now's not a good time, Petal. And if I'm being honest, I don't know if I can handle—"

"Aiden?" a feminine voice sang. "Where's the coffee?"

I tripped backward, stepping away from him and his apartment. "Who's that?"

A blonde appeared behind him, a senior I recognized from campus. "Who's she?"

Aiden didn't look at her. "My friend. Coffee's in the cabinet above the machine. I'll be back in a second."

She nodded, eyeing me a moment before vanishing.

He stepped outside. "Don't do that."

"Do what?" I croaked, riddled with disbelief.

"Look at me like I've broken your heart."

"You have." Until that moment, I hadn't realized someone else was capable of doing so. "The part that belonged to you, anyway." I turned and ran for the stairs, taking them two at a time and almost falling. I righted myself, swiping at the wet on my cheeks as I rushed past rows of doors toward the exit.

A hand grabbed my arm, stopping me. "That's not fucking fair, Stevie."

"What isn't?" Struggling to breathe, I spun around and glared. "Me being honest with you?"

"Exactly," he seethed, his top lip curling. "Not when it's a little too late."

"Whatever." I went to leave, and then I was against the wall, and Aiden's scent was everywhere, clouding my senses, blurring my vision.

"You don't get to just give yourself to some guitar swinging asshole, then show up here with your heart suddenly on your sleeve." The words were gritted through his perfect teeth, hard and desperate and tearing at my heart.

"I know, and I'm sorry," I said, tears bubbling. I smacked them away and pushed at his chest. "I really am. I'll just... I'll see you around."

He didn't move, and when I gathered the courage to look at his face again, I saw his eyes glassing and felt the hurt radiating from every muscled inch of his body. "You fucked me up, Petal." He chuckled, dry and weak. "No, you had me where you wanted me, fucking tied me down, then drove a Mack truck over my damn chest. You destroyed me."

I blinked, sniffing as I dared to raise my shaking hand to

his cheek. "I never meant or wanted to." His skin was warm and smooth, a stark contrast to Everett's clammy and prickly.

His eyes shut, a tear collecting on his long lashes. "I know."

Remembering the guest inside his apartment, I gave a weak smile when his eyes reopened. Taking the tear from his lashes, I licked it from my thumb. "Go, she's waiting for you."

His nod, the way he retreated, was a razor dragging over the bleeding organ in my chest. Still, I forced myself to say it one more time. "I'm sorry."

He walked away, and I made myself watch, knowing I'd ruined a chance at having something that wasn't only real but also healthy and beautiful. "Don't say that again, okay?"

"Why?" I asked, standing up straight from the cool wall.

He ran a hand through his finger swept hair. "It's a reminder that you have something to be sorry for."

"You're really going back to her?" I couldn't help but ask, knowing I'd all but sent him.

"Go home, Stevie."

"I don't want to."

In quick strides, he was standing in front of me again. Muscles rippled, and my eyes ducked to the basketball shorts hanging low on his sharp hips. "Why? Did he leave you again?" I glared, my mouth slack. "Make you a bunch of empty promises to get between your legs and then bail?" Any softness had left his voice.

"Don't," I pleaded.

"No," he snapped. "You made the mistake of telling me about him, and then I made the mistake of seeing it with my own two eyes. I won't be your second choice because some asshole couldn't make you his first."

He cursed when my face crumpled. "Fuck you, Aiden. You don't know nearly as much as you think you do."

"Yeah?" He inched closer. "Well, the same goes for you, heart slayer. I'm fucking in love with you, but you either can't see that, or you just don't give a shit."

My breath hitched, loud. "What?"

He laughed, dark and disbelieving, then jogged back to the stairs. "Jesus Christ. Just go home."

"Aiden, wait."

He didn't.

EIGHTEEN

AYING THE PAPER DOWN, I PLACED THE TIED ARRANGEMENT OF wildflowers, daisies, and petunias in the center, then carefully started wrapping them.

"You're hiding today." Gloria leaned against the doorframe to the back room. "You should've seen the way Mr. Ross's face fell. You know he comes in specifically on the days you work."

I snorted. "Yeah, to buy flowers for his wife."

"Doesn't matter. Sometimes, a smile from a pretty youth is enough to liven the weirdest of souls."

I smiled at that. "Is Sabrina back yet?"

"Nah. My money's on her stopping by the bakery to nab a donut."

"Diet's not going so well?"

Gloria laughed, a warm, scratchy sound. "She's been on a diet since I met her, but only when people are looking."

I loved the way they loved one another. "Has it always been this easy with you two?"

"No way, honey. You've caught us in our prime." Gloria hummed, and I set the flowers in the stand, moving on to wrap a cluster of multicolored dyed roses. "This got anything to do with a certain dark-haired fellow who hasn't stopped by with coffee for you this week?"

Aiden's blond friend, the salty taste of his lone tear, and the words he'd said to me hadn't left me alone for a minute. "Can I tell you something?"

"Let me flip the back in fifteen sign."

I trimmed the stems and laid out fresh paper, then she was back. "You know how my brother's in a band?" When she nodded, I continued, "The boy I love happens to be in it too. His best friend."

Gloria grabbed a stool, tugging it closer to the wooden bench. She adjusted her bright pink sweater dress over her gray tights, crossing her leather booted feet, then nodded. "Tell me everything, honey."

By the time I finished, her skin had paled, and her hand was at her chest. "There's something wrong with him," she said after a few minutes of staring into space while I finished another arrangement. "More than what you must be seeing."

"I'm pretty sure his parents are drunks and just horrible people. He had a younger brother. He, um, he died before they moved to Plume Grove."

Gloria made a sound of anguish. "He lost the only person who loved him unconditionally."

I didn't think it was possible to cry any more tears over Everett, but there I was, brushing more away. "He's so broken and lost, and I can't figure out how or where I fit among those cracks." I sniffed. "What's more, he continually pushes me away, and I just... I can't do it anymore."

Gloria got up and walked over with her arms out.

I went to them, letting the scent of incense and her fruity perfume calm my cresting emotions. "So you don't do it anymore. You can't squeeze your way into someplace that's not ready to make enough room for you. All that'll do is hurt." Her hand swept over my hair, and my arms tightened around her plump waist. "If it doesn't feel good, you let it go, and you find something that does."

Aiden was already in class on Thursday, and I hesitated, unsure whether I should take my usual seat beside him or move to an empty one on the other side of the room.

I stood on the stairs and let students pass me as indecision and fear had my heart tapping fast.

I'd seen him on campus on Monday with some of his team-mates, walking to the cafeteria, but if he saw me, he didn't let on. I could only stare then, just as I did now.

When I noticed I was one of the only people still standing, I collapsed into the closest seat, thankful no one was near me, even if that meant I was sitting right by the doors.

The professor arrived, and as he scrawled over the board, Aiden spun around, searching.

I ducked lower in my seat, forcing my eyes to my desk as I opened my book and clicked my pen into action.

"Mr. Prince, is there a reason you've decided to play musical chairs today?"

Looking up, my face flamed when I saw Aiden approach with his book and pen. "Yes, sir. It seems my girl forgot where we usually sit in your class and instead, sat someplace else." He dumped himself into the seat next to me, opened his book, and held his pen at the ready as half the class and the professor looked on. "I can't work properly unless she sits next to me. Ready when you are," he said.

Professor Clarence scratched at his graying beard, eyes bouncing to me, and his lips twitching with a barely contained smile. "As long as you're not wasting anyone's time." He nodded. "Very well, the plans we revised last week shall now be scrutinized further with the following method…" He tapped at the board, and my shoulders drooped.

Aiden wrote something in his book, then, keeping his eyes trained forward, he slid it toward me.

I glanced down at it.

Nothing happened with Nora.

Shocked, I mulled over his words, not sure whether to believe them. Then I turned to a clean page in my book.

Nothing?

Well, I mean, I tried... so some things happened. But I couldn't do it, so thanks for being the reason her friends all look at me like my equipment doesn't work.

I bit back a laugh, but the first part... I looked forward again, tapping my pen on my book.

It wasn't as if I had a right to be upset. I was the one who kept running back to a guy who did whoever and whatever he wanted. So could I really not forgive Aiden for making out with some girl named Nora? He'd put the brakes on being with her because of me. It was way more than Everett had ever done.

It was way more than I'd done for him.

Beneath my desk, his hand crept over my thigh, and I stilled, trying to steady my choppy breathing. Then, with butterflies flapping in my dipping stomach, my hand slowly crawled over his.

When class ended, he grabbed my bag after I'd put my things away and slung it over his shoulder before tugging me out of my seat and into the hallway.

"Where are we going?"

"To talk or make out. I'd prefer the latter, but I'm also happy to simply stare at you."

Passing students who caught some of his words did a double take, some laughing.

"Prince," I hissed, tugging his hand once we'd reached the sidewalk.

He stopped, and my tongue glued itself to the roof of my mouth as he crowded into me. "You're all I think about. Whether I'm asleep or awake, you're always there. And I was willing to wait, I swear. But I can't anymore." His Adam's apple shifted, his eyes taking on a vulnerable sheen. "It's all or nothing, Petal. So what do you say?"

I didn't hesitate. Didn't care that people were still coming and going in the building behind us. "All. Everything." I took both his hands, keeping my eyes on his. "Please."

His lips parted, lashes bobbing as he blinked rapidly. "Well, since you asked so nicely."

Then he was kissing me.

Not the chaste, flirtatious kisses we'd planted on one another's lips or cheeks before, but a breath-stealing, soul-igniting, tasting the tip of forever kind of kiss.

His hands cupped my cheeks, and mine flattened against his Henley-covered chest as our lips found a soft yet frantic rhythm. The type of rhythm that spoke of lifetimes instead of stolen moments. The type of rhythm that set my heart soaring, thudding against my chest the same way his was doing against my palms.

We broke apart when one of his friends passed, hooting, "Finally, you pussy-whipped motherfucker."

Laughing, I ducked my heating face.

Aiden ignored him, lifting it to press his mouth to mine again. "I don't want to ever stop."

"We have to," I said, his nose nudging mine. "You have another class."

"Fuck class, we need milkshakes."

I couldn't wipe the giddy smile off my face, the one that

matched the feeling swimming inside, making each step to the cafeteria lighter.

With his hand in mine, he ordered our usual shakes. When we found an empty table, one of his teammates swaggered over as Aiden took a seat next to, instead of opposite, me.

"I've never seen this egotistical prick have to work so hard to bag—"

"And that'll be all, Smithers."

The guy with apple red hair stuck his hand out. "I don't believe we've formally met. Aaron."

I took his hand, letting him shake mine gently before pulling it back. "Stevie."

"Yeah, I know." He grinned. "The whole team practically knows."

I could feel my cheeks warm yet again, but I laughed it off, and Aiden squeezed an arm around my middle.

I sipped my drink as he and Aaron talked about last weekend's game, then waved when Aaron wandered off. "Judging by the way you guys were talking, you won?"

"Yeah," Aiden said, taking a sip of his milkshake. "We won all right. Ever played?"

I shook my head. "My brother played for a season back in grade school."

Aiden stared at his drink for a moment. "He decided he was more interested in music?"

"Definitely, and soccer. Being in a band has been his dream since I can remember." I paused, then sucked a long sip of vanilla heaven. "Sorry," I said afterward. "I know the last thing you probably want to talk about is the band."

"You're wrong." He squeezed my hip, fingers digging, and I giggled. "If it involves you, no matter how much it might grate, I want to know about it."

I looked at him, studying those faint freckles over his nose and the hard set to his jaw. It loosened when he met my gaze, and he licked his lips. "You're almost too good to be true, Prince."

He leaned forward, ghosting his lips across mine. "I tried to fuck someone else when you broke me. I'm not perfect. In fact," he said, sitting back, "if it weren't for meeting you, I'd probably still be working my way through campus."

I knew what he was doing. "You can't make me hate you."

"I never want you to hate me. I just don't want to be compared to him. I'm not perfect, but what you're seeing, how we might make each other feel… of course it's going to seem that way compared to how things were with…" He stopped there, not needing or wanting to say his name.

"Everett," I said, needing to. "And I don't think you're too good to be true because I'm comparing you to him."

Aiden raised a brow, taking a drink.

I took it from him and set it down, talking low as he looked at me with humor dancing in his eyes. "I'm serious. I want you because you're you. All of you. The smartass, the player, the flirt, the guy who doesn't mince words ever, even when he's angry… all the bad as well as the good. All or nothing."

Our hands linked, and I leaned in to lick the froth from his bottom lip. His mouth stole mine, moving fast and hard, the taste of vanilla malt and second chances heady between our soft breaths.

"All or nothing," he repeated, pecking me before pulling away. "So…" He cleared his throat, shifting in his seat. "Your mom. She teaches music, so she can sing, right?"

I smiled at his clear discomfort. "She sure can."

"And your dad can sing, but you're the odd duck who can't do anything musically inclined."

"Hey," I said, laughing. "I play a mean triangle."

"I bet you do," he said, wrapping his lips around the straw and sucking.

I laughed again and finished my drink. "She'd love you, you know. They both would."

"Yeah?" he asked, nudging my shoulder with his.

I nodded, nudging him back. "Yeah."

My limbs were so tense, I could feel a knot forming as Aiden slid into home right before the tag was made to win the game.

The crowd, already standing, roared their applause. Their screams, clapping, and stomping feet rattled my skull.

Now that things had changed, I wasn't sure what to do when the game had ended, but I figured I'd just follow the crowd's lead. When they started dispersing, I trailed them out of the stadium and into the parking lot.

This was the first home game Raslow's baseball team had played in the month we'd been officially dating, and although Aiden had invited me out of town with him to the other two they'd played, I couldn't go due to work and studying for finals.

School would be out in less than a month, and I was a little shocked at how fast the time had flown. Especially when it used to drag—month to month spent waiting and pining for something that would never be. Since meeting Aiden, even when we were just friends, the days flashed by in a blur of smiles, laughter, flirtatious arguments, heated ones, nerve-tingling touches, jokes, and kisses.

We hadn't slept together yet, and I knew he was trying to give me time. That he was waiting for me to make the first move. And I was ready. I'd been honest when I'd told him I was done and that I wanted him. All or nothing.

The air was still balmy as we filed outside. The team appeared fifteen minutes later, greeting fans, friends, and loved ones.

My smile bit into my cheeks when Aiden snuck up behind me and spun me around. When my feet met the ground, I immediately cupped his damp cheeks, bringing his head down to mine. "You need to wear those pants tonight," I whispered.

"Oh, do I?" He grinned, then pressed his lips against mine in a hard, wet, and moan-inducing kiss.

"Let's go," I said, pulling away.

He didn't need to be told twice and waved to some of the guys on the team, only stopping a few times to shake some young kids' hands. My heart warmed at the way he made them smile with such ease, simply by being him.

He opened the door of his Audi for me before tossing his gear in the trunk. The vibrating hum of the engine did nothing to curb the excitement brewing between my legs.

"What are you doing?" I asked minutes later when he turned into the drive-through.

"Ordering us some burgers. I'm starved."

Opening my purse, I tried not to grumble and fished out my phone, finding nothing but the background picture of me and Adela. Sighing, I tucked it back inside and ignored the smirk I knew was sitting on Aiden's face. "I'm good, thanks."

Finally, burgers sitting in a brown bag on my lap, he turned back out onto the road. And a minute later, he turned into a gas station.

"What?" I sputtered.

He unclipped his seat belt, jumping out. "Need some gum and a Gatorade."

Frustration curled my hands as he strolled, all lazy grace, toward the bright entrance.

When he returned, I chewed my lips to keep my annoyance masked. It didn't work. When he tossed the gum into the console and the drink into the cup holder, and then just sat there, I snapped, turning to him to yell... I didn't know what because he was smiling.

My eyes narrowed. "Okay, what are you doing, Prince?"

"Not much fun, is it, Petal?"

Confusion creased my brows. "What?"

He tutted. "So impatient."

"Aiden," I warned.

"Waiting. It's not fun to be kept waiting, am I right?" He grinned. "Or am I fucking right?"

I groaned. "You're an idiot, is what you are."

He barked out a laugh, then finally started the car.

I seethed, even as laughter tried to burst free, the whole way to his apartment.

He had the place to himself, courtesy of his dad, and I was thankful for that when we finally got inside, and I exploded. "I thought you were okay with us being friends all that time."

Eating his burger, he tossed his bag by the door and his drink on the glass coffee table. He swallowed before talking. "Petal," he said through a laugh. "I was fucking messing with you. Come here."

"No," I said, and he raised his brows, shoving the rest of his burger inside his mouth, then uncapping his drink. "I needed." I stopped. "Ugh, I was..." I couldn't even say it and nearly stomped my foot as heat climbed up my neck to decorate my cheeks.

Chuckling again, Aiden took a long swig of his drink, swishing it around his mouth before he came for me. "Horny?" he supplied.

I nodded, feeling that excitement return when his eyes dipped over my face and settled on my lips. Who was I kidding? It never really left. Even when he made me mad, I still wanted him.

"Then we'd better fix that. I like seeing you angry-needy." He ducked, hoisting me over his shoulder. My Chucks flew off when I kicked my legs as he carried me down the maroon-painted hall to his room, where a large king-size bed decked out in black linens sat in the center.

Clothes lay strewn on the ottoman at the end, some on the floor, and a gaming console perched in tangles on the table below the large flat screen on the wall. I'd been in here before but never for long.

Never for this.

Dumping me on the bed, he made quick work of ridding me of my panties, then tugged my denim dress up and over my head. "You're too fucking beautiful for this world."

"Kiss me," I said, reaching for him.

"With pleasure." He climbed onto the bed, his tongue mating with mine, his fingertips driving me crazy as they brushed over every inch of skin.

When he moved them between my legs, I sighed with anticipation and relief. "Want them, do you?" he whispered against my lips.

"Yes."

He hummed, biting and tugging my lip as he fell back to the bed. I frowned, dismay settling in until he said, "Let me tell you what I want."

"I swear to God, Prince, if you play any more games…" I was so turned on, so frustrated, that I didn't even care I was naked. Vulnerability took a hike in the face of desperation.

Sitting up, he crooked a finger for me to come closer.

I shuffled over on my knees, which he gestured for me to spread, his hand climbing up my thigh. Two thick fingers trailed through me, and I shivered, needing more but not wanting his touch to leave.

"Now, what I want is for my fingers to be buried inside you and soaked."

Air wheezed out of me at the hoarse command and timbre to his voice.

"Sit on them." I did, and they slowly filled me. "Yes, fuck yes."

Feeling my heartbeat in every limb, I trembled as he dipped the fingers on his other hand into his mouth, sucking. Then, eyes heavy on mine, they met my slick flesh. With the slightest bit of pressure, they skimmed over my throbbing clit.

I was gone. "Shit, Aiden," I whimpered and moaned, fucking his fingers as I crashed and burned.

With a damp hand on my hip, he held me down when I tried to move away. "That's it, come completely undone, beautiful."

When the waves retreated and my vision cleared, I stared down into his adoring, lust-fogged gaze, then I climbed off and pushed him to his back. My lips found his, my hands sinking into his hair as I whispered, "I already have."

NINETEEN

LOOMING CLOUDS THREATENED TO STEAL THE MORNING GLAZE THAT bathed Raslow in golden warmth.

"No, we're doing fine," I reassured Mom, staring out the kitchen window.

"You always say that. Lord knows how many times we've helped Hendrix since he left. We can spare a little to do the same for you."

This was the third time she'd offered since I'd moved out and started college. I was being honest, though. Yes, money was tight most weeks, but I had enough to get by.

Still, I got the feeling she wanted to help, so I offered, "Well, I could probably go for some new clothes soon..."

"Excellent," Mom chirped, a door closed and noise echoed as she likely walked down the street to her building. "I'll drive up this weekend, and we can go shopping."

Shit. "But school's out soon, I could just—"

"Gotta go, my next client's probably already waiting for me. I'll see you Saturday morning." She made kissing noises, then ended the call.

I gaped at my phone, unsure what I was supposed to tell Aiden. After last weekend, we'd made plans for a repeat.

Puffing out a frustrated sound, I shoved my phone in my bag and left for work.

The morning passed with its usual rush, and Adela came by between classes to fill me in on the date she'd had last night.

"Sounds like that guy I went out with in high school." I snapped my fingers. "What's his name?" I smiled, remembering, and slapped my hand on the counter. "Clive."

Adela crinkled her nose, trailing her finger over the petals littering the wooden countertop. "I bet Clive's car didn't smell like stale Cheetos, but at least this guy tried to touch me."

"A hand massage, though?"

"I don't know what y'all are bitching about." Sabrina walked in from the back room, sorting through a box of cards. "A hand massage sounds divine." She plonked the box on the counter, and I snickered as I plucked a few cards out, placing them on the pile by the register.

"It was creepy," Adela said. "The first time the guy takes me out, and all he wants to do is love all up on my hands."

I eyed them. "You do have nice hands."

Sabrina hummed, grabbing them to inspect for herself. "Great cuticles, too."

Adela groaned, but I knew she was lapping up the attention.

The wind chime over the door sang, and I looked up from Adela's hands to find Aiden nearing the counter. He flashed that I-can-make-you-do-anything grin, edging in next to Adela, who was tipping her head back, brows raised high.

The sight of him in jeans and a worn leather jacket just about liquefied me where I stood.

Adela heaved out a sigh. "Warn a girl before you turn from sexy to drop-dead sexy."

His brows furrowed. "What?"

"The jacket," she supplied, finally lowering her gaze.

"One second." Sabrina walked around the counter, and Aiden's eyes grew when she raised her hands to his head. She swept some of his hair back, then pursed her lips. "God, it's like Scott Eastwood and Henry Cavill had a love child."

Aiden grinned, his features creasing with adorable confusion as he looked at me.

Sabrina caught it and laughed. "I'm gay, so don't worry your handsome little brain over it. But Gloria and I still love to look. And my," she said, quirking her lips at me as she headed for the back room, "you sure are fun to look at."

Aiden's cheeks tinted, and Adela visibly melted. "Oh, Jesus. Dump her gorgeous ass and take me out. But first, tell me, do you like hands and Cheetos?"

Aiden wiped a hand down his cheek. "I'm so lost right now."

Adela and I both laughed, and she patted him on the shoulder. "Probably for the best. Later, lovebirds."

I was still smiling when she'd left, then I turned that smile to Aiden, who was watching me with that electrifying intensity. Grabbing the flowers by the window, I walked around the counter and set them in a pot with matching arrangements.

Try as I might, though I didn't exactly try too hard, I couldn't erase the feeling that threatened to burst in my stomach whenever I thought of our weekend together. Whenever his eyes were upon me.

He was a gentleman, sure, but his filthy, sweet words as he got to know my body and helped me get to know my body in ways I didn't know existed haunted me.

I didn't know why I hadn't expected that. And I didn't know they—that he—would affect me so entirely. In ways so consuming, even when we weren't in the same room.

To distract myself, I fiddled with a cluster of petunias and daisies. "No class today?"

"Everyone's cramming, and besides, Tuesday's aren't the same, knowing you're not on campus."

"You should still be there, but I won't lie. I like having you here instead."

His arms came around me, and courtesy of my messy bun, he could rest his lips in the crook of my neck. "What can I say? You leave a lasting impression every time I see you."

"Still?" I pressed, leaning back into his hard body.

"Still." The warm silk of his lips pressed into my skin. Once, then twice. "I fear it'll soon be everlasting."

I think I sighed loud enough for him to hear, judging by the way his arms tightened around my waist. "I missed you too."

"Thank fuck for that." Another kiss, then his hand reached out and his fingers caressed the petals of a sunflower. "What is it about these flowers, besides the obvious, that you love so much?" If it weren't for the soft way he'd said it, I'd wonder if he were jealous.

I ignored the residual pang that made its ugly presence known at the familiar question. "I guess something about them makes me stop, and I'm not just talking in the physical sense. I'm talking about those moments that make us truly stop and take a proverbial seat. The ones that cause the whirring in our minds to fade into a distant hum." I drew in a sharp breath, admitting similar words I'd said to another man, a boy, all those years ago. "Does that make sense? I feel at peace. Grounded. Alive. Happy."

Aiden's chest rose and fell against my shoulders, and when he spoke, his voice was drenched in quiet affection. "I've never heard anything make more sense in my life."

We stood there for several minutes, his arms around me, as rain started to fall outside. Drops splattered on the window and in the mulch in the flower beds and pots outside. "So…" I cleared my throat, turning in his arms, but my voice was still scratchy. "How do you feel about meeting my mom?"

"Fucking ecstatic." And judging by the way his eyes sparkled, corroborating his words, I knew he wasn't lying.

"Are you sure I look okay?" Aiden ran his fingers through his already beautifully mussed hair. "Not too overdressed?"

I adjusted the lapels of his charcoal dress shirt, then eyed his dark denim jeans. "You're perfect, as always, so stop fussing."

"But I need to be better than perfect." I laughed, and he released a breath, nodding to himself. "Christ, I don't think I've been this nervous since I asked out India Peters in the second grade."

"Ha! I knew you started early." I rose onto my toes to steal a quick kiss.

We left the car and approached the café where I'd told Mom I'd meet her. She didn't know I was bringing Aiden until last night when I called, so we agreed to have coffee before he ditched us so we could shop.

Aiden stopped right outside the door, his hand clammy in mine. "You're sure about this?"

I was about to laugh again, but then I saw the paler hue to his face. I reached up, rubbing my thumbs over his cheeks. "She's going to love you. You and I both know that."

He nodded, releasing a shuddering exhale.

"Can we get some coffee now? Someone kept me up late last night."

He chuckled, nodding again, then held the door open as we moved inside the country styled interior. Brown timber tables were dressed in red checkered tablecloths, and the matching seats beneath them wore the same patterned cushions.

Seated in the back with a magazine on the table in front of her, Mom's hair was gathered into a clip, rogue curls sprouting over the top of her head like a fountain.

She looked up as we approached, closing the magazine as her smile spread.

"She's beautiful, just like you," Aiden said, a tad too loud.

A voice I wasn't expecting to hear, on account of Mom saying he'd had to work, came from behind us. "That they both are."

"Daddy." I spun, my hand leaving Aiden's as Dad picked me up and squeezed me in one of his usual breath-stealing hugs.

Setting me down, he tilted my chin to study my face. "You're looking good, Stevie girl."

"You too," I said, meaning it. His blond hair showed more evidence of gray, but his blue eyes were vibrant, happy.

"Not having any kids around to suck the life from you will do that," he said, turning to Aiden when he'd laughed.

"Aiden, right?" Dad held out his hand. "Brad."

Aiden was almost two inches taller than Dad. "Great to finally meet you, sir."

Dropping Aiden's hand, Dad's nose scrunched. "None of that, makes me feel old."

He gestured behind us to the table, and after Mom introduced herself to Aiden, patting his cheeks as she looked from him to me with a wide smile and wet eyes, we ordered drinks.

Within minutes of them arriving, Aiden had my dad in fits of laughter as he regaled him with tales of some of this season's blunders. Dad was more into football than baseball, but he still followed and watched a game now and then, and as they kept chatting, it was evident he was thrilled to be talking to Aiden.

Though I didn't miss the moments when he'd catch himself after laughing too hard and look at me as if remembering this guy was dating his daughter.

That was made evident when Mom said to Aiden, "Stevie's never even brought a boy home before. She wasn't much for dating growing up."

"Mom," I hissed, "unnecessary."

Aiden only grabbed my hand, peering down at me with his head tilted. "Oh, really?"

"Yep," Mom said. "And here Brad thought he'd be chasing them away with his set of unused golf clubs."

"I bought them for that purpose, actually." Dad sighed, then lifted a pointed brow at Aiden. "Though I guess there's still time."

Aiden chuckled, knowing he was joking, and we eased into casual conversation about work, classes, and talk of when I was coming home to visit.

"Hendrix called last week," Mom said, draining the last of her coffee.

Her words gripped my stomach, and I prayed it didn't show. Mom already knew enough. Knew exactly why I'd never had any real boyfriends.

"They've stopped in a small town a few hours south."

Dad nodded. "Apparently, they've scored a regular paying gig at one of the bars there, and they need the money."

Mom's lips pinched; her eyes trained on her empty coffee mug.

I knew, for as much as they both wanted Hendrix and the rest of the guys to live their dream, that their quest was starting to become a concern. Mainly financially. My parents thought the bug would've died by now. That their hunger would have waned, and they'd return home with new prospects.

I knew better. "Everything okay?"

Dad tapped his knuckles on the table, smiling a grim smile. "Just the drinking. Hendrix didn't sound so happy is all."

"He's drinking more?" I asked.

"No," Mom said, giving me an apologetic look. "It's Everett."

Beneath the table, Aiden's hand tensed tight around mine, and even though I knew it was wrong to need him where Everett was concerned, I was thankful for his grounding touch.

Within seconds, I shook the concern that threatened to soften the cracks Everett had caused, and I smiled. "I hope he settles down, then." I swallowed the remainder of my coffee.

Mom frowned, her gaze bouncing back and forth between me and Aiden, but then she quickly replaced it with a smile. "Well." She turned to Dad. "Ready for some shopping?"

Dad's expression soured. "Do I have a choice?"

We laughed, and even though it was the last thing I wanted to do after hearing about Everett, I gave Aiden a brief kiss goodbye, then headed into town with my parents.

TWENTY

THE SQUAWK OF BIRDS FADED WITH THE SUN, THE BUSY HUM OF town easing as sunlight prepared to change shifts with darkness.

I'd gone home, dumped the bags full of clothes onto the kitchen counter, then raced to the shower to rinse off the busy afternoon spent bouncing from shop to shop.

My parents credit card surely took a beating, but I'd tried to lessen it as much as I could by picking discounted items even when Mom caught on and scowled.

Stopping by Belladonna's to grab the pizza I'd ordered, I then raced back down the street. Shadows curled over the concrete with every step I took toward Aiden's apartment, six streets away.

Wiping the beads of sweat dotting my forehead, I rapped lightly on his door, hoping he was home. Too eager to see him after leaving with Everett lingering in his ears, I hadn't thought to check.

"Who is it?" he called.

"Me," I said.

A paused breath, then, "It's open."

I turned the handle, pushing the heavy door open with my hip, then kicked off my boots.

Walking farther into his apartment, I was about to call out when I passed the living room and saw him sprawled over his black leather sectional.

Something wobbled and tilted inside me at the sight of his marred brows. He stroked a finger across them, his lips rolling over each other as he tossed a baseball with his other hand, not looking as it fell into his palm.

"I come bearing pizza," I said, entering the room and setting it on the glass coffee table.

The smacking of the ball hitting his hand ceased, and his gaze moved to the box. "Pepperoni?"

"Duh." I smiled, but it fell when he didn't look at me.

Not sure what to do, I walked over to the couch, my knees resting against the cool material as I looked down at him. He was still wearing the same clothes he'd worn to meet my parents. "You okay?"

A sigh pushed past his lips, and he dropped the ball, finally giving me his eyes. "Just been busy being petulant."

I lowered my lashes. "Can I interrupt for something?"

"That depends. I rather like being mopey every now and then."

I couldn't contain my smile and crawled over him when he held his arms out. My forehead dropped to his, and then my lips fixed themselves to his mouth. "See, they loved you."

He didn't say anything, dragging his lips over mine.

Then I was flipped to my back, and he was tugging up my purple T-shirt dress. "I love you."

Dark and bottomless, his eyes flared, hooking into my chest and daring. The words were hanging on the tip of my tongue as his own caused my bruised heart to dance.

My legs opened wider, and I reached down to tug off my socks. "Show me."

Maybe it was the reminder of Everett, or maybe it was because by his standards, I was ready. Either way, as our clothes came off and he carried me down the hall to his bedroom, my legs around his silken hot skin and his lips glued to my neck, it was happening.

I was thrown to the bed, and I rolled onto my stomach, watching as he grabbed a condom and tore it open with his teeth.

The action had my thighs clenching, my teeth scraping my lip. "Wait," I said.

His brows rose in question as I scooted over to the side of the bed, swung my legs over it, and tried not to think about how brazen I was acting when I spread them open. I grabbed the back of his muscled thighs, pulling him close so that thick, long member bobbed and swayed in front of my face.

"Petal," Aiden started.

His mouth shut when I licked the salty drop beading on the tip. "This is the first time I've done this," I admitted, slowly lifting my eyes to his.

He swallowed, his hand coming to rest beneath my chin, and his thumb gliding over the corner of my mouth. "You're serious."

I nodded. "So I'm sorry if I suck, pun intended."

We both laughed, and then I took him as far as I could inside my mouth, and his laughter broke into a stream of curses.

He allowed me to find a rhythm that I was comfortable with, but I still gagged a few times as I tried to get as much of him inside my mouth as I could. I gave in and decided to just suck and lick to the best of my ability, reveling in the noises that dragged out of his throat when my other hand reached beneath to gently caress him.

"God, lie down." He stepped back, leaving my mouth with a wet sound.

"I wasn't done," I protested.

He grinned, shaking his head. "I will be soon, but even though I plan to come many times with you tonight, I don't want the first time to be in your mouth."

I licked my lips as he rolled the condom he'd been holding

in his hand over himself, then I did as requested and lowered to the bed.

He stroked himself as I eyed the twitching of his pecs, abs, and arms. He was barely restrained power, and having him crawl over top of me and swipe his fingers over the wet between my thighs was almost like having an out-of-body experience.

"You're magnificent," I breathed.

He thrust a finger inside me, then slowly pulled it back out, lashes heavy as he watched my reaction. "Magnificent?" I nodded, and he chuckled. "I haven't been inside you yet."

My legs wound around him, my hands roaming over the bumps in his arms and shoulders, feeling them twitch until I reached his face. "Then hurry up."

Pushing at my entrance a second later, he eased inside as our foreheads met. My body awakened further, stretching to accommodate, gripping and lubricating for more.

"Aiden."

"Mmm, you feel so fucking good." A stumbling breath peppered my lips. "This... I can't believe I'm finally able to do this." His lips grazed mine, his hips slowly pulling back before pushing forward again, deeper, as deep as he could go. "And holy hell, it's better than I ever could've dreamed."

"Aiden," I tried again, my voice struggling to rise over everything my body was feeling.

"Fuck," he said, seated deep and grinding his pelvis into mine.

"Aiden," I snapped, gasping as he continuously hit that perfect spot. "Shit."

His licorice eyes narrowed, and he lowered onto his forearms. "What's wrong? Am I hurting you?"

"No, you adorably, ignorant hunk of man," I sputtered out, my eyes closing when his hips stilled. I opened them, and blurted everything that'd been gathering, collecting, and coalescing since I'd met him. "I… I'm in love with you."

His breath washed over my cheeks, his own hollowing with the escaped rush of air. Then he blinked, a crooked slant to his lips. "My cock's that good, huh?"

I ignored the words, and instead, I listened to the vulnerability lingering beneath them. Moving my hands over his cheeks and into his hair, I pulled him close, nose to nose, until every breath we inhaled and exhaled was shared, and he looked at me.

"You're my best friend, and the best thing to ever happen to me," I whispered. "So yes, your cock is that good, but really, I'm just a chicken shit who's been too afraid to utter those words to someone again. Even if I've been feeling them for months."

"Months?" His voice croaked.

"Months."

He stared a full minute longer, then his arms swept beneath me, holding my chest to his as his hips started moving, and his tongue swept inside my mouth.

Beat for beat, our hearts pounded to each other through our slick flesh, and my nails dug into his back as he slowly carried me up the hill, then gently pushed me over the edge.

He followed, groaning his pleasure into my mouth as our bodies quivered and our hearts thumped like wild beasts that'd been caged for too long.

And afterward, as he lay half on top of me stroking the skin on my arm with his lips against the side of my forehead, he murmured, "Say it again."

I turned into him, smiling into his clammy chest. "I love you."

He sighed, his arm moving to my back, gripping me so tight, there was no space between us. "I love you too." He kissed my head. "I fucking love you too."

TWENTY-ONE

WE SPENT THE SUMMER JUMPING BETWEEN MY PLACE AND HIS apartment.

Aiden usually went home, but claiming he didn't have many people to see there besides his dad and some old high school friends, he'd decided to stay behind.

I had to work, but as much as I was starting to finally miss home, I wasn't ready to go back just yet. Mom understood when I'd called and told her I had to stay, but she made me promise I'd come home for Christmas and at least stay a few nights.

That I could do, and it became easier to look forward to after I'd asked Aiden to come with me.

Mom and Dad had visited last Christmas, but I couldn't continue to hide behind my job and Adela.

"It's serious, then." Adela smirked from the couch as I flitted about the apartment, collecting miscellaneous items I probably wouldn't need for the trip home.

"He's already met them," I reminded her, plucking up a paperback and studying it. I wasn't sure if it was mine or Adela's.

"Yeah, but sleeping under their roof?" She tutted. "You might be twenty, but in Brad's eyes, you're still his little boyfriend-less, innocent girl."

"Ew. Don't refer to my dad by his first name. It's weird."

"Calling someone mister who looks that good when he's pushing fifty just isn't right. I'm doing you and myself a favor."

I tossed the paperback down. "First my brother, now my dad?"

She licked her finger, turning the page in her book. "Not my fault your family has good genes."

A knock on our door had me walking over to hug her, then I pinched her arm for being a brat. "Merry Christmas, turd."

Her laughter followed me as I left. "I'd check under your pillows when you get home for that!"

On the other side of the door, Aiden's eyes were curious. "Ignore her," I said, heaving my duffel over my shoulder and grabbing my purse.

Aiden took it from me. "Merry Christmas, Adela."

"Merry Christmas, gorgeous."

I grumbled as we made our way down the steps to where his car was idling by the curb.

After opening my door, he took my bag to the trunk.

I slid inside and clipped on my seat belt, Aiden's cologne and the clean scent of his car loosening my tense limbs.

"So where exactly will I be sleeping?" he asked once we'd hit the highway, my hand wrapped in his. "In a cupboard beneath the stairs?"

I snorted. "Sure thing, Harry. Except we don't have stairs. One story."

He forced a pout. "One day, I'll get to live out my dream as The Boy Who Lived."

"You've been doing a lot of living, if you ask me."

That dangerous tilt shifted his lips as he swung a sweeping look over me. "True."

I was glad when he gave his attention back to the road. Months of dating, of letting him get familiar with every part of my body, still hadn't hindered his ability to make me blush.

I grabbed his phone to distract myself. Not only from him,

but from the fluttering fear and excitement that returning home for the first time since I'd started college erupted.

Scrolling through the mega long playlists, I skirted the heavy metal, RnB, and felt my stomach dip when I found Dashboard Confessional.

Aiden's hand squeezed mine, and as the guitar intro to "Hands Down" started, he glanced over at me. "No way," he said. "It feels like it's been years since I've listened to this song."

"Me too." It hadn't been that long, but it sure felt like it. "My brother wasn't a fan and used to poke fun at me."

Aiden mock gasped, and I giggled like a fucking sixteen-year-old.

We settled into the song, but when the chorus hit the second time, I almost jumped out of my seat when Aiden belted it out at the top of his lungs.

I doubled over laughing. How someone could look so good when they were doing something they were so terrible at, I didn't know, but at that moment, I knew I more than adored him. I felt more than a lot of things for him. Things that terrified and revived.

A love that rivaled another.

Dragging my eyes forward, I gave in and joined him for the last leg of the song.

Aiden, sucking in a loud breath, lowered the volume of "Arabella" by the Arctic Monkeys before we turned down my street. "Well, here goes nothing."

I smacked his arm, smiling. "Shush. You've already met them."

"I love it when you shush me."

I pointed at the house on the left where my dad's truck sat in the drive, ignoring the nudge in my gut and that pull from the house sitting across the street.

Digging stubborn claws in, I kept my gaze fixed firmly on my own house, and grinned when I saw the snowman Dad said he'd lost years ago half-lit up and moving side to side in the garden.

The sun had set, and we were welcomed with hugs, claps on Aiden's back, and a grin from Dad before we ventured inside.

"What happened to the snowman?" I asked, gesturing for Aiden, who was holding our duffels, to follow me down the hall to my room.

"Well, he'd been shoved up against an eave in the attic, so, uh, half the lights were smashed." Dad scratched the back of his head. "He's back now. That's all that matters, right?"

A soft laugh left me, and we put our things away in my room before joining Mom and Dad in the dining room for dinner.

We were halfway through our meals, discussing some of the classes I was taking this semester and Aiden's upcoming training, when Dad brought the conversation to an abrupt halt. "Hendrix's room is free."

"Dad," I tried not to growl.

Mom slapped his arm, scowling. "She's twenty. And I hate to break it to you, but they've been dating a while, Brad."

Looking at Aiden, Dad winced, muttering what sounded like a string of fucks under his breath.

Turning to Aiden, I found his eyes alight with humor. "I'll sleep wherever. Couch is fine, too." He nodded for emphasis. "Really."

Mom's expression warmed. "That won't be necessary. We trust you'll be on your best behavior while you're here."

Aiden took Hendrix's room, and I scowled at Dad, shaking my head as I stood in the hall and brushed my teeth. He tipped his hands up, then disappeared to his and Mom's room at the other end of the house. "Nice to have you home, Stevie girl."

Grumbling, I returned to the bathroom and spat, then washed my face. I waited one minute before I tapped on Hendrix's door.

Aiden jumped up from where he'd been sitting on the floor, throwing Hendrix's soccer ball. He dropped it and followed me out and past the bathroom to my room.

He was on me as soon as the lock clicked over. "I want to respect their wishes, but first, I just need something to tide me over."

"You're not respecting anything," I said, my breathing ragged as he yanked my nightgown off, my nipples beading under his hooded inspection. "Except my need to have you with me." I gripped his head, meshing my lips to his. "Deep inside me, wrapped around me ..." I licked his upper lip, then bit it. "All night."

"My Petal's wish is my command." He picked me up and tossed me onto the bed, then reached for his shirt while I reached for him.

The silver potted cacti that still resided on my windowsill glinted in the moonlight, and my desperation grew as an unwelcome sensation seeped in.

Flipping me to my stomach, Aiden spread my thighs and ass cheeks, raising me just enough to slide inside before falling over me to interlock our fingers. "Deep enough?"

He knew it wasn't. "Deeper."

He rose and sat down. I turned, and he tugged me over him, holding himself at my entrance, depthless eyes boring into mine as I sank down, the moan I tried to keep inside slipping free.

He stole my lips. "Quiet," he rasped, sucking on them.

"I'm trying," I panted.

He pushed me back, holding me there, and used his other hand to reach between us. "Right there?"

I struggled to nod. He was pushing and pulling my body off and onto his. "Yes."

His finger moved down, finding where we connected, and we both groaned as he stole some of the slickness and used it to toy with me again.

He ducked his head, leaning over to take my nipple. "Right there?"

"Aiden, fuck."

"There, then," he said, wicked satisfaction in his voice as he rocked his hips to the rhythm mine were hunting and continued to torture me with his tongue, body, and fingers.

I came apart, and he dropped me to the bed, my vision hazy and his mouth latching over mine to keep me quiet. Hard and furious, he pounded into me, then pulled out, coming all over my stomach.

The sight of him doing what he was doing... what *he* had done in this very room over two years ago, caused a twinge in my chest. But when I looked up, saw Aiden's head fall back as he emptied stream after stream of himself over my skin, his throat cording and his impressive chest heaving, the twinge fled, and I pulled him down to me.

"Petal, shit." He chuckled, semen sticking to both our stomachs.

"I love you, Prince." I kissed each corner of his mouth while he fought to catch his breath.

When he did, he smoothed some hair back from my face, eyes sated but still luminous in the dark room. "Music to my fucking ears."

Christmas morning was quiet compared to what years of memories conjured.

After gorging on large stacks of blueberry pancakes for breakfast, we took our coffee into the living room and opened presents.

Mom and Dad had gotten Aiden socks to use when he played, and after rummaging through his bathroom cabinet, searching for his cologne, I'd given Mom the name, and they'd bought him some more of that too.

I'd balked when I'd seen Armani stamped over the glass bottle, but Mom quickly said thank you and hung up before I could protest further.

I piled my stationery, body lotions, perfume, and paperbacks with Aiden's presents in my room, returning to find the living room empty.

"He's been abducted."

"Shit." I joined Mom by the window to peek into the backyard.

Dad was gesturing to the half-built gazebo, his eyes bright, while Aiden tilted his head, appearing invested in what he was being shown.

Perhaps he was, though I'd never seen him show a lot of interest in woodwork or any kind of construction. I made a mental note to ask him about it when we had a quiet moment.

"You look happy," Mom said a while later, peeling carrots and potatoes by the sink for lunch.

"I am," I admitted, and the buoyance, the ease in which I'd admitted those words reaffirmed it. "He's incredible."

"He adores you," Mom said, eyes on her task.

I grabbed a bottle of water from the fridge and seated myself at the dining table, my finger drifting over the familiar, time-worn grooves and scratches in the wood. "I love him," I said quietly, then laughed. "I never thought I'd be able to..." I trailed off.

Mom smiled over at me. "All it takes is the right person, and it can happen again and again and again."

I nodded, contemplating whether to admit something to her. "Can I ask you something?"

"Of course."

"Do you think you can fall for two different men, I mean really fall for them, and love them both at the same time?"

Silence lingered for a minute. "So you haven't stopped."

Not a question, and my eyes began to burn. It was a betrayal, but one I couldn't stop. One I was trying to ignore and move past. It had been easy for a while, as long as I didn't pick at the wound. "No." I tried to clear the gathering thickness in my throat. "I think it's unlikely I ever will."

Mom let that sit there for a minute before responding. "That doesn't mean you can't give yourself to someone else. And who knows," she said, her voice low. "Maybe, with time, it'll fade. One love becomes louder than the other."

"Louder than the other," I repeated. After a few moments of digesting that, I felt the need to reassure her. "I'm okay. I'm not devastated over him anymore. I just... it's still there, and being home makes its presence known."

Mom nodded, tossing the scraps after dumping the vegetables onto a tray to go into the oven. "Time, Stevie. All things take time." She paused, hands on the counter as she locked me in place with one of her assessing looks. "It's good to see you move on, though. As much as we love Everett, he just isn't capable of looking at you the way Aiden does. And you deserve to not only be looked at in that way, but also to be treated as if nothing is more important than you." She straightened. "You deserve to be someone's entire world. Their first and only choice."

I swiped at a traitorous tear. "I know." And I did know, but when the heart was desperate, it was capable of ignoring whatever it needed to.

When lunch was ready, Aiden and Dad came back inside. Aiden cracked open a beer and while offering one to Dad, informed him he was twenty-one, which made me smother a laugh. Mom cranked the carols up and sang along, her hips swaying as she delivered all the food to the table.

Dad waved Aiden off, taking the beer with a nod of thanks, then his seat next to Mom.

"Have you seen what he's built out there?" Aiden asked, drizzling gravy over my ham and vegetables before doing the same to his plate. "It's going to be good enough to sleep under."

"You know where you'll be staying next time, then," Dad said, chuckling when Aiden shook his head.

"Make sure it's finished, and you might just have yourself a deal." Aiden took a swig of beer, then glanced at me. "We can drag some sleeping bags out there. Maybe a blow-up mattress..." Lost in the excitement that glazed his eyes, shining in the dizzying wonder of his smile, I was about to nod when the front door opened with a bang.

"Well, that's why there was no welcoming committee," Hendrix yelled over the music. He turned the stereo down on the counter, and the rest of the band entered the room.

Dad almost choked on his beer as he set it down with a thud. It dribbled down his chin and beard. Standing, he wiped it away and greeted them all, Mom joining him.

And when Everett's form hovered in the entryway, clad in a torn white T-shirt, jeans, and combat boots, his hair reaching his shoulders and stubble drowning his rugged jaw, I did choke.

I never thought I'd see those green eyes contain that much emotion. The likes of which I couldn't even begin to name.

Aiden thumped me on the back, then rubbed it and handed me my glass of water.

Only when my lungs had recovered did Aiden turn around to take in the man whose gaze I could feel on my profile.

I swapped the water for Aiden's beer and drained it.

TWENTY-TWO

EVERYONE PULLED UP A CHAIR, EVEN SOME NEW GUY, WHO I struggled to recognize.

He reached over the table, offering his hand to us. "Rupert, or just Rupe. New bass player."

"Bass player?" I questioned, shaking his hand.

"Yeah, the guys held auditions while they were staying in my hometown of Glass Lake." He snatched a roll off the table, tearing off a chunk. "I watched every show, three nights a week, and so when I saw they were looking for someone, I just about pissed myself."

Mom's nose wrinkled, but she forced a smile when he glanced her way.

I looked over at Hendrix, who was seated next to Dad, his gaze avoiding mine as he said, "I was sick of it. Need to finally bust out the riffs I've spent half my life playing."

I felt Everett's stare like a weight sitting on my shoulders.

Aiden was concentrating on his food, but his nonchalant expression didn't fool me. The stiffness to his body screamed of displeasure.

Yet I couldn't stop myself from watching when Everett pulled out a stool at the kitchen counter and folded his large frame on it.

Riddled with scrutiny, his eyes skittered over everyone at the table, but they always returned to me, where they stayed the longest. When I caught them, and the veil of betrayal and anger fell, I saw the regret.

And I knew, this new bass player had nothing to do with Hendrix and his ego, and everything to do with Everett getting too drunk to play and sing at the same time.

I dragged my eyes away and forced down the food on my plate that suddenly had no taste.

Graham stood then and stabbed a finger at Aiden. "Okay, I can't handle it anymore. I know you from somewhere."

Aiden set down his fresh beer, giving Graham his attention.

Graham scratched at his jaw, his brows shaping. "Oh fuck. You play ball?"

"Baseball, yeah." Aiden's voice was gruff, but maybe only to my ears.

Graham clapped his hands. "My dad's a huge college ball follower. He's been watching every game they air of yours since you started."

"Wow, man." Aiden flashed him a genuine grin. "You tell your old man I said thanks."

Graham sighed. "He's not talking to me. I kind of ditched a full ride to hang with these shitheads."

"Speak for yourself," Hendrix mumbled, shoving a piece of ham in his mouth, eyeing Aiden with obvious curiosity.

Graham's eyes grew. "Wait a minute, I bet if you signed something for him, he'd at least look at me."

Aiden sat back, relaxing a little in his chair as he chuckled. "Sure."

I kept my eyes off Everett and placed my hand on Aiden's thigh beneath the table as I watched him sign a reindeer napkin with a Sharpie Hendrix had plucked from his back pocket.

"You guys just carry Sharpies around now?" I tried to joke as Aiden capped the marker.

Hendrix finally looked at me. "You've stopped hooking up with your brother's friends now?"

Dad cussed so violently, everyone at the table fell quiet.

"Well, shit, Sandrine. Just lay it all out there, why don't ya?" Dale said, getting up and clipping him over the head. "Get over it already. You'd screw her friends in a heartbeat."

"Would fucking not," Hendrix protested. "Besides, it's different."

"How?" I challenged.

"How?" Hendrix repeated. "Because Everett is practically family."

"Hell and holy shit on a fuck," Dad spewed. "You..." He coughed, struggling to look at me. "You and Everett?"

"On that note," Graham said, grinning from ear to ear with his napkin in hand. "We'll be going. Families who hate us to see and all that fun shit. Come on, Dale."

"What about the new guy?" Dale asked, pocketing his phone.

The new guy was eating another bread roll. "I'm good here or on the bus." Dad sent him a glare that had him saying, "On second thought, I'm great at charming the parents. Let me come with."

"I knew it," Dad said, a tad too triumphantly. "I tried to tell you, Brenna, but you wouldn't even hear it." He mumbled something about, "Telling me there's raccoon's in the goddamned attic."

Aiden's thigh turned to concrete beneath my hand, and I pulled it away.

Mom rolled her eyes and took a huge swig of wine.

Everett's gaze was still fixed on me, unwavering and turbulent.

I dropped my head into my hands.

"Merry fucking Christmas, fam-bam," Hendrix sang at the top of his lungs.

Aiden dug his tongue into his cheek as soon as the door to my room shut behind him. His hand rose, lips parting, as he tried to formulate words.

This happened over and over while I stood there, my chest and head hurting.

"Shit. Fucking shit, Stevie," was all he finally came up with.

"I didn't know they'd be here, Aiden."

He paced the short length of my room, arm flexing as he scrubbed a hand down his face. "I know. Doesn't change the fact they're here, though, does it?"

I sat on my bed. "We couldn't ignore them forever."

Aiden didn't seem to agree, his hand slapping to his side. "It would've been nice to try."

I said nothing, staring at the specks littering the brown carpet of my room.

Eventually, he joined me, and we both lay down on my bed, not touching, and staring up at the glow worms on the ceiling.

I closed my eyes, not wanting to stare at them either.

Orange mingled with pink over my bedroom walls, and I forced my eyes open as noise drifted through the ajar bedroom door.

Aiden must've draped the knitted afghan over me, but as I sat up, pushing hair back from my face, I couldn't see him.

Panic sharpened until I saw his duffel sitting next to mine by my sticker-covered wardrobe and heard the unmistakable deep sound of his laughter from down the hall.

What a mess. A tangled, acrid mess.

I used the bathroom, then went to the kitchen to grab a glass of water before gathering the courage to enter where the noise emanated from in the living room.

Hendrix, Mom, and Aiden were chatting and laughing, but there was no sign of Everett and Dad.

I smiled at Aiden when he flashed me a questioning look, and then I went in search of Dad, who was undoubtedly pissed.

Low voices filtered through the crack of the front door, and the orange glow of a cigarette caught my eye. I peeked out and saw Everett's shadow in a deck chair on the lawn near the bus. Dad was sitting in another chair beside him, nursing a beer.

A hand fell on my shoulder, and I startled, then realized it was only Mom. "Leave them. They're hashing it out."

"Is he mad?"

"He was," Mom admitted. "But mainly with me for not telling him."

"I'm sorry," I whispered, my voice catching.

She squeezed my shoulder, then grabbed my arm, turning me away from the door. "Nothing to be done about it now."

Anxiety rolled off me when I heard Dad laugh and mention my name, but I moved back down the hall, entering the living room with Mom.

Aiden scooted over on the couch, and I sank down beside him, his arm coming to rest around my shoulders.

"What's going on?" I asked.

"Your boyfriend was telling me about how he met you," Hendrix said, stroking his whiskered chin. "Smooth as silk, man."

"You did not," I said.

Aiden sipped his beer, tipping a shoulder. "Why not? It's a great story."

Hendrix fiddled with the pegs of his acoustic guitar, then tested the strings. "It is. Much better than the other one I heard."

"Hendrix," Mom warned.

"Chill, Mom." He plucked a fast tune, then slapped his hand over the strings with a grin. "I'm dealing with it."

"Deal a little faster. It's over and done with now."

Hendrix pursed his lips in a way that said he wasn't so sure, and Aiden cleared his throat. "You hungry? We had lunch left-overs for dinner, but I didn't want to wake you."

I poked his dimple. "I'm fine, Prince."

"What'd you just say?" A rough question from the entryway.

My hand fell from Aiden's face as Everett's paled beneath the Christmas lights strung from every corner of the room.

"What do you mean?" I asked, my spine pulling taut at the crazed look in Everett's eye.

"Him." He gestured to Aiden. "What'd you just call him?"

"Prince," I said, my cheeks heating. "It's, um, his last name."

Aiden's brows furrowed as Everett stared at him with an intensity that went beyond jealousy and resentment.

Then the beer bottle dropped from Everett's hand, foam dribbling onto the red rug as he disappeared.

The crash of the front door hitting the side of the house reverberated, and we all sat still as stone to the sound of his shouted cursing until silence fell.

"What the fuck was that?" Hendrix stood, moving to pick up the fallen beer bottle.

Mom was blinking in the direction Everett had gone.

Swallowing the knot that'd formed in my throat, I got up and fetched some wet towels for the rug and patted it clean. Once done, I went to Aiden, who seemed more confused than any of us, and took his hand. I didn't know what to say. That was an outburst none of us could explain away, so I tugged. "Come on. Let's go to bed."

"But..." Aiden hesitated, looking in the direction Everett had gone. "He's okay?"

That this man had the ability to be concerned for the very same guy he felt threatened by made my heart crash and burn as it melted with tenderness. "Yeah," I said, smiling through the tears that'd gathered. "He'll be okay."

"He's been a mess more than usual lately," Hendrix informed behind me.

I'd forgotten he was still there and turned around.

He set his guitar back on its stand, running his hand over his mop of blond hair. "Drunk all the time. And I mean all the fucking time. He's never not got a drink in his hand. He stopped playing guitar midway through a set just three weeks ago, and the only reason we haven't kicked him out is because we've built a following, however small, from his voice, and no matter how drunk he is, he never fails on that front."

"You can't kick him out," I said, fear spearing through me at what Everett would do without his one remaining saving grace.

"I know." Hendrix sighed. "I never could. I'd make him play the fucking harmonica before I did that."

"I'll meet you in bed," Aiden whispered, kissing my forehead, then leaving the room.

I looked from his retreating back to Hendrix as he picked up pieces of wrapping paper and tossed them onto the coffee table. "Hen, I'm sorry. It wasn't something I could help, even if I wanted to, but still, I'm sorry."

Hendrix kept moving, and I wasn't sure he'd heard me until he said, "It's just him, Steve." He straightened, dropping balls of paper to the coffee table. "He's like my brother, so of course, I love him, but... he's not for you."

I nodded. "I know that now."

"Do you?" Hendrix angled his head. "Because that guy"—he gestured out of the room—"Aiden, he's the kind of guy you need. Not some drunk who can't see past his own selfish bullshit."

He was right. It didn't negate that I'd love Everett anyway, no matter what he did, or that I couldn't be with him. Love was love, no matter how undeserving the person.

I stepped forward, holding my arms out. Hendrix raised a brow, and I laughed. "Don't leave me hanging."

His cheeks rose with his grin, and then he scooped me up, hugging me tight as I wrapped my arms around his waist. "You smell like an ashtray," I whispered.

He chuckled. "Don't tell Mom and Dad."

TWENTY-THREE

IDEN'S QUIET SNORES DID THEIR BEST TO LULL ME TO SLEEP BUT failed.

Carefully moving his arm off my waist, I climbed out of bed and padded to the door in search of water.

A quiet voice had the glass slipping in my hand and almost crashing into the sink. "Did you fuck him in the same bed I had you in?"

I put the glass in the sink and forced the water that felt more like cement to slide down my throat before I turned around.

He was standing in the arched entryway to the dining room, his shoulder pressing heavily into it, night shadowing his features.

Resolved to dust off his question, I walked by him. "Go to bed, Everett."

A warm hand snatched mine, pulling me back into his hard chest. "Answer me."

His hand was tight around mine over my stomach, and he used the other to move my hair aside.

As soon as his lips hit my skin, whiskey on his breath and shudders ready to roll over me, I pulled away. "Stop it. Where've you been?"

"Didn't think you'd care, Clover."

"God." I shook my head. "Okay, good night."

"Wait," he said when I'd almost reached the end of the hall. "I-I need to…"

I waited for him to say it, but I had no plans to make it easy for him this time.

"Please, just let me talk to you."

"Why?" I spun back. "It won't change anything. All it'll do is cause trouble I don't need."

"It's not about us." He blew out a wet sounding exhale, the next word croaked. "Please."

That did it, and I felt my shoulders droop. I adjusted my T-shirt and gestured for him to follow me into the living room.

He slumped on the couch next to me, and I scooted back, trying to put a bit of space between us.

His lips pinched as he watched me, and then his head flopped into his hands, fingertips digging into his scalp. "His name was Mason, my brother. He was only eight when…" He stopped, and I heard a strange buzzing in my ears, felt my pulse thud in my neck. "We were playing outside on the driveway where we used to live."

My hand went to my throat, and I struggled to breathe while I watched his back heave as his head lowered even more.

"He was on his scooter, and my parents were passed out on the couch after the bender they'd had the night before. It was a Saturday morning, so it wasn't so busy. I told him to wait while I went inside the garage to find his helmet. And next thing I knew—" He groaned. "Fuck." He drew in three breaths and seemed to hold them as he rushed out, "I heard him scream, and it-it… just cut off. Then a woman was screaming, and then sirens were screaming." His hands were squeezing his head now, growled words gritted through clenched teeth. "Everyone was fucking screaming as my baby brother lay dead behind some woman's SUV."

Tears collected and pooled in my eyes, and I did my best to swallow them, but they slipped out, falling silently down my cheeks.

"There was so much blood, Clover. S-s-so much, and I tried."
He coughed, wet and loud. "I tried to wake him up, but people
kept pulling me away from him, and then they took him in the
ambulance. They took him away, and I never fucking saw him
again."

"Everett," I started, not knowing what to say. If there was
anything of value I could say.

Then he fell against me, his head landing on my lap and
his arms winding around my waist. "You gotta understand. He
was all I had, all I had that mattered." He sniffed, his words tear-
strained. "And then I met you, Hendrix—all of you."

I ran my hand over his hair, feeling the grit, the sweat, and
wondering when he'd last washed it. "Does this have anything to
do with your outburst earlier?"

"Yes." He was quiet a minute, the shaking of his shoulders
crumbling my resolve. "Clover, his mom. Desiree Prince. She
was the one who hit him. She was high, and I don't even know.
Apparently, she's dead now, but she fucking killed him."

My hand, my entire body, stilled, my eyes drying as all the
dots joined.

Aiden's mom committing suicide. High. The screaming. The
guilt she would've felt... I looked toward my bedroom, to where
Aiden lay sleeping.

Or did lay sleeping.

He was standing in the doorway, his expression unreadable
in the dull lighting, staring at me and Everett.

Then he was gone.

Torn, I felt Everett shake again, his tears morphing into sobs
as I gazed down at where his head was still buried in my lap. Aiden
needed me, but Everett... he'd needed this for a long time. For
years, given the way he'd kept running through life, running away
from it, trying to outsmart the ghost's intent on trailing him.

And so with guilt piercing thorn-laden tendrils into my heart, I smoothed Everett's hair and rubbed his back while years of grief soaked my sleep shorts.

The rumble of Aiden's Audi penetrated some minutes later, and I heard his car take off down the street.

"Hey," Dad whispered, tapping me on the shoulder.

Forcing open my heavy eyelids, I squinted up at him and felt something draped over the bottom half of my body.

The lines around Dad's eyes and across his forehead tightened with his scowl. His disapproval aimed at Everett's snoring form. "What happened?"

"He didn't tell you?" I whispered, remembering how they'd talked outside.

"Some, but judging by the noises he made with you some hours ago, not all."

Everett groaned, rolling over and blinking his eyes open.

Shifting his hands to either side of my legs, he pushed himself up and to the other side of the couch with a loud yawn. "What time is it?"

"Time for bacon and eggs," Mom called.

My stomach, after not being fed dinner last night, growled. The thought brought me back to Aiden, and I sat up, darting around Dad and down the hall to my room. I knew he'd left, but he would've come back. It wasn't his fault, but I was sure it had upset him, more than upset him, to hear it all the same.

He never came back.

The sight of my lone duffel had me rushing to my purse to grab my phone. I had no missed calls, but I didn't let that deter me and hit his name before pressing the phone to my ear. My hand dug into my tangled hair as I reached his voicemail three times.

Giving in, I knocked some stray tears from my face and sent him a text. I asked where he was and if he was okay, then I made sure the volume was up loud and put my phone down.

The smell of bacon and eggs floated down the hall, but I grabbed a fresh set of clothes and locked myself in the bathroom.

Everything Everett had come clean about the night before, everything that'd happened because of it, not only with him but with Aiden just leaving, coalesced into a storm that thundered through my veins and sent my ass sliding down the shower wall.

I sat there a long while, tears streaming and my chest heaving until a knock sounded on the door.

"You alive in there?" Hendrix.

I sniffed, standing and quickly immersing myself in the spray. "Yeah," I called once I was sure my voice would remain steady.

I had to go. I couldn't stay here when Aiden was God knows where feeling who knew what. Everett needed me, yes. And even though I longed to ease all that ailed him, I couldn't. I'd given him all I could spare, and even that had probably been too much for Aiden. Besides, he had my family. I wasn't leaving him alone.

Not like I had Aiden.

I washed and toweled off before dressing in jeans, a black T-shirt, and a long cream knitted cardigan, then brushed my teeth and packed my things.

Everyone had finished breakfast by the time I entered the dining room and nabbed a few slices of cold bacon.

"Thanks for using all the hot water," Hendrix said, entering the kitchen with blue lips and a towel hastily wrapped around his waist.

"When did you get tattoos?" I asked, taking in the phoenix spread across his chest and the unfinished dragon head on his upper arm.

He stared down at them and shrugged. "On the road, few different places."

"Can you do me a favor?" I asked.

"If you hurry up and spit it out. I'm fucking shrinking by the second here."

"Ew, why?"

"Steve, come on."

"I need a lift back to school." As much as I loved Mom and Dad, I couldn't handle being in the car with them for that long and potentially talking about everything that'd happened. I needed to sort through it all on my own. Preferably in silence.

"Ugh." He scrubbed at his wet face, sighing. "Give me ten minutes."

I set my things by the door, then followed the sound of an acoustic melody through the living room and out onto the back porch.

Standing against the doorframe, I stared at Everett's back. He sat on the edge of the half-built deck, serenading the few birds in the trees lining the back fence with his abrasive, hypnotic voice.

It's funny how your eyes once shone
Brighter than any sky
While we were riding lows
During downward highs

It's funny how I can't seem to care
When I look around
And find no one there
Because when my feet hit the ground

It's just you
Yeah, just you

It's not a game,
It never was
I'd always thought
All this lying and dying
Was for the most beautiful cause

Until you cut me, baby
Then watched me bleed
Sliced me deep
As you stayed my feet
You cut me, baby
And then you cried
Promising there would be
No more goodbyes
You cut me, baby
Sliced me wide open
Never knowing, never caring
Just what might happen
Oh-ohhh

I know I'm trouble
It's written all over me
And I know it's a fucking handful
When you're only trying to
Live and love me

Really, it's okay
How I'll go and you'll stay
Because nothing,

I'm sorry, not even you
Can keep me contained
We both know it's true
Yeah, not even you

Until you cut me, baby
You just watch me bleed
Sliced me deep
As you stayed my feet
You cut me, baby
And then you cried
Promising there would be
No more goodbyes
You cut me, baby
Sliced me wide open
Never knowing, never caring
Just what might happen
Whoa-ohhh-oh

Oh, you don't get a say
Over whether I'll go
Or when I'll stay
No, not today

It's not up to you to decide
How far I'll sink
Or how far I'll climb
Yeah, you should know by now
I'll drift even if you're mine

Until you cut me, baby
Then watched me bleed

Sliced me deep
As you stayed my feet
You cut me, baby
And then you cried
Promising there would be
No more lies
You cut me, baby
Sliced me wide open
Never knowing, never caring
Just what might happen

Ohh-ohhh but now
Hush, hear me, baby
Listen, don't open your mouth

Next time you cut me
I'll be sure to bleed
All over your shoes
Before I fucking leave

It was new, or maybe it wasn't. It'd been so long since I'd seen them play.

Still, it scraped my chest raw. Every time he opened his lungs and his lips caressed words into song, words he'd never dare utter in everyday conversation, it moved me. This, though, this was different.

But even as that part of me that would always belong to him yearned and cried, the other part that belonged to someone else, someone who was probably hurting just as much as Everett, lifted my feet and carried me back through the house to the door.

His lyrics followed, stayed with me, until I closed the door to Mom's car and Hendrix started the engine.

TWENTY-FOUR

"**S**O, YOU AND EVERETT, IS THAT OVER NOW?"

How like Hendrix to ask such complicated questions at the very last minute.

I unclipped my seat belt and opened the door. "We never really began."

Leaning an arm on the steering wheel, Hendrix pondered my words, then nodded at the apartment building behind us. "That's not your place."

"No," I said, getting out and closing the door. I opened the door to the back seat, pulling out my duffel. "It's Aiden's. Thanks for the ride."

He flicked his hand in goodbye, driving off once I hit the sidewalk.

Heaving my bag up the steps, I ran over all the things I wanted to say until I reached his apartment. Steeling my spine, I dumped my purse and duffel to the ground and knocked.

Every word, every apology I'd formed evaporated when Aiden finally came to the door, opened it, then walked back inside his apartment.

I ditched my bags, following him. "What happened?"

"Care to elaborate?" he asked, stopping in the kitchen and ripping open a bottle of Jack Daniel's. His detached demeanor and the cool calm in which he poured himself a shot and threw it down his throat grated.

"You just leaving me there like that. What the hell was that?"

"Oh," he said, wincing as the whiskey probably burned on its way down. "Yeah, that was me walking away from something that just about destroyed me."

Anger vanished, waves of guilt taking its place. "Your mom—"

"I didn't know," he said, pouring another shot, then capping the bottle. "I mean, I knew, but I didn't know specifics. So yeah, I left. I needed to. But I came back." He tossed the shot back, slamming the glass down before rounding the counter. His chest was bare, his golden skin pulling at my eyes, along with the dip of his hip bones, of which his team sweatpants rode low on.

I shifted my eyes, forcing them to his face. An indecipherable emotion passed over it, hardening the sharp angles and darkening the two-day-old stubble littering his rigid jaw. "You came back?"

"Mmm." He strode closer, one slow step at a time. "I did. And you know what killed me more than finding out just how much me and your damaged guy have in common? Hmm?" I frowned, unsure, but he continued. "It was seeing you asleep together exactly where I'd found you, all tangled up as if you didn't have somewhere else you should've been instead." He stopped moving, eyes ablaze with fury, and his teeth gritting. "And you let it happen. As though what he'd told you and how it made him feel were all that mattered. Because who cares how I feel, right? Not when it was my unhinged mother who ruined his life."

"Aiden, no," I said, clearing my throat as razor blades tried to tear it. "No. I know it's a lot, and it looked bad, but I fell asleep." I laughed, disbelief and fear rattling the sound. "Does the fact I love you mean nothing?"

He leaned back against the counter, his tongue tracing

his lips and one bare foot crossing over the other. "Does it mean anything to you? Or am I just some kind of bandage you've done your best to wrap around all the shit he's put you through?"

"Wow," I wheezed out, unable to believe what he was saying, and the callous, cold way in which he'd said it. "You know what? Fuck you." I turned for the door.

"Oh, how quick you are to walk away," he said when I'd reached the threshold. "I can't help but think if I were him, you'd still be standing right in front of me, taking whatever I throw at you."

Anger returned, intensifying and curling my fingers. "That's not fair, and it's not true."

"Isn't it?" I spun around, and he leveled me with both his biting question and hard stare. "I'll tell you what's not fair, Petal. Waiting and then all but begging for you to give me a chance." His voice roughened, eyes glassing. "Waiting and all but praying that you'd fall for me even half as hard as I've fallen for you, and then..." His throat dipped. "Having to watch you hold and comfort the guy you loved first. The reason I couldn't and why I don't think I ever will be able to have all of you."

"Aiden," I pleaded, my tongue thick.

"No." The blunt word sliced sharp and deep. "You don't get to have us both. So who's it going to be?"

"Me and Everett..." I shook my head, taking a step toward him. "We're not anything."

He drifted forward, a sinister curl to his lip as he loomed over me. "That's the worst lie I've ever been told." Lowering his head, he whispered words that had my eyes shutting over tears. "Just because he doesn't see you every day, just because he's not fucking you, doesn't mean I don't see that."

Tears flooded and cascaded over my flushed face as I planted my hands on his hard chest and pushed him back. "How... h-how dare..." Unable to talk, I gave up and raced out of there.

His silence echoed louder than the slam of his door.

Ten days passed by with a speed akin to Mr. Ross's slow, unsteady gait.

After not hearing from Aiden the following week, I admitted defeat, dried my tears, and decided to call him. He didn't answer. Nor did he the twenty times I'd called and sent various texts since I'd failed to see him around campus.

I'd just left his place, knocking half a dozen times to no avail, when I realized I'd left my phone at work in my haste to get to his apartment and check on him.

Cursing myself out, I raced down the stairs and began the trek back through town. The whole not having a car thing was really starting to become a problem, no matter how small the town was.

On the sidewalk, I pulled to a stop so fast my breath skidded out of me.

Everett was leaning against the window of Petal Power, hand and face pressed to the glass as he peered inside.

"What are you doing?"

With a start, he turned, eyes almost as wide as his smile, and walked over. "Looking for you."

I traced every inch of his face, noting the clarity in his bright eyes, the healthier complexion, and the clean sheen to his newly trimmed hair. It still kissed his shoulders in dark blond waves, but it looked soft to the touch. My fingers tingled with the urge to check, but I backed up. "Why?"

A rough chuckle made those greens gleam, and he tucked his hands inside the pockets of his jeans. "Thought that'd be obvious."

"Nothing is obvious with you," I said. Guilt manifested at his pinched reaction, but this shit with Aiden was eating at me like a parasite, and although I didn't blame Everett, he was the reason my heart was pattering too fast in search for what it needed since arriving home after Christmas.

"I deserve that and more, and well…" Blowing out a breath, he swayed closer, letting his gaze wander over our surroundings, a gentle smile softening his lips. "I live here now."

The world turned a flat shade of gray, its vibrancy leaking from the buildings, flowers, and cars around us. It all fell, splattered onto the concrete with my stalled heart. My stomach filled with a swarm of jittery bees, even as it sank.

"No," I whispered, hardly a sound.

Everett's brows met. "Yeah, I leased a crummy apartment above the bar we played at last year. Cheap rent in exchange for playing a few nights a week. I've got interviews lined up with some places too."

I shook my head, my hand quaking as I pushed it into my hair and tugged, barely feeling the sting.

It was there. This was real. "But…" I stopped, then swallowed. "The band?"

"I left," he said with more calm than I ever could've imagined him saying those words. "They were probably sick of my drunk ass constantly fucking up anyway." He laughed, but it lacked humor and conviction. He took my hand, voice quiet. "It's time to quit running, Clover."

I pulled back. "So you decide to do that here?"

He tipped a broad shoulder, gaze hesitant but sincere. "You're my home. Being with you and sharing that with you over

Christmas… Well, it was many things. The main one, the most important one, being that it reminded me of that, yet again." His lashes lowered, then rose with his lips. "And if you're my home, where else would I go?"

I was tempted to pinch myself. Perhaps even punch myself. This had to be a dream, but I could smell him. Was it possible to smell people in your dreams? I couldn't remember.

"I'm with Aiden," I croaked out, not even knowing if that was true but wanting it to be.

Everett stared down at me, my words chasing that unfamiliar softness away and replacing it with the usual granite. "I know."

"I love him." I started walking backward, pointing an accusing finger at him. "You fucked me up, and then I met him, and I love him, Everett."

A green eye narrowed. "Who are you trying to convince, Clover?" The words weren't malicious, but his steps were filled with intent as I turned down the street, and he followed me.

My pace picked up as I rounded street corner after street corner, feeling him there behind me. When we reached the sidewalk leading to my place, I stopped and whirled on him. "Oh, my God, stop. Just go, please. I'm happy you've decided to better yourself, but that can't be with me. I'm happy now," I said, my voice cracking.

He kept walking until the toes of his boots nipped at my own, his hand reaching for my hair and tucking it behind my ear as his eyes studied mine. "Then why don't you look happy? Sound happy?"

"Because you'll no doubt mess everything up for me." I went to back up, but his arm looped around my waist.

His words were heated and resolute. "I'm not here to mess shit up for you. I swear. I'm here because I fucking love you. I've loved you for years, and there's nowhere else I want to be." He shook his head, and shocked, feeling as if lightning had struck my veins, my resistance collapsed, and I turned to mush in his embrace. His forehead lowered to mine. "Not anymore. I've tried to be anywhere and everywhere else, and it didn't fucking work, Clover."

Stunned, I didn't move until he kissed me, soft and gentle and full of the kind of promise that, once upon a time, I'd be desperate enough to believe.

But once upon a times were for dreams, and he was only capable of nightmares.

I shoved him off me, my voice a seething rasp. "Go to hell, Everett."

He grinned, undeterred, even as he retreated a step. "Been there all my life. So I guess I'll just make myself comfortable until you might want my company again." He winked, then passed a familiar black Audi before disappearing.

With my heart slamming against my rib cage, I forced my eyes to the apartment, then raced up the path.

All the air I'd been struggling to inhale since seeing Everett turned to ice, crusting my tongue and slicing into my throat when I saw Aiden.

Sitting atop the three steps outside my front door with his knees apart, he gazed down at a tiny velvet box between his hands.

After a minute that stretched into eternity, he sighed and snapped the box closed. "I've been drafted." Hollow words for something of that caliber. "I was going to tell you over Christmas, but I thought I'd buy this first." He chewed his bottom lip, still staring down at the box, then he enclosed it inside a fist. "Thought there was a good chance you'd want to come with me."

"I will, yes," I said without any thought at all and shifted forward. "Just let me…"

Rising from the steps, he refused to look at me as he passed, his cologne mingling with my fear as he stalked to his car. "I don't think so, Petal."

"Aiden, don't. Stop."

He didn't; he climbed into his car, and the sound of the engine starting unglued my feet.

Blind with terror, I ran to it as he backed up and waited to turn out onto the street. I slapped the window, my fingers smearing and streaking, clawing at the glass. They fell when he pulled out and sped down the street.

A silent scream scraped past my lips, and I dropped to the sidewalk, unaware of my surroundings. Uncaring of the noises I might have been making as his departure opened cracks that sent salty rivers flooding my cheeks.

Arms came around me, lifting, and then I was inside. The door was kicked shut, and before I knew it, I was being carried into my room and placed on the bed. The scent of tobacco and clean linen enveloped me as a gentle hand pushed the wet hair from my face.

"Did you know he was there?" I blubbered out. "Don't lie to me."

Everett's sigh stirred my hair. "I didn't."

The disbelief, the injustice, the regret—they wouldn't stop squeezing every breath, every heartbeat. Even when the tears dried.

Everett's chest vibrated against my back as he held me, and his abrasive humming eventually lulled me to sleep.

TWENTY-FIVE

FOR WEEKS, I CALLED HIS NUMBER, ONLY TO EVENTUALLY BE TOLD it'd been disconnected.

What had changed in a month that he could cut me out like that? In a way so permanent, I could already feel the scar.

Nothing had changed for me. Not even having Everett here, who checked in on me every day, had changed the way I felt about Aiden.

But then again, not even Aiden could change the way I felt about Everett.

Love was a messy, drunk-ass son of a bitch.

I didn't stop there. I checked his Facebook and caved after he'd been gone for seven weeks and sent him a message there. All that did was get me blocked, of which he made sure to do on Instagram too. But not before I saw him at some charity gala with a model named Latoya Adams draped over his arm in all her designer, uber-contoured glory.

It took me a while to even find out what team had picked him up. Google searches didn't provide much until the season had started, and I now caught myself watching a game I'd never cared much for just to catch a glimpse of him.

My fingers deftly wrapped the twine around the bridal bouquet, and I studied it in the light, scrutinizing every petal, every leaf, each visible stem before setting it on the stand and fussing some more.

"One might think that bouquet is for you with the way you

keep clucking over it like a mother hen." Gloria dumped a box of ribbon on the counter with a light thump, then smacked my hand away from the flowers.

I scowled but got to work on the ones for the bridesmaids. "I'd want it perfect if it were me."

It could've been me, a catty voice echoed. It was almost me. I snuffed it and sipped from my mug of warm tea.

"Oh look, Mr. Rugged is here again," Sabrina mused, dusting the shelves by the front windows.

Gloria shot me a look that I studiously ignored.

Sabrina and Gloria took Aiden's absence almost as hard as I had, and to say they'd warmed to Everett instantly would be a blatant lie. But they were cordial, and I could tell that the way he'd been coming by, doting in his own quiet way, was wearing them down.

They weren't the only ones.

I'd half expected him to bail after mere days of watching me mope around. Heartbroken or not, I was no longer a sure bet where he was concerned, and he knew it.

Yet he was still here.

Everett pushed open the door, causing the wind chimes to sing, and the smile that hitched his lips higher into those cheeks of his had me smiling back. It was strange to see this man show up with that same smile every day when he did nothing but leave, break, and ruin me. Part of me still waited, still poised in preparation for the moment he disappeared again.

"Clover." He nodded. Retrieving something from the pocket of his denim jacket, he then slid it over the worn countertop.

Placing my tea down, I grinned when I saw the tickets to *Breakfast at Tiffany's*. The cinema in town played old films one night a week in the springtime. We'd already been to see *Casablanca* and *Gone with the Wind*.

"Not a date," I'd told him the first time.

"It's whatever you need it to be, Clover."

Those words came back to me as I surveyed the tickets, my teeth denting my lip. "I'm not sure you'll like this one."

"That's what you said last time. We won't know until I see for myself, right?"

"Right." I smiled.

His eyes, clear and bright, smiled at mine.

"How's old Barney doing?" Sabrina asked, making her presence known.

Everett blinked, then nodded. "His leg's still acting up, but he's having no trouble barking orders from his chair in the corner of the store."

Sabrina snorted. "I'll bet. You tell him that one of those planter boxes we bought last month has already cracked. He needs to go back to the old supplier."

"Or we'll go through them ourselves." Gloria quirked a brow, then waggled her fingers before vanishing into the back room.

Everett tapped his fingers on the counter. "I'll pass it on tomorrow morning." He worked at the hardware store in town five days a week.

Sabrina rounded the counter, staring up into his face for a heartbeat and then patting his cheek. "You're looking good, boy."

Everett's eyes narrowed, but he maneuvered that roguish smile into place and thanked her.

Then he turned to me, leaning over the counter on his elbows, and my eyes traced the facial hair that peppered his jaw. Those emerald eyes penetrated, long strands of hair licking his cheek when he tilted his head.

I let him stare, busy staring myself, then laid my hand over

his. "I'm okay." I smiled when he didn't let up, laughing low. "I'll
see you at seven."

"Oh, yeah." Digging into his pocket, he retrieved a cheap
looking smartphone and set it on the counter. "Got a phone."

Shock held me still, but only for a few seconds before I
picked it up to put my number in.

"It's already there. Learned it by heart years ago."

I dragged a finger over the glass screen. "Well, I suppose
when you leave again, I'll at least be able to call you."

His brows lowered and his forehead creased. He pocketed
the phone and slowly backed toward the door. "Not going anywhere, Clover. You'll see."

"You hated it." I laughed as everyone in the theater stood and
made their way to the exit.

Everett stretched his arms over his head, then let out a loud
yawn. "I didn't hate it."

"You were bored."

He bobbed his head side to side, then pinched the air.
"Maybe a little."

I grabbed his hand, pulling him up. He didn't budge, and
instead, he pulled me toward him until I lost my balance and fell
into his lap.

"Ever." I planted my hands on his chest, my thighs cradling
his.

Taking their time, his own hands coasted up my back, eyes
firm on mine. "Been a while since you've called me that."

"I guess it has."

While nothing had happened between us since he'd decided

to upend his life and make one here, he'd still made no secret of wanting it to. We'd touched, though never like this, and some nights he even fell asleep on my couch with me after we'd watched TV, but I was holding back.

I was waiting, but I was no longer waiting for him.

As my fingers scrunched the crisp shirt he'd donned, and I felt him hard beneath me, I began to wonder why I was too scared to give him a chance.

Aiden wasn't coming back. He'd made it clear he wanted nothing to do with me. And not only that, but everything I'd ever wanted was finally within grabbing distance.

I just couldn't bring myself to trust it. To reach out and take it.

"I love you," he whispered, splitting me wide open as he leaned forward, hands cupping my ass and his lips running over my cheek.

He said it at least once a day, and the way he did so, with such conviction and no expectation, never failed to steal my breath.

Goose bumps erupted over my arms. My eyes fluttered as tingles ignited, a wildfire over every patch of skin he caressed. It felt too good to be touched, to be held, and with such reverence. Unbelievable that he was here. That, for the first time since I'd laid eyes on him, he was putting me first.

"Come on." Gently, he smacked my ass when I didn't move. "Let's get you home."

I climbed off, and he handed me my purse before nabbing our popcorn boxes.

He dumped them in the trash on the way out, and I was thankful for the warm air as we strolled outside.

"What exactly was it like on the road?" I'd heard second-hand tales from the band, but Everett knew that wasn't what

I was asking. I wanted to know what it was like for him, and I figured it was time to finally ask. To hear about the dream he thought might carry him away from all that haunted him.

He took his time to answer, and worry began to nibble. "You don't have to say anything if you don't want to."

"Don't do that," he said, a tad sharply.

"What?"

"Treat me like shattered glass. I won't break." He stopped, and I did too. "You're not that girl." He curled some of my hair behind my ear. "You're the girl who gets mad, asks me the hard questions even if I don't want to answer them, and gives me hell when I do something you don't like."

"Those were different times."

He licked his lips, inching closer. "Different times, maybe, but we're the same people, Clover. If you want to ask something, ask. In fact, I've been waiting weeks for you to."

I pushed his hand down and continued walking. "You could've been more forthcoming yourself."

"Not when I'm not sure if you're ready for that."

I nodded, and we walked in silence until we'd reached the street's end.

"It's every runaway's dream," he said, his voice soft but carrying in the still night. "Escapism at its best. But a lot of hard work too."

We wound around the corner, the sidewalk bathed a dull orange from the streetlights.

"The late nights, shit money—that's if you get paid anything—the constant traveling on a putrid smelling bus. And when we found a place that paid for regular shows, well, that was great, but I didn't want to stay in any one place too long."

"You'd start drinking more," I cut in as gently as possible.

"Mmm, exactly. And with the drinking came the wildness.

We all did it, sure. But I can't remember many nights, if I'm being honest." He slowed to light a cigarette.

"Does that scare you?"

"It didn't then." Breathing out a puff of smoke, he tucked his lighter and packet into his jacket pocket. "But now that I'm looking back? Fuck yeah. It sickens me."

I didn't want to ask what I needed to, but he did say not to sugarcoat. "Have you been tested?"

"Clover," he said, coughing. "Shit, warn me before you drop bombs."

I didn't laugh. "You said to ask whatever I wanted to."

"I did." He sighed, clearing his throat before taking another drag. "And yeah, got tested about two weeks ago. But I never fucked without protection."

"How would you know if you were always shitfaced?"

"Warranted, but do you really wanna know those specifics?"

I gave him a look.

Chuckling, he raked a hand through his tangled locks. "Fine. Besides the fact I just know, I'd see the evidence the next day. Either on the floor, seats of the bus, or in the trash if I was classy enough. But Clover, you—"

"Everett." I couldn't hear that.

"It's fucked up, but you were who I thought of each and every time, and so knowing I couldn't have you but still not wanting to risk fucking up, it was kind of just ingrained in me."

"That's… God, there are no words." I choked out a sad attempt at a laugh. "That you could just sleep with anyone while I barely looked at another guy until Aiden."

Now standing outside my place, he slipped his hand around mine and turned me to him. "You and me, we were never supposed to happen. Hell, I'm still pinching myself every day I wake up in this tiny ass town, knowing I'm in the same place as you."

His hold eased, thumb brushing mine, and my tense limbs drooped as I met his determined gaze.

"It ends now. It ended before Christmas. You're the only one, the only thing I want. Not the music, not the groupies, not the escape, not the recognition. You. Just me and you and forever."

"Forever," I echoed, tasting the word on my tongue.

Dropping his cigarette, he took my face in his cool hands, tilting it back to search my eyes. "We're still young and stupid, and we're bound to make more mistakes, but I'm tired of making the same ones. If you'll believe nothing else I say, then at least believe that."

With a lingering kiss to my forehead, he released me, and I watched him drift down the street until the shadows swallowed him.

TWENTY-SIX

THE INTERIOR OF ZOE'S WRAPPED ME IN ITS SMOKY EMBRACE, filling my nose with the scent of peanuts, stale beer, and cigarettes.

Neil, a guy from school, was manning the bar alongside its owner and namesake, Zoe.

Zoe was a single mom of three boys, her husband having skipped town when the youngest, Jeff, was born three years ago. The bar had once been her dad's, who warned everyone she was all bark with extra bite.

Everett was by the stage, untangling cable leads and chatting with some of the locals who frequented the run-down building most nights.

I sidled up to the bar, giving Zoe a smile. Her lips twitched, the piercing in her cheek shifting, and that was as good as it would get smile-wise.

Everett's attention was pinned on me when I asked for a soda and turned back to face the stage.

I raised my hand, fingers fluttering alongside my stomach as he gave me that devastating, hope-filled grin and then meandered between the tables, coming for me.

"Going to hang around this time?"

I licked my lips, quickly thanking Zoe for the drink she slid over, then let my eyes roam over the black shirt clinging to Everett's chest. When they reached his face, his own eyes sparkled, all knowing when it came to me. "Depends."

His brows jumped. "On?"

"On how well you play, I guess."

"Get on that stage, Taylor, or I'll be cutting the hot water again."

I pursed my lips at Zoe's threat, but Everett only grinned some more.

With a swipe of his fingers beneath my chin, he stalked back through the tables and finished setting up.

It wasn't the first time I'd come to see him play since he'd shown up in Raslow, but it was the first time I planned to hang around for the whole set. Not that he needed to know that.

Taking a seat on the stool with his guitar strapped to his back, Everett adjusted the mic stand. "How're we all doing tonight?"

Replies were hollered back, and while taking a sip of water, Everett nodded at an elderly man in the corner of the room. "How's that hip of yours treating you, Rog?"

"She's getting there."

Instead of a forced stage one, Everett flashed a rare genuine smile, swinging his guitar around. "That's what I like to hear." He dropped the bottle to the stage, then began to strum, bobbing his head and bouncing his knee as the crowd quieted.

The first song he chose was a popular one the band often played together, but even without them, and Everett singing at a slower pace, it was nothing short of chilling.

His ability to take a more upbeat rock-infused song with rivets of pop and turn it into a haunting, bluesy ballad had my mouth drying and my hand reaching blindly for my soda.

Lemon-scented rum,
In the barrel of a drum
We're brewing dreams

And I'd invite you because I kinda like you,
But I'm all tied up
In this feeling swinging from the ceiling
In my beat-up truck

Oh, we're like lovers, you and I,
But it's only for a night,
Because I'm wasted air
Sorry, there's no encore even if you want more,
Because I'm wasted, yeah

And I dare you, I honestly do, to find me here
Where the rooms are tight and the moon glows bright,
Let's get wasted there

Cherry-flavored pie
Shaped like a star in the sky
We're flying high
And I'd invite you because I really like you,
But I'm all shook up
High on this feeling that keeps on leaving
Like I give a fuck

Oh, we're like lovers you and I,
But it's only for a night, because I'm wasted air
Sorry, there's no encore, even if you want more,
Because I'm wasted, yeah

And I dare you, I honestly do, to find me here
Oh, where the rooms are tight and the moon glows bright,
Let's get wasted there
Yeah, get wasted there...

With his eyes closed, lips hugging the mic and thick fingers caressing guitar strings, he drowned the entire room with that hypnotizing, magnetic, gravel-stained timbre.

Watching Everett Taylor sing was an indescribable experience. One that took you right out of this world and set you in one where he only existed with you. It used to bother me that other people, that the entire world would get to experience that.

Now it bothered me that not many would.

He rolled through the band's most popular songs, adding his own perks to suit the lack of instruments, and even sang some new songs I'd never heard before.

Our skin, it heats
Without a moment between the sheets
Our eyes, they glow
Even without a trace of hope

Aren't you hungry, baby
Do you feel it gnawing
At your chest
Can you feel it clawing
So fucking restless

Only fucking you
Can sate this appetite
That keeps me awake
Oh, every day and night
So wrap me up real tight
In fake promises
As we forever wait
For a day too late

Our minds they tangle
Wondering dreaming
Hoping from every angle
And our hearts they'll break
Over and over
Because without a beginning
There is no closure

But aren't you hungry, baby
Do you feel it knocking
On your pretty little soul
Do you feel the sting as it pricks your skin
So out of control

Only fucking you
Can sate this appetite
That keeps me awake
Oh, every day and night
So wrap me up real tight
In fake promises
As we forever wait
For a day too late

They say no
And we scream yes
There's no middle ground
In this beautiful mess
But even if you don't
I swear I'll wait and I'll wait
Yeah, oh I'll wait...

Because only fucking you

Can sate this appetite
That keeps me awake
Oh, every damn day and night
So wrap me up real tight
In fake promises
As we forever wait
For a day too late
Always and always and always
Just a day too late

Shaken to the point of tingling, I felt my tongue dry and moisture pool behind my eyes.

His mind-clearing voice, accompanied by the smile he sent my way as he let the last notes echo into the mostly silent bar, had heat unfurling in my stomach.

And staring at those soul-infused green eyes, I forced myself to accept that no matter my resolve, or his own to better himself, nothing had really changed. Like the sun and the moon, we'd always revolve around one another, doomed to dance on opposing sides of fate.

After chatting with a guy who looked to be playing next, he joined me at the bar again but didn't order anything.

"So, good enough for you to see my new digs?"

I laughed, nodding, then he helped me down from the stool. My hand stayed clasped with his as he led me behind the bar and up a flight of steep wooden stairs.

We passed what looked to be a staff room, a storeroom, and a bathroom before reaching the end of the narrow hall.

Pulling out a set of keys, he unlocked the door. It squeaked as it swung open, and Everett gestured for me to go in.

Moving carefully over the scuffed, creaking wood floor, I peered around the tiny room, taking note of how little there was inside. Not that you could fit much. It was almost as small as my bedroom back home.

A twin bed sat pressed into the corner. A window with dirt-laced sheer curtains alongside it gave a view of the main street that cut through town below. A dusty set of shelves leaned by the far wall with a small TV, guitar picks, and various notebooks and pens atop it.

On the wall near the door was a small sink and a countertop that housed a tea kettle and white microwave. "Do you use the staff bathroom?"

Everett placed his guitar by the nightstand, then grabbed the cigarettes that'd been lying next to a framed photo and dug one out of the pack. "Yeah, it's not so bad. Has a lock."

I nodded, watching him sandwich one end of the smoke between those pillowed lips, then cast the other aflame.

He tossed the lighter down onto the scratched wood, the floor groaning as he walked to the end of the bed to open the window.

The photo frame pulled and stole my attention, and I moved closer to the bed, my butt bouncing on the unexpectedly springy mattress when I sat down and caught sight of whose picture was tucked behind the sheet of glass.

Mine.

I was seventeen, and judging by the creases that lined the image of my face, he'd clearly stolen it from a yearbook and had it folded up. "Sneaky."

"I had to," he said, so casual. "It's lived in my wallet the whole time we were away." Smoke encased his tentative question. "That freak you out?"

Did it? It surprised me, sure, but… "No."

Quiet settled, but it wasn't uncomfortable. At least, it wasn't for a minute. "You still think about him?"

Instantly knowing who he was referring to, I thought about how to answer that. Everett had been here, doting, waiting. As much as I no longer wanted to cut him open with words the way he'd done me, I still had to be honest. "I do."

Everett said nothing, the crackling sound of him inhaling tobacco filling the room.

"But I don't think he's coming back."

He made a low sound in his throat, then dropped the cigarette into an empty Coke bottle by the window. "Well, I didn't think I would either."

My smile was grim, my tattered heart beating faster at the thought of Aiden showing up, telling me he was sorry for running, and making it all better. As only he could do. It'd been over two months since I'd watched him snap that ring box closed, then drive out of my life.

The sound, the sight—it was still all so clear.

I'd like to blame it all on Everett, but that wouldn't be fair. Falling for two men might've been out of my control, but how I handled the love I felt for them was entirely up to me.

I released a sigh that rattled my lungs.

"I can't lie. I'm glad." Everett dropped to the bed, then fell back, the muscles in his arms contracting as he slid them behind his head to stare up at me. "I'm glad he's gone, but I'm sorry he's hurt you. More than that…" He reached for my hand, and I let him take it, let him wind our fingers together. "I'm sorry I ever left you in a position where someone else could swoop in and have you, only to end up hurting you too."

"Swoop in?" The calluses on his fingers tickled.

"Yeah. You're mine. I've already told you that." He graced me with a sad smile. "It's my fault you doubted me enough to forget."

My breathing thickened, and I tugged my hand from his. It fell to the bed. "I don't want to talk about this anymore."

"What do you want to talk about then?" There was no anger in his voice, just curiosity.

"Nothing." I stood, walking to the door. "I should head home."

He sat up and grabbed his keys. "You're not walking by yourself in the dark."

The night air was tepid, the streets quieting down as we weaved through town to the residential streets that surrounded it.

Thoughts of Aiden were pressing in. Thoughts of how long it might be until I heard his voice again. That deep laugh. Seeing that mischievous twinkle in his dark eyes. Thoughts that had me fearing if I ever even would.

Everett chased them away when he stopped by the playground and plucked a dandelion. "Come here."

"Cheap ass," I joked, smiling as he shifted my hair. He slid the stem behind my ear, then carefully maneuvered my blond waves around it.

"There." He cupped my cheeks, eyes bright beneath the silver moon. "That fucking smile."

I ducked my head, feeling sixteen all over again when my cheeks colored.

He tipped my chin up, his breaths coming fast, and the hold on my chin tightened as his eyes coasted into mine, crashing with fire. "The way I love you, I can't even tell you. One look at you, and every muscle in my body just fucking seizes." Letting go of my chin, his eyes still firm on mine, he collected my hand to lay it on his chest over his pounding heart. "Especially this one."

I had no choice but to soak in every rough word and felt them soothe the ache that never seemed to fade.

When I said nothing and just stared up at him with my

hand on his chest and my eyes wet, he shifted my hand to his lips, then dropped it.

We continued down the street, drifting into the next, and a myriad of complicated, conflicting emotions threatened to strangle me. "You're not drinking."

"I am, sometimes. Only when I need to."

His admission flattened, disappointment curling deep.

"Clover, I won't lie to you. You know that."

"Maybe working and staying at a bar isn't the best thing you should be doing right now." That was an understatement.

He chuckled, coming to a stop once we'd hit the steps to my place. "I do better with temptation close by." He winked, and I pinched my lips to keep from smiling. He never winked. He wasn't a winker.

"If you say so."

Reaching up, he brushed his fingers over my cheek, then backed down the path to the street. "I've got this, Clover. I swear."

I knew it would be a mistake to believe him, but I still did.

TWENTY-SEVEN

"**A**ND PRINCE STAYS HOT AT THE PLATE." THE COMMENTATOR'S voice rose above the sound of Adela making a smoothie in the kitchen. "Just look at those numbers, Abe."

"Ugh." I clicked the TV off, rolling onto my back to stare up at the living room ceiling.

"You need to stop watching already. Torture much?" Adela set a banana smoothie down on the coffee table, then fell over my extended legs, sipping her own.

"I'm done."

"Uh-huh," Adela crooned into her glass.

"So done."

"Told your mom yet?"

I shifted my legs beneath her, and she shuffled over for me to swing them off the couch. I sat up, dragging my fingers through my hair. "Last week. Dad saw a game on TV, and she called wanting to know why I'd never told them he'd been drafted."

"Awkward."

I snorted. "No, what was awkward was explaining the model who keeps showing up at his side." I forced my chest to deflate. "She knew then."

"I just can't believe it. Over a lousy kiss?"

"It wasn't just the kiss," I repeated for the twentieth time, picking up my smoothie.

"You and Everett have history. What human being doesn't have history with at least somebody?"

"Apparently not him." Though I knew that was a lie, and perhaps, it was Aiden's history with Darby that made him even more unwilling to stick around and fight things out.

I eyed Adela's lack of dance attire. "You're not teaching today? It's Saturday." She'd scored a new job teaching jazz and ballet to toddlers at a small studio in town three days a week.

"I'm ready to ditch them and try my hand at pole dancing."

"They're adorable." I tipped my glass back, my taste buds welcoming the sweet flavor. "Go get dressed."

She drained her drink, then rolled the glass between her hands. "In five. I need to psych myself up first."

I left her to her preparation, heading to the kitchen as I finished my smoothie. It was delicious and all, but I still needed caffeine.

A bang on the door had me quickly checking my morning hair in the window. I winced, then sighed when Adela made no move to get it and coasted down the hall.

I was still licking foamy milk from my upper lip when I opened it to find Everett on the top step, hands tucked in his ripped jean pockets and his work shirt on.

His eyes rounded. "Fucking hell. I'm trying to behave here."

I frowned, and then it dawned as I felt my nipples bead behind the thin layer of cotton covering my chest. I tugged at my tank, thankful I was at least wearing pajama pants.

"Good morning to you too." I crossed my arms over my boobs. "Shouldn't you be at work?"

"On my break. I started at five. Got something to show you, so go get dressed."

"What is it?"

"Clover, just hurry up before you get my ass fired."

I left the door open and raced down the hall, hearing him say to Adela, "What are you doing?"

"Mentally preparing."

"To dance with toddlers?"

She belted out a dry laugh. "Exactly."

After dressing in cutoffs and my Stevie Nicks T-shirt, I shoved some socks on, then rammed my feet into my floral Doc Martens.

Dragging a brush through my hair, I flipped my head forward and gathered it into a messy bun as I made haste to the door. "Bye, Del. Have fun with the babies!"

"Fuck you," she sang.

Everett and I both laughed, and he closed the door as soon as I barreled past.

"Where are we going?" I asked once we'd hit the sidewalk.

"My work."

With furrowing brows, I struggled to keep up with his fast pace. "Why?"

"Christ, Clover." He chuckled, grabbing my hand and hauling me along. "Can't a guy surprise you ever?"

"Not much of a fan of surprises."

"No shit."

I pulled my hand from his, and he snatched it back, kissing it.

We reached his work ten minutes later. "How long is your break?"

"Forty-five minutes."

I balked. "You would've spent more than half just coming to get me."

He dragged me around the side of the building. "Worth it, I hope."

I came to a stop when I saw the bags of mulch and gardening tools spread out on a yellow picnic blanket. Gloves, a wide brimmed hat, packets of seeds, and potted flowers.

"Barney needs this garden re-done. I've torn out all the weeds and laid it bare, but I thought you'd maybe want to do the rest."

It'd been years since I'd planted anything—since I'd left home—and I couldn't keep my smile from digging into my cheeks to save my life. Or the squeal of excitement that slipped out.

"I know it's not your own, but I just thought—"

"Shut up and hand me that shovel."

Everett's unfettered laugh was abrasive and music to the soul. After helping me get set up, and tearing open the bags of mulch, he plopped the hat atop my head. "I've gotta get to work, but I'll come check in if I can."

He wasn't able to come back until his shift was almost over, and the sight of him, sweat dotting his hairline and causing his shirt to plaster to every dip and mound of his chest, was enough to make me reach for the water bottle he had in his hand.

I drank greedily, then wiped my mouth before capping and handing it back.

"Wow." The word was a hoarse breath as he uncapped the water and surveyed the long row of California poppies I'd planted in front of what would be black-eyed Susans.

"You didn't waste any time, Clover."

I licked my already drying lips. "No, but I'll need to come back tomorrow after work to finish."

Barney trudged over, his gait still unsteady after coming off his bike. He whistled. "By golly, when the boy said he needed a favor, I didn't think I'd be the one benefiting."

"It's been fun." I slipped the gloves off. "I'll come back to-morrow if that's okay? I need to plant the last of the seeds and add more fertilizer."

"If that's okay?" Barney chortled, whacking Everett on the

back. "Where'd you find this girl? I had no idea Sabrina and Gloria were hiding a garden fairy in that little flower shop of theirs."

Everett scowled, which earned a laugh from me as I stood. "Call me Tinker Bell, and we'll need to have words."

Barney wheezed out a laugh, then waved us off, heading back inside the hardware store. "Hurry up, boy. We've got some crates with your name on them waiting to be unloaded before you leave."

Everett flicked his fingers over his head, indicating he'd be a minute. "Let me buy you lunch?"

I snorted. "Ah, no."

His lips parted, large shoulders dropping, and I smacked his chest with a glove. "It's after three, so I'll be buying you an early dinner."

His relieved smile colored my world, turning everything a shade lighter.

After showering, I sent Everett a text saying I'd meet him at his place, and that we'd eat at the bar.

He wasn't one for texting, and his replies were usually short and clipped, which never failed to make me laugh.

"You can't just respond with 'k'."

"Why not?" He dragged a fry through a puddle of ketchup, then popped it inside his mouth.

"It's not proper text etiquette."

He licked his lips, and my eyes dropped to them as he said, "Etiquette?"

It wasn't right for a word to sound so good. "Yup. It's rude. If someone makes the effort to reach out and ask you a question about your day, or hell, sends you a text about their shitty day, you can't simply say, 'that sucks,' or 'k,' or 'fine.'"

That glint in his eyes didn't dissipate. "Noted. When are you done with school?"

"Four-year degree. Two almost down, two to go."

Everett munched on more fries, his fingers tapping out a beat on the table. "You still want your own flower shop?"

"Or farm, I haven't decided."

"A farm would be wicked."

I smiled in agreement, barely daring to imagine it, when a middle-age guy, maybe older, in a crisp suit approached our booth. "You're not playing tonight?"

Everett took a bite out of another fry, offering a brief look at the stranger who was apparently not a stranger to him. "You're back."

The man smiled, then held out his hand to me. "Jack Keen. Keen Records."

My fry fell from my fingers, and I hastily scrubbed my palm over my cutoffs before shaking his hand. "Stevie."

His grin was all business but beautiful nonetheless. "Wonder?"

"Nicks." Everett took a sip of water, eyeing him over the rim of the glass.

"Even better," Jack said, gently releasing my hand.

A smile bloomed, but it wobbled when I saw the tightness in Everett's jaw. He was uncomfortable, at the very least.

"Have you thought about my offer?"

"Some." Everett lowered his glass. "Been a little busy."

Jack threw his gaze at me, giving me a quick once-over. "I see."

"You're interested in signing him?" I couldn't keep my mouth shut a second longer.

Everett sighed.

"Interested is putting it mildly. Perhaps you can talk some sense into him, Stevie." Jack shot me that devilish grin, then rapped his knuckles on the table, a business card sliding from between his fingers. "I'll be in the area another few days. Call me, we'll chat."

Everett didn't so much as nod, but his eyes dropped to the card, where they remained as Jack Keen waltzed past the bar.

Zoe looked from his retreating back to Everett and did a double take.

I shrugged when she gave me a questioning tilt of her head, then slid the metallic blue and black embossed card over to take a better look. "You don't want to." It wasn't a question.

"I don't want that lifestyle anymore, Clover."

"But you want the music." I tucked the card inside my purse, and he watched, lips rolling over one another. "Judging by the gleam in that shark's eyes, you could have whatever you want." I laughed, feeling a little lightheaded, then reached across the table to squeeze his hands. "On your terms."

"I just want you, my guitar, and some people to listen. That's it."

I nodded. "I get that. But just… at least think about it. You could do this for a living. A real, money in the bank, buy your own house and cars, not have to worry about Zoe's kids running up and down the stairs outside your apartment door, living."

His lips twitched. "They're not so bad."

"That's not what the bags underneath your eyes said when you told me they were trying to ride serving trays down the stairs."

He huffed out what would've been a laugh, but then swiped a palm down his face. "Let's leave it for tonight." His eyes teased. "'Kay?"

I snickered. "Fine."

He did laugh then, and we finished our food.

My attention stayed glued to my fries, but it was hard to eat, to think about anything other than the offer that could change Everett's life for the better.

Yet I was proud, so fucking proud of his ability to stare temptation in the face and say no because he didn't like the person he thought it'd make him become again. That didn't change the fact it was still an opportunity of a lifetime. It was everything they'd ever worked for.

And then the other reason hit me. "The band."

Everett exhaled a loud gust of air. "That too. Come on." He pushed his plate away, grabbing my purse.

I followed him upstairs, wondering how the rest of the band might take it if Everett accepted whatever deal this Jack guy might offer. I'd heard Hendrix was working at the local golf club and playing lifeguard on the weekends. Graham was studying at the local community college, and Dale was apparently trying to make it with his new YouTube channel. I had no idea what New Guy was doing.

Regardless of them knowing he needed it, it'd been a huge blow to the band, Mom had said when I'd asked how they'd taken Everett just walking away.

This would be yet another blow. One they might never recover from.

"Have you spoken to them lately?" I asked once we'd reached his room.

He shut the door, flicking the lock and tossing his keys onto his nightstand with my purse. "A bit. Mainly Hendrix. He sounds glad I'm doing well, not exactly ecstatic that I'm here with you, but he's not mad. Apparently, they're still playing at home when he can get them all together."

"He's singing?"

"Yeah," Everett said. "He's good, more pop-punk. Crowd would love it."

"Hmm." I flopped back onto his bed, bouncing a little. "I guess he is."

He grabbed my ankle, plucking my boots and socks off, then took a seat on the bed, shifting my feet to his lap.

I purred, actually purred, when he began rubbing them. "That's kind of gross, but it's so good I don't ever want you to stop."

A raspy chuckle flooded the room, knuckles kneading the flesh below my right foot. "I suppose you could say they're pissed. They truly believed we'd eventually make it, but being that we're friends, and they saw how messed up it made me, I think they're struggling with how to feel."

"Ha." I stabbed a finger at him. "They believed for good reason." That made me wonder, though. "Seriously, have you ever believed you guys were good enough?"

He swapped to my left foot. "Once upon a time, and we could've been, if I had taken it more seriously."

"The way you do when you play here."

"I'm just being me here."

"Well, that's what your new mate downstairs wanted." I groaned when his thumbs pressed beneath my toes.

"Shit." He groaned too. "Don't. Sounds like that make me desperate to be as deep as I can get inside you."

"Sorry." Yet my voice betrayed me as my body coiled tight. I cleared my throat and changed the subject. "Where's the bus now?"

"I think they've sold it."

I never would've expected that to sadden me, but it did. "Can I ask you something?"

"We've been over this. Just ask."

My tongue poked my cheek as I hesitated. "I know, but it's probably not something you want to talk about."

The bed dipped when he released my foot and came to lie down beside me. "Ask."

I fell back, rolling my head to face him. "Have you seen or heard from your parents since the first time you came back?"

"No." So carefully blank, his expression didn't change.

Still, my hands itched to comfort. "I'm sorry."

"Don't be." His teeth slid over his lip, the tiny chip in the front right one snagging my attention. "It's what I wanted, what I prefer, Clover."

Tickling fingers danced over the skin of my palm, and then interlaced with mine. "But they were better before..."

"Before Mason died?" His pitch deepened and lowered. "Yeah, but like I told you, nothing exceptional."

"I think being an exceptional parent would be kind of hard."

His top lip curved, lashes bobbing with his shifting eyes. "Your parents are exceptional."

"They're not perfect," I reminded him, "but they are kind of great."

"You don't need to be perfect to be exceptional." His words were but a low rasp, and it seemed like our faces had drifted closer. "In fact, the most brilliant people on earth are brilliant because of their imperfections."

It hit me like a rock slamming into my chest, robbing me of breath. I felt the dam begin to break, emotion coating my tongue. "Why was it so easy for you to leave me?"

His eyes flickered with pain, and his hand met the side of my face. "You thought it was easy?"

Unable to, I didn't answer.

He let out a short laugh, soaked in disbelief. "Clover, lying

to you, saying hurtful things to make you forget about me...
Next to losing Mason, those were some of the hardest things
I've ever done." His fingers whispered over my cheek. "Harder
than living in a house full of junkie drunks. Harder than stepping over glass ten times in the place I was meant to call a home
before learning to wear boots everywhere. Harder than having
my friends look at me with pity. Harder than having my dad hit
me until I grew old enough to fight back."

He blew out a tremulous breath that coasted over my lips.

"I didn't want you because I couldn't have you. I've wanted
you since I first saw you digging around in the dirt, planting and
nurturing. Since you smiled at me like I wasn't some grubby
loser outcast who'd just moved to town. Your soul"—his finger
brushed down my cheek, dipping over my chin and down my
throat, then landed on my chest over my erratic heart—"and
this beautiful thing inside here? It's pure sunshine, the best form
of warmth, and I'm sick of feeling like I have no right to it. I'm
sick of forcing myself to remain out in the cold."

I took his hand, bringing it to my mouth to kiss his scarred
knuckles. "Do you still think you're unworthy?" A wet laugh escaped. "Because that's the biggest load of shit I've ever heard,
Ever."

He grinned. "I'll never be worthy, but fuck if I even care
anymore. I want to deserve you, so I'm going to do just that."

Heat rushed through me, and the room seemed to shift
around us as I marveled at the admiration shining from those
green orbs. "Yeah?"

"Fuck yeah."

We moved at the same time, our lips meeting, teeth nip-
ping, and our hands clawing at our clothes. My teeth opened his
mouth for my tongue to skim inside and found his waiting.

A groan shook itself free of his throat, rumbling into mine

as he got my shorts unzipped and halfway down my legs. I flipped onto my back to kick them and my panties off, and he cupped my face, turning it back for his mouth to return to mine.

My hands searched and unzipped his fly while our tongues dipped and stroked in that raw, sensual synchronization they'd learned long ago.

Home. Kissing Everett, having his hands stroke over my thigh to my hip, raising my T-shirt, felt like coming home.

"Tell me," he said into my mouth as I tried to sneak my hand inside his pants. "Tell me you love me."

"You already know I do," I whispered. "I never stopped."

His eyes closed, a hissed breath cutting past his lips and over mine when I wrapped my hand around him. "God, I need you."

I moved my leg, and he took the opening, his fingers racing down my stomach, leaving chills in their wake to drift through my arousal.

Feather soft, he explored, evoking breathy sounds from me as I watched his eyes darken and felt him grow impossibly hard in my hand. A thick finger prodded at my entrance, gently pushing inside. A gleam lit his eyes, that velvet voice. "Look what I do to you."

I garbled out some kind of response, and his finger retreated, moving to my clit and circling.

Then he tore away, kicking off his jeans and briefs, and I laid on my back as he loomed larger than life above me, tugging off his shirt.

He'd filled out even more, probably since he'd stopped drinking so much and started working at the hardware store. Columns of packed muscle bunched as he lowered over me, his cock bobbing before the tiny hairs of his sculpted lower abdomen, and his hands lifted my shirt.

Strong yet gentle, they skimmed over my skin, lifting the material to my chin. He pulled it over my head, leaving it there as I felt his mouth drop to my pink laced bra.

Damp heat wrapped around my nipple, teeth pulling the cup down and hands pushing mine over my head.

Wrapping his tongue around one of the hardened buds, he grumbled out, "Fuck, I've missed these tits." He moved to the other, giving it the same attention while one hand left mine. It ended up between my thighs, and a finger dunked inside to fuck me, slow and deep.

It was heady, too much, being laid out like this. My legs spread as his fingers tortured and his hot mouth laved at my breasts. I couldn't see anything, only shadows through the material of the shirt that was heating with every breath I struggled to take. It heightened every touch, stroke, sound, and breath.

"Everett," I warned. "You'll make me come before—"

"I don't care. Soaked isn't good enough. I want you dripping. I want to hear it when I sink inside you." His breathing was growing labored, matching my own as he murmured against my skin, curling his finger inside. "When I fuck you, I want you shaking from what I've done to you, from what I do to you."

"Shit," I choked out, my body stilling as ripples of tingling heat spread from between my legs, shooting everywhere.

He gripped my quaking thighs, and then he was inside me in one quick thrust.

My legs clamped around his back, and I rode the heavy aftershocks his invasion caused to roll through me.

He tugged at the shirt, and I tore it off, throwing it to the floor as my desperate hands grabbed for his face. His lips caressed, his hips gyrating into mine, circling and grinding.

A groan penetrated my foggy thoughts every time he slid

out before driving back in. "I swear to God, Clover. It's just me who gets this heaven now." His lips brushed my cheek, moving to my ear to suck the lobe. "Understand?"

"You can't leave." I couldn't stop myself from setting my worst fear free. "You can't fucking leave, Everett."

He paused, his hips, his mouth—all of him—stilling, and raised his head to stare down at me.

Thumbing a tear from my eye, he shook his head, remorse lining his forehead. "I'm here to stay, Stevie. So tell me, are you all mine?"

My smile wobbled as I pushed thoughts of dark eyes aside. I wrapped my arms around him, then rolled, shoving his chest until he was on his back, and I was sitting on his cock. "Does it not feel like I am?"

My hips rotated, and he sat up, hands moving up my back to grip my shoulders and push me down until I swallowed all of him and all breath had fled my lungs. My head fell back, and his lips pressed into my throat. "Now it does."

Once I'd adjusted, I clung to his neck, my lips hovering over his as we both rocked our hips. A slow climb to ecstasy, an overwhelming sensation different from all the times we'd had sex before, but no less fervent in potency.

"So wet, so fucking warm." His voice was as soft as the fingers stroking my back, tangling in my hair, and coasting over my ass. There was no room between our chests, our hearts echoing the same frenzied beat. "Do you feel me everywhere?"

"Every-fucking-where." I gazed into his eyes, watched them ignite before his lips took mine, and I felt his finger glide down my ass.

I tensed. "Trust me?"

After a prolonged beat, I nodded.

He brought his fingers between us to my mouth. "Lick."

He groaned, hips jolting beneath me as I licked and sucked the two thick digits. "Your cunt tastes good, doesn't it?"

My breath hitched as heat crawled into my cheeks, and my body squeezed his in response.

He chuckled. "So god damn beautiful."

Our mouths met again, sliding over each other as his fingers found the tiny opening and began to rub. I jerked over him, and we both moaned.

He didn't push inside, for which I was thankful. I wasn't sure if I was ready or down for that, but the wet tickle of his finger was enough to make my thighs clench tighter around his hips, and all too soon, that tingling heat returned.

Our climax wasn't fast and swift, it wasn't pounded and beaten from us, but rather, coaxed through the slow reconciliation of our bodies.

My clit rubbed against him as he filled me deeper than ever before. I felt him twitch, felt the break in his exhale as his lips faltered over mine, and we barreled into shared orgasms that had us dissolving and melting.

Afterward, his forehead on mine and our skin sweat-misted, we clung to every sensation, our lips fused as it faded.

TWENTY-EIGHT

"**D**O YOU REALLY THINK THEY'LL BE UP FOR THIS?"
We'd borrowed Adela's car and were on our way home.

For the first time since I'd left last Christmas, I didn't dread returning. I felt only slight nerves for what might happen when we got there and told everyone the news.

My hand hugged Everett's as we traversed the back streets of Plume Grove, nearing the beach. "I think they'll play hard to get, but I'll give you back door entrance if they say no."

Everett barked out a laugh, then paused, glancing over at me behind his Ray-Bans. "Wait, seriously?"

He'd been trying to ease me into it in the weeks since we'd reunited and crashed together in a way that still sent ripples of warmth cascading down my arms. Every time since had been an adventure, had evoked sensations that'd laid dormant, waiting for his touch, but that first time… it'd felt like a new beginning. And I'd never felt a beginning shake me in ways like that. In ways no orgasm ever could.

"Seriously." I hoped like hell they were on board. Anything the size of his cock had no business trying to fit into a place as small as my ass. It didn't seem like a fun time to me.

Everett shifted in the driver's seat, releasing my hand to tug at his jeans. "Number one thousand and twenty-two."

"What?"

He spared his parents' house the briefest of glimpses before pulling into my parents' driveway. "The number of hard-ons you've given me when I'm around your family."

I clicked off my seat belt, reaching below my legs for my purse. "Only a thousand? We'll need to work on that."

"You're gonna be the end of me, Clover."

Grinning, I went to climb out when he grabbed me, pulling my face to his for those lips to kiss mine. "I love you."

"I love you." So surreal that after years of longing, of dreaming for this moment, it was actually happening.

I just prayed that walking inside that house together, making that big of a statement, didn't burst this feeling that kept expanding every time I was with him.

We made it to the porch steps before the door was flung open, and Mom came rushing out.

Her arms squeezed us both, her eyes glassy as she kissed our cheeks. "I've got no idea what you two are up to, but I'm just…" She blew out a breath, stepping back with her hand over her chest. "So happy you're all here again."

Dad stood in the doorway with a pensive look on his face as he studied me and Everett.

I forced my lips into a smile, and his features softened. More hugs were had, and he clapped Everett on the back, whispering something to him that sounded like, "You really don't wanna fuck this up, kiddo."

Inside, we followed them to the living room, where the rest of the guys, even New Guy, sat sprawled over the couches.

Hendrix on his beanbag, thumbs moving across the screen of his phone, muttered, "Not even kidding."

"I need me a job at the golf club," Graham said.

"You wouldn't score as well as Hendrix, man. Don't waste your time." Mom cleared her throat, and Dale's eyes widened before he pasted on that smarmy, mischievous smile. "Well, well."

Everyone looked up, and I went to remove my hand from Everett's, but his grip tightened.

"To what do we owe this pleasure?" Graham crossed one leg over the other, his polo shirt looking a little more snug as his arms spread over the back of the couch.

New Guy moved away from him a little.

"Enough with the Shakespearean shit." Hendrix slipped his phone away.

"That's not Shakespeare, you fucktard."

"Language, ladies," Dad said, taking a seat on the only spare couch, then gestured for Mom to join him.

"So are you two lovebirds going to take a seat?" Dale rubbed his brow. "Or do you wanna continue standing there like stunned mullets?"

We moved into the room and sat on the floor near the fireplace. I crossed my legs quickly, cursing the fact I'd donned a dress. "We have news."

"Yeah? Pregnant?"

Mom's eyes popped. "Hendrix."

Hendrix shrugged. "What else could this broken family meeting be about?"

Everett spoke then. "Keen Records. We've been offered a recording deal."

Silence permeated the room, thicker than the heat invading the opened windows.

Hendrix opened his mouth, closed it, then opened it again. "H-How?"

Everett shook his head. "That doesn't matter. What matters is Jack Keen wants us in the studio within the next thirty days. So"—he glanced around—"are we in?"

Everyone spoke at once, yelling, cheering, shouting, cussing, and then finally, Hendrix's voice broke over the commotion.

"Wait, wait, wait." He leveled Everett with a look colder than ice. "How do we know you're not bullshitting?"

I opened my purse, dug for Everett's phone, and handed it to him.

Dale tutted. "You finally got a phone and didn't even call? Harsh, man."

"It was only recent, and shut up, I don't know your number." Everett found Jack's name, then set the phone on speaker on the rug below us as it rang.

It reached voicemail, and Jack's voice echoed, "It's Jack, leave a message that won't waste my time."

Hendrix scoffed, collapsing into the beanbag. "Of course."

Everyone seemed to deflate, even Mom, who was pursing her lips with her hand tight in Dad's.

Everett didn't seem bothered and just twiddled his thumbs, waiting.

The phone rang, and he answered after the third ring. "Yeah."

"Sorry, man. Was racing to get back into the office in time. They all there?"

Everett's eyes lifted to the stunned faces of his friends, his family, and he grinned. "They're all here."

Jack's sharp laughter filled the room. "Okay, so what's the verdict, boys?"

"Then the old bastard had the nerve to say it looked like a pancake."

Sabrina choked on her laughter, coughing and sputtering as she wiped beneath her eyes. "Pancake ass. Oh, my dear lord."

I set the tape down, drumming my fingers over the counter-top. "How old are you two again?"

Gloria ran her hand over my hair as she flitted by the counter. "Never too old to joke about the shape of one's ass, my darling."

"Damn right," Sabrina agreed, still snickering as she bent down to sort through the cellophane. "He was right, though."

"You love it," Gloria shouted.

A text came through, and I nabbed my phone from beside the register.

Ever: If I have to listen to Dale and Jack fight one more time...

I smirked, then read the one he'd sent straight after.

Ever: Oh yeah. Have I told you I love you today?

The band had started rehearsing at a converted warehouse studio Jack owned. They were there from dawn until dusk, six days a week. Some nights, Everett didn't get home until almost midnight, judging by the texts he'd send. We weren't living to-gether, but I stayed at his place Friday through Monday. I'd hoped to spend more time with him now that school was out, but it seemed pointless to hang around in his room without him there.

The past month had been a whirlwind of band meetings, practices, and argument after argument. Mom and Adela had a good point, though, when they'd told me to steer clear and let them sort it out. They needed to clear the air in order to create and focus on what they all wanted. Left with little time, they only had enough material for half an album and failed to agree on anything new.

I began tapping out a response when another message came through, this time from Adela. I accidentally opened it but figured I'd respond quickly.

Adela: I'm fresh out of supplies. Can I steal some until I can get to the shop later?

Me: Knock yourself out.

Clicking back to Everett's message, I got halfway through typing a reply when it hit me.

I usually had my period at least a week before Adela got hers.

The phone slipped from my hand, clattering to the wooden surface.

Gloria glanced over her shoulder. "You okay?"

Then Sabrina's hand was in my face, waving. "Shit. What the hell is wrong?"

"I think she might faint. Quick, get the spray bottle."

"You get the spray bottle. You're closer."

Their hands started slapping at my face, and I pushed them off. "I'm fine. I'm fine. I just… I have to go."

There was no point in worrying until I knew for sure. These things happened. There'd been a few times when my period had been so light, I'd wondered what the point of it even was.

I raced into the back room for my purse. "I'm sorry. I'll be back tomorrow."

"Not if you're still as pale as a sheet of paper," Sabrina said. "Oh, hey, your phone."

I backtracked, mumbling my thanks as they watched me with mirroring looks of concern. "I'm okay," I repeated, hoping it was true, praying it was true. "I swear."

Then I was out the door, practically running down the street in my haste to get to the drugstore.

I purchased three tests, different brands, and didn't so much as glance at the young girl working the checkout as I threw a fifty-dollar bill down and scooped up the boxes, then dropped them into my purse.

One fell out as I was exiting the store, and I bent over to pick it up, when someone wearing familiar looking boots and black jeans beat me to it.

If I wasn't going to faint back at the shop, I feared it was about to happen now.

"I'd ask how you are, Petal, but I think I've caught you at a bad time."

TWENTY-NINE

WITH MY HEART SINKING LIKE A STONE, I TOOK THE BOX FROM HIS hand and shoved it into my purse as my eyes welled.

Then I turned around and kept on walking.

"Whoa, wait."

"Can't. As you said, bad time. And even if it wasn't, I've got nothing to say to you."

"That test says differently."

The words raced out, scraping over my tongue before I could think better of it. "If I am pregnant, we both know it's not yours."

Aiden stopped, and so did I. Passersby moved around us as color leeched from his face.

That freaking face that hadn't changed, save for the thick coat of stubble that now seemed to be a permanent feature.

His eyes, dark and impenetrable, closed, then reopened and focused on the ground.

"I'm sorry." It was a rasp. "But you've been gone for months, Aiden."

"Five months, which, apparently, is long enough." His chest heaved with a loaded exhale. "Everett?"

I didn't want to say it. Didn't like how even thinking the word felt like a betrayal. To both men. Even though I'd done nothing wrong other than fall for them both.

So I said nothing and left, holding my purse close to my chest until I was locked behind the comfort of our bright blue front door.

I slid down it, my purse falling to the floor, the tests inside spilling out as my hand sank into my hair, tugging.

Real. It was all too damn real.

I'd gone on the pill. I'd made the doctor's appointment after the first time Everett and I had sex in his tiny room.

Time sped by as I stared at the boxes, counting and measuring all the ways life would change if those tests were positive. Then it slowed when I thought about them being negative.

Either way, choices would need to be made.

What was Aiden doing here? The season wasn't over yet.

Squeezing my eyes shut at the thought of telling Everett that Aiden had returned, that I'd taken these tests, and that I could be pregnant caused an ache to bloom behind my skull.

I forced myself off the ground, forced myself to pick the tests up, and forced myself into the bathroom where I carefully read the instructions.

Ten minutes later, I was trying to swallow a knot the size of my fist as I stared at all three tests. All three—very much positive—tests.

I was fucking pregnant.

After letting the shock, fear, and a small kernel of excitement drip from my eyes, I spent the next hour with them as I tried to go over all the things I'd need to do next.

Number one was tell Everett, but he wouldn't be home for hours, and I wasn't about to text him news like this.

Number two was call the doctor.

Number three was call my mom and have her come and hold me until this mess got figured out.

Unfortunately, I could only do one of those, so I called my doctor and scored an appointment for the next afternoon after work.

I ran myself a bath, ignored Gloria's call, and sent her a text saying I was fine, then I curled up in my robe on my bed and stared at the wall.

Everett. The band. Aiden. My degree.

What the hell were we going to do?

Gentle hands brushed hair from my face, and I blinked open weighted lids to find Everett seated on the side of my bed.

His eyes were rimmed in red, exhaustion pulling at his plump lips. Golden light danced across the dusty blond hair curling around his face, bathing him and the room in peach as the sun approached the horizon.

"You finished early?" I found that hard to believe.

"You didn't answer my calls or texts."

Oh. I reached for my phone, but it wasn't there. It was in his hand.

"I got worried." The subtle note of wariness to his voice had hair rising on my arms.

I pushed them beneath me and rose to sit.

My hands shook, combing through my hair while I contemplated how best to tell him the news. "I, um, I need to tell you something."

He didn't move or speak for an extended minute, but then he handed over my phone and stood from the bed. "Does it have anything to do with Aiden texting you?"

"What?" I lit up my phone and saw what he was talking about. I had two texts from Everett, asking how I was, if I was okay, and then three missed calls.

Above those was a text from Aiden.

Prince: Pregnant or not, I still need to talk to you.

He hadn't gotten a new number then. He'd just blocked mine.

"Pregnant?" Everett roused my foggy brain. "Is that true?" With his eyes skating over my flat stomach, he began pacing my room, his undone laces slapping against heavy boots. "And how the fuck would he know?"

"I ran into him when I was leaving the drugstore today, and one of the tests fell out of my purse." I snorted. "Awesome timing."

Everett didn't laugh, not that I'd expected him to.

I sighed. "According to three tests, I am. I have a doctor's appointment tomorrow afternoon to confirm."

His pacing ceased. "You went on the pill."

"After we'd had sex. We didn't exactly follow the rules." I puffed out a half-laugh. "Ever."

That earned me a glimmer of a smile.

"Come here," I whispered. "Don't leave me alone in this."

"Fuck," he groaned, his hand in his hair as he returned to me. He dropped his hand, then dropped to his knees beside the bed. "I'm being a dick, only thinking about how I feel about this. I'm sorry."

While I wasn't exactly over the moon, the idea of having his child had beads of warmth planting in my stomach. "You don't want to go through with it."

His eyes widened, and he pressed his lips to mine, kissing me several times. "No, it's not that. I'm shocked, Clover. You and a baby, I would never have dared to hope for something like this. I just..."

"Just?"

He released me, and I watched the green of his eyes fade

as worry crept close to the surface. "I just hope I can be enough for you."

"Are you going to be here?"

"Yes," he said instantly.

"Then that's enough."

He frowned. "What about school?"

"I can finish online or after the baby is born." I smoothed my hand over his cheek. "Let's wait until I've been to the doctor before we get too carried away."

He nodded, turning to lay a kiss on my palm, then he lowered his head to my stomach, his lashes lowering as I ran my nails through his hair.

"You're tired."

He ignored my comment. "Aiden. Are you going to see him?"

He'd see right through my lies unless they held some truth. "I would love to hear what he has to say for himself, but I don't need to."

"Why?" Gazing up, he narrowed his eyes. "Why do you want to hear it?"

I swallowed, mulling over an answer that might make him understand, even if only a little. "He hurt me, Everett."

"I was there, right here." Anger laced his voice. "I know."

I nodded.

"Don't see him." The words were a rushed plea. "I don't want him anywhere near you."

"Ever," I tried.

"No. I know that makes me a controlling dick, but so be it." His eyes and his tone were hard. "No, Clover."

"You have nothing to worry about." The lie tasted foul on my tongue. I would never hurt Everett like that, but emotionally, when it came to Aiden, I still was. I still hadn't let go. And after seeing him that morning, I was worried I might never be able to.

"I do. You're not seeing him. What time is this appointment tomorrow?"

I blinked. "Three forty-five. But you have to be at the studio."

"I'll meet you there." He stood, pulling me off the bed, his arms banding around me as he sang low to my lips. "Now let's get you fed before I feed you my cock."

"So bossy and crass."

He squeezed my ass.

I laughed when he turned, causing my back to meet the closed door, and framed my face with his hands before devouring my mouth.

THIRTY

RUE TO HIS WORD, EVERETT MET ME AT THE DOCTOR'S OFFICE where they ran tests and called me back two days later for the results.

He made sure he was there for that too as the doctor gave us a rough due date of the tenth of February, then handed over a mountain of pamphlets. Which meant the lighter period I'd had in May wasn't just a light period. I'd been spotting, as I was apparently ten weeks along already.

I had a moment when I did the math in my head, counting back to when Aiden and I had last been together at my parents' house over Christmas. Then I laughed like a crazed woman, realizing how stupid the thought was. It was impossible. I was relieved, if only for the fact that every time I thought of Aiden, I still remembered the way he'd left me crumpled and discarded on the sidewalk at the start of the year.

After my unnecessary freak-out, I felt like the biggest idiot. Adela had a good laugh over it too. To say she was shocked when I'd told her I was pregnant would be an overstatement. She'd jumped off the couch, screaming with her arms in the air, hollering that Dale owed her a hundred dollars.

Now if I could just tell Gloria and Sabrina and maybe my mom without throwing up, that'd be fantastic.

As it was, I wasn't feeling nauseous, but my boobs ached, which I'd attributed to hormones when Everett had squeezed them too hard.

Turns out, I didn't need to say a word.

"You're pregnant," Gloria greeted, hands on her hips when I walked into work that Friday.

"Uh, hey?" I blinked; the door slammed behind me, wind chimes dancing.

"When were you going to tell us?" Gloria's eyes were doing that weird rounding thing they did when she was getting pissed.

"When you didn't look like you might kill me?" I offered a weak smile.

Sabrina finished with an arrangement, then set it down and opened her arms. "Oh, she's just messing with you. Come here."

I went to her, my emotions climbing as her scent and arms enveloped me.

Gloria clucked her tongue, then groaned. "Fine, but I wanted Aiden."

I could feel Sabrina give her the eyeball over my shoulder, and then Gloria was hugging me too.

I started blubbering like a baby, and they began to coo and pet my hair as I mumbled out incoherent things. "Didn't know. And I don't know if I'm ready. And Aiden's b-back. I'm not even twenty-one yet. And I don't want to see him. And oh, my God, I'm having a fucking baby."

The wind chimes sang as a customer walked in. "Um, I just came by to grab some—"

"Later, Allen," Sabrina said. "Shoo." The chimes sang again as he retreated. "Have you told your mom yet?"

"No." I stepped out of their embrace, thanking Gloria when she handed me a tissue. "I don't know how. Everett and me…" I blew my nose, then dabbed at the mascara trails beneath my eyes. "We've only just gotten to a place where we feel like we're finally able to do this."

"Having a baby won't make anyone mad at you, darling." Gloria rubbed my back.

"Your mom might even be excited," Sabrina offered. "When she gets over the shock of becoming a grandma of course."

"Not helping." Gloria glared.

"Why don't you head home for the day?" Sabrina tucked some hair behind my ear. "Put your feet up, or hey, maybe—"

The door opened again, and I looked over to see Everett walk in wearing a megawatt grin, the kind rarely seen on him.

It fell when he caught sight of me, and then he was rushing over, collecting me to him. "What happened?" His tone was sharp but not accusing.

Ensnared in the crisp clean scent of his black T-shirt with his arms around me, I struggled to remember why I'd been so worried. "I was just having a moment. I'm okay."

Framing my face, his hands tipped it back to search my eyes. "A moment?"

I nodded, sniffing and smiling. "I guess my hormones are going to be crazier than normal."

His thumbs brushed beneath my eyes, removing the wet smudges, and his lips pressed into a tight line. "You should've called me."

"It only just happened."

He peeked over my shoulder at Gloria and Sabrina, then returned his attention to me. With his hands brushing up and down my arms, he drew in a ragged breath. "I fucking hate seeing you cry."

"I'm sorry."

His brows furrowed, lips twitching. "Don't apologize."

"What are you doing here?" The way he kept bailing when he needed to be recording this album wasn't right. They'd barely gotten started, and I wasn't sure how Jack and the rest of the band kept allowing it.

Then again, it was Everett. He did what he wanted when he wanted to.

"I have something for you."

I tilted my head, my gaze questioning, then I looked at Gloria and Sabrina, who were wearing secretive smiles. They knew about whatever this was.

Everett clasped my hand, and his smile returned, curving his lips and warming my chest. "Come on."

Outside, I stopped on the sidewalk when he pulled a set of keys from his pocket and hit the key fob, unlocking a Volkswagen SUV. "Um..."

"It's yours," he said, opening the door.

"What?" I dragged my eyes from the excitement dancing over his face and carefully stepped closer to the red car. "It's mine?"

"Did you really think you'd be able to get around town with just a stroller?" He laughed. "We need a car, Clover."

Perched on the back seat was a baby seat, still in the box. My hand rose to my mouth, my eyes watering yet again. "Holy shit, Everett."

He rubbed my back. "Red. It was that or yellow, which they didn't have. I couldn't picture you in anything dull."

"How did you...?" I stopped, glaring at him. "You used your advance? God, Everett, that's to help you live until this album starts making some money." He couldn't work at the hardware store with the kind of hours they had to put in at the studio.

"It's fine." Sincere and firm, he said, "Trust me."

Those two words had my shoulders relaxing. Marginally. "You could have bought something cheaper. This would've been expens—"

"Clover." He groaned. "Would you quit riding my ass and get in the damn car?"

I planted my hands on my hips, ready to ream him out, then stopped when his mouth caught mine. His hands sank into my hair, and he kissed me until I could hardly breathe, let alone remember what I'd been worried about.

"Where are we going?" I asked after he'd tucked me inside.

"Studio. If I'm gone too long, they'll have a tantrum." He turned the car around and headed through town toward the highway. "Besides, I like it when you're there."

"Just..." My eyes were zigzagging everywhere. The gear shift, the stereo, the leather seats. "Wow."

"You over your shock enough to admit you like it?"

With my fingers gliding over the center console, where two bottles of cold water were perspiring, a small laugh tumbled out. "I fucking love it."

Everett slipped on his sunglasses. "I love you. Now drink some water. You've been crying too much."

I did as I was told, and for the first time since we'd found out about this pregnancy, I felt like everything really would be okay.

"I guess things are getting serious," Graham drawled around the butt of his cigarette, wearing a shit-eating grin as he watched us cross the lot to the refurbed warehouse.

"Mind your business, G." Everett lit up his own smoke, then waved at the door. "Head inside, I'll be there in a few."

Waves of heat curled over the ground, raising goose bumps on my skin. I pushed the door open, relieved the A/C was up high.

"Well, look who it is." Hendrix gave a slight smile from where he sat on a blood red leather couch, tuning his guitar. "How you doing, Steve?"

"Good." I turned in the open plan space. "Where is everyone?"

A thud from the window across the warehouse made me jump, and there was New Guy and Dale behind the window of the control room, waving.

"How's it coming?"

"Slow," Hendrix grumbled.

"Why? Something happen?" I moved to the couch, taking a seat near him.

"These things take time. A lot more work than any of us would've guessed, but aside from that." He eyed me a moment, then shook his head. "Your boyfriend keeps happening."

About to ask what he meant, I paused when a guy I didn't know came in through a side door with a headset wrapped around his neck. "Ready yet?"

"Yeah, he's back." Hendrix stood, looping his guitar strap around his neck.

The guy nodded, heading into the control room with barely a glance my way.

"Did he seriously buy you a car?"

My hands became interesting, and I ran my fingers over each other. "He did."

Hendrix laughed, a low, gruff sound. "Well, at least he's doing one thing right."

"What's that supposed to mean?"

"It means exactly what I said, Steve." He sighed. "Look, I'm over it. I really am. You two being together. But he's the master of half-assing shit, and you know it."

"He's been working hard," I tried to defend.

"Right. When he's here, and when he's here, he's only half here."

"I'm pregnant," I blurted.

"Excuse me?" Hendrix backed up a step, his eyes layered with exhaustion, bulging. "For real?"

I nodded. "We found out about a week ago, so it's my fault he's probably been distracted."

Hendrix scrubbed at his mouth. "Huh."

I wasn't expecting him to be happy about it, but it felt good to tell him the truth instead of hiding it for a change. "I'm not quite three months along yet, so…"

Hendrix nodded. "Yeah." He nodded again. "Yeah, I won't say shit. Mom and Dad know?"

I brushed my hands over my blue polka-dotted skirt. "Not yet. We've been trying to wrap our heads around it first."

"What about school?" he asked. "You're what, only halfway done?"

"Hendrix, don't."

"Don't what? Remind you of the life this kid will be interrupting? The one my asshole friend keeps interrupting?"

I stared up at him, beseeching. "I'm happy. He makes me happy."

Our gazes stayed locked a minute, and I almost lost the precarious hold on my emotions when his eyes misted. "'Kay, Steve." A smile crawled into place as he walked over and chucked me under the chin, his guitar pick poking into my skin. "If you're happy, I'll try to ignore the bullshit and be happy too."

"Thank you," I croaked, rising and wrapping my arms around him, sneaking beneath his guitar.

His fingers glossed over my hair, and he whispered, "Just don't let him treat you like shit, all right? Promise me."

"I won't, and he's not. I promise."

We stepped back, and he rammed his hands into his hair, pulling it in two different directions as he chuckled. "An uncle. Well, shit."

"What's happening?" Dale's voice boomed into the room. "Let's go already."

I glanced over to see him flapping his hands in the window. "I guess he's still taking his job as momager seriously?"

"Fucken' oath, he is." Hendrix flipped Dale off. "But in all honesty, we'd be worse off without him."

"Agreed," Everett said, entering the cavernous space and striding toward me.

"The only time I wanna see those flimsy ass fingers move is when you're bent over your guitar, asshole. Time is money, and you're all fucking wasting it." A shriek from the speakers followed Dale's shouted words, and I winced, rubbing my ear.

Everett took me by the waist, and I kissed his chest, whispering, "Hendrix knows. I told him." Craning my neck back, I found his gaze riddled with questions, but I just smiled. "He's okay. You need to go." Looking like he was about to protest, I stabbed a finger at his chest. "I'll be here, and I'll be fine."

He exhaled a frustrated breath but conceded and grabbed his guitar, which had been lying on the couch, before following Hendrix into the adjacent room.

I took a seat again, realizing I'd left my purse at work. But it didn't matter.

When that recording light came on, I rested my head back against the couch and relaxed.

THIRTY-ONE

ALKING THROUGH THE SHOP AND OUT INTO THE DARKENING street, I checked my phone. A missed call from Aiden had my steps faltering as I neared my car.

I thought he would've left. But he'd tried to call at least every second day over the past few weeks and had even sent texts. I ignored them.

I didn't want to dish out the same treatment he'd fed me, but things with Everett were good, and no matter how much I longed to speak to him, to just hear his voice and see how he was doing, regardless of what'd happened, I didn't want to mess that up. We'd even scheduled my first sonogram for early next week.

I stared at his name a moment longer, then pushed the temptation away and drove home.

Pulling over outside the house, I grabbed my bag and jumped out, then almost screamed when I caught a dark figure standing near the hedges lining the walkway to my front door.

With a hand over my pattering chest, I murmured, "Aiden?"

"Figured the only way to get you to see me would be to wait for you at sunset like a true stalker." His attempt at humor fell flat, and he raked a hand over his thick hair, which had grown out on top, but was cropped close to his scalp on the sides. "I'm sorry, Stevie."

"I watched a couple of your games," I said, for lack of anything else to say. "You're doing great."

"Was," he said with a sigh. "I don't know if I'm going back."

My feet shifted, my keys digging into my palm. "You're under contract. You have to."

"My dad's one of the best attorneys in the state. You think he'd let me sign something without an escape clause?" He chuckled. "Besides, some little blonde thing was taking up too much room in my brain."

I blinked. "But the model…"

Grimacing, that dimple popped in his cheek as he tucked a hand in his pocket. "You fucked me up, Stevie. For the longest time, I didn't think I'd ever want to see you again."

"Yet you're here." A gentle statement.

"I'm here."

I cleared my throat. "I thought you would've left after, well, you know."

"Finding out you're pregnant with that asshole's baby? Yeah, I thought I would've too. I tried, but I don't know, something stops me every time."

It hurt. It cut and burned me to say it. "Don't let that something be me, Aiden."

His dark eyes caught mine, locking tight. "You don't get to tell me what to do or how to feel."

I was being plucked at the seams. Everything that I'd tried to bury resurfaced within minutes. "I need to get inside." I made to walk by him, but he slid his hand around my wrist.

Voice low, with vehemence shouting at me through his eyes, he said, "I don't care if you're having his kid." He bit his lips, then shook his head. "No, I do fucking care. It kills me, Petal. But I can't just stop loving you because that's happened. I wish I could, but I can't."

Tears blurred. "Stop."

"No, so I'm here. I'm here until you're willing to talk to me."

"There's nothing to talk about. At the first sign of trouble, you left. You blocked me from your life completely."

"So he can do that to you for years, but I can't fuck up once?"

"Fuck you, Aiden. That's different." I tried to pull free, but his grip tightened.

"It's not, and you know it. Yeah, his brother died. That's fucking terrible, but it doesn't give him a right to stomp all over you because he's still saddled with guilt."

Horrified, I wrenched my wrist free. "You're a real bastard, you know that?"

"You're only saying that because you know it's true. My mom died when I was just a kid. Do you see me acting like a self-absorbed shithead?"

A shallow laugh left me. "Yeah, actually. I do."

His eyes closed, and he set free a loud exhale. "I'm sorry. It's just—"

"How about instead of trying to make your absence seem more acceptable than his, you just fucking apologize and admit you were wrong? Because you were, Aiden. You were wrong to judge what you saw before giving me a chance to explain. You were wrong to leave me broken on the sidewalk as you drove away. And you were wrong to ignore me for weeks on end when I so desperately needed you."

I stopped, drawing in a burning breath as tears rimmed my eyes. "You were wrong because I wanted it to be you, and all I wanted was you." My voice caught. "But then you left."

"Stevie." He grabbed my face. "Don't cry. Fuck."

My head flopped to his chest, and the scent of his cologne had me shaking as I tried to steady my breathing and push everything back down.

"I fucking love you," he whispered, choked. "You're having his baby. I don't know how to compete with that, but I can't leave."

That broke the spell, and I moved back. "I'm not asking you to compete with anything."

Panic struck his expression. "You're right. What I did was beyond messed up, but you have me by the balls. You have since the day I first saw you. I didn't want to share your heart, so I needed to see if I could shake you."

"All or nothing," I said quietly, a pinching tightness clamping around said heart. "Turns out, I'm not exactly able to just stop loving someone."

Aiden stepped forward, the moon highlighting the pained angles of his cheeks. "I can try—"

A throat cleared down on the sidewalk, and my blood ceased flowing, every muscle in my body freezing as Everett came into view. "You can fuck off now."

Aiden closed his eyes. When he reopened them, that troublesome glint had reappeared. "I'm good where I am, thanks."

Everett's jaw turned to stone as he eyed where I stood on the steps, then he marched over, getting right up in Aiden's face. "I was being polite, so let me rephrase that. Get the fuck out of here before I rip that smarmy smile off your pretty boy face."

My ears began to ring.

"Aww, you think I'm pretty?" Aiden drawled, stepping chest to chest with Everett. "You're kind of sweet for a drunk."

With a growl, Everett shoved Aiden, hard, and I raced down the steps, screaming at them to stop. "Cut it out. Aiden, go home."

"Sure." He steadied himself, then brushed his hands down his chest, eyes thinned on Everett before he flashed me that crooked smile. "You know where to find me, Petal."

"The fuck did he just call you?" Everett headed for Aiden's retreating back.

"Everett, stop." I forced as much as I could into the words. "Please."

They were still evenly matched in height and weight. But even though Aiden was likely fitter, stronger, Everett knew how to throw his weight around and fight dirty.

Thankfully, he stopped, shoulders tense, and watched Aiden zoom down the street in his Audi.

Hardly daring to breathe, I waited for him to turn around.

Crickets pierced the air, the warm breeze doing nothing to wash away the cold icing my skin.

With his back to me, Everett's question hit my ears, a threatening but soft cadence. "Do you still love him?"

Chills swept up my arms and wrapped around my vocal cords.

No sound came out of me, even as I opened my mouth to... what? Try to reassure him in some way? I didn't want to lie, but I didn't want to admit the heart-searing truth we'd skated over these past few months either.

A self-deprecating laugh rumbled out, and he turned, pinning me where I stood with a glacial fog filming his green eyes. "You can't even lie to me, can you? Just once." He lowered his head, his hand sinking into his hair. "Fuck, Stevie."

Panic forced my feet into action when he took off, rounding the corner. "You said you wouldn't leave."

He stopped but didn't look at me. "I'm not going anywhere, but I can't be near you right now."

Then he was gone, and me and my malfunctioning heart were on our own.

A whole day passed before I was finally able to breathe easier.

I rushed to pick up my phone. "Hello?"

The sound of guitars and laughter filled the background, and then his voice. "Clover. Tell me you love me."

"I love you. I'll always love you."

His heavy exhale swamped my ear. "I'll pick you up after we get done. You're staying at my place tonight."

He hung up, and I smiled, setting the phone down.

"I take it everything is right again in the world?" Adela asked, towel drying her hair in my doorway.

"Yeah," I said, ignoring the prick that stabbed at my chest. "I think it is."

She gave me a weak smile before walking away.

THIRTY-TWO

F AIDEN WAS STILL IN TOWN, I DIDN'T KNOW.

I hadn't seen him since he'd shown up on my doorstep last week.

Everett and I were supposed to attend a sonogram appointment tomorrow, but he couldn't get time away from the studio until the following Saturday, so even though he'd urged me not to, I'd rescheduled. So it'd happen a little later than it should, but it would be okay.

Everything was going to be okay.

The festering anger and hurt that lingered with my inability to let go of Aiden completely seemed to have faded. At least, I hoped it had. We were communicating, even if that mainly involved our bodies and our gazes. Everett was too tired to think straight most nights when we finally met up, let alone string a heartfelt sentence together.

Walking into Zoe's, I glanced around the half-filled wood and brick interior, taking note of the young woman singing on the small stage. Zoe was the only one manning the bar, so I didn't bother her with questions of Everett's whereabouts and headed upstairs.

He'd given me a key to his apartment with the car, explaining that I could now drive over and wait for him to finish if I wanted to.

I wanted to. Especially tonight, seeing as I hadn't heard from him all day. That wasn't exactly uncommon, but he'd usually text one of his annoyingly blunt messages if he couldn't talk.

I unlocked his door to the scent of Lysol and tobacco, and it shut behind me with a creaking thud. His bed sat unmade, a half empty pack of cigarettes laid open on his nightstand next to a bottle of Advil.

I dumped my purse on the crumpled gray sheets, then went in search of one of his shirts—my favorite thing to wear when I stayed over. He hadn't done washing in a while. Opening and closing the drawers, I found precious few items. A glance at the basket by the door displayed a pile of clothes still waiting for attention.

There was a washer and dryer next to the bathroom right outside, and I decided I'd get to those after changing. My bra was starting to chafe, and most days, I couldn't wait to get it off as soon as I'd put it on.

Plucking out a soft gray shirt that'd fall to my thighs, I began to slide the drawer shut when something rolled to the front.

With my stomach turning, I picked up the bottle. Brown liquid sloshed around as I inspected the contents. Not even a third remained.

He'd had a drink or two since we'd been together, but nothing as hard as this. Usually just a beer with dinner if we'd eat out.

But this… this was expensive. Though I supposed having a large sum of money in the bank and little time to spend it meant splurging on a decent bottle of whiskey wasn't exactly hard.

It hit me then. The nights I didn't see him, the clean scent of mint on his breath when I did. I dropped the bottle back in the drawer and closed it. Then, even if it felt like I was crossing a lot of lines, I searched the wardrobe where he kept one or two good shirts, and a pair of Vans and work boots—his combat boots always glued to his feet.

Nothing.

Lowering to the floor, I peered beneath the bed, but only spied a few dust bunnies and one lone sock.

Falling to my butt, I was about to give up, and told myself to get over it, when my head fell back. My hands raked through my hair as I pulled in three deep, measuring breaths.

The air vent.

Grabbing the only chair in the room, reserved for his guitar, I dragged it over, checking its stability before carefully standing and pulling the vent open. I stuck my hand inside, knocking something over. Clanging sounded as I reached for it, and I winced as a bottle rolled out, smacking me in the head before I caught it in time to stop it from crashing to the floor.

Another bottle of Jameson, this one almost full.

Not needing to check whatever else laid inside, I put the bottle back, then closed the vent and hopped down.

After tucking his T-shirt away, I rubbed my throbbing head and locked the door on my way out.

Uncertainty plagued me. Unsure what to say to him, seeing as he never said he'd stopped drinking entirely, just that he wasn't doing it all the time anymore, I couldn't find a way to reason with what I'd found, or if I should bring it up with him.

There was a good chance he'd be upset I'd gone snooping.

There was also a good chance he'd only been drinking on the odd occasion when he needed to.

There was a good chance of anything when it came to Everett Taylor.

Yet I could still feel the weight of the almost empty bottle of Jameson in my palm, long after I finally fell asleep.

The next morning, I woke to the sound of my phone ringing.

Sunlight exploded through the open blinds, spraying rays of light over the shadows in the corners of the room.

"Clover?" He sounded tired. "I'm so fucking sorry. I fell asleep at the studio; we lost track of time."

I smacked my lips together. My eyes closed, sleep lingering on the fringes of my mind as what I'd found last night in his apartment tried to wake me up. "It's okay. I figured as much when I came over and didn't hear from you."

"You're at my place?"

"No." I cleared my throat, then turned onto my side, yawning. "I came home."

Quiet hovered over the line. "Did you sleep okay?"

"Would've been better if you were here."

A sigh left him. "Tonight. I promise."

"Whatever you say, rock star."

He chuckled, then paused, coughing. "Sorry. Fuck me, I feel like I've been on a ten-week bender without the partying to show for it."

There might've been no party, but he was clearly hungover.

I tried to laugh, but it wasn't going to happen. "I need to get ready for work. You should get some breakfast. Drink some water."

He hummed. "We're starting, but I'll grab something in a bit. Don't forget the vitamins."

I smiled, picturing the stern look on his face when he'd bought them for me. "Okay. Oh, and I need to go bra shopping."

"Yeah?" He sounded more alert.

"Uh-huh. Mine are getting too tight. I think I need maternity ones." It was times like this I'd wished I'd told Mom already, but Everett was great about making sure I had everything I needed. Still, I made a mental note to call her once we'd had the first scan done. Once I had even more confirmation that this wasn't some crazy, farfetched dream.

"We'll go this weekend."

"You sure? They're probably not going to be all that sexy."

"Fuck sexy. I want my tits taken care of."

I did laugh then and cursed at his ability to make every worry he'd caused fall away with just the sound of his voice.

"What time is the sonogram tomorrow?" Adela called from the bathroom.

"Two," I said around a mouthful of Doritos.

"And Everett is going?"

"Yup." I grabbed the remote, clicking through channels.

Adela exited the bathroom in a cloud of perfume and hair-spray. "How fucking exciting. Are you finding out the gender?"

"Too early for that, but yeah. Don't exactly have the funds to go out and buy stuff that's not yellow or green once he or she arrives."

She fluffed her hair with one hand, a sly smile on her face as she checked her phone with the other. "Okay, don't wait up." She kissed the air, heading for the door.

"Same guy?" I called, shoving another Dorito in my mouth and crunching. She'd been seeing some guy from the dance studio where she worked. I'd met him once as he was leaving our place and still pulling his shirt on, and though he'd been in a hurry to leave, he seemed nice and pretty into her.

"His name is Bentley, and yes." The door closed, and I gave my attention back to the TV.

My phone beeped, and I dusted flavoring onto my pants before snatching it from the coffee table.

Prince: How're you feeling?

I stared at those three words, confused.

Me: You're still here?

Prince: I said I would be. But I flew back to Atlanta for a meeting. Got in this morning.

Huh. My fingers hovered over the keypad, the little letters teasing with their infinite ways to cause trouble.

I locked my phone and set it down, dropping the remote when I saw *Jaws* was on. I then did my best to immerse myself in cheese supreme goodness.

Banging on the door woke me, and I startled into a sitting position, the bag of Doritos falling from my lap to the floor.

An infomercial was playing on the TV, and I squinted at the time on my phone. It was almost one in the morning. I'd passed out hours ago. I was falling asleep earlier and earlier each night.

Bang, bang, bang.

I frowned at the missed call notification from Aiden and the five missed calls from Everett before dropping my phone and forcing myself up.

Carrying my half empty glass of water with me to the door, I took a long sip before checking the peephole. Golden hair and a stubble-lined cheek stared back at me.

I opened the door, and Everett all but fell through it, stumbling into the hall table and cussing as he tried to right himself. "Holy shit, where'd that come from?"

"The thrift store," I said, still trying to wake up and take in what was happening.

Everett chuckled, shaking a finger at me before continuing down the short hall into the living room. "You're funny, Clover. Funny and beautiful."

Closing the door, I set my glass down on the hall table and followed, my stomach souring. "How much have you had to drink?"

"Only a little." Everett flopped onto the couch, then kicked off his boots. When he tried to yank off his socks, he fell to the floor with a thump.

"Only a little?" I asked when, groaning and laughing, he made no move to get off the floor.

I walked over, and he turned his eyes up at me. He squinted, shying away from the bright globe in the ceiling above us. "Yeah, but listen. Don't be mad, 'kay?" Rolling side to side, he tried to get up. "Just, just… don't be mad. It's really fucking all right." Then he stilled, his face paling. "Oh, shit."

Vomit flew out of his mouth, flooding the hardwood floor and dribbling down his chin as he coughed. "Jesus," he wheezed, coughing some more. "Haven't done that in a while."

My heart screamed and shattered, but I couldn't move. I just stood there, watching as he struggled to keep from puking again.

"Come on," I said, trying to stop my frenzied emotions from entering my voice, and reached for his arm. "Let's get you cleaned up."

He slapped a hand to the floor, then slipped, not realizing he'd put it in his own vomit, and slid into the puddle of brown mush on his back. "Aw, fuck."

Aw fuck, indeed.

Not once had I felt the urge to puke during this pregnancy, but that did it.

I turned and bolted down the hall, making it to the toilet just in time to hurl all the Doritos and the cucumber sandwich I'd eaten hours earlier into the porcelain bowl.

I could hear Everett muttering to himself, and I took a moment to make sure my stomach had settled before rinsing out my mouth and splashing some water onto my face.

He was going to need a shower, so I grabbed a spare towel and one of his shirts from my room and set them on the vanity.

When I returned to the living room, he was on his stomach, but otherwise, he was exactly where I'd left him. In his own vomit.

I shook him, poked him, and tried to gently slap his cheeks, but he wouldn't stir.

Panic sliced sharp, and I gripped his arm in both hands, tugging him up with every bit of strength I possessed. "Everett, shit. Help me out here." I tried to joke to stop the barrage of tears strangling my throat.

He groaned and moved to sit up. "Clover?" He stared down at the floor. "Fuck. What the hell?"

"You vomited, and now you need a shower."

He stared at it for a moment, then started gagging.

Jesus Christ.

Finally, after throwing up one more time, he crawled toward the hall, slapping a puke-covered hand onto the wall to help himself up.

I was right there, my arm going around his waist to help support him.

We made it to the bathroom before I felt him teeter, and I glanced up to find his eyes were shut. "Everett," I screamed as we both went down.

Pain radiated up my side and through my elbow, and he grumbled out a string of curse words, rubbing at his forehead, which I think smacked into the toilet seat.

Wincing at the pang in my elbow, I crawled over to him and undid his jeans.

"Do you need me, Clover?" he slurred out.

I ignored him. Sex was the absolute last thing on my mind as I yanked at his fly, then tugged.

When I had his pants down to his ankles, I pulled off the sock he hadn't managed to remove earlier. Then I pulled the pants from his body, almost flying back into the bathtub.

And he was passed out again.

Sighing and feeling a tightening in my stomach, I left him there in his briefs, black T-shirt, and with his head slumped against the wall. I needed some help.

Adela didn't answer, and though I considered it, it was too late to call Gloria and Sabrina. Not only that, but they'd only just started warming to Everett. He didn't need their judgment right now.

With the band staying near the studio, at least an hour's drive away, that left only one other person.

After staring at the screen of my phone for a few minutes, I unlocked the door for him, then returned to Everett. I turned on the shower, hoping the steam would help rouse him. Maybe sober him up a little.

"You okay?" I heard from the door not even five minutes after I'd called, explained, then hung up.

I met his dark gaze and swallowed over the knot constricting my throat, making it hard to breathe. "I'm sorry."

He shook his head. "I've got this. Go sit down."

I hesitated as Aiden walked over and hauled Everett from the ground.

Everett woke up, limbs flailing, as Aiden carefully maneuvered him into the bathtub.

"What the shit?" Everett shot confused eyes from Aiden to me, but the confusion wasn't enough to hide the betrayal. "Don't touch me."

Aiden backed off, and Everett slid into the tub, his shirt clinging to his chest as he wiped his hands over his face and let the water rain down on him.

"I'll get him some water."

Aiden followed. "You're bleeding."

The glass almost slipped from my hand as I turned the tap off. "What?"

Aiden grabbed the water from me, then, with eyes full of fear, he gestured to my ass.

I reached behind me, no room for shame as fear invaded, and felt it. "No."

Aiden took the water to the bathroom, and I heard more cursing, followed by the shower shutting off.

He returned with my purse and a towel, but I couldn't move. "Let's go." Shifting me to the sink, he rinsed the blood from my fingers.

"But Everett…"

"Fuck that." He turned off the tap. "Something isn't right, Stevie. Forget him and think about you for a minute." Then he led me out of the apartment, closing the door behind us.

THIRTY-THREE

'D THOUGHT I WAS DOING OKAY WITH THE IDEA OF BECOMING A mother, but it had been a lie. A carefully constructed lie to not only put on a brave face for Everett but also for myself.

For the dreamer who hadn't had a chance to fulfill his dream yet.

For the woman I was still growing into.

And for the baby who was probably better off raised by monkeys.

I had no idea what to expect or what to do. I'd only ever seen babies in passing on the street, in the mall, and in places like the doctor's office.

Until then.

Until I saw the little blob of a human being growing inside me on that dark monitor. The tiny thud of his little heart sent shockwaves rippling through me, solidifying and strengthening a bond I didn't know existed, and bringing tears to my eyes.

I could do this. I would do this.

"Everything looks fine to me. Sometimes these things happen when the body is under a lot of stress." The young doctor with a ginger beard wrote me a prescription. "When's your next scan?"

"Tomorrow's my first one."

He looked up from his pad, his cloudy moustache shifting. "You're fourteen weeks, going on fifteen in a few days, Ms. Sandrine."

I nodded, wiping goo from my stomach with the towel he'd handed me. "I know. Life got in the way."

"Well, fortunately everything is looking great. But in future, I would recommend getting to those on time."

Sitting up, I thanked him as he took the towel and tossed it into a trash can beneath his desk, then handed me the small piece of paper. "For any cramping pain. What were you doing before this happened?"

The paper felt cold in my hand. "Helping a friend." I couldn't meet his eyes as I explained carefully, "She came home drunk, and it got messy. She needed help."

The doctor was quiet for a solid minute, and the lie became a corrosive taste filming my tongue.

Was I ashamed? No, but I was worried—riddled with concern over Everett's actions tonight, and feared things were getting worse. I was about to turn twenty-one. Admitting I had a drunk boyfriend, playing into the young mom stereotypes and raising red flags, wasn't what I wanted or needed right now.

I'd gotten everything I needed, what mattered, so I thanked the doctor one last time, the door closing with a barely audible snick behind me.

Out in the hall that led to the waiting room, I paused. Aiden's eyes were closed, his head tilted back over the seat. His long, powerful body was slouched, legs spread, and his hands sitting over his white T-shirt covered stomach.

The searing ache in my eyes worsened, and I bit my lip as he scraped a hand over his thick hair, his whiskered jaw shifting while his eyes remained shut.

A brief glimpse of the room said I wasn't the only one staring. An elderly woman and a young group of girls sat on the other side, their gazes bouncing over him every chance they could sneak.

The ache blistered as everything I'd kept hidden below the surface began to crest.

He'd come without a second thought, without question, and without judgment.

The towel I'd wrapped around me, in case I'd bled some more, sat on the seat beside him, where I'd waited in terrified silence before getting called in.

He'd held my hand but otherwise stayed quiet, knowing that there really weren't any words to say. Yet when my name had been called, I'd rushed to the opened door and left him behind. I couldn't take him in with me. Whether the news had been bad or good, it didn't seem right.

His eyes opened as my footsteps neared, but he showed no sign of being hurt by any of this. Only concern. He rubbed his face, his lashes sticking to one another. "Are you okay?"

I let the tears tumble free, nodding.

He straightened, frowning as he stood from the seat. "Then why are you crying?"

"Because I saw him, heard his heartbeat."

A twitch to his lips, then he smiled, reaching out to brush my tears away with his thumbs. "He? You know already?"

I sniffed, unable to contain my smile. "Not for sure, but I just do."

His smile softened with his chuckle, the harsh edges of his face relaxing, thumbs still feather light over my cheeks. It was wrong but felt too good to put an end to. "Let's get you home, then."

"Why are you really here, Aiden?" I asked once we were inside his car. It wasn't an accusation, but a question that'd been plaguing me.

"You know why." A sigh escaped, but before I could berate him for potentially ruining his career, he continued, "It's okay. I've been granted leave. They weren't happy, but they're letting me return next season. I have some meetings close by and on Skype. Besides, I needed to wrap things with the apartment."

"Right." The thought of him leaving, of not seeing him again, stole my breath and threatened to send a fresh wave of tears.

The streets were dark and abandoned, and the time on the dash read four fifteen in the morning. We'd not been off the highway long, the silence strangling, when Aiden pulled over onto the side of the road.

He hit the hazards, then turned to me, hard gaze unwavering. "What are you doing, Stevie?"

My mouth opened and closed, my heart pounding.

"With him. Yeah, you love him, I get it." The words were pained, slicing between his teeth. "But I know you love me too, and this can't keep happening. You're having a baby, for Christ's sake."

My voice was hollow. "I know."

"Leave him. You don't even need to leave him for me, just…" A noise of frustration echoed through the car, his fingers pinching the bridge of his nose. "He's no good for you."

"He's been okay," I said, feeling sick that I needed to defend Everett. That I needed to defend him to Aiden of all people. "He was doing okay, but I don't know… I don't know what happened."

"There doesn't need to be a reason. If he wants to drink, he'll find any reason. That's what addicts do."

"That's not fair." But he was right. He was right, and I hated it. Hated that I knew it before he'd even said anything, and now he was unearthing it, bringing that knowledge into the light.

And now that it was out, I could no longer bury it. I couldn't act like none of this was happening and that everything would be okay.

"What's not fair is bringing a child into this world with an addict for a parent." The pain in his eyes, the conviction in his soft voice, slammed me in the chest.

And I knew then, he wasn't just saying this for me. He was saying it for him. "Is this about me anymore?"

He sat back, the tense stance he'd taken deflating. "It is. My mom has nothing to do with this."

"She does. And I agree with you, Aiden, I really do, but it feels like giving up."

"On him? Or on some fucked-up dream you've harbored for years?"

"Are we ever supposed to give up on our dreams?" The words whispered out of me, and I winced as they reached his ears and caused his features to ice.

"If they only end up hurting you, then yeah, you give them the hell up." He flicked the hazards off, but I grabbed his arm before he could put the car in drive.

"I'm sorry."

He recoiled, and I pulled my hand back. "You can't stay there with him."

"He's probably asleep." At least, I hoped he was. Weary, I sank back into the seat. Hating the way we'd just left him, I felt a kaleidoscope of conflicted feelings for the broken man inside my bathroom. Mostly betrayal, worry, and anger.

"You didn't answer my question."

I wasn't sure he heard me when I whispered, "Because I don't know the answer."

He put the car in drive, then pulled out onto the moon-glazed road.

That ache twisted deep as I watched Aiden from the kitchen window, and he finally drove away.

He'd told me to call him if I needed help, but that was it. With a million things I wanted to say, but having no room and no right to say any of them, I'd just thanked him, collected the towel and my purse, then climbed out of the car.

I picked up the glass I'd left earlier, draining the contents while I tried to think about what I needed to do first.

Everett's snores traveled down the hall, and though I knew there was probably a huge mess to clean up, exhaustion urged me to bed. Where I stared at his sleeping face, the peace that'd settled over it, until the darkness took me too.

I woke to a blazing sun, its heat curling the hair around my forehead, and Everett's palm sticky on my hip. Lying on my back, I felt his hand sweep over my stomach, then stop.

And then I heard it.

The near silent sound of rasping breaths heaving out of him, and wet beads falling to my skin.

My hand reached for his hair, fingers resting over the tangled strands. "He's okay."

His tears came harder, and then his arm curled around my waist, his face pressed into my side.

Exhausted in every possible way, I closed my eyes and eventually collapsed back into sleep.

I woke again later that afternoon. This time, save for the four-leaf clover sitting on the pillow beside mine, I was alone.

My lips hitched as I picked it up, feeling the smooth texture of its leaves between my fingers. Getting up, I walked to my bookshelf and set it next to a framed photo of Everett that I'd taken two months ago at the bar. He'd been playing and smiling into the mic. He'd looked happy, at peace, and I was ecstatic I'd captured that moment forever.

I'd missed my appointment, and as I ate an extra-large helping of Froot Loops, I called them back to reschedule yet again. Thankfully, they had an opening before the week was out.

It was then I noticed the floor had been cleaned. The scent of pine cleaner staining the air.

I kept eating, checking my phone as I did, as a feeling came over me. One that worsened when Adela came home from work, hungover and grumbling about her date.

Her words penetrated, but as I opened a text from Aiden asking how I was doing, she snapped her fingers in front of my face. "Earth to Stevie fucking Wonder."

"Sorry," I said. "So it's small, but you came, right?"

She took a seat on the other side of the table, shoved her hand inside the cereal box and threw a handful of dry Froot Loops into her mouth. "True." She groaned. "It still sucks, though. He's exactly my type. Fun and smart with a little bit of asshole sprinkled over the top."

I smirked, then blew out a breath while I responded a quick *fine* to Aiden.

Prince: Fine? The universal word for not fine is fine.

Me: I'm okay. Just tired.

I watched the bubbles come and go as Adela kept chewing cereal, and he hesitated with a response. Finally, they stopped. I left my phone and took my bowl to the sink.

"Hey, you called me pretty late last night. What was that about?"

It was on the tip of my tongue to tell her, to explain everything that'd happened, but as I rinsed the bowl and placed it and the spoon in the dishwasher, I swallowed the words. "I was just looking for a new light bulb. All good."

She hummed. "I hope you didn't get on any chairs."

"I was fine." I gave her a look and then made my way to the shower.

Shampoo swirled down the drain, soapy bubbles mingling with fresh sheets of water. The sound of Everett's regret, his torment, wouldn't leave me alone, and haunted me as I dressed and ran a brush through my hair.

Giving in, I returned to the kitchen to get my phone and tried to call him.

He didn't have voicemail. When it rang out, I tried to distract myself with a book on the couch while Adela watched *Dirty Dancing* for the hundredth time.

When she'd gone to bed, the lie I'd told lingered over my skin like a frosted breeze. Everett still hadn't called, so I tried again.

Then I tried Hendrix, who didn't answer but sent me a text.

Hendrix: At studio, can't talk right now. Is Everett with you?

I didn't even respond. The book tumbled from my hand to the floor as I got up from the couch and grabbed my keys and purse. If he wasn't at the studio, then where was he?

I hated it. I hated that the first place that came to mind after what'd happened last night was the bar.

Anger scorched like a blazing trail of fire, tightening my hands around the steering wheel as I parked in the half-filled lot of Zoe's.

I thought, judging by how he'd acted that morning, that he'd realized he couldn't do this anymore. But as I pounded up the steps to his apartment, unlocking the door and swinging it open, I discovered just how wrong it was to assume anything when it came to Everett Taylor.

His bed had been stripped, the mattress turned on its side. Some of his meager belongings sat in two boxes in the corner. The window was wide open, the gauzy curtains swaying in the summer-night breeze, erasing his scent from the room.

"Oh, good." Zoe's voice stopped the hurt from pouring down my face. "Can you take his shit? He said he didn't want it, but he's got journals filled with lyrics in one of those boxes." She snapped her gum, and her cheap perfume stuffed itself up my nostrils. "Seems kind of wrong to throw them out."

I turned to her. "He left?"

Zoe's mouth gaped, and for the first time since I'd met her, I saw what looked like pity flicker through her sharp brown eyes. "Well, yeah. He dropped off the next two weeks' rent, took a bag and his guitar, and just walked out."

I swallowed, bile turning my stomach and clawing at my throat. "He…" I gripped the doorframe to steady myself. "What time?"

Zoe scratched at her temple. "Ah, maybe around midafternoon?" Pausing, she forced out a gruff laugh. "Wait, so he didn't tell you he was moving?"

"No."

"I figured he might've found a better place to stay at. Yours even, seeing as you're having a baby and all."

I placed a hand over my stomach. "You knew?"

She rolled her eyes. "Girl, please. I've got more kids than I know what to do with. And I looked just like you've been looking these past weeks, scared as shit, every time I found out their deadbeat dad had knocked me up again."

I shook my head, trying to clear the black invading my vision. "He's gone."

"Gone?" Zoe repeated, her thin penciled brows rising. "He didn't look to be in a good way, that's for sure."

"He's not." The nausea grew talons. "If you hear from him, will you tell me?"

"Wait, so he for real just left you?" she asked. "Son of a bitch. Want me to burn his shit?"

I looked back at the boxes, the chasm named Everett cracking wide open. "No. Wherever he's gone, he'll probably come back." Eventually. Even if eventually would no longer wait.

"Fucking hell." Zoe sighed, marching into the room and stacking one box on top of the other. "Well, you better not take his stupid ass back when he does. I'll carry these down for you."

I smiled at the rare act of kindness, knowing it was from a place of solidarity. But I couldn't stop the shock, the disbelief from seeping into each heavy step to my car.

My phone rang as I drove home, the film over my eyes making everything a blurred haze. I hit answer on the steering wheel, my heart hoping and praying for his voice.

"Stevie, fuck. Either answer the phone or just text me and tell me you don't want to talk." I said nothing, swatting tears as disappointment hit me like a tidal wave. "Stevie?"

"I'm here," I strangled out. "Sorry."

"Where are you?"

"Driving. I'm heading to the studio."

Aiden paused. "You're crying."

"Seems to be a recurring thing lately." I laughed, bitter and wet. "He's gone. Again."

Aiden cursed. "Don't keep driving, please. I'll meet you at your place."

The sound of his keys jangling reached me. "No, I need to talk to them. I need to see if they know where he went."

"Stevie," he warned.

"I'm going, Aiden."

Another round of cussing. "Fine. At least let me take you."

"No. You've been dragged through this enough." I sniffed. "Since you first fucking met me."

"That's my choice. Now go to your place, and I'll meet you there. It's dark out, and you're in no state to be driving."

Ugh. I almost screamed, but I did as he said and turned around.

I sat in my car until Aiden's roared into the space behind, and then I got out and climbed inside as he held the door open for me.

"Are you sure you want to be around me right now?"

He clipped on his seat belt, then threw a U-turn and drove down the street. "Rain, hail, or shine, Petal."

My lungs were about to collapse, my breathing erratic. Too fast and too shallow. "He left… he fucking left."

Taking my hand, Aiden squeezed it. And I was thankful he didn't say anything when he had a million reasons and a glaring, golden opportunity to say I told you so.

"What are you going to do when we get there?" Cars zoomed by on the highway, heading home from work, and on my thigh, his hand curled around mine.

"Try to get some answers."

"Would they even know anything?" The question was hesitant, as though he could feel everything coiling inside me, winding tight and ready to explode.

"They'd have to. He was recording an album, for shit's sake. He can't just up and leave them without saying something to someone."

Aiden chose silence for the remainder of the trip. When we neared the turnoff, I blinked back the burn in my eyes.

Aiden finally spoke, voice low. "He's done this before."

"This is different." My own voice was quiet, weak. Defeated. "He's usually leaving with the band, not running away from them." From all of us.

Only me. He only ever ran from me.

The row of warehouses came into view. We reached the lot, and I barely waited for the car to stop before jumping out and marching across it to the doors, pushing them open.

They didn't budge, and I growled, slamming my hand down on the buzzer repeatedly until Graham's voice came over the intercom. "Little sis?"

"Where is he?"

"Ah…" A beat of silence as Aiden stood at my back, then, "Let me get your brother."

A minute later, Hendrix walked outside, his eyes widening as if he'd just realized it was night. "God, any longer in this bunker, and we're all going to turn into pasty vampires."

"Everett," I rushed out. "He left the apartment at Zoe's and paid out his rent."

Hendrix let out a long breath, his gaze moving from me to Aiden and back again as the rest of the band filed out behind him. Heaving out a pained sound, he rubbed a hand over his forehead. "Motherfucker."

He could play dumb all he wanted, but I knew that spark of recognition in his eyes. "Hendrix, tell me. Where is he?"

"I don't know, Steve. I swear."

Rage colored my vision, and I shoved at his chest, screaming,

"Bullshit." My hands slammed down, and he did nothing to stop me, just stood there as I hit his chest again and again. "You're lying. One of you has to know. You'd know, he's your best fucking friend." Tears choked my voice. "He can't do this to me again. Not again. I can't..." Hands pulled me back, turning me into a warm, hard chest as the fading screams became a garbled, keening sound. "He can't. Not this time." I gasped, gritting out, "Not this time."

Aiden's hold tightened, and I sagged against him, then he was half carrying me back to his car. The door slammed and the engine started, cool air blowing over my skin as he stood outside, talking to Hendrix.

My hands ripped into my hair as I lowered my head to my knees. I remained locked that way until Aiden helped me out of the car at home.

THIRTY-FOUR

THE DAYS PASSED, CARRYING YEARS OF HISTORY IN A TAUNTING cycle.

Fleeting snippets of time mingled. The good and the bad and the heartbreakingly horrible moments all coalescing into a multicolored web of something so beautifully imperfect, it was a wonder they ever existed at all. That we'd ever existed at all.

Love was supposed to forgive all things. Of that I was a strong believer. But what happened when love was only capable of taking so much? What happened when the bad started outweighing the good, and the good was never meant to be a song sang to completion?

We'd ended time and time again, yet we'd never really started. And now we had. We had a beginning and an ending, and the pain was infinitely harder to carry than before, to swallow like a foul-tasting pill and trudge onward.

I wasn't sure which was more difficult to admit. That we were never meant to make something whole out of something too broken, or that it was time to give up, once and for all.

He never answered my calls, and as the first day of his absence rolled into the second, it became clear that his phone was either off, discarded, or disconnected.

Aiden had taken me home after the murky events of me losing my shit outside the studio. He'd laid down behind me on my bed, listening to me cry for another man. Just like that other man had done when Aiden had left me in a similar position. He didn't touch me or say anything, but his presence alone soothed more than it shamed.

Still, I wished I could have turned it off. That I'd done something to make it easier for him, but that was impossible. In fact, misery had pulled me so deep, I'd forgotten he was there until he'd set a bottle of water and a mug of tea on my nightstand, then kissed my forehead before Adela took his place.

He'd left after that, and I hadn't heard from him since. Not that I could blame him or find it within me to care enough to call.

Adela remained a force of quiet strength in those first few days, flitting around the apartment to fetch me food. Not only did she remind me to shower, but she also took me to my first sonogram.

I was numb, too numb. And though the sight of my baby caused a ripple of happiness, of excitement and love to unfurl in the darkness, it was too bittersweet to appreciate the moment in its entirety.

He was missing it. Wherever he was, whatever he was doing, he was going to keep on living without his child in his life. He would miss everything.

But that was his mistake. No longer would I cling to throbbing memories of him or the hope that always straddled my every decision where Everett was concerned.

No more.

The phone rang three times before she picked up. "Honey, hey! One second, I've just got a student here finishing up."

I waited as Mom set the phone down, my eyes falling from the stark white ceiling of my bedroom to the colored scarfs hanging over my lampshade and bookshelves. The yellow dress lying over the bright blue ottoman by the window. The purple and floral Docs and red Chucks by the chair near the door. Why was everything so damn bright?

"You there?"

"I'm here," I said, a hoarseness to my voice I couldn't clear.

"Are you all right?"

I assumed Hendrix hadn't yet told them. My best guess was he was too busy trying to figure out what to do with a half-recorded album.

"No." Sorrow dripped into my voice, my veins, my very bones. "I need you."

She didn't hesitate. "I'll be there by tonight. Should I pack a bag?"

"Please."

"I think it's a great idea." Sabrina patted my shoulder.

Gloria snatched the pamphlet, slipping her pink glasses on. "Strengthens the body and calms the mind." She hummed. "Well, it couldn't exactly hurt, could it?"

Adela had suggested it after hearing some of the moms in her tiny tot's dance class discuss it. I took the pamphlet back, drumming my gnawed off nails on the picture of a glowing pregnant woman. "School starts next week, though."

"So?" Gloria perked a brow.

"So I'm going to get busy." I was five months and starting to show, but as much as I loved my tiny bump, I couldn't lie and say I wasn't nervous about attending school again.

Mom had encouraged it, reasoning the more credits I had, the easier it'd be to return if I wanted to after the baby was born. I wanted to, and though it wasn't exactly rare to see moms on campus, pregnant or with babies in tow, I considered maybe working more instead. I'd need the money, and I could hopefully finish my degree online.

Sabrina and Gloria were too quiet. "What?"

Sabrina sighed. "Not to sound like an evil old crow, but you're no busier than what you were when he was here. You have that time available to you now, so use it for yourself." Her voice was stern but not uncaring, which helped the dose of tough love go down a smidgen easier.

"Okay." I admitted defeat, staring back at the pamphlet. "I'll consider it."

They smiled, and Gloria even offered to come with, just as the door opened and Aiden strolled in.

I couldn't wipe the shock off my face if I tried. Last I'd heard when I finally vacated the dark cloud Everett had left raining over my head and texted him, he'd gone back to Atlanta.

"What are you doing here?" I smiled, feeling some of the heaviness ease off my chest.

He tucked his hands into his pockets, grinning at Sabrina and Gloria, who tittered and waved before disappearing into the back room. "Was passing through, thought I'd check in."

"Uh-huh." I was still smiling, enjoying that I could as I took in his dimpled smirk and the way some of his dark hair sprinkled over his forehead.

He drew in a breath, releasing it with his words. "So, actually, I'm keeping the apartment."

I blinked, my heart kicking. "What?"

He tilted a shoulder as if making such a monumental decision wasn't a big deal. "I figured you'd need help looking up gory birth videos, someone to fetch your ice cream in the middle of the night, and to remind you that even when you can't see your toes, you're still the most beautiful thing in the world."

"Prince," I breathed, swallowing hard. "You're too damn sweet, and I don't deserve it."

"Stevie, don't give me that—"

"No," I whispered, not wanting to say it but knowing I had to. It hurt, like razorblades lining my throat, as I forced out, "You can't drop your life for me. You'd only be wasting your time." His mouth tightened, but I raised my hand and pushed on. "I can't. I'm done. Not just with Everett but with the entire male species at this rate."

"I wasn't implying you bend over and lift that fluffy skirt for me."

I stared down at my favorite pink ruffle skirt, then raised my gaze to his with my mouth hanging open.

A light chuckle flitted past his lips, but it didn't match the pinch of darkness I saw flash in his eyes. "Kidding, Petal. My dad needs me closer to home for a while anyway to help with a few things. And I thought it'd be a good opportunity to make sure you're doing okay. Friends. We did it once, so we can do it again, right?"

I lifted a brow.

Another smirk, then his teeth sank into his lip. "Right." He sighed. "Okay, well, I'll be around if you need someone to help shave those lovely legs of yours."

"Aiden."

The door open, sunlight streaking the paint specked concrete floor, he gazed at me over his shoulder. "Yeah?"

"You're too good to be true." I meant every word. I loved him. Boy, did I love him. But I'd spent too much of my life being in love, and I was sick of the way it seemed to cause more pain than happiness. If my goal in life was to make others happy, to fill people's eyes and souls, and my own, with beauty, then I couldn't keep slamming heart-first into misery.

My words had his lips tilting up, then he winked and sauntered out the door.

THIRTY-FIVE

AIDEN WAS BACK IN TOWN THE FOLLOWING MONTH, BUT I HADN'T seen him.

Our dialogue took place via text messages, and I often dodged his calls, if only to avoid the temptation to crawl inside his comfort. It was enough that it helped whenever I saw his name light up the screen of my phone.

Mom and Dad were waiting for me after class, and I hustled outside the lecture hall, my hands wrapped around my almost six-month bump as I tried to contain my excitement.

A few double glances and whispers of speculation had circulated—were still circulating—as people caught sight of my stomach, but nothing could steal this feeling from me. Not today.

It was the small things, I'd come to realize in the weeks that'd dragged by, that would help me continue when all I wanted was to stay curled beneath my duvet and shut the world out.

Though I suppose finding out the gender of my baby was no small thing at all.

"You're still so sure it's a boy," Mom said next to me in the waiting room, encouraging me to drink more water.

My eyes grazed the blue gray walls, the crisp white furniture, and the receptionist desk, seeking distraction. "My bladder is about to burst."

"Keep drinking, or we might not get a clear picture." Mom licked her finger, turning the page of a magazine.

"It's a boy. This will just confirm it."

"Have you thought of any names?" Dad crossed his ankles, stretching his arms over his head.

To say he was impressed when Mom called him from my place after she'd arrived to stay with me would be a lie. But over the two weeks she was there, he gradually came around. Still, the rigidness to his jaw when his eyes met my stomach conveyed exactly how he was feeling about Everett's disappearance.

He was mad as hell, but knowing it wouldn't make me feel any better, he was trying not to let it show.

"No," I said, ignoring the fact that not once had Everett and I even talked about names.

"Am I late?" Hendrix burst through the door, causing a few patrons in the room to lift their gaze.

He saw us and visibly relaxed, the door closing as he came to sit beside Dad. "Sorry." He dragged a hand through his hair, exhaling. "I sped the whole way here."

Mom reached over to smack him with the magazine. "Idiot."

"What? I wasn't about to miss it."

I smiled at him, my chest warming when he winked.

We'd had dinner together last month, where he'd sworn he had no idea Everett was leaving or where he'd gone. The taut pull of his mouth and shoulders and the dull sheen to his eyes accompanied regret-laced words over not being able to get in touch with him. To try to make this right for me.

I'd told him that wasn't his responsibility, and that making the best album he could with what they had was.

Since then, even though he'd been swamped at the studio, he'd made a point to check in each week. Even if it was just to have some snacks delivered to my place with a card that never failed to make me laugh.

"Ms. Sandrine?" A brunette with a kind smile appeared in the waiting room.

We all rose, and Mom took my hand, her gaze searching as I expelled a loud breath. "You okay?"

Okay was the last thing I felt. But with my family surrounding me, something told me I was going to be, so I nodded.

"Let's find out what you got in there," Hendrix said, his arm looping around my shoulders as we headed down the hall.

"Will your landlord let us paint the room blue? You really should just move back home." Mom dunked a fry into her ketchup. "Think of how gorgeous Hendrix's room would look as a nursery again." A wistful smile played on her lips.

Dad grinned. "What a time warp that'd be."

"Don't worry about how I'd feel or anything." Hendrix mock pouted.

I bumped him. "It's okay. I'm staying here. You know, where I have a job, school, and Adela. It'll work out."

"There are only three rooms, though. Adela won't mind you using the other as a nursery?" Mom asked.

I laughed. "She's already dumping boxes of diapers in there every time she gets paid."

Something moved across Hendrix's face, but he was quick to wipe it away. "Who's getting the crib?"

"I will," I said. "They're expensive. I'm not expecting anyone to foot the bill."

"No." Dad's voice was firm. "You'll take the help we give you. This is our first grandchild, not charity."

I swallowed thickly, nodding at him and drinking my water.

Mom patted my hair. "You need to let us spoil him, or I'll be annoyed. Annoyed and spoiling him anyway."

I set my water down, then fanned my face. "Stop, hormones. God."

Everyone returned to their food, and Adela just about burst my eardrum when I answered her call and told her I was having a boy. "Jesus."

"Sorry, but oh my God." She panted, sounding as if she was running. "This is so perfect. Okay, gotta go. Things to do."

"Like what?" I asked cautiously.

"Oh, you know. Just maxing out my credit card in Target."

I rolled my eyes, then closed them over the threat of gratitude. "Love you."

"Love you more." She hung up, and I read a text from Aiden that'd come through twenty minutes earlier.

Prince: What's the verdict, Petal??

Me: boy. :)

Bubbles danced as he tapped out a response, then disappeared. It happened four times before he finally responded.

Prince: I'm fucking thrilled for you.

"You could hear her scream from the next state," Hendrix drawled, fingers tapping over his phone. "The guys say congrats."

Not sure what to make of Aiden's text, I placed my phone back inside my purse. Then I mentally slapped myself. It wasn't his baby, and I was lucky he still wanted anything to do with me. "She's already on her way to the mall. And tell them I said thanks."

Mom and Dad laughed, and after a few beats, I let myself laugh too.

My chest throbbed, and I sighed out a stuttering exhale.

Hendrix watched me, slipping his phone away. I wrangled my face into something passable, then directed my gaze to the rain-soaked street outside the café.

"Progress with the album?" Mom asked.

"Good, it's, um... well, it took a bit to wade through, but it's working out now."

"Sounding good, I'll bet."

Hendrix drummed on the tabletop. "It's coming together, yeah."

Hearing the unease in his voice, I turned to study his blank features. "What happened?"

Dad cleared his throat. "They've changed course."

Slowly, I blinked, my attention still fixed on Hendrix as he struggled to look at me. "What do you mean?" I hadn't meant for it to sound accusatory, but nonetheless, it happened.

Hendrix's shoulders drooped. "We didn't have enough to finish without him. And Jack said—" A look at Mom had Hendrix shutting up.

"Go on," I urged. "Jack said what?"

Mom made a whining sound.

My heart and voice hardened. "Just tell me."

Hendrix didn't balk at my demand. He merely slouched back in his seat, defeated. "Jack said Everett has made some new agreement with him. He's not on the album. Yes, his lyrics are, but he wanted off." He spread his hands. "So instead of making us repay the advances, Jack was willing to give me a shot as lead vocalist. We should be able to wrap it by Thanksgiving."

A screech sounded as I pushed my chair back, but I didn't stand, only concentrated on trying to breathe. "He spoke to Jack." *Of course, he did*, a sinister voice said. Music first, Stevie last. "Jack knows where he is?"

"If he does, he's not talking. All we know is that Everett paid some of his advance back, and he's signed over the music to us." I watched Hendrix's booted feet shift over the cracked tiled floor. "He basically sold his songs to us."

I couldn't fucking breathe. "And he just let Jack do that? That's his music, Hendrix. He wrote most of that album." God knows why I was still defending him, why I cared when just the thought of him made me want to slam my head against the table. "It's his."

Hendrix raised his hands. "Hey, cool it. This was Everett's decision, and I imagine he'll get paid future royalties for the music, so don't worry."

"I'm not worried. I…" I stopped, my hands sinking into my hair and tugging. "Ugh." Jack had spoken to him. He'd gotten a phone call.

I was carrying his baby, and all I'd gotten was a useless four-leaf clover.

Mom was in front of me, helping me up. "Let's get you home."

I let her, and even though I didn't need it, I was grateful for the touch. The support. I needed something to keep me tethered to the here and now, so as to not lose my damn mind in the middle of the day, in the middle of a café, surrounded by the lunch crowd.

My purple maxi dress fluttered around my legs, and I placed a hand over my stomach as Dad grabbed my purse.

And then I felt it. Through the barrage of feelings assaulting me all at once, I felt it. "It wasn't gas," I said aloud.

Hendrix coughed out a laugh. "What?"

I'd called Mom earlier that week, unsure whether the baby was moving or not. A Google search had said it could be gas while some forums disputed it was, in fact, the baby moving.

Mom's eyes were bright with unfettered delight crawling over her face as her hands came to my stomach, and she felt it too.

They all crowded me, and everything melted away. Hands pressed against the tiny flitting movement on the left side of my stomach.

"Holy shit," Hendrix said.

Tears of joy trailed down my face, joining the smile that dug deep into my cheeks.

Holy shit was right.

THIRTY-SIX

"**T**HIS SEEMS KIND OF BIG." I FOLDED THE ROMPER WITH elephants printed on it.

Adela plucked the tags off some blankets. "Babies don't stay tiny for very long."

Sadness swamped me, the little nudges in my belly trying to chase it away.

"You've been doing better," she said, taking a seat beside me on the floor of our spare room. Which would soon house more than a chest of drawers, diapers, and piles of baby clothes. "What's up?"

"Just..." How much was he going to miss? I was sad, not for myself, but for him. Our baby.

Adela made a sound, understanding. "That's not your burden to bear. You didn't tell him to leave; that was all on him."

"Where do you think he is?" I'd pondered that, my imagination trying to place him in various places. But knowing what he'd been like every other time he'd left me behind, I shut the curious quest down.

"Busking his way through the South? Who knows." She sighed. "Sometimes..."

When she trailed off, biting her lip, I frowned. "Sometimes what?"

Her hands smoothed over the blue and green floral blanket on her lap. "I sometimes wonder about you and Everett; were you ever truly meant to be?" My back stiffened, but she continued with a nostalgic smile. "But then I remember the way he looked at you, especially since he moved here, like you were the very air he needed to breathe, and he didn't have enough. Then I'll wonder how he could hurt you. If he looked at you like that, how he could continue to put his own needs first?"

The desire to defend him had faded. "I know."

"Either way"—she moved her hand to my stomach, smiling down at it—"this baby was born from love. It will know only love. And that's enough. It's always enough."

"Don't make me cry, or I'll nipple cripple you."

She laughed, then nodded, her eyes wet as she patted my cheek. "You're going to be just fine, Mama. You'll see."

Three sharp knocks echoed from the door, and I made to get up, but naturally, in my state, Adela beat me to it.

A minute later, Aiden appeared in the doorway, carrying two milkshakes. Adela reached around him, snatching one and grinning, then bounded out of sight.

Aiden blinked, then shook his head. It tilted when he studied me, his mouth curving.

He'd been over a few times since my scan last month, and I hated seeing him. Almost as much as I loved having him near me. Every lingering look and fleeting smile tore at my insides. I could hardly stand to see him, yet I couldn't seem to deprive myself of it either.

I soaked in his tight fitted jeans and T-shirt with his team's logo in the corner.

Sweeping a hand into his hair, he stepped deeper into the room. "You're glowing."

The word glow spiked thorns, but I took the compliment with a smile, my attention focused on folding the rest of the washed clothes in front of me. "So are you. Lots of time in the sun?"

He huffed, lowering to the ground beside me and leaning back against the wall. The scent of his cologne seemed more potent. It enveloped me like a cloud, making me dizzy. "The team's finished now."

"I saw. Sorry about the loss." They'd made it to the semifinals, which he'd flown back for. I'd watched it on TV last week.

Aiden bent his knees, clasping his hands around them. "We had a good run. Besides..." Humor roughened his voice. "I think I spent most of the game, hell, any game, pinching myself, so it definitely could've been better."

"Pinching yourself?"

His head rolled to face me. "It still trips me out. That I actually get to play with and against some of the best players in the world."

Lost in the swirling dark depths of his eyes, the curl and dip of his lashes, and the dream-like quality to his voice, I was held immobile. I shook my head, refocusing on the clothes. "You deserve to be there, and you know it."

"Yeah, I guess I'm just lucky they're giving me another shot." He fell quiet, and I felt his warm gaze as I sorted the washed from the unwashed, then started ripping off more tags. "I've missed you."

I hesitated, wanting to say I'd missed him too, wanting to say so many things, but my tongue grew two sizes bigger, and then his phone rang.

He pulled it from his pocket. "Hey, Dad."

He sipped from the milkshake that'd been sitting beside him, then handed it to me as he smiled at something his dad said.

I took it, almost moaning. Vanilla heaven rolled over my tongue, sliding down my throat.

I drank while he talked, and was about to get up when he

said, "She's good. I'm at her place now." His tone turned irritated. "Fine."

A rich, gruff voice sounded. "Stevie?"

My eyes widened, and I looked from Aiden's smirk to the voice in his hand. "Uh, hi, Mr. Prince."

"Cooper. Aiden tells me you're having a baby boy. Just putting it out there, Cooper's a fantastic name."

I laughed. "I'll take note of that, thanks."

"Welcome. So I'll be in town next Friday, and I'm taking you both out to dinner at that new restaurant. One of my clients owns it."

My heart thundered as I threw a helpless glance at Aiden. His grin said there'd be no saving me from this. "Sure. You do remember we're not actually together anymore, right?"

"Like I give a shit. Meet me at seven. I need to go; some asshole just dumped bad news on my desk."

The line disconnected, and Aiden put his phone away as he stood. "Your dad seems, um…"

"Forceful? Entitled? I know." He held his hand out.

I ignored it. "Aiden, I can't do this."

He lowered to the floor, crouching in front of me and searching my eyes. "It's just dinner. My dad's been wanting to meet you for the better part of a year now. Appease him, or I'll probably never hear the end of it." He pouted. "Please. For me?"

I grumbled. "Those puppy dog eyes should be illegal."

"Quit busting my balls. Let him spoil you with all the fancy food you could dream of."

He offered his hand again, and after a second, I let him haul me up off the floor. "Well, damn, Petal." His throat bounced as he gazed down at my stomach.

I flattened my hand over it, my white lace summer dress

clinging to the soccer ball-sized bulge. "Gets bigger every time I wake up."

"I'll say."

I slapped him, and he snickered, bringing my hand to his lips.

As his smooth mouth encountered my skin, we both paused. The skin on my arms prickled, and my stomach dipped.

He released me, clearing his throat. "Anyway, I need to head home and unpack. Only just got in this morning."

I nodded, my hands bunching at my sides as he strode from the room, and I heard his booted steps fade down the hall.

"Now raise them to the sky. That's it. Breathe in…. and release."

I did my best to follow the instructor's guidance but found myself three seconds behind every time.

"Try yoga, they said. It's relaxing, they said," I whispered beneath my breath.

Liza must have had supersonic hearing. "What was that?"

"She was just saying she wishes she didn't eat those onion rings last night." Adela made a face, her hands and arms following every move like she was a born yoga Jedi.

I scowled at her, then smiled at Liza as if to say, *what can you do?*

"You shouldn't be eating onion rings while you're pregnant. Deep fried food is not healthy for the baby."

"Oh, boy," I sighed out between a small crack in my lips.

Adela snorted.

Rolling up our mats, we tried to contain our laughter. "I don't even like onion rings."

"Shut up. It was the first thing I could think of."

"Onion rings?" She helped me up.

"I've wanted some all week. Damn diet."

I half-rolled my eyes. "As if you need to diet."

We patted our faces with towels, then headed for the door. "I do with your pregnant ass bringing home all these snacks."

"I never said you had to eat them, especially when I bought them for myself."

"I'm not eating them." I shot her a look, and she waved a hand. "Well, I haven't this week."

We stopped at a row of chairs outside, stuffing our things away and grabbing our keys. When I looked up, sipping from my water bottle, a row of pamphlets caught my eye.

My doctor had recommended birthing class, but I hadn't thought much of it. Mom said she'd never bothered, giving me a spiel about how our bodies had been designed for the task, and that it wasn't necessary.

I plucked up an information booklet. "Think I should go?"

Adela popped the top on her bottle. "If you want, but if that Liza is running the show, you're buying me onion rings."

Smirking, I tucked the booklet inside my purse.

THIRTY-SEVEN

Me: How fancy are we talking here?

I stared at the array of dresses on my bed, waiting for Aiden's response.

Prince: Go all out, Petal. As long as you're comfortable.

That was the problem. At almost seven months, I had limited options and even fewer maternity dresses that would be appropriate for fine dining. I blew some curls from my face, then began putting away the dresses that wouldn't work to narrow it down.

Frustrated, I walked over to the mirror, inspecting the light makeup I'd donned and trying to think.

I was making this into too big of a deal. It was just dinner. We weren't even together, so why should I care what his dad thought of me?

I groaned, marching back to the bed and collecting my phone.

Me: What are you wearing?

"Fuck it," I muttered, selecting the dark blue floaty satin dress. I'd just slipped it on, adjusting it over my stomach and fussing with the beaded straps when a text came through.

Prince: Why don't you open the door and find out.

"Little shit." But I was smiling and quickly stuffed away the other two dresses before snatching up my purse.

Adela was out, attending a party near campus, so the apartment was uncomfortably quiet as I hobbled down the hall to the front door.

Aiden was wearing a white button-down, and the top buttons were unfastened, granting a glimpse of golden skin. Black slacks sat low on his hips, and his feet were clad in leather.

"Well, now I feel woefully underdressed," he murmured, and our eyes met.

I tried not to blush but felt heat erupting in my cheeks anyway.

I shifted back, allowing him in. "I was about to say the same thing to you."

"Sure, you were." He bopped me under the chin, then bent low, inhaling my hair.

I shoved him, but it was halfhearted at best. "Quit, creeper."

"Stop being so delicious then."

It was an odd thing to be turned on, to want a man who wasn't the father of the baby residing in your body. Odd and conflicting and frustrating.

I shut the door as Aiden meandered into the living room. "Let me grab some shoes."

In answer, he folded himself onto the couch, flicking on the TV.

I'd barely slipped the black sandals onto my feet when another knock sounded on the door.

"Want me to get it?" Aiden called.

"Please." I huffed out an annoyed breath, trying to get my swelling foot inside the faux leather straps.

"What the fuck are you doing here?"

At the sound of that voice, my hand slipped from the shoe, my foot sliding in as I rose on unsteady legs.

"I could ask the same of you. Kindly fuck off now." The door slammed, and I didn't think I breathed at all, racing down the hall to find Aiden outside the kitchen.

"Is that…?"

His brown eyes flickered, waves of emotion surfacing and fading. The most prevalent being anger. "It's him."

I drew a shuddering inhale, then let it barrel free when Everett pounded on the door. "Open the door, you fuck."

"I don't know what to do." My voice and the fluttering of my heart were weak.

Aiden's lips pinched, and then he started pacing. "I can't make that decision for you."

Why did it suddenly feel like I was standing upon a precipice, where one wrong move could cost me more than I might be able to bear?

"Aiden—"

"You can't leave him banging on your damn door all night. Answer it, or I'll tell him to get lost again."

I knew he wouldn't leave, not until he saw me, which was only reaffirmed when he shouted, "I'll stay out here all night, Stevie. Not like I've got any place to be."

What was he doing? Just showing up here like this and knocking on my door like nothing had happened?

As if he hadn't left me for months.

Anger had my hand gripping the door handle, and I pulled it open to find Everett stubbing out a cigarette, his duffel bag slung over his shoulder. "You didn't last long this time."

A wisp of a smile shaped his lips when he turned and saw me, then it fell, his mouth opening and a harsh breath caving his chest when his eyes dropped to my stomach.

They glassed over, and he took a staggering lurch forward as though he'd reach out and touch it.

I stepped back, clinging to the door to keep me upright.

He met my gaze then, his own still wet, his corded throat constricting. "You're the most beautiful thing I've ever seen, but that stomach, our baby... holy fuck, Stevie."

He stepped forward again, and I held out my hand. "Don't touch me."

Scraping a hand through his hair, he blinked, and, feeling Aiden at my back, it seemed to register.

He didn't look drunk, but he did look different. His stubble clipped back, showing the square angles of his shifting jaw and his complexion. It was sun-kissed and clear, almost as clear as his bottle green eyes that changed as each second ticked by. From relief to joy to regret, and finally, settling on anger.

"He needs to leave. Now."

"*He* is taking me to dinner." Why I felt the need to stab him a little deeper and twist the knife, I didn't know. No, wait. I did. He'd ruined me, flayed me open time and time again. Then left me half dead on the ground for the flies to feast on what remained. Now he was back and making demands? "You're the one who needs to leave."

Thick brows gathered. "You're not even going to ask me where I've been?"

"Like it'll be much different to all the other times."

He flinched, a sharp laugh escaping as he rubbed his jaw and swayed back. "Right, of course."

"You fucking broke me, Everett. For the last time."

"Stevie," Aiden cut in.

Everett growled. "I broke you? I show up here, after missing you for months, and this same asshole is still trying to take what's mine."

"You two need to talk," Aiden said, gently clasping my arm. "I'll only make it worse."

Then he was shouldering by Everett, stalking down the paved path to his car.

"Jesus." I ran my hands through my hair, disbelief attacking every breath. "I swear you plan this shit. You always wait until I'm functioning like a semi-normal human—"

Everett's voice lowered, his chest heaving as he visibly tried to calm himself. "Did you get my four-leaf clover?"

"Fuck your clover. If you think what I need is a weed in place of a supportive partner who won't bail on me, you're even more delusional than I originally thought." The words tore out of me, cutting and slicing, jagged and loud, and had Everett's expression blanking.

"You think pretty damn highly of me, don't you?" he asked, tone dry.

My voice was caked in tears. "I once thought the world of you. I thought there was nothing you couldn't do, that you were magic just waiting to be discovered. But every chance you got, you set that adoration, that love on fire and never stuck around to watch me burn." My words cracked. "So no, Everett. The days of me thinking highly of you are over. And you've got no one to blame but yourself." I marched forward and stabbed a finger at his chest. "So don't you dare do this. You don't have the right to look at me like that or make me feel guilty for something that you did."

Stealing my hand, he nodded, his fingers shaking around mine. His next breath, loud and defeated, sagged his shoulders. "I deserve your anger. Your tears. Your hostility. But I can't..." He swallowed, the sound thick. "I can't be near you right now."

"What?" The word wheezed out of me as he dropped my hand. "What did you fucking expect after being gone for months?"

"Not this." His head shook. "Not seeing you with him." From the same ripped jeans he always favored, he procured a pack of cigarettes, and lit one. "And if I don't walk away now, it'll unravel everything I've worked so hard on."

Mystified and crazy pissed, I shouted at his retreating back, "Where the hell have you been?"

"Rehab, Clover." Ash flicked into the air behind him. "Fucking rehab."

Rehab.

Long into the night, that one word plagued me, sending me tossing and turning as I tried to get comfortable with the wiggling human attached to my insides.

For all these weeks, he'd been getting help? Then why didn't he tell me that? Why didn't he tell me anything, instead of leaving me with nothing but a useless weed and a bleeding heart?

The next morning, I slipped on a maternity shirt and maxi skirt as soon as I'd eaten, and with exhaustion weighing every step, I decided he no longer got to make the decisions.

He didn't answer his phone, so climbing into my car, I called Hendrix. "Is he with you guys?"

"Steve, yeah, but—"

"No buts. Tell him if he moves, I'll skin his balls."

Hendrix made a sound of surprised disgust, and I hung up.

About to turn out onto the street, I stopped, feeling the anger fade. The fuel that fired my soul and revived the broken remains of my heart emptying.

I put the car in park and slunk back into the seat, staring out the front windshield.

Gold and red leaves twirled across the sidewalk, the breeze swooping and carrying them until it lost its strength and sent them tumbling with gravity's will.

I sniffed, swiping at my nose, and then I called Hendrix back. "Fuck, Steve. Way to turn me off my breakfast."

"Sorry. And never mind. I was just…"

"Angry?" he offered. "Look, I get it. But he's not at the studio. He's staying at Graham's apartment."

"Oh."

"Did he tell you where he'd been?" he asked.

"He did, but I don't know if I believe him, or if I should even care at this point."

Hendrix said nothing for a moment, then his voice gentled. "Believe him, Steve. I know he's fucked it all up, probably countless times now, but he's a deeply wounded guy. One who's been fighting to find some kind of healing."

Everything he said penetrated. It burrowed into the part of my heart that wanted Everett to be the best version of himself he could be. The man I knew he was capable of being.

"You've forgiven him," I said. "Just like that."

"No." His laugh was gruff. "No way, but I see it. I see what he's been trying to do, what he's done for himself these past few months, and I respect that." Lowering his voice, he mumbled, "Doesn't mean I didn't slug him in the gut for how he left you."

I smiled through the wobbling of my lips. "I need to go."

"Call me if you need anything. I'm heading to the studio in a beat, but I'll have my phone with me when I can."

"Thanks," I whispered, ending the call.

Back inside, I lowered to the couch and contemplated calling Aiden. God, what a mess. Would he even want to talk to me? There was only one way to find out.

He didn't answer, and trying not to feel dejected, I slouched back, curling my legs into the cushions.

My phone rang.

"Hey." Just that one word sounded wary, poised and prepared for the worst.

"On a scale of one to one million, how much do you hate me?"

His chuckle fell flat, but I took some comfort in the fact I'd made him laugh a little. "I could never hate you, Stevie. Though some days it'd make it easier if I could, for sure."

I licked my dry lips, closing my eyes. "I'm sorry, Prince."

A ragged breath had my eyes opening. "I take it he's not there."

I hated what that implied. That I treated him like some dirty secret. "He left not long after you did."

A harsh pause preceded his next words. "Shit, Stevie."

I scrambled to change the subject, to keep from begging him to come over. "Did you tell your dad I was sorry?"

He laughed then. "The sly asshole didn't even show up."

"What?"

"Yeah, when I got there and saw no sign of him, the server rushed over and told me that dinner for two was courtesy of Cooper Prince."

I couldn't contain my smile. "He set us up?"

"Yep."

My smile and heart tilted as I pictured him seated there alone. "I'm so sorry."

The pounding of my heart thickened when he took his time to say, "Hey, I have to go. I have a Skype meeting in ten minutes."

"Okay." I nodded even though he couldn't see. "Sure, yeah."

Another lengthy silence fell, followed by a murmured goodbye before he disconnected.

Rolling onto my side, I moved my hand to my stomach as the baby protested the shift in position, and I stared at the blank TV.

THIRTY-EIGHT

I ATTENDED SOME BIRTHING CLASSES WITH ADELA, BUT BETWEEN school, work, and the ache that never left my pelvis every time I walked more than a hundred meters, I barely had the energy to even think about giving birth to a tiny human.

I was petrified. Therefore, kind of thankful for how busy I was. It left little time to give much power to those fears.

Since showing up on my doorstep over a week ago, I hadn't seen Everett, and after speaking to Adela and my mom, who were riddled with conflicting opinions over the reason he'd been gone, I decided it was probably for the best.

He wanted to get better, as far as I could gather, and that meant staying away from me. That was fine, but I wasn't chasing something I wasn't sure was any good for me anymore.

And Aiden, well, he wouldn't so much as respond to my text messages. That was probably for the best, too.

Waving goodbye to Gloria, I stepped into the light sun shower and struggled with my textbooks and purse, trying to dig my keys out.

The books disappeared from my hand, the scent of tobacco smothering as Everett stomped on his cigarette and started walking to my car.

"Um," I started.

"Unlock the car, Clover."

Scowling, I did, tucking my purse in the back seat with my books.

All the while, Everett leaned against the car, his arms crossed over his chest. "You're still attending class."

"Why wouldn't I be?"

His lips twitched. "Because you're having a baby in about two months."

"I'll keep attending until I can't, not that it's any of your business." I tugged my sweater down when I felt the breeze rush beneath to tickle the skin of my stomach. "Thank you very much."

Unmoving, he stared, his bottom lip sliding beneath his teeth.

Within seconds, I grew increasingly uncomfortable, unnerved, my feet scuffing over the concrete. "Can I help you with something?"

"You really don't want me to answer that."

I ignored the jolt to my chest. "Fine. I'll be going then."

"Being there, making that kind of decision, it was fucking voluntary."

I'd started rounding the car but paused with my back facing him.

His tone deepened, lowered, became rougher. "I couldn't hear your voice every other week and focus on what I needed to do. I know myself, Clover. I know I'm an alcoholic, but I also know I'm addicted to you."

Something splintered inside my chest. I turned, mouth agape, and my heart thrashing.

"I know that you, just as you always have"—he pointed a finger at me—"take up most of my thoughts, my strength, my entire heart—everything."

My throat closed, a tremor racing through my hands. "You could've told me before you left."

"I could've, yeah, and that's on me, but you're not listening.

I'm a fucking alcoholic, Stevie." I flinched at the harsh words, and he let out a sardonic laugh. "That's right. We both know it, but it still sucks to hear it out loud, right? I didn't know if I was going to commit. If I'd last longer than a week in there, let alone the duration I stayed."

I blinked away tears. "What made you stay?"

"Mason." His voice lowered. "I stayed for me, for you, and for that baby in your stomach, and because I was just a fucking kid doing the best he knew how when my world was taken from me."

He'd talked through it. "You spoke to someone?"

"Numerous someones, but yes, I spoke. And once I started, I couldn't stop. Everything. My deadbeat parents, Mason's death, meeting you, the music—all of it. It needed out. It needed a safe place to land. Only then could I start wading through the shit-fest I've made of my life."

I felt my lips quiver. "Your life isn't shit."

"I know that," he said, tone and expression softening. "Christ, I know that. But I was this parasite, leeching color and happiness, leaving trails of empty promises and broken pieces everywhere I went." His voice cracked. "I knew it had to stop. I knew when I moved here, and I was honestly trying. But the night you could've lost our baby, because of me and my reckless decisions, I knew I wasn't trying hard enough." He straightened. "I had two choices, Stevie."

"And what were they? Leave me or leave me?" I desperately wanted to haul those words back, but I couldn't, so they sat there, simmering in the air between us.

He didn't balk. "Walk away from those I continued to hurt for good, or find a way to stop hurting them."

I shook my head, the light smattering of rain melding with the tears falling down my cheeks.

"You're allowed to get mad. You're allowed to fucking hate me for all I've done to you, but what you're not allowed to do is stop loving me."

"Enough. I need to go," I said, finally realizing we weren't alone. Some passersby had stopped or were gawking over their shoulders at us.

"Wait," he said, rounding the car when I climbed inside.

I groaned as he held the door open, leaning in. "Please, Everett. Just let me go."

"Never." He grabbed my face, pulling it to his lips. The smooth warmth of them meeting my forehead sent shivers biting. "Never. It's you and me, and I love you."

He swiped his hand over my stomach before backing out and closing the door.

The weeks dwindled by, and on the days I was working, Everett dropped off lunch or dinner, causing Gloria's and Sabrina's brows to rise as he swaggered out the door without saying a word.

"Strange man," Sabrina murmured.

"But sweet," Gloria added.

A week before Thanksgiving, I came home to find Adela wearing a shit-eating grin on her face.

I wasn't driving home for Thanksgiving. Too pregnant and with too much to do, I'd asked Mom and Dad to come to me instead. Hendrix and the band were busy wrapping the album in the studio anyway, so Mom took the opportunity to not wash dishes pretty well.

"Where did that come from?" I glared at the stained crib sitting against the wall in the center of the room, a mattress tucked inside.

"Everett."

I almost tripped over the alligator rug, and Adela snorted, grabbing my arm. "No face planting while preggers."

"Noted." Inching closer, I skimmed my fingers across the shined edge of the dark wood. "Wow."

"Yep. And before you get mad, I told him no, but he said he'd assemble it out on the street for all he cared."

I bit my lip to keep from smiling. "Asshole," I mumbled.

"Extreme asshole." Adela laughed.

I tried to picture it, our baby asleep inside the crib his dad had built for him. It nearly brought me to my knees, so I stepped back, taking a seat in the rocking chair I'd found at the thrift store.

"You don't look happy."

"I'm not unhappy," I defended, drawing the words out.

Adela picked up the snow globe on the dresser, shaking it until the confetti-like pieces rained mists of white glitter over the little village inside.

I'd lost count of how many times I'd sat in this room late at night, doing the same thing with the globe, exactly where I was sitting.

"A state of in between, then." Her pouty lips tilted. "Better than sad. Where's Aiden?"

He hadn't been around for weeks, but that was probably my fault.

"He's gone home for the holidays. He said he'd try to catch up with me in the new year."

Adela said nothing to that, and I studied her pinched expression. "He's blowing me off, isn't he?" I'd feared that was the case, but I couldn't bring myself to admit it. The thought of not having him in my life was unfathomable, though it wasn't as if I'd asked him to hang around. "I'm pregnant, Del. What am I supposed to do? Ask him to be with me while I have this baby?"

"I'm sure he would say yes if you did."

I knew that, and that was what had stopped me. It wasn't fair, not for him, not for Everett. Not for anyone. "I'm having this kid, getting my flower farm, and raising him with the help of a hundred goats."

She laughed, then sobered. "So Everett seems really good. His face as he looked at all this stuff…" she trailed off, and I wished I could've seen it. "No one told him he was having a little boy."

"Shit," I hissed, my eyes closing briefly.

Adela hummed, tapping the glass globe.

I groaned, scrubbing my hands over my cheeks. "What the hell am I supposed to do here?"

"You mean, who are you supposed to pick?"

"I can't do that," I blurted without thinking. "I've been just fine on my own anyway."

Adela set the snow globe down beside the framed photo of me and her. "Let's face it, Stevie. Yes, you're not with either of them because it's what you need right now. But it's also because you know…" Her brow arched. "You know if you give one of them another chance, this is it. You kiss goodbye to one love for another."

My stomach dipped and tears burned. "Why do you need to be so right for?"

Her laughter was soft and lacking humor as she left me with everything I'd been trying to ignore.

THIRTY-NINE

"WHERE'S YOUR BOYFRIEND?"

I looked over at the doorway, capping my highlighter. "How'd you get in?"

"Answer my question, and I might answer yours."

I scowled, and leaning against the doorframe, Everett flashed a small glimpse of his teeth.

"He's not my boyfriend."

His tongue crept over his upper lip, eyes narrowing. "We've danced this dance before."

I contained a snort, bookmarked my page, and shut the textbook. "Except this time, I'll be dancing on my own." I gave my eyes to his. "Answer my question."

"Adela told me where you keep the spare key."

"Traitor," I spat.

"You're carrying my son; I need to know I can get to you in case of an emergency."

"The only emergency you need to worry about is my inability to hold liquids in my body for longer than twenty minutes." I cringed, swinging my legs over the bed. "So kindly get lost while I take care of business."

He was in front of me in an instant, an arm around my back, and his other sweeping under my knees, lifting me into the air. "Holy shit, put me down."

He didn't. He carried me to the bathroom, where he set me down carefully, then backed out.

After shaking off the shock, I did my business, washed my hands, and returned to find the room empty.

He was in the nursery. "You didn't tell me we're having a boy."

"Correction, I hadn't gotten around to it, and then you found out yourself by sneaking in."

He was eyeing the crib. "Do you like it?"

I sighed, leaning into the doorframe. "I love it, but you didn't need to—"

"You should sit down." His gaze assessed me. "God damn, how on earth did I get so lucky?" I didn't think he'd meant to say the muttered words aloud.

Damn him and those green eyes that conveyed such stark sincerity, speaking clearer than words ever could. I sniffed, doing my best to ignore how he affected me. "You got lucky a few times, but now your luck has run out." I tried not to waddle as I moved over to the rocking chair and failed.

"If you say so." His eyes were glued to my stomach, longing, adoration, and something else making my tired heart want to leap into his hands.

Annoyance surged. The way he could still make me feel like I'd fallen for the first time every time he looked at me—like he was at that moment—wasn't fair.

"What do you want from me, Everett? Because every time I think I've figured it out and that you'll be happy, that maybe you'll stay this time, I turn around and you're gone again."

A dry laugh filled the small room. "I don't think you're ready for this conversation right now."

"What, because I'm pregnant?" I scoffed. "I've survived everything else you've put me through; I can handle a few measly words."

"Fine." With his jaw clenching, he slammed a fist on his

chest, shocking me. "What I want is for you to fight for me the same way I've fought with everything I have for you. I want you to believe in me the same way you used to when we were kids. But more than that, I just want you to acknowledge that I'm trying. Every. Fucking. Day. I'm trying to be the best version of me that I can. Not just for you. Not just for our baby. But for me."

My feet, that'd been gently rocking me in the chair, stopped as his declaration—the pain and desperation that leeched from it—electrified every part of me.

He sighed, a hand plunging into his hair as defeat weighed heavy from his limbs. "I've gotta go."

I hated myself for saying it, but I couldn't stop. It was as if I was standing on the edge of my emotions, looking down into a swirling black abyss. "It gets hard and you leave. Typical."

He paused in the doorway, his back rigid beneath a green Henley. "Got an appointment with a therapist I'm seeing."

"Oh." Guilt slammed into every nerve ending, stiffening and rendering me breathless.

He hesitated a moment, rapped his knuckles on the doorframe, then disappeared.

The sun dipped below the horizon, sending shadows swaying on the walls before I finally wiped away the tears, made a sandwich, and ran a bath.

Steam clouded the air, my eyes tracing its billowing path to the ceiling while my toe reached for the faucet, turning it off.

"They say it's not so great to sit in a hot bath while you're pregnant." His voice startled me, water splashing as I scrambled to cover myself. "I've adored, licked, sucked, rubbed, pinched, and dreamed about those tits. Hide if you want, but it's a wasted effort."

Heat painted me pinker than the water, and I folded my arms over my chest. It was covered in water and leftover bubbles, but still. "You haven't seen them like this." I hated how insecure I sounded, yet I wanted to smear the salt on a little harder. "They've changed." I cleared the edge in my throat. "A lot."

When Everett didn't respond, I let my eyes meet his, and what I found there, the longing and heat, caused my thighs to clench. "You're carrying my child, any change that causes would be nothing short of breathtaking."

Fuck him and his way with words.

I turned away, my feet sliding over the lip of the tub as I sank lower into the water. "You're back."

"Evidently." His smile could be heard in his voice, and I clamped my teeth together.

"Your appointment went well?"

"About as well as those things can go." He sighed, and my eyes bulged, stomach flipping, when he entered the room and took a seat beside the tub.

"Don't worry about my privacy or anything, will you."

"You left the door open, and like I said"—he lifted a muscled arm, finger skimming the water—"it's not good to take hot baths while you're pregnant."

"A girl needs to have some form of relaxation while carrying a squirming human around every day." His smirk drew my gaze. "Besides, it's not that hot."

"I know."

"Since when did you become an expert on pregnancy anyway?"

He leaned back against the wall, rubbing his wet fingers together between his jean-clad knees, still staring at me. "I had some free time in rehab and wanted to use it wisely. You also need to quit eating those fish sticks."

I tossed my head to the side. "Oh, come on."

"I'll find you a sufficient alternative."

My brows shot up. "You will, will you?"

"Yep. I've got a meeting with Jack tomorrow, but I'm heading to the grocery store afterward. Sick of the microwaved bullshit Graham eats."

I wanted to ask about Jack, about why they were still talking when Everett was no longer part of the band. I wanted to ask why he was here, pushing all my buttons. I wanted to ask so many things, yet I didn't. "You used to eat that microwaved bullshit all the time when you stayed at the bar."

"That was before I got used to three cooked meals a day."

"How'd you pay for it?"

"Rehab?" I nodded, and he dropped his eyes to the green tiled floor. "Jack. I paid back half of my advance. When I left the facility, I went to set up one of their payment plans, only to find out the sneaky bastard had already taken care of it."

I wasn't sure what to say. "What kind of label executive does that?"

Everett shook his head, a small laugh escaping. "That's exactly what I said. I owe him, so we're meeting to talk about some things."

"You're going solo?"

"No," he said, stern and instant, then scratched at the whiskered shadows lining his jaw. "I think he wants to buy more songs. Have me write for some of his artists."

"Holy shit," I breathed out, forgetting for just a moment how upset he'd made me as happiness, bright and overpowering, bloomed for him.

I saw him try to tame his disbelief, the smile, but he lost the battle. It transformed his face, lightened his eyes, loosened his shoulders, and had him shaking his head again. "Yeah, but we'll see."

The baby stole my smile and my breath, elbowing or kneeing me in the ribs.

Everett was right there when I opened my eyes, his own filled with concern.

"It's okay. He's just moving."

"Is it supposed to hurt?" The fear in his voice melted some of the ice encasing my heart.

"No, it doesn't hurt. But it can get uncomfortable as hell sometimes."

He reached for the water, then stopped himself. His eyes, loaded with a silent plea, locked with mine.

I nodded, exhaling slowly as his fingers breached the surface and whispered across my stomach.

"Jesus, Clover," he rasped, his hand gliding over the taut skin, following the baby's movements. A limb protruded, and his eyes grew two sizes, stealing a laugh from me. "That's insane."

I shifted in the tub. "He doesn't seem to want to quit, especially when I'm trying to relax."

"He's a tiny dancer." A soft smile lifted Everett's lips, his attention fixated on my stomach. "How is it possible to love someone you've never even met?"

Something clogged my throat, quaking my response. "I know."

"Hey, little buddy," he crooned, some of his long hair falling to curtain his face. I wanted to push it back, to see every slice of emotion that harnessed his features. "You need to settle down."

He was met with a kick, and I laughed.

My laughter broke when Everett started humming a slow melody, voice rough and jilted from disuse. His hand rubbed and lulled me into a state of relaxation. The kind I hadn't felt since before he'd left.

I never wanted the sun,
I only needed a little warmth
And you said oh, darling,
You live in a world where you can have both...

Silent tears flowed as he sang. There was no way to stop them, so I didn't. I let them tumble. And then I let Everett help me out of the tub, wrap me in a towel, and scoop me up.

Lowering to the floor, he didn't try to placate me.

With his arms tight around me, unyielding, I fisted his shirt and sobbed into the skin below his neck.

FORTY

HAULED MY BAG OUT TO THE CAR AND INTO THE TRUNK, REARRANGING gift bags full of presents. It was too awkward, so I hadn't bothered with wrapping this year, but I doubted anyone would care.

"Shit," I hissed when I remembered I'd forgotten my heartburn medication.

I spun smack into Everett's chest. "Looking for these?"

I snatched the bottle from him and tucked it in the side pocket of my overnight bag before shutting the trunk.

He stopped me, gently moving me aside to find a spot for his own bag. "What are you doing?"

"Were you just going to head home and not have me go with you?" He closed the trunk, brows raised.

"Well, yeah." I'd figured if he was joining us for Christmas, he'd grab a ride with Hendrix or someone. "And how'd you get my pills?"

"I've seen you take one after dinner whenever I'm here, so I got you some more."

He'd been coming by at least four nights a week to cook. After the third time, I gave up trying to send him away. He could cook, and I couldn't handle being on my feet for long after three in the afternoon. Adela was all for it, the traitor, and even made remarks about stealing him from me.

Everett didn't seem to care when I said there was nothing to steal. Nothing seemed capable of swaying him and his overbearing presence.

Almost every day, he continued to insert himself in front of me. Part of me wondered if it was merely because I was carrying his baby, or because he was trying to make up for the way he'd continuously damaged me. Either way, I didn't have the energy to overthink much these days and often passed out with my computer right after dinner.

"Thank you." I backed up, then went to lock up before climbing in the car.

Of course, he was in the driver's seat, but I wasn't going to protest when it was getting harder to maneuver the watermelon that was my stomach behind the steering wheel.

"How are you feeling today?"

"Huge, tired, and eternally hungry." My grumbling made him smile, which he failed to hide.

My nose twitched as I caught a whiff of his clean scent and the undertones of tobacco. He still smoked but was careful not to do so around me anymore.

"One more month," he reminded me.

My cheeks vibrated as I blew out a huge breath and rubbed my bulge. "It's going too fast, but at the same time, I can't wait to have my body back."

"You still doing the birthing classes?"

Adela had told him when he'd asked over dinner the week before last. "Yeah, but I missed the last one. Had to study."

"You're going to do great."

I wished I had his confidence. But there were only two ways out of this situation. My vagina or a knife. And quite frankly, I didn't like the thought of either.

I was tempted to ask him where he'd been yesterday and the day before, on account of not seeing him at all. But sounding needy was the last thing I wanted, especially when I didn't want to need him.

It was an ever-present, maddening ache; loving two men and not being with either of them. Aiden hadn't called in weeks, and though I'd texted him this morning to wish him a Merry Christmas, he never responded.

As if knowing where my thoughts had veered, Everett's hands tightened around the wheel.

"How're things going with Jack?"

"Good," he clipped, then sighed through his nose. "I've got three contracts already lined up, and I started back at the hardware store last week. Just part-time to help until the money comes through."

That explained a lot. "Congratulations."

"Yeah, it's all finally happening."

The comment had me pausing, and with my eyes widening, I loosened my seat belt and turned to face him. "Wait a second."

"Waiting," he said with a twist to his lips, then overtook someone on the highway.

"You never planned to record the album, did you?" My voice was quiet, realization dawning with every word I uttered. "You did it for them."

"It was their dream, not mine."

My chest squeezed. "God, did you plan to go to rehab?"

He shook his head, laughing a little. "No. I had hoped I could fix my shit on my own. That I wasn't an alcoholic but merely a guy with a past he'd rather forget."

I blinked what seemed a thousand times. "Not showing up, flaking on them... What were you trying to achieve exactly?"

"I wanted Hendrix to take control. To do what he was always meant to—kick me to the curb and take my place." His laugh was gruff and short. "But he had too much faith in me and love for me, and therefore, hope that I'd come through and do my damn job."

"Why didn't you just tell them?"

He thought about that for a minute. "Many reasons. The main one being they're my friends. My family. No matter what I've done, they would've remained loyal, and that loyalty might've torn them apart. They didn't need me, but they needed to figure that out on their own."

"Yet that might not have happened."

"No," he agreed, "which fucked with my head. They weren't supposed to keep waiting on me. They were supposed to take the opportunity presented to them and steal it for themselves. To make sure everything they'd worked so damn hard for would be theirs. I took a gamble, not knowing whether it would pay off, but in the end, it somehow did."

"You son of a bitch," I exhaled out. "Music is your life."

His scowl deepened, pulling at his pillowed lips. "It's part of who I am, and for the longest time, I'd thought it'd be my ticket out of hell, the thing that'd save me, but it's not my life, and it didn't save me." He swallowed. "I had to do the saving myself."

The wind seeped into the cracked open windows, whistling and chilling, while all he'd said tried to sink inside my whiplashed heart and brain.

"Clover," he said, soft and direct. "Music is my passion, but you're my first and greatest love. Combined, you both help heal and hide all that festers. But it wasn't enough. The guilt I've carried for years wouldn't let that be enough."

A haze filmed my eyes, and I shut them to clear it. "I'm so fucking proud of you, and I'm so fucking upset with you."

Everett's hand grazed mine on my lap. "That's okay, and that's enough heavy."

I stared out the window to the blurry green and gray that lined the road as he scrolled through the options on the screen, then selected a song.

When that familiar intro began, my eyes drifted closed once

more. The temptation to bang my head against the window erupted. Memories of the past collided with the soul-shaking present.

Yet as Everett kept singing "Start Me Up" by The Rolling Stones, it became harder and harder to linger in the gloom. And it only worsened when he kept hitting restart until I finally caved, laughing while I gave him what he wanted, and joined in.

It was midafternoon by the time we reached my parents, and Everett rounded the car, insisting I stay put until he did.

His hand was strong around mine as I used it to help pull myself out of the seat, a yawn howling from me. "You need a nap."

"Ugh." I nodded. "I so want a nap." Another thing pregnancy had changed about me. It'd turned my non-nap-loving self into a serial napper. I could happily nap for only ten minutes, so long as I snuck one in.

"My babies!" Mom hurried over, arms wide as she tried to squeeze us both in a gripping hug. My stomach made that a little hard, but she didn't seem to care.

Dad grasped my face, inspecting it before saying, "You look tired, Stevie girl."

"God, thanks."

He grinned. "Still beautiful, so don't be hating."

"Don't say *don't be hating* and we should be fine." I kissed his cheek, then did my best not to waddle across the lawn as I headed inside.

He was right. I must have been tired since even one look at the gardens in desperate need of love didn't so much as slow my feet.

Everett brought our bags to my room. "Don't worry, I'm on the couch."

I didn't have the energy to say anything. I crawled onto my bed, comforted by the scents of home, and passed out to the sound of Everett's soft chuckle.

A gentle wobble of my shoulder, and my hair shifted from my face. "Dinner's ready."

I was instantly up, earning me a rich bout of laughter as I tried to orientate myself with my surroundings.

Home. My old room.

I swung my legs over the side of the bed, not bothering to fix what I was sure was one hell of a bird's nest atop my head before pushing myself up.

Everett took my arm, halting me. I frowned, then groaned with mortification when he swiped below my bottom lip. "Lovely."

"Even when you drool, baby."

I shoved him playfully, and he grinned, moving for me to amble out and down the hall. The scent of food tugged me one way while my bladder screamed for me to veer into the bathroom.

"I'll prepare you a plate. Go use the bathroom."

I grumbled beneath my breath, then shut the door on his smiling face to do my business.

Everett was heaping sausages and salad and cobs of corn onto my plate when I plucked out a chair and all but collapsed into it. "Smells so good."

I yanked it from him and got started, ignoring the laughter my parents tried to contain.

"Your mom was all about the ribs when she was pregnant with you." Dad cut into his sausage, then speared some salad. "Lost count of how many late-night trips I made."

"She wants anything she can pour gravy on," Everett said, drizzling some over my food.

Mom was watching us with a sparkle in her eye, and I smiled back, ignoring the way it grated. Trying to ignore how I was the only person in the room who still seemed to harbor any ill feelings toward the man next to me.

A honk outside had Mom's fork dropping with a clatter, and Dad looked up just as the front door opened.

"Hola! We come bearing Christmas carols." Hendrix skidded into the kitchen, waving his phone in the air. Graham, New Guy, and Dale came crashing in behind him.

As everyone said their hellos, Hendrix readied his phone, and as Hendrix's voice filled the room, singing Everett's lyrics, I couldn't stop myself from observing Everett.

His knife and fork were suspended midair, his jaw slack as he listened.

Hendrix watched, excitement warring with trepidation, waiting for the same reaction I no doubt was, but it never came.

"Well, I'll be fucking damned," Everett said through a laugh, dropping his utensils and shoving his chair back.

Back thumps and half hugs were had as one song rolled into the next, and the guys dragged stools from the kitchen counter to the table.

Mom's eyes were glossed, a lone tear rolling down her cheek, elbows on the table, and her hands clasped beneath her chin. Even Dad appeared choked up, his smile tilting as his attention stayed fixed on Hendrix's phone.

When Everett returned to his seat, I dropped my knife and lowered my hand beneath the table, linking my fingers through his. Where they stayed as we listened to the rest of Orange Apples' debut album.

Graham went home to see his parents, and New Guy joined him.

"What's his name again?" I asked Everett when they'd left.

He rubbed his brow. "Ron. No, Raymond." He cursed. "Rupert?"

I laughed and heard my phone from my room, but I was too comfortable on the couch, the lights on the tree hypnotizing as we watched *Home Alone* after dinner.

Everett got up, returning a minute later with my phone and an expression made of ice.

I took it from his outstretched hand and watched as he flopped into his seat at the end of the couch. He didn't lift my feet to his lap again, and instead, he ran his hands through his hair, staring daggers at the TV.

I looked down at my phone and saw why.

Prince: Merry Christmas, beautiful. I'll be back next week, and I think we should talk.

Hesitation held my fingers immobile over the screen. The feeling of eyes on me sizzling my already jumpy nerves.

Me: I'll be home.

Even though there was so much I wanted to say, I let it go and locked my phone.

Everett's eyes followed its journey to the floor, and I loathed the feeling that sending just a text message evoked. That slithering, scaly guilt.

After five more minutes, the tension drifting between us threatening to drown, I heaved myself off the couch and headed to bed.

I was pulling my pajama top down over my belly when Everett walked in, shut the door, and set my forgotten phone on my nightstand.

I pursed my lips. "You're mad."

"Understatement."

I pulled the sheets back, taking a seat on the bed. "I'm not with him, Everett. And for the record, I'm not with you, either."

"Keep telling yourself that," he bit out, kicking off his boots.

"Excuse me?"

"I said, keep telling yourself that."

"Fuck you." I sent a finger at the door. "The couch is back that way."

"I love you, Clover." His words were low but soaked in feeling as he stood before me, tilting my chin up to his face. "I'm in deep, all yours, ruined from the inside out." His grip firmed when I made to wrench away, and he sucked my gaze to his. "In a world hell-bent on destroying me, fate handed me you. And I'll be damned if I let anyone fucking take you from me."

The cool air turned warm, and I tore my eyes from his blazing ones. "Love isn't everything. It's not what I need from you."

He fell to one knee, his hand reaching behind him. "I wasn't going to do this until tomorrow, but no matter how long you leave me waiting, I need to do it now." A velvet blue box popped open, revealing a platinum band pillowed among red inside.

"Everett." The word was a warning and a wish, wrapped in one.

"You can keep holding me at arm's length, or you can

forgive me and let me love you the way I need to. The way I'm desperate to with every breath this life allows me to take. Eventually is ready and waiting for us, Clover. And though I'll never feel as though I deserve you, I'm hoping like hell you're ready to grasp it, so we can finally make it ours."

This love, our love, it was an entity all on its own. It stalked us wherever we roamed; a living, breathing beast that wouldn't rest until it won. Until it was just him and me, saddled in its unshakable, never-ending embrace.

Yet I couldn't form one of the two words I needed to say. I couldn't take one of the two options presented to me. All I could do was stare at the gleaming ring, at the possibility of a future that lay uncertain.

Would he leave again? Or had everything that'd happened with us, and to him, led him to this place where he could speak of forevers and mean it with every inch of his being?

I wasn't sure. All I knew with certainty was that I was crumbling, my walls teetering and collapsing, one by one.

And still, I didn't make a sound.

Well, hopefully my dad won't curse up a storm when I tell him I got my sixth ticket for the year. I figure he'll be okay when I tell him the story of how it led to meeting my future wife...

The memory of his voice impaled, sliced open everything I'd tried to keep contained, and ruined me.

"Clover? Fuck." Everett set the box down on the nightstand, then climbed onto the bed and pulled me to his chest. "It's okay." He soothed, his fingers wiping at my wet cheeks. "You don't need to answer me right now. But I had to ask, to take this step and make myself clear, that's all. I need you to know what my intentions are." He continued to swipe at my cheeks, speaking softer now. "It'd always felt like a dream, thinking I'd one day get to ask you to be my wife, but now that

I can touch it, picture it, and believe in myself, I had to ask. I had to."

"I'm sorry," I whispered, lowering my head to his chest. "I love you, I do, but—"

"Shhh." He kissed my forehead. "It's okay." It wasn't. I could hear it in the strain of his voice and feel it in the thundering of his heart against my cheek. "Take your time."

A knock sounded on my door; Mom's voice hesitant on the other side. "Everything okay?"

"Yeah, we're okay." Though there wasn't a trace of conviction in Everett's answer.

FORTY-ONE

WE ARRIVED HOME THE DAY AFTER CHRISTMAS, AND ALTHOUGH Everett doted on me and smiled and laughed at all the right times with the family, my non-answer plagued him.

It was in the shadows that swept across his eyes, turning the vibrant hue of green a shade darker. I wanted to erase it—the anxiety, the hurt, and the disappointment.

I wanted to, but I didn't.

"Darling," Sabrina said two days before the new year would arrive. We were inundated with orders for parties, weddings, funerals, and the list went on. "You should be sitting while you're doing that."

She dragged the stool over, and I thanked her as I sat and finished tying off the stems.

"You look like you're either about to go into labor or jump off a cliff."

I snorted, then coughed, then groaned. "Everett asked me to marry him."

Gloria's head peeked out above the cupboard on the other side of the counter. "Say what?"

Sabrina's gaze was heavy as if she was trying to peel back my skin to look inside my muddled brain. "You didn't answer him."

Gloria gasped. "Oh, boy."

"He left me. Again. While I was pregnant, mind you," I

grumbled, tossing the knife down. "Seems like everyone but me is ready to forget about that."

"We're not the ones in love with the guy," Sabrina said. "Grudges, betrayal—they burn longer and brighter, and can last a lifetime where love is concerned."

"Amen." Gloria jerked her head, then lowered it, rummaging through the cupboard again.

"Unless, of course," Sabrina said with a casual air, "you decide to forgive."

I chewed on that, tasting how sweet it would be, and almost fell into the tempting notion. I'd done that one too many times. "I don't trust him."

"Don't trust him not to leave you, you mean?"

I nodded, leaning over to grab the tape out of the drawer.

"You don't need to answer him, you know," Gloria said. "My sister, Clara, kept her first husband waiting two years before she agreed to marry him."

"Didn't he die a year later?"

Gloria moaned. "Seriously, Sabrina?"

Yeah, seriously? I shot her a look, and Sabrina winced, hands filled with flowers, upturned. "Whoops."

My lips itched with the urge to smile. "While I appreciate you guys wanting to help, I can't decide right now. So… I'm just not going to."

"Ever? So you're saying no, then?" Gloria asked, shock painting the question.

"No, I'm not saying anything."

The two women were silent for a solid few minutes, but I could feel them biting their tongues and groaned again. "Out with it."

"You don't need to marry him to forgive him. To try again."

"What she said." Gloria raised a hand in the air, shaking it.

My own stopped moving, and I lowered the bouquet to the countertop. "I know that." I did know that, but I was still stuck. Maybe it was self-preservation. Maybe it was Aiden. Maybe it was hormones running amuck.

Or maybe it was because, as Adela said, once I took a step too far in one direction, it was done.

Something began while something else ended.

Over.

The new year brought no clarity, only more anxiety.

And with my looming due date, I knew I couldn't keep living in tangles. Yet there I was, staring at a text from Aiden asking me to see him later at his apartment, and tied up in knots.

"Hey," Everett said, tapping on my opened bedroom door. "I got some more snacks, and the drug store had a sale on wet wipes."

"Oh, thanks."

He shifted on his feet. "Are you busy?"

In answer, I locked my phone, setting it down as I gestured for him to come in. "What's that?"

Everett stared down at what looked to be an album in his hands. "A photo album."

I straightened as much as I could, and he sat beside me, the bed dipping.

The album looked old. Dust stains speckled the black leather and lined the page edges. "It's yours?" He nodded, hands tight around it. Too tight.

"When did you get it?"

"At Christmas. Broke in when they were asleep."

Oh. "Your parents?"

A defeated sound fled him. "Seems the same old, same old, but I didn't care. I just wanted this. I'd kept it tucked beneath some loose floorboards in my room and thought you might, um…"

"Look at it with you?" I suggested when his hands shook.

"Please."

Fire licked at my chest as I absorbed his determined expression, which was fixed on the album. His brows puckered, and he sucked his lips between his teeth. "Here," I said, patting the spot next to me and gently taking the album from him.

He scooted closer, and I laid it over our legs, my heart racing as I opened the front cover and found a picture of Everett in dirty overalls, aged two, on the first page. "You adorable thing, you." I scratched at some dust covering the picture so I could see his golden blond hair and carefree smile.

Everett was silent as I kept turning the pages until, eventually, I came across a photo of a newborn baby snuggled next to him on a threadbare couch.

"Mason," I breathed, my finger caressing where his head lay tucked next to Everett's leg. He had no hair, but as I turned page after page, Everett deathly still beside me, I saw him morph from a helpless newborn, into a crawling baby, a toddler, and then into a little boy.

He had the blondest hair I'd ever seen, almost white, and the same color eyes as his big brother. "So much like you."

Everett was a silent force, and when I glanced at him, I discovered he couldn't speak. His eyes were wet, his face pale, and I shut the album, then put it on the nightstand beside my phone.

"Come," I said, lying down and smacking the pillow beside mine.

After blowing out a wet sounding breath, he pinched the bridge of his nose with a groan, then joined me.

I stared into his eyes, willing away the sheen to them that stabbed at my heart. "Did your therapist ask you to do that?"

"Yeah." A dry, vacant word, his eyes someplace he'd probably rather not be. *One step at a time*, I surmised. He'd endured enough over the past ten minutes.

"Kiss me."

The present snapped back into his face and transformed it into a perplexed frown. "Clover."

"Kiss me," I repeated, my fingers gliding over and up his arm, causing a shiver to follow.

"I can't," he said.

My racing heart skidded to a brutal halt. "Why not?"

"Because," he said with a glimmer of a smile. "I need to know you forgive me before I take anything else from you."

My eyes stayed on his for an interminable amount of time, and each pound of my heart became louder the longer I replayed all he'd done. And then the gentle, earnest adoration in those green orbs had me checking myself. Severely.

"I find myself doing this thing," I said, needing to be honest, my heart bleeding and waiting for someone to staunch it.

"Oh yeah?" The raspy timbre ignited goose bumps.

"Yeah." I shifted closer, my huge belly touching his. "I don't know when exactly it happened, but somewhere along the way, I stopped seeing the good. Or maybe I blocked it out in order to hold onto my bruised feelings to better protect them next time. Either way, it's time to admit I've been shortsighted." My hand reached his face, my fingers ghosting over the harsh rise of his cheekbone and feathering over the hair lining his jaw. "You've got so much good in you, Everett Taylor. So fucking much. But the things you've done to hurt me... they outweighed the good. Or so I thought."

He kissed my fingers when they reached his lips, and I smiled, sniffing as I let it all tumble to the surface. The tummy flutters, the secretive smiles, the afternoons spent pretending to do his homework, the jumping through my window, and the unbending way he looked at me when no one else was around, and filled my every waking thought. He'd been my dream since I'd first laid eyes on him, and I gave up on him when he'd turned into a nightmare.

"They don't outweigh it. Your heart is too big, your soul too magnetic. And I guess what I'm trying to say is that I believe in you. I always have, and I probably always will. Not just because I love you, but because you're worth believing in."

His hand met mine over his cheek. "Clover."

"Can we name him Mason?"

"Christ," he said, sniffing back tears. "Really?"

I worried my lip. "If you want?"

"I want," he said, a tear escaping his eye. "Thank you."

I caught the tiny bead, brought it to my lips and rubbed. "Can you kiss me now?"

His gaze tracked the movement, and he huffed out a humorous breath, then leaned forward, his hand holding my face.

"Just so you know." With my lips over his, I stopped, my fears lingering between us, needing more. "You can fuck up, make mistake after mistake. I don't, and never will, expect perfection. What I do expect is you. Here. With me. No matter what."

I heard him swallow. "No matter what. Through whatever kind of hell, I'll be right beside you, loving you."

It felt like I was standing on the edge of eternity, staring it in the eyes as another darker pair flashed through my mind. It could've been beautiful, what Aiden and I had, but it wasn't what I needed.

And though I knew it would hurt, I couldn't run and hide from this.

Already, I knew the years would pass and that ache would dull, but it would probably always linger. I could live with a dull ache, but I couldn't live with a gash that never stopped bleeding.

All thoughts of Aiden vanished as my lips found the smooth, familiar curve of Everett's, and we both sighed, our mouths parting with the sound, then melding again.

After a minute, I whispered into his mouth, "That doesn't mean I'm saying yes."

He grinned, lips fusing to mine. "Not yet."

My boots crunched over some loose gravel in the parking lot, the streetlamps casting the surrounding cars and building ahead in patches of black and orange.

Everett wasn't thrilled with what I was doing. No, scratch that, he was probably pacing the floor of the living room, waiting for me to get home.

But I wasn't going to lie to him, and I wasn't going to do this any other way. He understood that, even respected it, but still, he respectfully fucking hated it.

"You're a sight for sore eyes."

I paused near the steps, only just realizing Aiden was sitting at the bottom with his hands between his bent knees.

"Hey."

"Hey." He stood, striding toward me with slow, purpose-filled steps. I backed up to the wall, Deja vu rattling my heart. "I'm sorry," he rasped out, his eyes swimming into mine. "So sorry."

"You had places to be. I get it."

"No." My heart sank. "I did, but I could've opted out. I've just… I've been a coward."

"You're no coward, Prince." I tried to infuse some light into the heavy that'd settled between us.

It wouldn't budge.

He chuckled, dark and graveled. "The idea of losing you? Well, I think it was easier to bear by avoiding the situation. You can't end something that's not happening. But I'm done with that. With being afraid of losing. I can be what you need me to be and then some."

"Aiden," I warned.

His hands cupped my cheeks, his head dipping, forcing my eyes to his. "Give me a chance. A real, honest to God chance, and I'll never once make you regret it."

God. I didn't know what I'd expected, but it wasn't this. My heart shredded, tore right down the center, and fell to the ground beneath our feet.

"I can't do that."

"You can. You fucking can." His hands tightened. "I just got sick of picking up the pieces, of feeling like I'm second best. I'm not, and we're more than that. I know that now, and you know it too."

"We were always more than second best. You were always more than that." It needed to be said because it was nothing but the truth.

Hope danced and swayed over his features, and I felt a part of myself slip away, knowing what I had to do. "I'm sorry."

"It's okay." His thumbs caressed my cheeks, and before I could draw breath, his lips were on mine.

I let myself have it, that one tiny taste of what I'd be walking away from.

A best friend. A lover. A future filled with mischievous smiles.

When his head angled and his tongue tried to pry my lips apart, I pushed him back. "No, I mean I'm sorry, Aiden, because I can't..." Tears blinded, sending me rocking on my feet.

His hands fell, slapping to his sides as what was happening registered. As what he'd seen on my face, perhaps found on my lips, sank deeper.

He stumbled back, a hand pulling at his hair, a stream of unintelligible curses flung at the concrete and brick surrounding us.

"I'm sorry, so sorry." I kept repeating myself, over and over, hoping he'd hear, hoping he'd know how much I meant it, and hoping he'd see how hard this was.

"No." He froze, leather jacket bunching as he stood eerily still. "Say it. Say what you want, Stevie."

I shook my head. "Don't, Aiden."

"Don't?" he thundered, spinning to level me with a look of utter devastation, one I'd remember for the rest of my life. A harsh laugh preceded his words. "If you can't say it's me, when I'm standing here, fucking begging for you to, then we already know the answer, don't we?"

I could do nothing. Nothing but chant those useless words. "I'm sorry."

He roared, hand slamming into a glass window in the brick wall beside me.

Glass showered like rain, mingling with the echo of my scream.

And then something wet trickled down my thigh, my panties flooding and clinging. "Oh, shit." I staggered, thinking I'd peed myself.

Aiden's face paled, and he stared in horror before using his uninjured hand to retrieve his phone from his jeans.

Hurried footsteps sounded. Then Everett's voice, strangled and layered in anger, bounced off the walls. "Don't bother, I've got her."

Slowing, he reached me in a few rushed strides, taking my hand and checking my face. "You can walk?"

I nodded, and he led me back to the car, laid down a towel he'd been keeping in the trunk, and helped me in. "You came."

"Jogged over as soon as you left." His laughter was silent. "Did you really think I was going to be able to wait?" His hands were tight around the steering wheel. "That I'd let my pregnant girl just go visit her ex in the dark?"

"You don't trust me."

"No, it's him I don't trust. And I just… I don't know. I had this feeling. Don't give me shit, okay? It's a damn good thing I listened to it."

As a sharp pain splintered and began to band around my midsection, I lost any will I had to argue with him. Not that I had much to say in the first place.

Mason Hendrix Taylor was born at three thirty the following afternoon, welcomed into the world via the form of a knife to the stomach after keeping me in limbo for hours on end.

I'd survived better than I thought even though every time I coughed, it felt like I'd tear my stitches and my insides might leak out.

Staring into his tiny, scrunched face, brushing my fingers over the golden tuft of hair on his head and the planes of his rosy, round cheeks, I fell in love for the third time in my short life.

And I knew that love, combined with the love of the hovering male who wouldn't leave my side, would be enough.

It was strong enough to fill cracks and cover scars, to ease the bruising left behind, and I had hope that it'd have the power to eventually heal. To release me from the curse I'd willingly walked into.

On our last night in the hospital, I stirred when I felt the soft touch of lips resting upon my forehead, and inhaled a familiar scent. With my heart thudding hard, I forced my eyes to open in time to see Aiden's dark form slip soundlessly out of the room.

To fall in love twice was a beautiful rarity.

To be in love with two men at the same time was a cruel twist of fate.

Your soul was split right down the middle, a piece of you stolen forever.

Some people walked through life never having tasted the essence of falling in love. Some people fell over and over again until they finally fell the right way and found something true.

I didn't know if I'd done it right or wrong.

But as I dragged my aching eyes to Everett, dozing in the chair by the window with our son curled into the crook of his arm, I knew I'd travel any path all over again if it would lead me back to them.

My only wish, the one that would keep me awake for years to come, would be for the lost piece of my soul to one day feel that way too.

EPILOGUE

Everett
One Year Later

T HEY SAY ALL THAT GLITTERS IS NOT GOLD.

Well, I begged to fucking differ.

Since the first time I'd laid eyes on Stevie Sandrine, her sunshine had branded me with its warmth.

It took her six months after Mason was born to finally wear my ring and another six months to convince her we were getting married today.

In a field of sunflowers and mismatched pastel painted chairs, I felt those stubborn ripped pieces of my soul stitch back together.

There'd been days growing up when all I could do was stare at her and listen and wait for any sound of her. Never in my wildest dreams did I think I'd one day be able to say she was forever mine.

I was born in shadows, and she'd radiated nothing but light.

Our journey hadn't been easy, but nothing worth having was ever easy to attain. And although there were days I'd catch her staring out the window, lost to her own thoughts, I knew she didn't have any regrets. As much of an asshole as I was, as much as I needed her, I wouldn't have let her choose me if I didn't feel it was what she'd truly wanted.

All I'd ever wanted was for her to be happy, to keep that

glow of hers alive, and I gave up on believing I couldn't be the one to do that. I now knew differently. I'd always known differently. I'd just been too lost to the past to think clearly of a future or think I'd even deserved one.

But I did. I do.

And there she was, gliding toward me, glittering and golden, encased in an ivory lace gown.

Beaded flowers danced in the sunlight over her chest, and I watched, mesmerized, as the flowers morphed into silken waves that draped and dripped below her breasts, shimmering and swaying over the curves of her hips while hiding those willowy legs.

Catching a glimpse of her boots, I felt my throat thicken, and my eyes swung up to meet hers.

Her vivid blues, glossed and lined with dark lashes, shimmered with her smile.

My chest heaved and I clenched my hands together as the breeze tugged some of her long golden hair aside. A crown of daisies perched atop her head, and fuck if that didn't just about send me over the edge.

But then she frowned, her head tilted a fraction, her smile waning. "What's wrong?" she mouthed the words.

Fuck. "Nothing at all," I mouthed back.

Her brows puckered, but she turned to her dad, kissing both of his cheeks.

Brad's eyes were wet, his smile shaking as he handed her over to me. Before he could—to hell with the rules—I took his hand, pulling him close to hug, and whisper, "Thank you."

"Jesus, kid. Don't make me blubber like a baby."

Smiling, I held him close another second, then released him, winking at Brenna, who'd been crying since she'd claimed her seat in the front row.

She laughed, then her face crumpled, and she blew her nose again.

Seated near Brenna, Sabrina had her arm around Gloria, who'd given up on drying her eyes.

Finally, I looked over at Clover, who was biting her lip, trying not to let the tears in her eyes spill down those beautiful cheeks. I offered my hand. "Ready?"

Nodding, she released her lip as her hand slid into mine and squeezed. "You look dashing."

"Dashing?" We took our place in front of the celebrant, and I glanced down at my almond-colored suit, new boots, and white dress shirt.

"Sexy?"

I raised a brow.

"Handsome?"

"Getting warmer."

She grinned, and her lips quivered, her voice choked and sincere. "You look like you belong with me."

The celebrant cleared her throat.

I ignored her.

"Better," I said and brought Stevie's mouth to mine.

"No freaking way." Stevie's eyes widened at the stage set up beneath the dome-like tent we'd hired.

The wedding and reception were held at a flower farm a half hour's drive north of Plume Grove. Which hid among deserted farmland just a ten minutes' drive from the beach.

The elderly couple who owned it had stopped hosting weddings here years ago. But after showing up on their doorstep with Stevie and Mason in tow, they took one look at Stevie's dazed expression and caved before I'd even opened my mouth to beg.

"Did you plan this?" she asked, as Hendrix started singing "Start Me Up" by the Stones.

I switched Mason to my other knee, handing him another slice of apple. "Maybe."

"Come to Pa," Brad said, stealing my kid.

He went willingly, his apple falling to the grass as he kicked his legs and smiled down into Brad's face.

"Shall we?" I stood, holding out my hand.

"This is some first dance," Stevie murmured into my neck once we'd reached the cleared space, and I'd pulled her body flush with mine.

"You don't like?"

Her laughter fluttered over my skin, warming and drugging. "It couldn't be more perfect."

Grinning, I stepped back to spin her around and couldn't help but wonder if I truly was the luckiest bastard alive when she threw her head back and laughed.

We weren't alone for long. Mason, who'd just started walking, toddled over, his arms wrapping around my leg. With my brows raised, I gazed down at him.

"Bup, bup." He bounced, arms reaching, green eyes huge and pleading.

Releasing Stevie, I lifted Mason high into the air, then held him as we continued to dance. Albeit with a lot less romance, but plenty of laughter.

Stevie

Four Years Later

The sound of the piano downstairs snuck through the floor-boards of the second floor where I was busying myself with cleaning up the kitchen after dinner.

Everett had made chicken stir-fry, my current favorite, and then needed to retreat to his cave to finish one of his latest creations.

He still worked with Jack and some of the artists at Keen Records, especially Orange Apples, being that Hendrix wasn't one to write more than a few songs before running out of steam.

Which was what he'd called it. Hendrix had yet to have his heart broken, or fall in love, and so that was how he chalked up his inability to write about the subject matter.

Everett didn't mind, and neither did the rest of the band. If you asked me, I saw through every loaded word of bullshit for what it was.

Hendrix, all of them, still wanted Everett's input. Not only that, but they also wanted his presence. To spend time with him how they used to. Even so, Everett ran his own business, composing from our large basement for a variety of artists, movies, and even some television shows.

That didn't mean I wasn't doing what I loved, too.

Peeking out the shutters of the kitchen window, I watched the last drops of sunlight leak into the sunflower fields beyond the house.

We purchased the farm eighteen months ago when Everett noticed it'd come up for sale. The elderly couple who'd owned it had now moved on to a retirement village near their family.

We weren't looking to buy a house. In fact, after living in the apartment for a year with Adela while I'd finished school, we'd purchased our first home. It was a beautiful, modern two-story monstrosity, and although I didn't love it, I was grateful for what it provided. Our own space.

Yet when I remembered how it'd felt to step foot onto Sunny Nights, the name of our farm, before our wedding here, I'd shoved the phone into Everett's hand, and said, "Make it ours."

And so he did.

This home held everything our hearts needed to thrive—music, peace, beauty, character, and love.

My soul had never felt more alive or more at peace as it did when I drove down our dirt-packed drive or walked through our back door and took in the outside view, the crisp air sinking into my lungs, my being.

It was hard for darkness to seep in when nothing but light surrounded you. Yet things hadn't been perfect, and I hadn't expected them to be. But Everett had kept his promise.

He'd relapsed two years ago after I'd had a miscarriage. It didn't happen when I would've thought it would. He'd been nothing but a solid pillar of support throughout the entire traumatic event, but I should've known that even weeks after, he could fall. Yet even when he did, he never left. He started attending meetings and began seeing his old therapist, Ted, again.

Now, he was content to meet with his sponsor should the need arise, and he made sure he saw Ted once a month.

Orange Apples were due to return from their first world tour in two weeks, and we were bursting to hear about their time on the road. They'd made it. They hadn't been some overnight success, but over the past five years and after releasing three albums, their latest climbing the charts, they'd grown a following that was beginning to engorge their egos, and they were only just getting started.

The phone rang, and I quickly checked on Mason, who'd

SERENADING HEARTBREAK | 361

been coloring in front of the TV after dinner, only to find his crayons deserted, and the door leading downstairs cracked open.

Smiling, I rushed to grab my phone from the countertop, not expecting a business call this late and frowning at the unknown number.

I wouldn't say business was booming, but I had enough to keep me busy. Still, I called them back, moving into the living room.

I sank into the couch as a breathless, "Hello?" hit my ears.

"Hi, sorry I missed your call," I said. "This is Stevie from Sunny Nights."

"Oh yes, hi," a woman said. "I'm sorry to call so late, but work has kept me swamped, and I need all the sunflowers I can get for my wedding."

"Congratulations." Leaning forward, I plucked up a crayon and a sheet of half doodled on paper. Yeah, I ran a tight ship. "When do you need them by?"

I heard a male laugh in the background and felt my neck and shoulders lock. "Two months."

I bit my lip, unsure, but positive I didn't want to let her down. "I'll have to take your name and get back to you, if that's okay?"

"Sure. Did I scare you? Because as many as you can spare would be perfect."

I wrote that down. "We'll make it work. I'm just waiting for some babes to grow a little more is all."

"Babes?" Her smile echoed in her voice. "I love that."

I laughed a little. "I call them my other children. So let me grab your details and I'll call you this time tomorrow?"

"That'd be great. It's Darby Prince, and this number is best."

My spine pulled taut, and leaning back, I tucked my hair behind my ear.

"Hello?"

"Sorry," I said. "Sometimes we get bad reception out here. Um, that's an awesome surname."

Her laughter was pattering rain and butterfly wings, a chime that both lit and burned my chest when she sang, "It's my husband's. This is our second wedding."

Unsure what to say, I blurted, "You don't sound old enough to be getting married for a second time."

"Well, this one is for his dad. We eloped last year."

I blinked, shaking my thoughts away. It couldn't really be... And then a muffled noise, followed by airy breaths. "Are you getting off this thing at some point tonight?"

"It's your fault I have to do all this in the first place," she said without a trace of scorn, only affection.

"Mmm, hurry up."

"Sorry," she returned. "My husband's a dick."

He wasn't, and we both knew that. Smiling, I tried to keep the tears from my voice. "No worries. I'll call you tomorrow."

We hung up, and I stared, unseeing, for the longest time at the phone in my hand.

Happiness warred with agony. Relief muddled with regret.

Locked inside the bathroom, I slumped onto the closed toilet seat, listening to the sound of Mason clunking on the piano downstairs while years of pent-up guilt poured down my face.

He was happy.

He was married.

He'd returned to that someone who'd already stolen half of his soul, and he'd reclaimed it.

Wiping the wet from my cheeks, I headed downstairs and stopped in the doorway, watching Mason.

He'd left the piano and was now watching his father from

the couch in the corner with curious green eyes as Everett scrawled in his journal at his desk.

Some people were stronger on their own.

Some people were stronger due to the people they surrounded themselves with.

I'd always known Everett was capable of the former, but all along, I'd also known deep down, I longed to be beside him when he flourished. Though to deserve that, I'd had to learn to accept him at his worst. I wanted to deserve him the way he so desperately fought to deserve me, and that was something I would never lose sight of again.

Everett Taylor had taught me many things during this roller coaster love of ours, the most prevalent of all being courage. When things get hard, you don't run away, and you don't give up. You plant two feet into the ground, remember the roots you've grown, the life and love you've nurtured, and you fight.

He was capable of magic. Not only due to his talent, but in the way he could still make me feel, even after all these years, like I was the only soul on earth worth knowing. His love revealed itself in his smile, his stalking eyes, his voice, his unwavering quiet strength and determination, and in his touch.

Souls were bound to knit to others. And where Everett was concerned, mine had stitched to his a long time ago.

We were never supposed to make something out of moments. We were always meant to build something out of lifetimes. And I couldn't see us parting and thriving for long on our own in any of those lifetimes.

Even when we fought it, we were destined to collide, and we forever would until we quit trying to let go of something that refused to unthread.

He wasn't his mistakes or his past, and I wasn't mine. Like so many of us, he was a culmination of disastrous, wondrous decisions that'd made him exactly who he was supposed to be. The man he'd grown into was worth it all. The man he'd grown into was who I'd always seen behind those damaged eyes, and now that he could see that too, there was no stopping him.

There'd be no stopping us.

In his torment, during the darkest years of his life, we'd found one another. Now, together, we wouldn't just be happy, we would no longer hide or be afraid.

Nothing could haunt us anymore.

Sensing eyes on him, Everett dropped his pen, then turned and pinned me with his soulful gaze. His lips hitched, and he crooked a finger for me to go to him.

My feet carried me over the beaten wood flooring and straight into his lap.

Pushing some hair off my face, he furrowed his brow, and his mouth tightened. "What's wrong?"

"Nothing," I said, meaning it.

His thumb brushed over my still damp lashes. "Bullshit. You've been crying."

"Hormones, and they're happy tears," I said, nodding for emphasis.

He stared a minute longer, then rubbed my five-month pregnant stomach. "You promise?"

Leaning forward, I pressed my lips to his, hearing Mason snicker behind me. "I promise." His mouth slid soft over mine, and I whispered, "Everything is perfect."

The End

Enjoy *Serenading Heartbreak?*
You might also enjoy *Bloodstained Beauty*…

Fresh out of college and headed straight for my dream job, I
didn't think things could get any better.
Then I met my dream man.

In an instant, my happy ever after had begun.
The life I'd stumbled into was beautiful, and the man I loved
was perfect.
But perfection comes at a cost, and I'd slumbered through all
the alarms.

Then I met my nightmare.
The man whose bright eyes held untamed darkness.
The man who disarmed me with his peculiar behavior.
The man whose cold, merciless hands shook me awake.
In an instant, questions started to dismantle my happy ever
after.

But whoever said the truth would set you free was wrong.
It wasn't going to repair the cracks in my naive heart.
It wasn't going to caress my face with comforting hands and
reassure me it was all just a dream.
No, the truth shoved me down a rabbit hole, and I landed in the
lair of a real-life monster.

Available now

STAY CONNECTED

Facebook page
facebook.com / authorellafields

Instagram
www.instagram.com / ellafieldsauthor

Website
www.ellafields.net

ABOUT THE AUTHOR

Ella Fields is a mother and wife who lives in Australia.

While her kids are in school, you might find her talking about her characters to her cat, Bert, and dog, Grub.

She's a notorious chocolate and notebook hoarder who enjoys creating hard-won happily ever afters.

ALSO BY
ELLA FIELDS

Frayed Silk

Cyanide

Corrode

Bloodstained Beauty

GRAY SPRINGS UNIVERSITY:

Suddenly Forbidden

Bittersweet Always

Pretty Venom

MAGNOLIA COVE:

Kiss and Break Up

Forever and Never

Lies and Goodbyes